The Emissary

Fredrick Hudgin

Novels

The End of Children Series:
- The Beginning of the End
- The Three-Hour War
- The Emissary

Ghost Ride
School of the Gods
Green Grass
Sulfur Springs

Short stories

A Rainy Night
Ashes on the Ocean
Being Dad
Get Them OFF!
Nice Day for a Ride
The Chair
The Last Salute
The Longest Ride
The Mission
The Second Chance
The Wiz
They Don't Have Christmas in Vietnam
When Is a Kiss Not a Kiss

Poetry Collections

Four Winds
Old Dreams and Young Adventures

Fredrick Hudgin

The Emissary

Book Three of

The End of Children Series

This is a work of fiction. Names, characters, places, and incidents either are the product of the author's imagination or are used fictitiously, and any resemblance to actual persons, living or dead, business establishments, events, or locales are entirely coincidental.

All names, measures of distance, time, temperatures, and math have been converted into their common English equivalents for ease of understanding.

The cover is a picture of the Cat's Eye Nebula as viewed by the Hubble telescope. I felt it closely resembled what the people in the shuttle would have seen when they viewed the magnetic arms of Gargantua. It is from the website Hubblesite.org. NASA has given permission to use the pictures on that site as public domain. NASA and Space Telescope Science Institute (STSci) asked on their website to be acknowledged for the use of their pictures.

In Chapter Six, I encourage you to play each piece of music as it is mentioned—the links to the music are listed at the end of the book. While the written word can create wonderfully powerful images, no words can do justice to this music. Perhaps someday I will be allowed to include virtual hyperlinks from your story hologram to the audiovisual parts of my stories. If you have no interest in classical music, skip that part and continue with the adventures of Freddie and Jeremiah.

The Emissary, Book Three of The End of Children

Copyright 2017 by Fredrick Hudgin

All rights reserved. No part of this book may be reproduced, scanned, or distributed in any printed or electronic form without permission. Please do not participate in or encourage piracy or copyrighted materials in violation of the author's rights. Purchase only authorized editions.
ISBN-13: 978-1541056206
Printed in the United States of America

For my wife, first reader, and source of great ideas:
Melvina

"Moral courage is the most valuable
and usually the most absent characteristic in men."
General George Patton

Prologue

What Has Gone Before

Three graduate students in physics at Stanford University, Lily Yuan, Kevin Langly, and Douglas Medder, discover how to open a wormhole after Lily has a dream that tells her how to do it. A wormhole is a hole in our universe that goes from one place to another, bypassing everything between them, including the distance. When the students open their first wormhole, an alert is sounded by the wormhole detectors that were planted on the moon fifty thousand years earlier during the time when humanity was raised up from apes to people. We are evaluated to see if we are ready, as a species, to begin trading and interacting with the other peaceful species who inhabit much of our galaxy.

The evaluation examines us to see if we have accomplished the five basic milestones of acceptance into the Ur, the loose government of the sentient species of the galaxy. The milestones are: ending war, controlling capitalism, ending pollution, ending resource depletion, and ending overpopulation. We fail to pass their evaluation. Now that we have wormhole technology, there is no way to stop us from developing starships and spreading our warlike attitudes and greed throughout the galaxy. Because of this, humanity is selected for elimination. The aliens release a virus that has no other side effects beyond turning off our ability to have children.

In another couple of hundred years, mankind would have figured it all out and passed the evaluation. But the dream was planted by someone who wanted humanity to be evaluated (and failed) before it was ready. Finding out who did it, why they did it, and how to undo the judgment, while the clock is ticking, becomes the race of our lifetime.

Without the stabilizing influence of parenthood and a future beyond the current generations, civilization begins to erode. Wormholes and a by-product, Dark Energy Portals, could have been a new dawn for humanity. Instead, they are turned into weapons that lead to the third world war—the Three-Hour War. Using Rosy technology (so named because of the rosy aura the energy emits) to deliver bombs with pinpoint accuracy, in three hours, the military capacity of the world is cut by three quarters, the supporting infrastructure of civilization is destroyed, and the governing bodies of almost all the countries in the world are eliminated.

In only Canada and the United States do the leaders escape.

The governments of Canada and the United States slowly reinstate themselves and attempt to suppress the anarchy that has swept their countries after the Three-Hour War. Once government and peace are reestablished, the bigger problem of asking the Galactic government for a second chance is revisited. But before we can get humanity's death sentence reversed, we have to make the Galactic government listen to us. The problem is, no matter how hard we wave our hands and shout, all we get back is silence.

As a last resort, a young woman volunteers to be sent on a suicide mission in a capsule that will pass the alien moonbase and exit the solar system. She has ten days of food and no way to return to Earth. She will die unless the aliens intervene. Her name is Leann Jenkins.

Chapter 1 – The Emissary

"Captain Xanny, please come to the bridge." Lieutenant Nussi's voice came through Xanny's personal communicator. The page interrupted the captain from responding to yet another request for information from Grock Corporation.

He turned away from his email hologram, grateful for any excuse to escape for a few minutes, and floated onto the bridge. He was an octopus with an anti-grav unit underneath him that provided support and propulsion. As he entered, everyone turned back to their work stations. They had obviously been paying attention to whatever had prompted Lieutenant Nola Nussi, his communications officer, to call the captain to the bridge.

"What's going on, Nola?"

The bridge was silent, a very unusual state. They obviously knew more than he did about whatever the situation happened to be. Lieutenant Nussi was a female primate with black hair, orange eyes, and green skin. Her head was a little larger than what is "normal" on Earth.

"I think you need to listen to this, Captain." She pressed a button. The face of a dark brown Earth primate with close-cropped curly hair appeared on her hologram. He was wearing a white shirt and the piece of cloth many of their leaders wore around their necks. Captain Xanny had seen the face many times before.

"Captain Xanny, I am George Robbins, the President of the United States. We are sending an unarmed, solo emissary to meet with you. She has no way to return to Earth. If you allow her to continue past your base on our moon, she will run out of food in ten days and die soon after that. She wants to meet with you and the Galactic government to discuss how our death sentence can be reversed. Please, intercept her capsule and allow us to begin a dialogue with you. Her name is Leann Jenkins. She is a student at one of our universities. She volunteered for this mission. Please, don't let her die."

The image of President Robbins disappeared and was replaced by Leann's image. Every hologram on the bridge displayed a pretty, young primate female—auburn hair, clear sun-tanned skin, white teeth, and forest-green eyes.

"Hello, Captain Xanny. My name is Leann Jenkins. At this moment, my capsule is passing the moon. It's on an exit path to leave our solar system.

"Since the bombs the countries of Earth threw at each other destroyed most of my world's military capacity, infrastructure, and governments, the governments of the United States and Canada are apparently the only ones still functioning on our planet. I have a message to the Ur from the President of the United States and the Prime Minister of Canada. It's my job to try to demonstrate to you why humanity needs a second chance. I thought I would start introducing myself to you by telling you about my childhood. ..."

Captain Xanny listened for a while. "Is she really on an exit trajectory?" he asked Lieutenant Nussi.

"Yes, sir."

"Analysis," he called out.

"Yes, sir," a voice responded over the intercom.

"Do you pick up any radiation from the capsule? Anything to indicate it has any weapons on board?"

"No, sir. It has only a Hore energy portal and the radios. It has a linked-Hore radio transmitting back to the planet's surface. I've done a scan of the capsule. It has no propulsion capability and no weapons of any kind. Besides the tiny Hore communication portal for the linked radios, it has no capability for Hore portal evacuation. She's in that capsule until she dies or someone retrieves her."

Leann had worked her way up to high school and was starting into the period when her father discovered his prostate cancer.

"Keep me posted of any change in her status. I will be in my quarters."

"Yes, sir." Lieutenant Nussi didn't take her eyes off the feed from Leann's capsule.

Captain Xanny floated back to his quarters. Leann's image was on every work station hologram he passed. It was even on in the canteen where there was standing-room-only as the off-duty crew silently watched Leann's monologue.

It was every crew member's worst nightmare to be abandoned in a lifeboat with no means of rescue. Yet here was a person from a primitive world who volunteered to do just that on the nonexistent hope the people who condemned her species to death would somehow save her. After two-and-a-half years on boring quarantine duty, Leann's message filled a void of drama and empathy that had been completely missing for the crew. Everyone hated being the people who were killing a species. And now the species had a face—a young, pretty, apparently innocent face, named Leann Jenkins.

"This won't turn out well," Captain Xanny muttered, going back to his cabin and the never-ending message queue from corporate headquarters.

……………………………

The convoy of a California DOT snow plow truck and three heavily armed pickup trucks left Reseda at 1 A.M. driving up The Old Road. The Old Road paralleled what was left of Interstate 5. The patrol consisted of seventeen Marines split across the four trucks, a driver, a truck commander, and, in the back of three of the trucks, one person for each gun. Marine Gunnery Sergeant Jeremiah Silverstein was commander of the Cal DOT snow plow truck that led the convoy. His corpsman (medic), Chief Petty Officer Freddie Harris, was commander of the last truck.

The pickups had been modified from the stock Ford F-450s with which Jeremiah's team started. On two of the trucks, a .50 caliber machine gun was mounted above the cab and an M-60 machine gun installed at both back corners. In place of the .50 caliber gun, the third truck had a six-barreled, electric-motor-powered Gatling gun known as a minigun. The minigun could fire two thousand rounds a minute, thirty-three rounds a second. It fired so fast the tracers, spaced every fourth round, appeared like a tongue of fire. A canopy covered the beds of the trucks. Holes were cut for the machine gunners to stick their heads through to shoot the machine guns. The sides of the beds had been armored to three feet above the bottom of the bed and across the roof. Quarter-inch-thick metal sheets were inserted into the doors with sand bags lining the bottom of the bed and the floor in each cab. The co-pilot could pull a rope to bring another armor plate up from the hood to protect the driver from bullets through the windshield. A large, black, armored grill and bumper replaced the shiny chrome one Ford produced. The radiator and wheels had been protected by more armor plating. Even the Cal DOT snow plow truck was painted and armored to protect the occupants, engine, and wheels.

The trucks were no longer pretty, but they kept Jeremiah and his crew safe as they slugged their way through northern Los Angeles and the San Fernando Valley.

The crew named each of the trucks—Brutus, Popeye, and Satan for the gun trucks, Sabre for the snow plow—then they painted them for maximum shock effect to inspire fear in those whom they attacked. The Marine flag was prominent on both sides, along with skulls, crossbones, fierce teeth around the grill dripping blood, caricatures of each truck's namesake in Marine uniforms crushing the stupid people who resisted them, and on the side they painted a gallows with a hanging body for each of the bad guys they killed bringing law and order back to greater Los Angeles. All three of the trucks had many of the gallows on their sides. The last touch had been to put a loud speaker on the front bumpers to talk their adversaries into giving up before the trucks killed them.

The trucks were so intimidating that, many times, all Jeremiah and his crew had to do was show up. Suddenly everyone was a law-abiding citizen who greeted them with open arms.

About halfway to Santa Clarita they encountered a barricade across the road. Jeremiah used the spotlight on Sabre to check out the area around the barricade. There were no lights visible beyond the headlights of the trucks and the spotlight on Sabre. The moon hadn't come up yet. The valley they were in was pitch black. A house was next to the road. Five armed men in camouflage and ski masks stood across the road with their guns at the ready.

Jeremiah pulled up the microphone on his PA system that was connected to the speaker on the front bumper. "This the US Marines. Remove your road block and lay down your arms. Do it now. You will not be offered a second chance."

Several of the men turned to the man in the middle. He motioned the men to remain in place. He put a megaphone up to his mouth. "You are trespassing on private property. You may pay the passage fee of one hundred dollars per truck or turn around."

"Lay down your guns and remove your road block. We are the beginning of the military efforts to reestablish law and order in this area. You have done a good job protecting yourselves. Please obey us and continue to be part of the solution. This isn't worth dying for. We're on your side."

The men looked to the man in the middle again for guidance. He was the obvious leader of the group. The leader lifted the megaphone to his mouth again. "We don't need or want your help. Pay the fee or go back the way you came."

Jeremiah picked up the microphone for the truck-to-truck radio. "I am going to pull off the road, like I'm going to turn around. Pass me and take up a triangle formation with Satan in the middle at point. Beware of people in the trees. I'd be willing to bet they have some snipers set up. Watch out for people in the house. Maybe we'll get lucky and these guys will back off. Safeties off, everyone."

Sabre pulled off the road, shielding the rest of the trucks from any fire coming from the trees beside the house. The other three trucks pulled up, Satan farther in front. Popeye and Brutus were on each side, a little back from Satan.

One of the men laid down his rifle and held up his hands.

"What are you doing, Tom?" the leader screamed at him. "That is DESERTION!"

"FUCK YOU!" the man screamed back, just as loudly. "I've had it with your make-believe military bullshit. These are the MARINES, you moron!" The man pointed at the trucks. "They are the real deal! It's over!"

The leader whipped his rifle around and shot him. The .50 caliber gunner on Brutus put three rounds into the leader, dead center. The bullets knocked the leader twenty feet back from where he was standing and sprayed his organs all over the road behind him. Everyone else put their weapons down and held up their hands.

A woman's voice screamed from the house. She ran into the road, cradled the body of the leader, and started wailing.

Freddie got out of his truck. "Time to go to work," he muttered, pulling his combat medic kit from behind the seat. It was a backpack. He slung the kit over his shoulders so he had both hands free and approached the woman carefully while the gunners in the trucks continued to watch everyone. This situation was a powder keg. It could blow up in their faces in a split second. Freddie's rifle was not pointed at the woman, but it could be in a moment.

"He's dead, ma'am," Freddie said to her.

"And you bastards killed him!" she moaned, rocking back and forth, clutching the man's body to her chest.

Freddie talked to her, trying to calm her down. "We told him to lay down his weapons and remove the road block. He chose to fight instead. He shot one of his own men."

"This is our land! You have no right to be here."

"This is the land of the United States, ma'am," Freddie said, trying to defuse the situation. If she kept talking, he could keep it from escalating. "We are US Marines. We are Americans, just like you. We are tasked with reopening this road and restoring law and order. If you'd like, I'll help you move him off the road. We need to pass."

He saw the "crazy" in her eyes. She wasn't listening. He started to say, "Don't do it, lady." But before he could get the words out, she pulled a pistol from inside her man's jacket.

"Pass this! You cocksu ..."

Freddie shot her through the head before she could bring the pistol up. She fell on top of her man and lay without moving, their blood mixing together on the road beneath them.

They were dead. They could wait. Freddie ran over to the other man who had been shot. He wasn't dead, but he would be shortly without some serious medical help. The man lifted his hand toward Freddie, then passed out.

"Call Reseda for a medevac, stat!" Freddie shouted to Jeremiah.

The bullet was through the man's abdomen, probably his spleen. He was bleeding profusely.

"Just as well he's unconscious," Freddie whispered. Now he wouldn't have to use anesthesia. Anesthesia on a person going into shock was always a crap shoot. Freddie set the medic kit on the ground and opened it up. He rolled the man on his side, pulled up his shirt, and opened up his abdomen with a scalpel, roughly paralleling where the bullet passed through. It was like the Mississippi River inside, with blood instead of muddy water. Freddie rolled him over to empty out the blood, then found the artery and vein going to the spleen and put clamps on them. He began looking for other damage. One of the ribs in his lower back was shattered as the bullet exited, but he wouldn't die from that. At least the bullet missed the liver, stomach, and pancreas. He started two saline drips, squeezing the bags to push the saline into the injured man.

"Where's that chopper?" Freddie bellowed in frustration, forcing the saline into the man with both hands as fast as he could. The man's pulse was fast and shallow. He was going into shock.

"Four minutes out," Jeremiah shouted back.

"Turn the trucks around so the headlights light the road behind us. It'll give them somewhere to land where they can see."

Jeremiah moved the trucks. The rest of the team was clearing the house and tearing down the barricade across the road. The men who had barricaded the road were helping.

The medevac helicopter set down in the lighted part of the road behind the trucks. The med-techs ran to Freddie with a stretcher.

"Male, middle-aged. 30-06 round through the abdomen. Got the spleen. I clamped it off. He's still open. Two liters of saline in. He needs whole blood stat. Goin' shocky."

"Got it," the lead said. They positioned the stretcher next to the man. "On my call. 1-2-3." They transferred him to the stretcher picked him up and ran to the chopper. The chopper lifted off before the door was closed for the flight back to Reseda. Freddie watched it go, wondering how many more people like this they would encounter. There was no reason for this to have happened.

He searched the bodies of the dead man and woman. He found their IDs, photographed each one, then returned the IDs to their wallets and pockets. Freddie signaled Jeremiah he was done.

"You got the video of that?" Freddie asked Jeremiah.

"Yep. Saved." Jeremiah agreed. Their battalion installed dashboard cameras on all four corners of the trucks. These were Americans. Americans knew about courts. The Marines were making sure they were ready. The feeds had already defused several complaints against Jeremiah and his trucks.

The convoy began moving toward Santa Clarita again. Brutus was the last truck in the convoy. It stopped and Freddie jumped into the passenger seat, then they continued down The Old Road. Freddie set his kit beside him where it was in easy reach for the next time.

... ...

"We need to get another message off the ship," Zarqa risked whispering to Flug. They were not alone in the canteen. Two arachnids were talking quietly in the corner.

Sergeant Zarqa Shaia and Corporal Flug had been on the pirate ship, *Easy Wind*, for over three months. Captain Xanny smuggled them on to search the ship's servers for proof that the pirate captain, Fey Pey, planted the dream in Lily Yuan and, along the way, try to glean who paid him to do it and why.

Flug was a heavy-worlder—fully two hundred kilos with maybe a two percent body fat. Flug's world was three times the mass of Earth. So was the gravity. People who lived on a "heavy world" tended to be large and muscular, weighing twice to three times what a "normal" Earthling weighed.

Zarqa was as small as he was big—think spring steel. Underestimating her was very easy and very dangerous.

Flug glanced over at the two arachnids, not sure what to do. It was always dangerous to talk about sending a message off-ship when no one else was within earshot—even the walls had ears on this starship. To risk such a conversation with people nearby was insane. And Zarqa knew this. The only reason she would take such a chance was she must have found the smoking laser (proof of Fey Pey's participation in the dream plant).

"Meet me in the thruster maintenance room in five minutes," he whispered, then picked up his protein drink and walked away without another word.

... ...

When they arrived at the settlement, Rebecca found Jonathan, Caitlin, and their two children living in her husband's house. Jonathan and his family escaped the anarchy in Fresno, coming to the mountains where they squatted in the first unoccupied house they found—Rebecca's. The house Rebecca and her friends were building was part of the deal Rebecca made to move Jonathan et al. out of her house so she could live there until her husband, Jeremiah, returned to her.

She met the four people who were helping her as she traveled from L.A. to the settlement after the Three-Hour War. They were Tony Blackeagle, Russell Duke, Juan Strickland, and May Chung.

Russell had been a computer programmer before the Three-Hour War. He served in the Navy during the Gulf War. He was short, wiry, blonde, crew cut, with a soul patch and goatee. Juan was tall, skinny, Hispanic, and clean-shaven. He claimed he could build anything with wood and nails. May was Vietnamese and a little stocky. She had long, straight black hair she kept in a ponytail down her back and a recently-healed three-inch scar across her left cheek from a knife fight in Stockton after the Three-Hour War. She was also Tony's girlfriend. Tony was a Native American—pureblood Crow. He was huge—fully six feet nine inches tall. His eyes could be soft and gentle or hard as ice, as the Viet Cong fighters discovered during his three tours in Southeast Asia. His white hair, seamed face, and grace of movement camouflaged a savage ferocity that hid under the surface.

The cinder block foundation on the new house had been laid in and the framing of the walls was complete. The rough plumbing stuck up through the gravel on the floor.

"When can you guys put the roofing on?" Rebecca asked.

"We can start tomorrow," Tony said, looking up at Juan and Russell who were sitting on the top of the wall waiting for the next roofing joist to be passed up. "We have to finish cross bracing the roof joists. Once that's done, we can put on the roofing plywood. Been a lot easier if we'd had trusses."

"Yeah, well, it'd be nice if a cement truck would show up to pour the floor, too. Those bags are going to be a lot of work."

"Can't wait to have it dried in," Juan called down. "Then we won't have to worry about the weather."

Tony snickered. "Juan, it's May in central California. It's gonna be hot and dry. And guess what? It's gonna be hot and dry tomorrow, too."

"Exactly! Once we get the roof on, we can work inside in the shade. This sun is killin' me." Juan paused to wring out the bandana he had tied around his forehead. "May, I need some water up here."

May climbed the ladder with a Thermos-full of the watered-down lemonade they used for rehydration and energy. "Water break, everyone!"

"What are you going to do about fixtures for the bathroom and kitchen, Rebecca?" Tony asked, sipping the glass of lemonade May gave him. "As soon as we pour the slab, I can start installing them."

"I found a guy who's selling me all of the fixtures in his parent's house: the lights, the bathroom fixtures, the sinks, everything. His parents died last year and the house was sitting empty. All he wanted was five hundred dollars. He said any money was better than no money. Then I offered him another five hundred dollars for the appliances. He said 'Hell Yeah!' I got a chest freezer, a fridge, a stove, a washer, a dryer, and a water heater. He even included the dishwasher. *I* don't have a goddamned dishwasher. Now Caitlin's going to have one."

"How about kitchen cabinets?"

"Cost me another hundred."

"Damn. That was a sweet deal. Why did he want the money so badly?"

"I don't know—for drugs, I expect. He had sores on his face and kept scratching his arms like bugs were crawling on them."

"You didn't pay him yet, did you?"

"Half down and the other half when we pick up the stuff. And I got a receipt. One of you will have to come with me to help take them out of the house and put them on the trailer."

"I'll go," Tony said. "I think I'll bring May's shotgun with us. That guy might decide he wants more money while we're taking out the fixtures."

"Then I'm going, too," May declared coming back down the ladder. "My shotgun doesn't leave without me being attached to it."

"Yeah, good idea. Jeremiah would approve," Rebecca agreed. They never left the settlement without being armed.

Rebecca closed her eyes and wished her husband with her again. She did this many times a day. After the Three-Hour War, Jeremiah left the settlement to search for her among the chaos in Los Angeles. He had not returned. No one knew if he was dead or alive.

"We'll need the cabinets before we frame the interior walls," Tony saw what was going on inside her. He was trying to distract Rebecca from her grief. Every time she mentioned Jeremiah's name, her eyes filled with tears. "We have to build the kitchen around them."

Rebecca got a grip on herself. "I'm bringing them back with me on this trip. We have to yank them, the fixtures, and the appliances out of that house. Should take most of the day. The cabinets are painted robin's egg blue."

"Oh, well," he chuckled. "It is what it is. I hope the appliances work. We'll have to keep the fridge upright when we transport it. The compressor will fail if we don't."

After the bombs, the housing industry dried up faster than a puddle of water in the Mojave Dessert. There were no banks to lend money, no government to oversee the industry, no Internet to search for what you wanted, and no suppliers to sell them to you. The only inventory that the unlooted stores had left was what they hadn't sold from their stock before the war. Many stores started offering used goods that they acquired locally. But money still worked for the time being. Probably because no one could figure out what to use in its place. How many eggs would it take to buy a dishwasher?

Rebecca sighed. "I guess I need to borrow Liam's truck again."

Liam Johansson did not like her. Since she returned from L.A., he attacked her verbally every chance he could. He had reason to feel that way. Rebecca had been arrogant and unfriendly when Jeremiah brought her up here before the bombing. When she left, she had taken all of Jeremiah's money and their only car, a Lexus SUV. Now, she paid the price for that unfriendliness and arrogance every day.

"Do you want me to do it?" Tony asked her gently. "Maybe he'll be a little more polite if I ask him."

"No. I'll do it. He never tells me 'no.' He just likes to see me grovel."

Tony called up to Juan and Russell, "Do you guys have enough to keep you busy 'til we get back?"

"Yeah," Juan said. "We got plenty to do."

Rebecca and Tony walked to Liam's house. Liam was sitting on his front porch reading a book.

"Hi, Liam," Rebecca said to him amicably.

"Rebecca," he said, never looking up from his book.

"We need to use your truck and trailer to pick up the fixtures, appliances and kitchen cabinets. Is that OK?"

"What do I have to say about it?" he replied. "It's only my truck."

"I'll fill it up in Sonora. There's still a couple of gas stations selling diesel."

"See that you do."

"Are the keys hanging on the wall?"

"I hope so. You were the last one to use it. Did you put them back?"

"Yes."

"Then they're still there." He made no effort to retrieve the keys.

"Can I get them?"

"I suppose you can. You appear to be an adult, capable of movement. You have fingers and an opposing thumb."

"*May* I get them, Liam?"

"Here they are, Rebecca," Amy, Liam's wife, said to her, coming out the door with the keys. She gave Liam a frustrated look and handed the keys to Rebecca.

"I ought to be back sometime this afternoon."

"Park it back where it is now."

"OK. Thanks, Amy. Thanks, Liam."

Liam continued reading his book without acknowledging Rebecca's departure.

... ...

Dr. Sridhar Hehsa, Director of the CDC in Atlanta, Georgia, stared into his microscope. Another failed test. It was coming—he felt it. He waited patiently for the ovum to die. This new line of research had been so promising. "The end to the Baby Stopper Virus"—it had a ring to it, a wonderful, ecstatic, jump-in-the-air ring to it. For three years, he dedicated his life to this quest. He might as well have been searching for the Holy Grail, for all the good his efforts had done him and the world.

The clock on the wall said eight minutes had passed since the sperm penetrated the ovum. Still not dead. Only one sperm penetrated so far. The other sperm cells were trying, but they could not penetrate the ovum wall.

"How about some tea," Dr. Hermann Splendt suggested. "Want some?"

"I will walk with you," Sridhar said, getting up. "This ovum will die, with or without me watching."

"You are becoming so negative, Sridhar," Dr. Splendt laughed. "Cool it with the negative waves. You have to *believe*. Believe it will happen and it will surprise you."

"That sounds very Indian, Dr. Splendt. Are you sure you don't have roots in the subcontinent?"

Hermann shook his head. "Not likely. You may not have noticed, Sridhar, but I have long blonde hair, blue eyes, and Arian features. I am pure German. My mother and father escaped eastern Germany as the Russians invaded at the end of World War II. Father worked for Hitler making germs. The US was only too happy to let him in. They put him to work making germs for the US at Edgewood Arsenal in Maryland."

They returned from the canteen fifteen minutes later with cups of hot Earl Grey tea. Sridhar sighed and made himself check the ovum. He was braced for another dead attempt. Instead of the dead zygote he expected, he saw a vibrant, healthy one. The other sperm cells had given up trying to penetrate.

"It can't be," he muttered, making sure the ovum he was studying was the same one he left in the microscope. He leaned over the microscope again. The zygote was still alive. The two pronuclei were plainly visible as was the polar body.

"OK, this is good," he whispered, refusing to let excitement rise in his heart. "Let's see if it survives a week. If it's alive in a week, then we might be onto something." He put the incubation flask back into the incubator.

… … … … … … … … …

Kevin stopped by mission headquarters to check on Leann's progress. "How's she doing?"

Lily was sitting at one of the consoles. "She's explaining who she is and why she's doing this."

"How's her trajectory?"

"Dead on. The launch was perfect. We're using the moon to slingshot the capsule into its departure path."

"Her new trajectory will keep her in line of sight with the moon at all times? Right?"

"Yep. It looks perfect. She's already above the solar plane."

"Anything from the aliens?"

"Not yet. We don't know if they are picking it up, ignoring her, or simply don't care."

"Where's the feed going to down here?"

"All the bases on Doug's Rosy Internet, including the Canadians. The women are cheering her on for being so brave. The men are cheering her on because she's so hot. She's a hit."

Leann's face was on every monitor in mission headquarters.

Kevin and Lily watched for a while.

"She's pretty good," Kevin said. "I don't think I could make being an undergraduate sound so interesting."

Lily watched without comment for a while. "She's doing a terrific job. We got to be friends while she was preparing for the trip. I hope this doesn't turn out to be the waste of a life. I've lost enough friends."

... ...

Leann focused the camera so her face was centered in the monitor. Her capsule was speeding past the alien moon base, about fifteen thousand kilometers above the surface of the moon. "Now that you know who I am. I want to begin my presentation of the worthwhile things created by the human species by reading a play written by a man who lived over four hundred years ago. His name was William Shakespeare. He wrote a play that spanned four days and was set in a town named Verona, six hundred years ago. It is a tragedy about two young people who fall in love and whose families are deadly enemies.

"The lead characters are Romeo and Juliet. Romeo is the sixteen-year-old son of Lady and Lord Montague. He has a cousin, Benvolio, and two friends: Mercutio and Friar Lawrence, a priest in their church. Romeo grows over the course of the play from someone who is more in love with the idea of love to someone who is willing to die for his beloved Juliet.

"Juliet is the beautiful thirteen-year-old daughter of Lord and Lady Capulet. Her cousin is Tybalt. Her nurse is her closest friend. Like Romeo, over the course of the play she grows into a woman of remarkable strength and resolve, pursuing Romeo and overcoming all obstacles that come between her and the fruition of her love for him. She becomes the reason for Romeo's metamorphosis into a person capable of deeply loving her back."

She continued with an explanation of the other characters in the play.

....

"The play begins with the onstage commentator explaining what led the characters to this situation." Leann took a deep breath and began.

> In the beautiful city of Verona, where our story takes place, a long-standing hatred between two families erupts into new violence, and citizens stain their hands with the blood of their fellow citizens. Two unlucky children of these enemy families become lovers and commit suicide. Their unfortunate deaths put an end to their parents' feud. For the next two hours, we will watch the story of their doomed love and their parents' anger, which nothing but the children's deaths could stop. If you listen to us patiently, we'll make up for everything we've left out in this prologue onstage.

In the palm of her hand she hald the remote control for the two cameras. Leann faded one camera and started the other, effectively changing scenes.

"Sampson and Gregory, servants of the house of Capulet, enter the stage together. Sampson begins the dialogue:" She activated the other camera, beginning the scene."

> "Gregory, I swear, we can't let them humiliate us. We won't take their garbage. "

She switched cameras, giving the audience a clue that the actors had changed. "Gregory responds," she told the audience, then made her voice lower. She zoomed the second camera into a close-up of her face.

> "No, because then we'd be garbage men."

She dropped the explanation of who was talking and used her voice change and camera change to identify the characters and continued the dialogue. Her performance was a combination of storytelling and acting. When a scene began, she explained to the audience where the scene was taking place and who the characters were.

....

"Romeo enters Capulet's orchard and sees Juliet on the balcony. He is alone."

Leann altered her voice to Romeo's and put on his hat. She tilted her head up to where the balcony would have been and sees Juliet.

> "But, soft! What light through yonder window breaks? It is the east and Juliet is the sun."

....

Leann bent over the imaginary Romeo after she woke in the tomb.

> “What’s here? A cup, closed in my true love’s hand?
> Poison, I see, hath been his timeless end.
> O churl, drunk all, and left no friendly drop
> to help me after? I will kiss thy lips.
> Perhaps some poison doth hang on them,
> To make me die with a kiss.”

She kisses Romeo with her back to the camera.

> “Thy lips are warm.“

She made a noise by moving her leg against the pilot’s console, then looked toward it, startled.

> “A noise? Then I’ll be brief.”

Juliet picked up Romeo’s dagger.

> “O happy dagger, this is thy sheath.
> There rust and let me die.”

Leann plunged the make-believe dagger into her chest, took a step toward Romeo’s body, reached out to him, and then collapsed on the floor. She lay there without moving while she triggered the camera feed to fade on the scene where Juliet finally joined her beloved Romeo.

A few minutes later Leann ended the final scene with the prince reflecting on the coming justice, brought about by the tragedy of Romeo and Juliet.

Leann had read and acted the entirety of William Shakespeare's *Romeo and Juliet* without any other actors or stage hands. She starred in the play in her sophomore year at Georgetown. This time she had to play all of the parts herself, changing her voice, body language and a few pieces of costume to represent the various actors and actresses. When she couldn't play a part, she read it like a story book, explaining what they meant to the audience. She used the two camera feeds, controlled by the device in the palm of her hand to control the scene and perspective changes. She had rigged a monitor to be her teleprompter in case she forgot a line, but it hadn't been necessary. She memorized the entire play when she was a sophomore.

This had been a phenomenal performance, worthy of the finest actors in the industry. And now it was done. Leann slowly climbed to her feet. After she selected *Romeo and Juliet* as her dramatic piece to present to the aliens, she spent countless hours over the course of a month rehearsing every evening with the drama teacher at the University of Calgary. Without his advice and feedback, Leann's attempt would have failed herself and the world.

"I would like to thank my coach and mentor at the University of Calgary," she said to the camera. "George Flamé spent every evening for a month helping me prepare this presentation of *Romeo and Juliet*. To my knowledge, it has never been performed in this way." She took a breath, realizing the play was, indeed, finished. "I need a few minutes before I can begin my next selection." She pressed the privacy timer that turned off the feed to the transmitters to the alien moon base and Earth. No applause greeted her. No feedback of any kind to bolster her emotional exhaustion. She staggered back to her bed and collapsed on it, asleep before her head was on the pillow.

… … … … … … … … …

At the University of Calgary, George Flamé sat with his drama class as Leann ended her performance. They had watched without a sound since Leann gave her opening remarks. When the camera winked out, there was silence. George started clapping. The class joined in until everyone was standing and shouting, "Bravo!"

When the applause died down. Professor Flamé addressed the class.

"You have just witnessed a performance that may have saved humanity. I would like to propose a tough goal for each of you in your careers as performers, writers, directors, and producers. Here it is: be better, reach for the brass ring, don't ever be satisfied with 'good enough.' If Leann hadn't tried something never done before, no one would have believed you could, let alone that it would succeed on such a grand scale. It's your job to do the same thing in your chosen field of drama. Never accept 'It can't be done.' Class dismissed."

... ...

As Leann's performance ended, Lieutenant Nussi sat in front of her hologram, tears running unashamedly down her cheeks. Every other hologram on the bridge, throughout the ship, and on the moon base was displaying the same ending.

Even Gwerny, the tough old Mellincon, cleared his throat and left the room before he embarrassed himself by any display of emotion.

Captain Xanny sat in his captain's chair on the bridge. He had enjoyed the performance as much as everyone else. "What would I do if I were the prince?" he asked himself. Then he wondered, "What can she give us after that? What if the next piece is even better?" Then wondered, yet again, "Who is it that wants to kill this species? And why?"

Already recordings of Leann's performance were spreading through the galaxy as the emails left the ship to loved ones everywhere.

Chapter 2 – If Only

"President Robbins, the base chaplain is here to see you."

President Robbins was surprised. *What now?* he asked himself. "OK. Show him in."

The door to the president's office opened. President Robbins stood and walked around his desk to shake the father's hand. "Father Acosta, what can I do for you?"

"Could we sit and talk for a moment, President Robbins?"

"Sure, I have five minutes."

They both sat. The father was silent for a moment, then began, "I'd like to talk about the content of Ms. Jenkins's presentations to the aliens."

"*Romeo and Juliet* was terrific, wasn't it?" President Robbins gushed.

"What is the purpose of her presentations?"

"To show the aliens we aren't a bunch of gun-toting, knife-wielding cretins who want to rape and pillage the rest of the galaxy. She has selected a series of poetry and prose she thinks has a universal beauty and appeal."

"President Robbins, what document has more beauty than the Bible? Why isn't she reading passages from the Bible?"

President Robbins realized where this was going. He wasn't a particularly religious man. He attended nondenominational services because he was expected to do so by the public of the United States.

"Which passages would you want her to read, Father? Should we have her dwell on Leviticus where God tells us over and over how to offer animal sacrifices or murder gay men? Should I have her read from Numbers about how he killed the Egyptians' first-born sons? Or the seven angels with the seven plagues in Revelation?"

The good father glared at President Robbins coldly. "I would have thought the Gospel of Matthew would be appropriate."

"I'm sure they would want to hear about the damned being tortured forever, about doing it his way or else. I'll bet they bring us into their loving arms after that one."

"Do you believe in God, President Robbins?"

President Robbins returned the hostile gaze of the priest, not sure how to proceed. "Yes I do, Father Acosta. I believe in a loving God who helps us and guides us. I believe in a God who lets us choose our path, then shows us why what we did was a good or bad choice. But if you'd like Leann to read from the Bible, why not the Qur'an and the Vida's also? There are more Muslims on Earth than Christians. She is supposed to be representing all people on Earth, not just the Christians in the United States. Within the borders of our country, we have large populations of Muslims, Hindus, Sikhs, Buddhists, Wiccans, and Native Americans. Why shouldn't we read from their holy books as well?"

They were both quiet for a moment, their faces red.

President Robbins broke the silence and said gently to the father, "I am assuming the aliens have their own religions, perhaps hundreds, even thousands of different religions from the thousands of species in the Ur all over the galaxy. What makes you think they would have any more tolerance of our religions than you have for my own perception of our God? I can't imagine any more nonproductive thing in our efforts to convince them to give us a second chance than to try to present one of our religions as the only way to Heaven."

Father Acosta started to say something, then stopped, at a loss for words. After a moment, he stood. "I will tell my congregation of your decision. They may not view your perspective as benignly as I am required to do."

President Robbins stood also. "I have no problem with what Leann has selected. Until she reads something that does not present the 'good' and 'beautiful' of humanity, *all* humanity, I will not intervene."

Father Acosta stood and left the office without saying another word and without shaking the president's hand.

… … … … … … … … …

"Professor Flamé, was it your idea or Leann's to perform *Romeo and Juliet* with Leann playing all of the parts?"

Michel Stern, a reporter from the Calgary radio station 98.5 FM, Virgin Radio, had asked him for an interview after Leann credited the professor as her coach and mentor. He agreed.

"Leann is an amazing woman. When she came to me with the idea, my first question was 'Why?' I didn't know Leann and couldn't imagine any reason that someone would want to perform *Romeo and Juliet* in this way. Then she explained her objective and asked if what she wanted to do was even possible."

"I was ready to show her the door when she stood and did three famous lines from three different characters in the play so well it gave me chills. I have directed, acted in, and watched *Romeo and Juliet* more times than I can remember, perhaps forty or fifty times. When she did Romeo calling to Juliet in the garden so well, I decided to see what else she could do as a single actor. The more we rehearsed and experimented, the more excited I became. But I was completely unprepared for how well it turned out. Leann may have created an entirely new way for Shakespeare to be performed. I've already started experimenting with *A Midsummer Night's Dream.* Now all I need to do is find someone else with as much multicharacter talent as Leann has."

Professor Flamé paused for a moment, then took a drink of water. As he set his glass down, he continued, "May I ask you a question, Ms. Stern?"

She looked up from her notes in surprise. "Of course, Professor."

"What did you think of the performance?"

She put her pen down with a thoughtful expression. "I was a Journalism major in college. I went to King's College in Halifax. This was my first *Romeo and Juliet.* The only thing I wanted to do when it was over was watch it again. My boyfriend and I finally agreed on something. We both loved it."

… … … … … … … … …

The bulkhead door closed. "Flug?" Zarqa whispered.

"I'm here. What's so important that you would risk compromising us?" Flug still could not believe Zarqa had spoken about getting a message off-ship in the canteen with other people around.

"I found out two things. We have to send them to Captain Xanny."

"What are they?"

"Fey Pey didn't meet with Envoy Gart-Disp."

"Who did he meet with?"

"The king of Glycemis."

"Really?" Flug was amazed. "I thought the king issued a shoot-on-sight order against Fey Pey. He was supposed to have knocked-up the king's daughter."

"He did. I mean he does. Publicly. I guess it was all a cover story."

"What did they say together? Why did they meet?"

"The king hired Fey Pey to plant the dream. He even had a witch transferred to Fey Pey's ship to do the actual plant. Her name was Ruatha. She was from Zindarr."

"Why did they do that? Why did they plant the dream? I don't see what's in it for them to take such a chance."

"That's the second thing I need to tell the captain."

"What? Holy shit! You found out why they did it! Why?"

"They raised up one of the aquatic mammals on Earth."

"You said that in the past tense. You mean they already did it? Before the primates are even gone?"

"That's what I'm saying. That's why they stayed away from Earth for the week after they left Glycemis. The king gave them the DNA for a species of aquatic mammals on Earth. The DNA was modified by the genetic scientists on Glycemis for the raise up. Fey Pey's crew needed a week to incubate the Species Inoculation Virus for the inoculation distribution. They released the virus when they came to Earth to plant the dream."

"Wow! That is wrong on so many levels."

"I guess they were tired of being the only aquatic mammals in the Ur. We have to get this to Captain Xanny."

"Yep. Now I understand what was so important."

The bulkhead door opened. "Arrest them," Fey Pey commanded. He was an aquatic mammal also. He floated into the room surrounded by a cocoon of water two inches thick. An antigrav device under his belly supported him and gave him locomotion.

Zarqa pressed a button on her tunic.

… … … … … … … … …

"Leann, that was an absolutely amazing performance!" Lily Yuan gushed. The two of them talked every day before Leann did the transmissions of prose and poetry to the aliens. In the time Leann prepared for the trip in the capsule, they had become fast friends.

"Did it come through OK?" Leann was having breakfast.

"Yes, it did. Every military base on the network is buzzing with how great a job you did. I have a message from your drama coach at the University of Calgary."

"What did he say? Wait! Is it bad? I don't think I want to know what he said if it's bad."

Lily chuckled. "Well, if someone said those things about me, I'd frame them. You decide." Lily cleared her throat and began reading. "Leann, I've never seen anyone play any of those individual parts as well as you did each one. And you did them all equally well. Amazing performance. Standing ovation! Bravo! If that didn't save humanity, nothing will. Your heroism has set an example for the men and women of the world. Your biggest fan, Professor George Flamé."

Leann clutched the chair in front of the console, closed her eyes, and let the relief sweep over her. Of all the people of the world, Professor Flamé's opinion was the one she dreaded the most. Without even knowing it, she started to weep. Great tears ran down her cheeks. It worked! Her reading was a success!

When she got herself under control again, she straightened her shoulders. A soft smile filled her face. "Please tell him how much his kind words meant to me. I hope I can keep doing as well. Because to not succeed is something I won't even consider."

"Well, if you liked that one, wait until you hear what President Robbins said." She cleared her throat and began. "'Leann that was marvelous! Thank you so much for choosing *Romeo and Juliet*. It was a stellar performance. Paula and I were both in tears at the end. We await your next selection with approval and anticipation.'"

Leann took another breath, wiped her eyes, and prepared herself mentally for the day's reading.

"Have I told you how much I admire what you are doing?" Lily asked. "I do. I wouldn't have the guts to do it."

"You have a child, Lily. She needs you more than anything else. And if this works, I'll be able to have one of my own."

When she felt she was ready, Leann pressed the transmit button, turning on the feed aimed at the moon base.

... ...

"She's transmitting again!" the cry sounded through the ship on the shipwide PA system.

All holograms on the ship and moon base were instantly switched to Leann's channel.

A composed and confident Leann Jenkins greeted them. "Hello my friends. I guess my telling of the story of *Romeo and Juliet* exhausted me more than I realized. I planned to start earlier than this. Today I would like to present some poetry and prose created by some people from Earth. I have three selections for you, two by men and one by a little girl.

"My first selection is by a man who lived a hundred and fifty years ago. His name was Walt Whitman. He presented a sexual side to his poetry, considered by many to be obscene when he wrote it. His writing was banned in many places. Now it is considered to be way ahead of its time. Here is a poem that doesn't rhyme. It doesn't have a ponderous rhythm. It talks about something as banal as the mating of two eagles, large raptors that live on Earth. Whitman uses them as a metaphor to present the beauty of the independence of the female and the male spirits. When eagles mate, they are both airborne. Their union has the appearance of a violent confrontation. They join claws at a high altitude and fall together with their wings flailing until just before they strike the ground. They break apart, then fly to their separate destinations, never to see each other again.

"Here is *The Dalliance of the Eagles.*"

> "Skirting the river road, (my forenoon walk, my rest,)
> Skyward in air a sudden muffled sound, the dalliance of the eagles,
> The rushing amorous contact high in space together,
> The clinching interlocking claws, a living, fierce, gyrating wheel,
> Four beating wings, two beaks, a swirling mass tight grappling,
> In tumbling turning clustering loops, straight downward falling,
> Till o'er the river pois'd, the twain yet one, a moment's lull,
> A motionless still balance in the air, then parting, talons loosing,
> Upward again on slow-firm pinions slanting, their separate diverse flight,
> She hers, he his, pursuing."

"How different this is from how many people view the sexual encounter. This was a joining of equals, not one that was brought about by dependence or subservience of one gender to the other. When it was done, each of the participants went their separate ways, pursuing their own goals."

Lieutenant Nussi stood in front of her hologram, raised her fist, and shouted, "YES!"

The other females around the bridge nodded in agreement. The males weren't sure how they felt about the selection.

....

"My next piece is by another man. His name is Robert Frost. He was a young man when Walt Whitman was finishing his life. This poem is called *Mending Wall.* Frost used common words and clear expressions to write about complex things. This is a poem about two neighbors walking the property line between their homes and repairing the damage winter has done to the wall separating their properties. But in a larger sense, this is a poem about barriers, both physical and emotional. Here is *Mending Wall.*"

"Something there is that doesn't love a wall,
That sends the frozen-ground-swell under it,
And spills the upper boulders in the sun;
And makes gaps even two can pass abreast.
The work of hunters is another thing:
I have come after them and made repair
Where they have left not one stone on a stone,
But they would have the rabbit out of hiding,
To please the yelping dogs. The gaps I mean,
No one has seen them made or heard them made,
But at spring mending-time we find them there.
I let my neighbor know beyond the hill;
And on a day we meet to walk the line
And set the wall between us once again.
We keep the wall between us as we go.
To each the boulders that have fallen to each.
And some are loaves and some so nearly balls
We have to use a spell to make them balance:
'Stay where you are until our backs are turned!'
We wear our fingers rough with handling them.

Oh, just another kind of outdoor game,
One on a side. It comes to little more:
There where it is we do not need the wall:
He is all pine and I am apple orchard.
My apple trees will never get across
And eat the cones under his pines, I tell him.
He only says, 'Good fences make good neighbors.'
Spring is the mischief in me, and I wonder
If I could put a notion in his head:
'Why do they make good neighbors? Isn't it
Where there are cows? But here there are no
cows.
Before I built a wall I'd ask to know
What I was walling in or walling out,
And to whom I was like to give offense.
Something there is that doesn't love a wall,
That wants it down.' I could say 'Elves' to him,
But it's not elves exactly, and I'd rather
He said it for himself. I see him there
Bringing a stone grasped firmly by the top
In each hand, like an old-stone savage armed.
He moves in darkness as it seems to me,
Not of woods only and the shade of trees.
He will not go behind his father's saying,
And he likes having thought of it so well
He says again, 'Good fences make good
neighbors."

"So does the speaker really not like walls? Why then does he join his neighbor for their once-a-year rite of repairing them? I believe he gets some comfort from the annual effort, making it a game and teasing his neighbor about why the wall should exist at all. While he apparently resists the need for the wall, he willingly interacts with his neighbor while they walk the fence line. How many of us have our own walls that we have erected so we don't have to venture beyond them? We rail at them. We criticize their need. But deep down, we're glad they are there."

She paused a moment to let that sink in.

"My last selection is a little longer. It was written by a girl named Anne Frank while her family was in hiding during a war that raged across our world many years ago. She was a member of a group of people known as 'Jews.' They had been singled out as 'disposable' by the German people who invaded her country. After the occupation of their country took place, Anne's father, Otto Frank, decided to move his family and another family, the van Daans, into a hidden apartment in his office building. Anne was thirteen years old. Just before they went into hiding, Anne had been given a diary for her birthday celebration. In it, she recorded her innermost thoughts, joys, and fears while the two families waited for the end of the war and freedom from their self-imposed incarceration. Anne's diary spans the two years the two families hid together in that little loft. Their crowded life together was full of arguments and danger. Many times they were hungry and cold, but they dared not leave the safety of the apartment. Anne's story is one of hope against all adversity. Hope that refused to fade while the occupying army tore at her country and killed her friends. I read for you, *The Diary of a Young Girl.*"

> "Saturday, 13 June 1942
> On Friday, 12 June, I woke up early at six o'clock; it was my birthday. I'm not allowed to get up then, so I had to wait until quarter to seven. Then I went down to the dining-room, where Moortje, my cat, welcomed me. At seven I went in to Mummy and Daddy, and then to the sitting-room for my presents. The nicest present was *you*—my diary! There was a bunch of roses on the table, and lots more flowers and presents arrived for me during the day. Daddy and Mummy gave me a blue blouse, a game and a bottle of fruit juice which tastes quite like wine! At school, I shared out some cakes with my friends, and I was allowed to choose the game that we played in the

sports lesson. Afterwards, all my friends danced round me in a circle and sang 'Happy Birthday.'

....

"How wonderful it is that nobody need wait a single moment before starting to improve the world.

....

"We aren't allowed to have any opinions. People can tell you to keep your mouth shut, but it doesn't stop you having your own opinion. Even if people are still very young, they shouldn't be prevented from saying what they think.

....

"Everyone has inside of him a piece of good news. The good news is that you don't know how great you can be! How much you can love! What you can accomplish! And what your potential is!

....

"It's difficult in times like these: ideals, dreams and cherished hopes rise within us, only to be crushed by grim reality. It's a wonder I haven't abandoned all my ideals, they seem so absurd and impractical. Yet I cling to them because I still believe, in spite of everything, that people are truly good at heart.

....

“What is done cannot be undone, but one can prevent it happening again.

....

“Whoever is happy will make others happy too.

....

“I must uphold my ideals, for perhaps the time will come when I shall be able to carry them out.

....

“I don’t think of all the misery but of the beauty that still remains.

....

“Nature makes me feel humble and ready to face every blow with courage!

....

“When you are on your bed at night just analyse all the happenings you have been go through whole day and learn from your mistakes, you will be a better person then.

....

“How wonderful it is that nobody need wait a single moment before starting to improve the world.

....

"In spite of everything, I still believe people are good at heart.

....

"Everyone has inside of him a piece of good news. The good news is that you don't know how great you can be! How much you can love! What you can accomplish! And what your potential is!

....

"I don't think of all the misery, but of the beauty that still remains

....

"Whoever is happy will make others happy.

....

"In the long run, the sharpest weapon of all is a kind and gentle spirit.

....

Leann looked grimly into the camera. "This is the end of Anne's diary. The Franks and van Daans were arrested by the occupying police on August fourth, three days after her last entry. Anne died that winter of a disease while she was in one of the German prison camps. Her body was thrown into a mass grave and never recovered. She was fifteen years-old. The war ended soon after she died and the criminals who started it were punished. Her diary was found and preserved by one of the people from her father's business. Anne's father, Otto Frank, was sent to a different prison camp from Anne's. He survived the end of the war and returned to the little house where he and his family hid for those years. He spent the rest of his life publishing and promoting his daughter's memoir in the hope that people would see the horror of war and never let it happen again. The little apartment Anne lived in for those two years was turned into a shrine. It is visited every year by people from all over the world who want to see for themselves where the little girl, who refused to stop hoping, lived. Most of the visitors offer a prayer that the leaders of our world never let this happen again."

... ...

Captain Xanny stayed in the canteen where he had watched Leann's reading with most of the off-duty crew. Unlike her other performances, this one was greeted with complete silence.

"How could they have produced this work?" one of the analysts finally asked. "They are primitive primates! Primitives don't feel these things."

"This is the same story as Nansi Mwettr," another added. "My mother read that story to me when I was a child."

Nansi Mwettr was the hero of childhood stories about the atrocities of war. Her story had been made and remade into countless movies in hundreds of languages. It was the popularity of her story that led to the public outcry that, in turn, led to the creation of the GSCB. The GSBC had established the evaluation process and milestones that were used to fail humanity's admission to the Ur. No other story could have made the crew question humanity's failure more than this one.

Chapter 3 – Make a Great Movie

The emergency aid camp was set up in what was left of Charlottesville, Virginia. The people waited in line at the mess tent. There was none of the joking or even nervous talking that normally accompanied the arrival of help in an emergency. The survivors had the ten-thousand-yard stare of people who experienced an event that was so massive and so traumatic that their minds shut down its ability to absorb any more. They looked ten thousand yards away because what was next to them was beyond belief.

The troops from Fort Bragg served the people who survived the evacuation of the radiation, land, and water. No one spoke. People ate because they didn't know what else to do. Nothing would ever be the same for them.

According to their stories and pictures, a wall of water, a mile high, rushed in from the Atlantic Ocean to fill the forty-five thousand square miles of the United States that had been suddenly sent into the sun. That wall hit the foothills around Charlottesville like a billion-ton battering ram, removing granite mountains that were a hundred million years old like they were made of mud and dust.

Then all that water returned to the sea carrying with it homes, people, cars, roads, electrical transmission towers, dams, factories, bridges, stores, farms, churches, gas stations—pretty much everything humans put in place. A lot of the land that was left after the tsunami blasted in was sucked back into the hole. Every survivor had their own story about how they survived and how countless others had not. Children, wives, husbands, parents, pets, livestock—swept away while the survivors watched, helpless to prevent it.

Crews from Fort Bragg moved among the survivors, taping and questioning them to make a record of what happened and to prepare a briefing for the president. The same interviews were taking place all around the new shoreline that ran from New York

City to Harrisburg, Pennsylvania, to Petersburg, Virginia, all the way to the northern edge of the Barrier Islands of North Carolina.

… … … … … … … … …

"Is that where we're supposed to meet them?" Freddie asked Jeremiah.

They arrived at the shopping mall at Santa Clarita where they were supposed to meet the friendlies who were going to help them take over the valley. The front of the Walmart across the parking lot was destroyed. Someone had burned it after everything that could be stolen was carried out. The smoke stains above the doors made the storefront appear to be the vacant eyes of a skull.

"Yeah." Jeremiah continued to study the storefront with his infrared night vision goggles. Other than a mild glow from the rock on the front of the store as it continued to cool from the day before, no other heat sources were visible. "We've got another half hour to wait before the rendezvous."

"If they come at all," Freddie finished.

"Yeah, well, there's always that."

The four trucks in the convoy parked in a circle, nose to tail, like the wagon trains of old. The motors and lights were off. Freddie was very quiet, unusual for him.

"You did a good thing back there, Freddie. That woman would have killed us all."

Freddie didn't say anything for a while. Finally he spoke into the silence, "I fucked up. I should have found a way to calm her down. She didn't need to die."

"There was nothing else you could have done. She was psycho." Jeremiah spit on the ground. "No one could have stopped what happened. From what I saw, she and her husband were cut from the same psycho cloth. Good riddance."

"My head knows that. My heart's not convinced."

"That guy we left in charge, now he'll do a good job." Jeremiah searched the parking lot again with his night-vision goggles.

"I hope so. I wouldn't want there to be another road block when we go back through."

While they waited for the friendlies to show up, Freddie studied the stars above the parking lot and wondered how his children were doing in Montana.

"His" children, he laughed at himself. Wilson and Shannon were his assigned wards in the Sterile Heritage Protection Site (SHIPS) where children, uninfected by the Baby Stopper Virus (BSV), were being raised to populate a colony on another planet. Freddie was uninfected also. He had been a hundred yards underwater serving on a nuclear sub when BSV was released. For two years he happily raised ten newborns, gestated inside chimpanzees and bonobos, close genetic cousins of humans but unaffected by BSV. Then the Three-Hour War struck. The SHIPS he had been assigned to was blown up. Freddie was able to escape the destruction with only Shannon and Wilson of his ten toddlers. The other eight perished in a huge explosion. He found shelter for the three of them in an abandoned house. The people in the neighboring farm, Ray and Andrea O'Flynn, discovered them after six months and brought them to their house where they lived until President Robbins issued his call for all military men and women to report to their nearest base for assignment. Leaving those children with Ray and Andrea had been the hardest thing he had ever done.

He pulled out his cell phone and turned it on. The faces of Shannon and Wilson in his arms looked out at him. Andrea took the picture the day he left their ranch.

"Are you guys happy?" he asked the children in the picture. "Will you remember me?"

A battered pickup drove into the parking lot and stopped about a hundred yards away from the Marines' encampment.

"Heads up," Jeremiah said to the team. "I hope these are the good guys."

He needn't have bothered alerting the rest of the Marines. The clicks of safeties going off sounded from all four of the trucks.

The pickup flashed its lights twice, then twice more.

"It's them. Rawlins, bring them in."

Lance Corporal Rawlins picked up his M-4 carbine, climbed down from his position as one of the M-60 gunners in Popeye, and cautiously began his walk to the pickup. The rest of the team covered him and watched in all directions for anyone else to appear.

Everyone saw Rawlins jump into the back of the pickup. It drove over to the Marines' trucks. A man got out of the cab with his arms up.

"I am unarmed," the man announced loudly. He was middle-aged. Maybe a little older than middle-aged. He had a short beard with salt-and-pepper hair.

Rawlins climbed out of the bed and did a quick pat down. "Yep. He is."

Jeremiah walked out from the trucks. "I am Gunny Sergeant Jeremiah Silverstein. Are you Carlos Sanchez?"

"*Sí*. That would be me. Welcome to Santa Clarita."

… … … … … … … … …

"Captain Xanny, please come to the bridge."

Lieutenant Nussi looked up in surprise as she lay in her bunk reading. She wasn't on duty, but she decided she might be needed on the bridge as well. She got there before Captain Xanny.

"What's going on, Kletra?"

"We've received a 'Captain's eyes only'," she told Lieutenant Nussi. No one was allowed to access a Captain's-Eyes-Only message but the captain and Lieutenant Nussi, his Communications Officer.

"Good job, Kletra. I'll take over your station. You are relieved for a few minutes."

"Great! I need to pass waste." She got up from the comm station and walked off the bridge.

Captain Xanny floated in moments later. "What's happening, Nola?"

"Sergeant Donax has received a 'Captain's Eyes Only'."

"What does it say?"

"Everyone leave the bridge," Lieutenant Nussi ordered.

The crew filed out and closed the hatchway.

"I don't know. I haven't seen it yet."

"Well, then play it."

Lieutenant Nussi pressed a glowing red light on the comm hologram. The emotionless computer voice read the message

"We have been discovered. Fey Pey didn't meet with Envoy Gart-Disp. He met with the king of Glycemis. The king hired Fey Pey to plant the dream. He transferred a witch to Fey Pey's ship to do the actual plant. Her name was Ruatha. She was from Zindarr. In addition to planting the dream, Fey Pey has raised up one of the aquatic mammals on Earth. That's why they stayed away from Earth for the week after they left Glycemis. The king gave them the DNA for a species of an indigenous aquatic mammal on Earth. The DNA had been modified by the genetic scientists on Glycemis for the raise up. Fey Pey's crew needed a week to incubate the species inoculation virus for distribution when he arrived. They released the virus when they came to Earth to plant the dream."

"Xxjllpedrsss!" Captain Xanny said angrily to the air.

Lieutenant Nussi blushed at the expletive. She had never heard Captain Xanny use such a foul word before.

"I'm sorry, Nola," he apologized, after realizing he said it out loud. "The only reason we would receive that transmission is if they have been killed. Zarqa would have known sending that message would be their death sentence. What a loss!"

Lieutenant Nussi was silent. Zarqa had been a close friend of hers. They served together for over five years. "It was a linked-Hore transmission, sir. Fey Pey won't know what was in the message, only that it was sent."

"That's even worse," the captain said sadly. "If they aren't dead yet, they will be tortured to find out what was in the message and to whom it was sent. You don't want to know what kind of tortures a scum like Fey Pey can dream up. Encrypt that message and put it in my personal storage. I'll be in my quarters preparing a letter to Zarqa's and Flug's next of kin."

"Yes, sir. Do you want me to forward the message to Corporate Headquarters?"

Captain Xanny pondered her request for a moment. "Not yet. All we have is a radio transmission from someone who, I suspect, isn't alive anymore. Before we can make this public, we'll need some incontrovertible proof. This could lead to a galactic war. Unless we want to be caught in the crossfire, we will have to be very careful about this. Let me consider our options. I'll let you know."

"Yes, sir."

Captain Xanny paused before he opened the hatchway to let the bridge crew back in. "Wasn't there a news story on Earth a while back about an aquatic mammal that was behaving strangely? Something about a primate boy being rescued?"

"I don't remember it, sir. I'll do a search."

"Let me know what you find."

"Yes, sir."

... ...

Rebecca looked with satisfaction at the progress they had made building the house for Jonathan and Caitlin. The roof was on. The siding went on a couple of days ago. The windows were in and sealed. All that remained, to get the house dried-in, was to install the doors. Inside, the place was chaos. Cabinets, appliances, fixtures, and lights were piled everywhere along with wire, connection boxes, outlets, rolls of red and blue plastic water lines, fittings, connectors, insulation, and tools. After some reluctance at the beginning of the project, Jonathan was working harder than anyone else.

"So, Jonathan," Rebecca asked, "do you want to shim the front door in or do you want me to do it? It's the last door. When the front door's in place, the house becomes a home."

"You do it. I never got the hang of shimming them damned doors. Whenever I do it, they come out crooked and the doors don't close right."

"OK. Or I could show you how to do it right."

Jonathan glanced at her out of the side of his eyes, spit, then sighed. It was hard for him to ask a woman for anything. But Rebecca was unlike any woman he ever knew. "I *would* like to know how to do it right, if you don't mind."

"I don't mind at all. Then you can do the interior doors when we get to them." Rebecca picked up a handful of shims. "Get the door. I'll get the level, a hammer, and a utility knife. It's easy once you know how to do it. We'll need some foam sealant, too, since this is an outside door."

Fifteen minutes later, the door was shimmed in place. It opened and closed perfectly.

Jonathan was thrilled. "Why, there wadn't nothing to that! A kid could a done that."

"Everything's easy, once you know how to do it," Rebecca agreed. "Can you put in the foam to seal it in?"

"I believe I can." He picked up the can of foam sealant, then hesitated. "Rebecca, how did you learn how to do this? Women don't know this sh ..." he stopped for a second, then finished with "stuff."

"My dad was a carpenter." Rebecca smiled at the memory. "I helped him build our house in Half Moon Bay."

"I prob'ly woudda liked 'im."

"And he would have liked you, Jonathan. He loved working with his hands." She picked up her tool belt. "OK. I'm going to help Tony. He's stringing the water lines to the bathroom."

... ...

"Today I'm going to read a book my friends on Earth recommended to me. Before I left, I asked them what books meant the most to them among all of the books they read. The hands-down favorite was this one. It was written almost a hundred and fifty years ago about a time, fifty years earlier, in my country's past when slavery was still allowed. It wasn't long after this period that we had a great war that ended slavery and gave those enslaved people full citizenship and the right to vote.

"This is a story about a boy growing up next to a huge river. It was written by a man named Samuel Clemens, who lived his boy-years in a little town much like the one in the story. It's a love story, an adventure story, a murder story, and a hero story. I give you *The Adventures of Tom Sawyer*. It opens with Tom's Aunt Polly calling to him."

> "'TOM!'
> No answer.
> 'TOM!'
> No answer.
> 'What's wrong with that boy, I wonder? You TOM!'
>
> ...
>
> "'Mayn't I go and play now, aunt?'
> 'What, a'ready? How much have you done?'
> 'It's all done, aunt." '
> 'Tom, don't lie to me—I can't bear it.'
> 'I ain't, aunt. It is all done.'
> Aunt Polly placed small trust in such evidence. She went out to see for herself; and she would have been content to find twenty percent of Tom's statement true. When she found the entire fence whitewashed, and not only whitewashed but elaborately coated and re-coated,
>
> ...
>
> "'– and as the doctor fetched the board around and Muff Potter fell, Injun Joe jumped with the knife and ...'
> Crash! Quick as lightning the half-breed sprang for a window, tore his way through all opposers and was gone!

> …
>
> "'Turn out! Turn out! They're found! They're found!" Tin pans and horns added to the din, the population massed itself and moved toward the river, met the children coming in an open carriage drawn by shouting citizens, thronged about it, joined its homeward march, and swept magnificently up the main street roaring Huzzah after Huzzah.
>
> …
>
> "So endeth this chronical. It being strictly a history of a boy, it must stop here; the story could not go much further without becoming the history of a man. When one writes a novel about grown people, he knows exactly where to stop—that is, with a marriage; but when he writes of juveniles, he must stop where best he can.
>
> "Most of the characters who perform in this book still live, and are prosperous and happy. Someday it may seem worthwhile to take up the story of the younger ones again and see what sort of men and women they turned out to be; therefore it will be wisest not to reveal any of that part of the their lives at present."

… … … … … … … … …

Captain Xanny chuckled to himself. "History of a boy has to stop before it's a history of a man! Hah!"

He turned back to his email queue and groaned. It was cancer! His email account had caught the dreaded mail-inbox cancer! No matter what he did, it kept getting bigger. While he replied to one after another, he kept remembering scenes in Tom Sawyer.

He daydreamed a moment between emails. "Make a great movie," he mumbled, thinking back to the court scene with Injun Joe, then the cave scene with Becky. He grinned again at Tom getting all the other kids to pay him so they could paint the fence. "I wonder if that would work around this ship? Maybe someone would pay *me* to reply to my emails!" He sighed again as he opened the next email.

"Please explain why your supplies forecast was two percent under what you requisitioned." Captain Xanny groaned. "Is it too late to tell them I wanna be a pirate again?"

Until Captain Xanny became a legitimate species miner employed by Grock Corporation, he had led a semisuccessful career as a very illegal, very unregistered species miner and pirate.

Chapter 4 – ¿Qué Paso?

Her communicator broke the silence of her ambush. "Lieutenant Fibari, please attend me in my quarters."

Fela was irritated at the interruption. She was leading a practice exercise in repelling invaders from the airlocks of the starship.

"Sergeant Tannl, continue without me."

"Yes, sir."

She leaned over to his ear so only he could hear. "I have a second group of aggressors ready to enter by another airlock to attack these guys from behind. I want these guys in a cross fire. Kill yourself and see who takes over."

Sergeant Tannl chuckled. "Got it."

"Here's the activation link. Press it when you want the other group to attack."

Lieutenant Fibari was feline with gray and black stripes, about fifty kilograms and one and a half meters from her whiskers to the tip of her tail. Half her left ear was gone and an old scar that was actually three parallel scars, began on her right shoulder, continued diagonally across her back, and ended on her left flank. She moved with a peace and grace that belied the ferociousness that earned her the position of Ship Sergeant-At-Arms aboard GSMS-77, the Grock Corporation's species mining starship commanded by Captain Xanny.

She padded into Captain Xanny's quarters and sat down next to him. "You wanted to see me, sir?"

"Fela, is the shuttle still set up for long distance travel?"

"I believe so, sir. I told the maintenance people to leave it as it was when we returned from our last trip."

"Good. I want you to go back to Taramon and deliver a message to Zuna for me. This is top secret and must happen immediately. I can't leave or I would do it myself."

"What is the message?"

"It's in this crystal. No one but Zuna or her mother will be able to open it to get the message. Deliver it into Zuna's hands—hers and no other's."

The crystal was mounted in a ring. Lieutenant Fibari slid the ring onto a middle toe of her front right paw. The crystal was about the size of a pea. She had never been one to wear jewelry. The ring felt odd.

"I want you to take one more person. You choose. Someone you trust completely. Someone who can handle the shuttle as well as you. Someone who can use the armaments and do a jump. When you get to Taramon, leave that person on the shuttle while you deliver the message. Zuna will ask you to transport her somewhere else. Take her wherever she asks. After she's done, she will want to return to Taramon. Take her. Be prepared for the unexpected."

About a thousand questions were clamoring for attention in her head, but she decided Captain Xanny would have told her more if he could. There was a reason she was being kept in the dark and it was probably for her own safety. That concerned her more than the trip. What could be so secret at a pirate play planet?

She got up. "I should be able to leave in half an hour."

"Good. All communications between us must be done by linked-Hore radios. Bring a spare."

"Yes, sir." Fela walked back to her quarters.

"Who should I bring?" she asked herself. The answer was obvious. She went back to the airlock drill. It was finished. Sergeant Tannl was giving a wrap-up critique to the aggressors and defenders as they sat around the briefing room.

"When I died, no one took over. You were completely disorganized and got killed. You deserved it. Who should have taken over?"

Corporal Mixx pursed her lips and raised her hand.

Sergeant Tannl smiled at her, then spun around the room and glared at another person. "Wrong! It should have been you, Sergeant Vue. Where the hell were you?"

"I had to take a leak. It was only a drill."

"We will run another drill tomorrow. Sergeant Vue, if you have to take a leak during that one, you will turn in your sergeant stripes. As far as any of you are concerned, this is real. You better hope this is as real as it ever gets for you. Otherwise you wouldn't be sitting around talking about what you did wrong and I would be writing letters to your next of kin. If you don't want to play by these rules, find a job in another department. Are we clear? We are training so you can stay alive in case it ever does get real."

Sergeant Vue wasn't used to being chastised by a fellow sergeant, especially in front of the rest of the team. He gave Sergeant Tannl a dirty look but didn't say a word as he got up to leave.

Lieutenant Fibari spoke up. "Sergeant Vue, you are assigned to moon base. Pack your bag and get down there. You have thirty minutes to clear the ship."

"There's no defense functions down there," he complained. "Everything's automated. I'll be bored shitless."

"Well, considering you won't be on defense, that shouldn't be a problem."

"You're firing me?" he asked in disbelief. "Over a drill?"

"Should have done it months ago. Don't know why I didn't."

"This is Kroll-shit. I want to see the captain."

"Be my guest. But if I were you, I'd suck it in and go down to moon base. The last person who complained about my orders was fired on the spot and returned to Grock. She's working in a cafeteria on Oort now."

Ex-Sergeant Vue left the room without saying another word. Lieutenant Fibari turned to Corporal Mixx. "Corporal, you are now Sergeant Mixx. You will run the exercise tomorrow." She studied the rest of the team in silence for a moment. "Tomorrow we will run an incoming photon torpedo drill. Amaze me. You will run the drill without either myself or Sergeant Tannl being present. Consider us casualties. Dismissed. Sergeant Tannl, please remain behind."

Everyone filed out, looking with compassion at Sergeant Tannl. They were sure he was going to get reamed for letting the exercise get out of hand.

After the last person left, Fela closed the door to the briefing room

Sergeant Tannl tried to explain. "Lieutenant, I apologize for not keeping track of Sergeant Vue. He was a flake. I should have expected him to do something stupid."

"The mistake was mine in not getting rid of that idiot months ago. I kept hoping he would improve. All he would have done was get everyone else killed." She could see the shock in his eyes. "You did exactly what I told you to do. But that's not what I wanted to talk to you about."

Sergeant Tannl cocked his head and waited. This wasn't turning out like he expected, at all.

"I want you to go with me to Taramon. I have to deliver a message. You will remain on the shuttle at the spaceport. We have to leave in twenty minutes. This is a volunteer mission only. You do not have to go and no record will be made if you decide to turn me down."

"I am assuming this mission is not without danger?"

"I am assuming the same thing."

"Count me in," he said without hesitation. "To tell you the truth, it's been a little boring around here lately."

"Yeah, well, sometimes boring is good."

"And sometimes it's just boring," he said with a smile.

Lieutenant Fibari laughed out loud when he said that. She had said those exact words to Captain Xanny two years ago, just before she sent Earth's under-construction starships into the sun. "Meet me at the shuttle in twenty minutes, ready to go."

… … … … … … … … …

"My last prose reading is a story that has captivated the imagination of humans, young and old, since it was written. It is an adventure story written of the time before radios, airplanes, and electronic navigation, before boats used great engines to move them effortlessly across our oceans. It is about sailing when sailing meant taking your life in your hands and praying the winds would blow your little boat safely to far shores. The captains of these brave ships fought their way through huge storms, hostile natives, unknown waters, and pirates to explore faraway lands on the hope of finding treasure and bringing it home. No one is entirely good or entirely bad in this story. So before I begin reading, I must get into the spirit of the book."

Leann got out a black scarf with a skull and crossbones on the front. She tied it across her forehead, then put on large gold earrings and opened a bottle of rum. She poured an inch of rum into a glass, held up the glass to the camera.

"I will begin with the pirate's toast." She downed the rum and chanted in a throaty voice, "Fifteen men on the dead man's chest—Yo-ho-ho and a bottle of rum!—Drink and the devil had done for the rest—Yo-ho-ho and a bottle of rum!"

She put down the glass, poured another inch into it, then said into the camera, "I read for you Robert Louis Stevenson's *Treasure Island*."

"Part One: The Old Buccaneer. It begins at a small inn on the shore of a country called England. The inn is named the Admiral Benbow. We meet the young man who is telling the story. His name is Jim Hawkins."

Leann took a breath, another drink of rum, then started.

> "Squire Trelawney, Dr. Livesey, and the rest of these gentlemen having asked me to write down the whole particulars about Treasure Island, from the beginning to the end, keeping nothing back but the bearings of the island, and that only because there is still treasure not yet lifted, I take up my pen in the year of grace 1700 and go back to the time when my father kept the Admiral Benbow Inn and the brown old seaman with the sabre cut first took up his lodging under our roof.

…

"Just then a sort of brightness fell upon the barrel, and looking up, I found the moon had risen and was silvering the mizzen-top and shining white on the luff of the foresail; and almost at the same time the voice of the lookout shouted 'Land ho!'

…

"'The captain's wounded,' said Mr. Trelawney.

'Have they run?' asked Mr. Smollett.

'All that could, you may be bound,' returned the doctor; 'but there's five of them will never run again.'

'Five!' cried the captain. 'Come, that's better. Five against three leaves us four to nine. That's better odds than we had at starting. We were seven to nineteen then, or thought we were, and that's as bad to bear.'

…

"I turned to run, struck violently against one person, recoiled, and ran full into the arms of a second, who for his part closed upon and held me tight.

'Bring a torch, Dick,' said Silver when my capture was thus assured.

> And one of the men left the log-house and presently returned with a lighted brand.
>
> ...
>
> "The next morning we fell early to work, for the transportation of this great mass of gold near a mile by land to the beach, and thence three miles by boat to the Hispaniola, was a considerable task for so small a number of workmen. The three fellows still abroad upon the island did not greatly trouble us; a single sentry on the shoulder of the hill was sufficient to ensure us against any sudden onslaught, and we thought, besides, they had more than enough of fighting.
>
> ...
>
> "The bar silver and the arms still lie, for all that I know, where Flint buried them; and certainly they shall lie there for me. Oxen and wain-ropes would not bring me back again to the accursed island; and the worst dreams that ever I have are when I hear the surf booming about its coasts or start upright in bed with the sharp voice of Captain Flint still ringing in my ears: 'Pieces of eight! Pieces of eight!'

Leann closed the book, looked into the camera, and said in a throaty pirate voice, "Aye, me hearty. Yo-ho-ho and a bottle of rum!" She drained the rest of the glass, turned over the empty bottle of rum, then turned off the camera.

... ...

Captain Xanny watched the signal end in silence. The story had filled him with memories of his own pirate days. He took a deep breath, trying to remember the clean smell of an ocean breeze and the taste of a glass of liquor in a smoky bar, then slipped into his anti-grav unit and floated to the canteen. It was full of people doing the pirate toast with their protein drinks: "Fifteen men on a dead man's chest—Yo-ho-ho and a bottle of rum!"

The crowd was having great fun talking about what it must have been like to sail on one of those old ships.

A gunner's mate who had been in Captain Xanny's pirate crew stood with one leg behind him like Long John Silver. He grabbed hold of another mate and started a soliloquy by memory, using Leann's gravelly Long John Silver voice in a loud whisper, so everyone could hear. "Now, you look here, Jim Hawkins, you're within half a plank of death, and what's a long sight worse, of *torture*." The old mate swung his head around and stared at the audience like a cornered dog. "They're going to throw me off. But you mark, I stand by you through thick and thin."

"Well done!" "Good job!" "Amazing!"

Captain Xanny shook his head. "Glaxcy, I think you missed your calling."

"Ay and many a fat wallet, too! Arggghhh!" Glaxcy hobbled out of the room like he had a wooden leg and an imaginary cane.

"Whoo hooo!" "Encore!"

Glaxcy returned to the doorway and continued his gravelly whisper, "I'm going now to find that wench and her bottle of rum. No one should look that fine and drink alone."

As one being, everyone turned to look at Captain Xanny. He hung his head, hating the words he had to say. "The company said 'No!' I asked, but they won't let me go get her." The words stuck in his throat. He was as taken by the young woman and her stories as the rest of the crew. This was the fourth day of her ten-day mission.

Then an idea popped into his head. "We have recordings of her performances, right?"

There were nods all around the room.

He put on Long John Silver's voice, "Well then, me pirates, there's more'n one way 'a catchin' a treasure ship! Send those stories to all yer friends and tell them to send 'em to all their friends. And tell 'em about the pretty girl in the capsule. We'll see who can't get permission, arggggh!"

No one told him they were already doing that and had been since Leann's first day. Across the galaxy, copies of Leann's performances were going out to friends of friends of friends. Each day the spread of them grew wider. With each performance, Leann's plight was known and important to a vastly growing number of interested people. *Romeo and Juliet* had made its way into the Imperial Palace. Reality TV had finally come to the Ur.

... ...

Princess Tablique ran into the room where her grandfather, Emperor Cabliux, and his councilors were meeting. Like the emperor, she had greenish skin, white hair, orange eyes, and her head w was a little larger than "normal" on Earth.

"Grandpa, have you seen the new movie from that little world at the edge of the galaxy?"

The princess was the star of the emperor's life. His councilors knew their meeting was temporarily on hold.

"What world is that, my dear?" the emperor asked, picking her up and setting her on his lap.

"I don't know the name. Erd or Erth or something like that. The movie was of a single girl acting all the parts. It was so sad, Grandpa! She fell in love and he fell in love and their families were enemies and they kept trying to escape together, but no one would let them and they came up with a plot to escape together, but they died instead." She looked up at her grandfather. "Grandpa, please watch it with me."

The emperor turned to his councilors. "Gentlemen, this can wait. I have pressing business."

They nodded, bowed, and withdrew. The emperor stood, carrying his granddaughter in the crook of his arm. "Where is this movie, Tabi?"

"On my hologram. That arachnid, Huni, I met last year at school? She sent it to me. She got it from her friend. Oh, Grandpa, you're going to love it!" She hugged the emperor.

He hugged her back. *I already love it,* he thought to himself.

They walked into his granddaughter's room and sat in front of her hologram. Tablique pressed the play button. President Robbins's face appeared.

"Captain Xanny, I am President Robbins, the president of the United States. We are sending an unarmed, solo emissary to meet with you. She has no way to return to Earth. ..."

The princess started to press the fast forward button to skip over Leann's introduction.

"Wait, Tabi. I want to hear this part, too."

"OK, Grandpa. It's just a guy introducing the story teller. Then she talks about her growing up. It's not very long anyway."

Fifteen minutes later Leann got to the end of her introduction. "Now that you know who I am, I want to begin my presentation of the worthwhile things created by the human species by reading a play written by a man who lived over four hundred years ago."

His granddaughter clapped her hands in excitement. "This is it! This is *Romeo and Juliet*!"

Three hours later, Emperor Cabliux the Twenty-third, emperor of the sentient species of the galaxy and equal in power to the Ur, sat silently in front of the blank hologram. His granddaughter was snuggled in beside him on the big comfortable chair. She had fallen asleep during Leann's performance. He hadn't bothered to wipe the tears still running down his face. He got up quietly, being careful not to disturb his granddaughter. He tucked a blanket around her on the chair and savored her innocent happiness. This story could have been about her in five or six years. Political intrigue was no stranger in his court.

"What would I have done if I had been the prince?" he whispered, as he watched Tabi sleep. "Would those two have ended up dying anyway? Could I have prevented it somehow?"

Out of curiosity he spoke to the hologram. "Hologram, when was this movie created?"

"Four days ago," the hologram answered.

"Well, that gives me six more days to find out what's going on." He walked out of Tabi's room and closed the door softly.

"Polu!" he called out as he walked down the hallway toward his councilors' meeting room.

"Yes, Sire." Somehow Polu always knew when to be nearby.

"I want a presentation on that species that was selected for elimination." The emperor's voice was cold as ice. "It was on Erd or Erth or something close. I want to know why they were selected for elimination and who did it. Start with the GSCB. Do it now. And I want to find out everything you can about a Captain Xanny. That's all I know about him is his name. He's probably enforcing the quarantine around the planet. I want this presentation by the end of the day. I will not accept any reason as to why it can't be done. Use any resources you need."

"Yes, Sire." Polu loved making waves in the emperor's name. And this one sounded like a tsunami.

... ...

Day three of the zygote and it was still not dead. It was entering the compaction phase that precedes differentiation. Sridhar didn't know if he should be ecstatic or braced for failure. None of their other zygotes survived this long.

"Dr. Splendt, please be coming to check this test." He stopped himself. He was speaking Hinglish again, English words with Hindu phrasing. He always did this when he was excited.

Hermann walked over to him. "What have you got, Sridhar?"

"This ovum didn't die. It's entering compaction."

Dr. Splendt wasn't convinced. "Are you sure this is the one from the latest test?"

"Yes. I checked twice."

Dr. Splendt leaned over the microscope. "I'll be damned. Perry was right! Changing gene 348-9a1 was the secret! I didn't give it a snowball's chance in hell."

"Wait," Sridhar cautioned. "Let's let it get to a week before we begin celebrating."

Dr. Splendt considered Dr. Hehsa's request. "Yeah, you're right. A lot can change in the first week. But you'll forgive me if I allow myself to get excited, just a little. The real test will be if it will implant successfully. If it implants, there will be some serious celebrating."

"But please don't tell the rest of the team. At least not yet. I don't want them to give up on their projects. One of them might also find an answer we will need when ... excuse me, *if* this fails."

"My lips are sealed," Hermann said solemnly, with a twinkle in his eyes.

... ...

President Robbins sat with his staff as they viewed the pictures and interviews of the destruction around what was now being called the Gulf of Washington. After the segment on the Gulf was complete, General Rheem, the president's military attaché, presented pictures of the nuclear reactors, radioactive waste sites, and where the US nuclear weapon arsenals were warehoused or, more precisely, where they used to be warehoused. Now, the sites were just holes. Some filled with water from nearby rivers or lakes.

The president listened without comment or expression until the presentation was complete.

"They even 'collected' nuclear-powered ships that were bombed during the war," General Rheem continued. "My staff believes they are removing all sources of active and potential radiation pollution."

The entire room was silent as the impact of the photographs sank in.

After a moment, Patty Kendricks, President Robbins's chief of staff, said into the quiet, "They're cleaning house."

President Robbins looked at her for a moment without understanding. He was having trouble keeping his temper under control. First his starships were thrown into the sun, then the Three-Hour War knocked most of the world out of commission, now the country's capital and a huge part of the east coast was gone along with countless friends, neighbors and cohorts. "Care to elaborate, Patty?"

"I think they've written us off. The twenty-some-odd million people that were sent into the sun were going to die anyway. So who cares? Not the frigging aliens! I think the aliens are just getting the world, our Earth, ready for the next species. They're cleaning house—cleaning up the mess we've made of this world. We're just in the way now, slowing them down from starting another species in this world-sized Petri dish. They're throwing us out with the garbage."

"Jesus!" General Rheem said in disbelief. "That means we can expect this to happen again and again? Are chemical contamination sites next? How about our major cities? Are they going to be 'cleaned up' as well?"

President Robbins was furious. "You mean beyond Washington, Philadelphia, Trenton, Richmond, Newark, Harrisburg, Petersburg, Norfolk, Atlantic City, and forty-five thousand square miles of US soil? And there's not a damned thing WE CAN DO ABOUT IT?" President Robbins slammed his fist down on the table in frustration.

He was angry. He knew he didn't make his best decisions while he was angry. Twenty-plus million people—friends, enemies, good people, bad people, adults, children, white, black, brown, yellow—all gone. And the people around the table were looking at *him*, depending on him to find a way out of this mess. *Calm down, George. Think—don't react!* The words were like a mantra. He repeated them silently several times then sat back in his chair. "I wonder if they got *Chernobyl* and *Fukushima*, too?"

"Probably," Patty said, smiling sadly. "And I suspect we won't have to worry about cleaning up Hanford or Santa Susana anymore."

General Rheem answered him also. "Based on what we see around the US and Canada, I would say there's a pretty high probability they got *all* the nuclear reactors, all the nuclear bombs, and all sites with nuclear contamination."

President Robbins was quiet for a while, his hands steepled in front of his mouth. "Well, if they got our nukes, they got everyone else's too. We can replace the generating stations with dark energy generators on a much more local, cost effective basis. The electrical distribution grid was too vulnerable. It was a national liability. And those nukes were an accident waiting to happen. If we can't use 'em, no one else can either. I, for one, am glad they're gone." He looked around the room. "It is what it is, people. Let's get on with the business of resurrecting the United States. How's Leann doing? Any contact yet?"

... ...

"Mr. Sanchez, what can you tell us about the situation here in Santa Clarita?" Jeremiah was still trying to figure this guy out. Was he part of the solution or part of the problem?

Carlos pondered how to answer that question. "West of I-5 it has calmed down. We have stopped the looting all the way west to Stevenson Ranch and north to Six Flags. The people living in those areas have joined in with us and no one goes in or out without someone vouching for them. We hung a couple of rapists who snuck in and that shit stopped quick. Their bodies are still hanging in plain sight as a warning to anyone else who feels the urge. The east side of I-5 is a free-for-all. The good cops are dead and the bad cops joined the gangs. Santa Clarita proper and Newhall are being systematically looted by three gangs: the El Monte Brothers, Rojo Diablo, and Free Clarita. Any law that can be broken is being broken on a daily basis: rape, murder, sexual slavery, robbery, assault, kidnapping, extortion, burglary, you name it. When people come to the west side to get to safety, we make them turn in their weapons and they have to join our militia. We have a training course. Once they complete the course, they get their weapons back and are on probation. We've only sent one person back."

"Why did you send him back?"

"*She* was sent back because she was a *puta mentira.* That lying bitch wanted to do nothing but stir up trouble between people up here. We figured she had been sent by one of the gangs to do just that."

"What do you think is the best way to tackle the east side?"

"I think you should hit the headquarters of Rojo Diablo. They are the biggest gang over there. Take them out and the other ones will take off like the *putos* they are."

"Can you provide some support in the attack? We are only four trucks."

"Can you get some more people from the other side of the mountain?"

"How many do you think we'll need?"

"I have about two hundred people, counting women and the teenagers over fifteen. Rojo Diablo has about three hundred members. The other two have around a hundred each. Any chance of an air strike on their headquarters? I could help you guys paint it."

"I'll call. Aircraft are in pretty short supply. Last I heard there were only three gunships in the whole of L.A. They were getting used nonstop in San Berdoo and Riverside. What kind of armaments do the gangs have?"

"All we've seen are small arms: pistols, rifles, shotguns."

"Automatic weapons?"

"A few. We figure most of them came from the police departments. The ones they have are M-16s and a couple of automatic pistols. I haven't seen anything heavier."

"How about people up in the hills around Santa Clarita and Newhall? Are they joining in the looting or keeping the looters out?"

"Don't know. No one from up there has contacted us. We hear shooting in the hills occasionally, but we don't know who it is or what they're shooting at."

"Let me call headquarters and update them. I'll see about the gunship."

Jeremiah returned fifteen minutes later. "No dice on the gunship. They're fully committed for at least another week. Do you think we could sneak some charges into the HQ that we could remotely detonate?"

"Well, you *gavachos* couldn't. These gangs are Chicanos. But my people might be able to do it. What have you got?"

"Kilogram blocks of C-4. We have enough to blow a city block."

"*Chinga!*" Carlos was impressed. "That'll give those *pendejos* somethin' to think about!"

"Do you think you could draw the layout of the building they're in? Doors? Windows? Basements? And the surrounding area? Where they have roadblocks?"

"*Sí*. We have all of that."

"I have one guy I want to send along with your emplacement team. He'll make sure the charges are where they'll do the most good."

Carlos didn't like the sound of that at all. "You can't send a white guy in there. They'll eat him alive. He'll blow the whole operation."

Jeremiah turned toward Brutus. "Freddie, come out here a minute. I want you to meet someone."

Freddie walked over to Carlos. "Yeah, what's up, boss?"

"You speak Spanish, right?"

Freddie looked back and forth between Jeremiah and Carlos.

"*Sí, ¿Qué pasó?*"

Carlos asked Freddie in Spanish, "Where are you from?"

Freddie could see this was some kind of test. He answered in Spanish, "San Antonio, Texas. Why?"

"Are you Mexican?"

"No, I am Colombian. My mother brought me to the United States when I was a boy."

"His accent is wrong, but he's Colombian. I think it will be OK." He turned to Freddie. "Harris? What kind of name is 'Harris'?"

"It's my father's name. What kind of name is 'Sanchez'?"

Carlos chuckled. "It's my father's name. Please tell me you have some tattoos."

Freddie hesitated, then pulled off his protective vest, jacket, and shirt. He was covered on both arms and most of his torso. He flexed his huge biceps and a woman's ass wiggled provocatively on his arm.

"*¡'Ta bueno!*" Carlos approved. He pointed to a ragged scar on Freddie's back. "Was that from a knife fight?"

Freddie touched the scar, still red and puckered, remembering the night the bombs destroyed the SHIPS and he carried Wilson and Shannon for hours through the Montana countryside in the moonless night while he was in shock from blood loss and cold. "No. A piece of shrapnel from the Three-Hour War."

Jeremiah decided it was time for some serious planning. "Let's come up with a plan and a timetable. I'd like to do this tomorrow tonight."

Carlos called the rest of his team from his truck where they were waiting. They walked together to the gun truck, Satan, where they started studying the maps, deciding who was going to be where, and when they had to be there.

...

"We need to give them a chance to surrender," Jeremiah told Carlos.

"OK. *You* can go ask them. The last guy I sent to talk to them came back a little light headed."

Jeremiah didn't understand. Carlos drew his finger across his throat. "They cut his head and his dick off and hung him upside down and naked, from one of the light poles next to the overpass on their side of the freeway. He's still there, or what's left of him. The crows had a big time feeding on him."

Chapter 5 - Coffee and Breakfast

Emperor Cabliux listened impassively to the presentation by nervous bureaucrats about why humanity had been selected for elimination. Their images paraded across the hologram in front of him.

"Failed their evaluation." "Selected for elimination." "Primates, after all."

"Where is Envoy Gart-Disp?" he asked coolly.

"I don't know, Sire," the last talking head said. "He doesn't ask my permission to travel. As you know, envoys have the authority to travel when and where they want."

"Has anyone told him I'd like to talk to him?"

"I left a message on his personal communication link. He has not responded."

"Thank you."

The emperor pressed the end button on the hologram and sat in silence for several minutes. The "wrongness" of this selection for elimination screamed at him. A dream! Someone planted a dream! The only people who knew how to do that were the witches. And that meant Kallisha on Zindarr. She had promised not to get involved in this kind of intrigue if he left them to their own devices on Zindarr. Now a whole species had been selected to die. The image of that young primate female performing that play appeared in his dreams last night. "We don't want to die like Romeo and Juliet!" her image had screamed.

The emperor sighed. Nothing to do but ask and *he* had to do the asking. He pressed the comm link on the hologram.

"With whom do you wish to speak, Sire?" the hologram asked.

"Kallisha on Zindarr."

"One moment, I will connect you."

"Emperor Cabliux," a sleepy voice greeted him a moment later. "Give me a minute to wake up."

"This won't take long, Kallisha. You may leave the video off."

"How may I help you?"

"A dream was planted in a female primate on a planet at the edge of the galaxy. This led her to invent wormholes, which led the species to be evaluated prematurely and failed. They have been selected for elimination."

"A dream? Planted? When? Who did it?"

"I was hoping you would know."

"I know nothing about it. But, by the Goddess, I will find out."

"This could compromise our 'agreement'."

"Give me one day. I will get to the bottom of it. Who knows the details?"

"Contact a Captain Xanny. He's enforcing the quarantine around the planet. He works for Grock Corporation. He should be able to fill you in. I am forwarding all of the information I have collected so far."

"I just received it. Thank you."

"Time is of the essence, Kallisha. I want an update in twelve hours."

"I will call you in twelve hours. Good night."

"Good night."

The hologram was silent again. The emperor pressed the comm button again.

"With whom do you wish to speak, Sire?" the hologram asked.

"Grock Corporation Headquarters."

"One moment, I will connect you."

"Grock Corporate headquarters. How may I direct your call?"

"I want to speak to the chairman."

"Chairman Grolik is busy. Would you like to leave a message?"

"No, I would not. This is Emperor Cabliux. Interrupt him."

He heard a cough, then a laugh. "All right, Jerrup. Quit screwing around."

"Turn on your video," the emperor told the receptionist.

Her picture appeared in the hologram as he was sure his did on hers. "Interrupt the chairman," the emperor instructed her again.

"Yes, sir. I mean, Yes, Sire. I mean ..." Suddenly the emperor was on hold.

A moment later a male voice came on the line. "Emperor Cabliux, so nice to hear from you again. How is the Empress?"

"She is not why I called, Chairman Grolik. I want to know about one of your incubation planets. Eth or Erth. They were selected for elimination."

"Ah, yes, Earth. As usual, it means dirt in their language. That is what they call their planet. Third planet out from sun EB-31-21-98, as I remember. Such great potential. Such a shame they were selected for elimination."

"What's this about a dream being planted? Why was that done? Who did it?"

"We don't know the answer to any of those questions, Sire. Envoy Gart-Disp was very upset that he failed the species. It was obvious they were sabotaged, but, without proof someone did it, he felt he had no choice. They had already started building starships and they failed to pass all five GSCB milestones. The planet fell into a worldwide war about two years after the quarantine was put into place. Destroyed most of the world governments, militaries, and infrastructure. Only two major governments were left functioning."

None of this was a surprise to the emperor. An elimination decree did tend to upset the status quo of a species. "There's a primate from the planet in a capsule trying to establish communication with Grock. Why has she not been acknowledged? Why weren't the species allowed to present their case? Why weren't they given a fix-it period?"

"I don't know, Sire. This is the first I've heard about them even asking."

"Find out about it. I want an update in twelve hours."

"I'm sure there is a good explanation for this."

"I can't wait to hear it. Goodbye, Chairman Grolik."

"Goodbye, Sire."

… … … … … … … … …

Leann pressed the transmit button on her console.

"Today marks the end of the first half of my trip out of this solar system. At the end of the day today, I will have travelled three million miles away from my home trying to convince you to give humanity a second chance.

"Yesterday's reading of *Treasure Island* concludes the poetry and prose portion of my presentation. Obviously with seven billion members of my species, I have not even scratched the surface of the agony and ecstasy our poets and writers over the centuries have captured and will be lost if humanity is allowed to perish. The passages I read were some of my personal favorites.

"Today I will begin your introduction to the musical efforts of humanity. I am no musician so I will be playing recordings of the musical works of various composers. I thought I would start with a mélange of artists presented as a movie. The making of movies on Earth started a little over one hundred years ago. This movie is a cartoon that was created to introduce children to the great music of the last two hundred years. It was a first on so many levels. It was one of the first movies created in color. It was the first movie to showcase great music for its own sake instead of as a soundtrack for a drama. It was the first time cartoons were used with great music and allowed both genres to expand. It was the first time a cartoon was created that appealed to both children on their level and adults on their level at the same time. It was the first recording using two channels, giving the playback the sound of a concert hall performance. I would like to send a video and audio feed together from my playback device so you may enjoy the movie as it was created. I don't know if you are receiving them or if this is even in the realm of possibility. If you could respond with some kind of signal, I will know you are able to receive the broadcast. Perhaps a flash of a laser I could see from my little capsule.

Within minutes the moon base and starship lit up in her observation port like the Fourth of July over Disneyland. At least a hundred different lasers flashed in her direction.

"OK" she said in relief, finally getting some feedback from the aliens. "I'll take that for a 'yes'." She switched the feed from the cabin camera and microphone to her computer and pressed the play button on the playback software. "I give you *Fantasia*."

... ...

"Taramon Traffic Control, this is unregistered starship *Black Swan*." Lieutenant Fibari was on the radio this time.

"Hello, *Black Swan*, back so soon?" the operator at TTC responded with a giggle. "'Mining' must have been good lately."

"Would you believe our captain left his wallet at a bar in Pirate's Alley?"

"I'd believe almost anything about Pirate's Alley. They don't let us go there. It's only for you 'miners'."

"We need a parking orbit, then a position in the landing queue."

"You are assigned obit 41W-09. Call back for a landing queue assignment once you get settled into your orbit."

"Acknowledge orbit 41W-09."

"*Easy Wind* is here," Sergeant Tannl said, studying his hologram. He was browsing the ships registry at the port quartermaster's site. "They're still registered as *Russell Shoal*. I wonder if Zarqa and Flug are still on board."

"If they are, it's just their bodies. But they are probably part of a sun by now."

"I liked Zarqa," Sergeant Tannl said sadly. "Flug was OK. I never got to know him very well. Zarqa and I ate lunch together every day."

"Both of them were good people. Flug was the best combat sergeant I've ever met. Get ready to jump to our parking orbit."

Tannl set the coordinates. "Ready."

Fela pressed the jump button. They no sooner got into their assigned orbit than the radio on the shuttle cracked alive. It was the Grock emergency channel. Lieutenant Fibari hadn't even known it was on and monitoring.

"Can anyone hear me?" a woman's voice asked.

She pressed the talk button. "This is Lieutenant Fibari. Who is this?"

"Zarqa and Flug."

Sergeant Tannl gasped. "It's them! How can they still be alive?"

"What is your situation?" Fela asked.

"We're in a holding cell on *Easy Wind*. Fey Pey is using us to negotiate with the people who are after him. We're his insurance policy."

"How are you talking to us? Where did you get a radio?"

Zarqa's voice came back on. "I had a bionic radio implanted before I left. It doesn't have much range, but no one knows it's there."

"How can we help?"

"Show up with an army of Ur storm troopers and bust us out."

"There's just me and Sergeant Tannl."

"Tannl? Tannl from the ship?"

"Yep, Zarqa," Sergeant Tannl replied. "It's me."

"Did Captain Xanny get the message I sent?"

"Yes, he did. He's trying to find proof for any of it," Lieutenant Fibari told her.

"I have proof. Get me out of here and a lot of people will go to jail."

"Let me work on a plan. I'll call you back."

"I'll have to call you. My radio can only talk for ten minutes a day."

"Then call me back tomorrow."

"Bye. Bye, Tannl."

"Bye, Zarqa." Sergeant Tannl was obviously upset. He turned away from Lieutenant Fibari until he regained control.

Taramon Traffic Control came back on the radio. "*Black Swan*, are you ready for your approach to Spelie Cove and Pirate's Alley?"

Lieutenant Fibari pressed the comm button. "Yes, we are."

The coordinates to the entrance to the approach path to Spelie Cove came through. She set up the jump computer and pressed the jump button.

… … … … … … … … …

Chief Petty Officer Freddie Harris walked behind a teenage girl, maybe fourteen, that Carlos said would lead him in. They entered a building and walked up six flights of stairs, then stopped at a door.

"What's your name?" Freddie asked the girl.

"Josephina," she replied. "This is the roof. There are two guards. Be careful."

Freddie eased open the door. Neither guard was in sight. He stepped out onto the roof. He saw the first guard sitting on a chair reading a magazine. He was staring at the centerfold. The second guard was pissing by an air conditioning unit. He threw a knife at the first guard. It hit him in the throat. The guard stood in surprise and pulled the knife out. A spray of blood from his carotid artery gushed all over his chest, then he fell over. The second guard heard Freddie walking up behind him.

"You'll have to wait, *puto*. I'm almost done."

He felt Freddie's knife slide across his neck. "Whaaaatght"

Freddie held him until he quit struggling.

The girl came up behind him. "You're pretty good. Almost as good as Rebecca."

"Who's Rebecca?" he asked as he studied the building across the street with his binoculars.

"She saved my life. Some bangers in Mission Hills knocked me out the morning after the bombs dropped. They held me naked on the ground, takin' turns doin' what bangers do with naked girls. She killed two of them and made one of them give me his clothes. She brought me to my uncle in Santa Clarita."

"Sounds like a good friend. What happened to her?"

"She went up to the mountains to find her husband. His name was Jeremiah."

Freddie turned to look at her. "Not Jeremiah Silverstein?" Jeremiah had told Freddie all about the mountain hideaway and about trying to find his wife before he gave up and re-joined the Marines.

"Yes. Do you know him?"

"Yep," he said, shaking his head. "It's a small world."

Jeremiah will want to know this, he thought, filing it in the back of his mind. Freddie had a few more important things to worry about right now. He resumed studying the building. The construction was cast concrete. That meant he would have to blow the supporting columns at the bottom and the building would collapse like a stack of records.

"Can we get into the basement?"

She thought a moment. "Maybe. I used to play in that building when I visited my uncle. A cousin of mine lived over there." She pointed to another building. "This one was always empty. Sometimes we were able to sneak into the basement. There's a door on the other side that goes down. If it's not locked, we can get in."

They walked back down the stairs, then across the street. Freddie pulled out a quart of tequila from his backpack, took a swig, put his arm around Josephina, and started singing a Mexican love song.

The guard next to the alleyway Josephina led them to held up his hand. "Hey, *pendejo*! What do you think you're doing?"

"Getting drunk and getting some *culo*. What're you doing?"

"I never seen you before. You can't be here. What's your name?"

Freddie's knife was at the guy's throat before the guy could lift his gun. "My name is Death!" Freddie hissed in Spanish in a voice as cold as ice, then he laughed. "You wanna drink?"

"*Sí*," the guard's voice cracked. "I'd love a drink." The man was clearly terrified.

"You take the bottle. I got the woman. See ya." Freddie and Josephina walked down the alley past the guard.

Josephina put her arm through Freddie's. "You are one *hombre malo*!" she giggled. "You even had me going."

"Where's that door?" he asked.

"Right up here." She indicated some steel doors set at an angle into the alleyway. They were locked with a padlock and hasp.

Freddie reached into his backpack and pulled out the bolt cutters he brought along. They came in handy for special ops everywhere. Although Freddie never finished Seal training, he was very sought after by Seal teams as a medic. He had participated in more Special Ops missions than a lot of Seals.

He opened the doors, let Josephina into the basement, then closed the doors quietly behind them. In fifteen minutes, the C-4 was placed.

Freddie pressed the transmit button on his radio. "Charges placed. Timers are set for five minutes from now."

They were walking back to the door where they had entered when it opened.

He heard his radio crackle to life through his ear bud. "Is everyone in position?"

"Satan in position." "Brutus in position." "Popeye in position."

"Did they go down here?" a voice asked from the alleyway.

"I don't know, Rubio." Freddie recognized the voice of the guard. "They walked down the alley and disappeared."

"Julio, Serra, check it out."

Two men came down the steps from the alley.

Freddie heard Jeremiah's voice loud and clear from the PA system in the trucks. He was broadcasting from all three of them simultaneously. "Rojo Diablo, this is the US Marines. Your building is surrounded. Lay down your weapons and come out into the street with your hands in the air."

There was silence. "What the fuck?" said the voice of the leader. "Bullshit! Get up here, you guys."

The two men ran back up the steps into the alley. The sounds of semi-automatic and automatic weapons fire came back through the open doorway.

Freddie heard Jeremiah's voice on the radio. "OK, people. Let's do this. Freddie, get out of there!"

The sounds of heavy automatic weapons came through the ceiling of the basement. Freddie heard the minigun on Popeye start up. He could only imagine the shit storm going on above them. Both .50s were working with the M-60s going off intermittently.

"Come on, Josephina. We have to go!"

They reentered the alleyway. Two people were barricaded where the guard shack had been. Freddie ran up behind them. They were firing at Popeye as it rolled slowly down the street toward the building. Freddie shot both of them. Bullets were flying everywhere. The seconds were passing way too fast while Freddie waited for a break in the fire fight. He kept glancing at his watch. Finally he decided they couldn't wait any longer. They were out of time. In two minutes the building would blow and this area would become one big fireball. He touched the comm button on his vest.

"Popeye, this is Freddie. I am next to the building in the alleyway. I took out the two guys that were shooting at you." Freddie picked up a plastic bag lying in the gutter and waved it. "I'm waving a plastic bag."

"Roger Chief, we see you."

"I have Carlos's niece with me. We're going to run toward you for a pickup. Cover us."

"Come on in. We've got you covered."

"Let's go!" Freddie said to Josephina. "They're going to cover us. You first. I'll be right behind you."

All of the machine guns on Popeye opened up at the buildings around them. Freddie and Josephina bolted from the guard station toward the truck, weaving from side to side. Freddie saw a movement in a broken-out storefront window. He sprayed it with his M-4. They reached the back of the truck. The armored panel swung down and an arm reached out for them. Josephina was pulled up into the back. The arm reached down for Freddie. He was pulled up as a bullet hit him in the back, just above his right kidney. The armor door clanked closed behind him.

"Son of a bitch! That hurts!" Freddie had forgotten that getting shot with a vest on hurts like hell. He rolled over and yelled at the driver, "I'd get the hell out of Dodge before that building blows."

"Clear the area!" Freddie heard the driver announce over the radio. The truck went into reverse and the motor revved. When they were clear of the blast zone, Freddie pressed the transmit button on his radio. "Popeye clear."

"Brutus clear." "Satan clear." The other drivers responded.

The building exploded as Satan was announcing "clear," showering the surrounding buildings with cinderblocks, timbers, and dust. The outside walls of the building remained in place. Freddie pulled himself up from the floor of the truck and stared at it in disbelief.

"I must be losing my touch," he grumbled, wishing his back didn't hurt so much.

Then, like a sand castle being hit by an ocean wave, the building walls collapsed inward, leaving a pile of rubble where they had stood a moment before.

"OK, everyone," Freddie heard Jeremiah's voice over the radio. "Let's clean up the garbage."

… … … … … … … … …

The phone next to President Robbins rang. He had been sound asleep, dreaming about his wife and a horse ride on their ranch in the Finger Lake region near Ithaca, New York.

"Robbins," he answered the phone.

"President Robbins. This is Captain Xanny. We need to talk."

President Robbins was instantly wide awake. He had been waiting two-and-a-half years for this phone call and said what he had practiced over and over: "What can we do to get our death order reversed?"

"I don't know. I've been trying to do that since I started the quarantine. But we have a more pressing problem."

"Are you going to retrieve her?"

"I cannot. I have been ordered not to interfere."

"So you're going to let Leann die?"

"Well, that's why I'm calling. I have an idea that might save her and not break my orders."

"I'm listening."

"Four thousand years ago, an agent from my company visited Earth. He disabled his landing craft so he could stay for a while. As far as I have been able to learn, his craft is still on Earth. I would like *you* to retrieve it and rescue Leann."

"Where is it? Four thousand years ago? Does it still work?"

"It should need some minor maintenance. I would send a crew down to show your people how to repair it and train one of your pilots to fly it. You must do all of the work on the lander."

President Robbins wasn't going to miss this opportunity. "When this is done, can you and I talk about how to fix our elimination order?"

"Yes. When this is done, I will tell you everything I've found and perhaps together we can discover a way to reverse the decision."

"Where is the lander?"

"In a country you now call Iraq, near the present day town of Nasiriyah."

"Nasiriyah? ... Dammit!" President Robbins swore in frustration. "We have no way to retrieve it. We have no aircraft that can fly there and fly back. Everything was destroyed in the war."

That made Captain Xanny pause. He had been so sure this would work without violating any of his orders from Grock.

"Could you bring it to us?" President Robbins asked.

"We have no way to transport it either. My shuttle is away on other business. All I have left are lifeboats. A lifeboat does not have the capacity to lift a shuttle."

"Can you fix it there?"

"That area of your world is still in turmoil. It would be dangerous for both my maintenance crew and your people."

"Let me talk about this with my staff. Maybe they can come up with a solution. How can I contact you?"

"Just send us a transmission like you have so many times before. Your government seems to know how to do that. I will contact you again."

"You mean you have received our attempts to contact you?"

"Of course."

"Why didn't you respond?"

"I was ordered not to."

"What changed? Why are you contacting me now?"

"No one wants Leann to die. This is a fine legal line I'm walking, President Robbins. I have been prohibited from responding to your overtures for communication. With this transmission, I am not responding to your requests. I am contacting you about something else entirely."

President Robbins thought about what Captain Xanny had said. Before he entered politics, the president had been a lawyer for most of his adult life. He saw the captain was taking quite a chance in contacting him. "I will send you an update within hours. It will be informational only. It will contain no request for a contact or meeting."

"Excellent! Thank you, President Robbins. I so hoped we could work together on this." The line went dead.

President Robbins jumped out of bed, pulled on his robe, and pressed the intercom next to his bed.

"Yes, sir," a sleepy voice answered.

The president glanced at the clock on the nightstand. It showed "03:21 A.M."

"I want a meeting of the National Security Council in one hour. Call everyone and get them here."

"Yes, sir." The sleepiness was gone from the voice in an instant.

"And we'll need coffee and breakfast for everyone."

"Yes, sir."

"And invite that Air Force captain, the one who piloted that F-35 when we went to Canada. I think her name was Marshall."

"I will, sir."

Chapter 6 – The Battle of Santa Clarita

When Lieutenant Fibari walked in to the Cauldron and Kettle, it felt different from the last time, less oppressive, more jubilant. It was more brightly lit than before and a lot more booths were occupied. She heard excited talk from some of the booths. People were obviously enjoying themselves. None of the booths were displaying ominous scenes like Fela had seen before.

The facial recognition software in the hostess hologram recognized Fela. "Welcome back, would you like the same booth as before?"

"I need to see Zuna," Fela whispered.

The hostess hologram pixelated for a moment, then came back into focus. "She is ... preoccupied. Would you like a booth to wait on her availability?"

"I don't have time for that," Fela whispered. "Tell her I must see her. Tell her it is about Zindarr."

The hologram of the hostess wavered again for a moment, then recoalesced and froze in place for a full minute.

"As you wish," the hologram said, reanimating again. "Please follow me. Zuna will meet with you now."

They walked to the back of the restaurant, then through a door that appeared in a blank wall. The hologram led them along a maze of corridors until they stopped in front of a nondescript door. The door opened and the hologram disappeared. Zuna was waiting inside, obviously irritated. She was a young hyena with white and red stripes.

"What do you want? What's this about Zindarr?"

"Captain Xanny gave me this to give to you, and only you." Fela pulled the ring with the crystal off her toe and put it on the ground in front of Zuna. "He said you would know how to open the message."

Zuna sniffed the ring. "It smells like one of mother's spells."

She drew a rune in the air above the ring. Nothing happened. She made a second rune. Still nothing happened. Zuna snorted in disgust. She sighed, picked up the ring in her mouth, and closed her eyes. A moment later she spit it out.

"Mother, that was sneaky," she whispered.

Zuna said a word Fela had never heard and drew a rune at the same time. A hologram of Captain Xanny appeared.

"Zuna, your mother taught me how to create this message. I have received a transmission from two of my people whom I was able to smuggle aboard Fey Pey's ship, *Easy Wind*. Unfortunately, they paid for the message with their lives. Here is what they said. Before Fey Pey went to Earth to plant the dream, he met with the king of Glycemis. The king hired Fey Pey to plant the dream and raise up a species of aquatic mammal. He gave Fey Pey the modified DNA to put into the SIV for the raise up. The king brought a witch with him to do the actual plant. Her name was Ruatha. She was from Zindarr. When they got to Earth, Ruatha found an appropriate female and planted the dream. Fey Pey released the virus."

"That's what this is all about?" Zuna asked in disbelief. "Getting another aquatic mammal species into the Ur? For that they were willing to sabotage an entire species?" Zuna was appalled that a witch had apparently been a willing participant in this. "I must consult with my coven to determine the correct response. You may wait in the restaurant." She picked up the ring in her mouth, walked out the door, and turned right.

The hologram hostess was waiting for them in the hallway. "The restaurant is this way." It indicated left. Fela looked in the direction Zuna disappeared. The hallway apparently went on for hundreds of yards without doors or windows. It was softly illuminated. Zuna was nowhere in sight.

Fela followed the hologram back to the restaurant and sat in a booth. A buxom blonde witch brought her a bottle of queetle, set it in front of her and left. Fela pulled out her communicator and contacted the lander.

"Hello, Fela," Tannl's face greeted her.

Fela had told him not to use her title of "Lieutenant Fibari" while they were on Taramon. "I am waiting for my contact here to decide if she will help us or not. How are you doing?"

Tannl tried to keep a straight face. "Only two attempts to approach the lander so far. I singed a Mellincon a little. He decided he didn't want to take our lasers after all."

Fela chuckled at that one. "OK. I'll let you know when a decision is made." She ended the call.

The walls of the booth were displaying a plain from Fela's home. The sky was greenish-blue. A small lake was next to her with some water fowl swimming about a hundred feet out. The sun was high in the sky with one of the three moons near it. A shaggy six-legged predator came down to the shore of the lake to drink. After it was done, it stared directly at Fela with water dripping off its chin, then turned back the way it had come and walked slowly away.

The morning turned into afternoon then evening. Fela switched to water after her third bottle of queetle.

Zuna was waiting at her table when Fela returned from the toilet.

"I need to go to Zindarr. Can you take me?"

"Sure. But it'll cost you."

Zuna was suddenly wary. "Cost me what?"

"Flug and Zarqa are on Fey Pey's ship, *Easy Wind*. They're the ones who found out about Fey Pey, the king on Glycemis, and Ruatha. It's orbiting Taramon. We need to rescue them before we leave."

Anger crossed Zuna's face for a second. She started to say something, then stopped. A thoughtful expression replaced the anger. "Fey Pey's ship, huh?" She stared at the wall for a moment, deep in thought. "Give me a second."

She padded into the back of the restaurant, then returned a few minutes later. "Yeah, we can do that."

"What do you mean 'we'?" Fela asked. "Do you mean me and you or something else? My lander only holds six people. You, me, and Tannl make three."

"We don't need anyone else, at least not on the lander. Six will be plenty of room." Zuna was almost laughing.

Fela was pretty sure she didn't like that Zuna was laughing.

"Are you ready?" Zuna asked, getting up.

"Yep." They left the restaurant and took a shuttle to the spaceport.

A crowd was around the lander. A Mellincon with a patch of burned hair on his ass was pointing at the lander and raising hell. A spaceport policeman was listening to him with a bored expression on his face.

"Any problem, officer?" Fela asked innocently.

"This Mellincon says whoever is in this lander shot him with a laser as he was walking by."

Fela pulled out her communicator. "Tannl, send me the feed of the Mellincon so I can display it." She pressed a button on the communicator. A hologram appeared in front of them. It showed the Mellincon approaching the lander, glancing around and loitering nearby for a good five minutes. He would approach the lander, then move away, watching the outside cameras as they followed him. Finally he attempted to remove one of the lasers. The second laser swiveled around and fried his butt.

The policeman turned to the Mellincon. "I think you should thank the guy inside for using low power. If it had been me, you'd be ash in the wind instead of your ass in the wind. Get out of here."

The Mellincon made a rude gesture, spit in the shadow of the lander, then stalked away waving his arms and swearing.

"Are we free to go, officer?" Fela asked.

"Yeah. Get out of here before he sneaks back tonight and you get to fry him for real. Then I'd have to do the paperwork and miss my dinner. Plus you'd have to pay for the cleanup and that smell never seems to go away."

"We were just leaving."

The policeman got back into his shuttle and left. Fela and Zuna walked into the lander after the entrance port opened.

"So what's the plan, Zuna?" Fela asked. "How are we going to get both Zarqa and Flug off *Easy Wind*? I don't think it will work if we show up and say 'please'?"

Zuna glanced at the pilot's holo to get the time. "Can you get there in fifteen minutes?"

"Depends on Taramon Approach Control." She turned to Tannl. "Do we have an exit queue position?"

"I was just going to ask for one," he responded.

"Go do it." She turned to Zuna. "What do we do when we get there?"

"I'll tell you then." Zuna sat down and put her safety harness on.

Taramon Approach Control gave them an immediate departure window. Tannl lifted off the lander and accelerated. He retrieved the stored coordinates for their parking orbit and pressed the jump button.

Fela retrieved the coordinates of where *Easy Wind* was in her orbit, entered them into the jump computer, and waited for the signal from Zuna. Zuna pulled her communicator out, counting with the seconds ticking off. "Jump now," she said to Fela.

Easy Wind appeared about two hundred yards away from them. The shields were up on the lander. Fela expected a salvo of lasers to strike out at them. Nothing happened. *Easy Wind* might as well have been an asteroid.

"Use that port to enter," Zuna said, pointing to one.

Fela aligned the lander with the portal and got a seal. After the pressure equalized, the portal opened. She still couldn't quite believe no one was firing at them. The portal door of the ship opened onto an empty corridor. Fela's laser was out and ready.

"Do you know where the brig is?" Zuna asked, stepping into the corridor.

"Yes. It's this way." She holstered the laser and started running down the corridor, feeling a massive déjà vu. She hadn't been on *Easy Wind* in fifty years. "Where is everybody?" she called over her shoulder.

Zuna was right behind her. "We have to get your people and leave before everyone wakes up."

"What did you do?"

"My coven put them to sleep," Zuna responded, smirking. "Don't piss off a witch ... but we have to be clear of the ship in ten minutes or it won't be nearly as much fun leaving as it was getting here."

"Why only ten minutes?"

"Two members of the coven were away. That was the best we could do on such short notice."

They got to the brig. "Zarqa! Flug! Where are you?" Fela shouted.

No one answered them.

Fela grabbed the ID badge of the sleeping guard and opened all the cells. Zarqa and Flug were in two of them. They were sound asleep and wouldn't wake up.

"Dammit. I didn't think about that," Zuna said, angry at herself. "How much does he weigh?"

"Two hundred kilos, more or less."

"I can't carry him. We couldn't carry him together."

"I remember there's a first-aid station nearby." Fela started scrolling the ship's interior using the terminal at the guard station. "We could use the anti-grav gurney from there to carry them."

"There's an anti-grav gurney right there in that locker," a voice said behind them.

Both of them spun around, lasers out. A young primate female was standing in the doorway of one of the cells. There were shadows under her eyes that looked like she hadn't slept in a long time. She emanated a profound sadness.

"Who are you?" Fela asked. "Why aren't you asleep?"

"I'm Ruatha. That spell was pretty easy to defuse. Unless I miss my guess, getting them out of here before the spell expires is going to be close. Maybe you should hurry up a little."

Fela got the anti-grav gurney out and set it up. They rolled Flug and then Zarqa onto it and pushed them back to the pressure lock, running when they could. Even though the gurney carried the weight, the momentum of their mass made them have to slow for each turn.

Ruatha stayed in the lock. "Aren't you coming?" Zuna called from inside the lander. "We have room."

"No," she said sadly. "The king of Glycemis planted a photon torpedo on Zindarr before he kidnapped me. If Fey Pey wakes up without my being on board, he'll detonate it. Everyone I love will perish. I have to go. Find that torpedo and evacuate it into clear space." Ruatha slammed the portal closed and ran back to the brig.

Tannl pulled up the escape jump coordinates he had put into the jump computer before they approached *Easy Wind*. He started to accelerate away from the star ship. A laser beam hit their shields, then a second one. Tannl pressed the jump button. A third beam went past them into space a hundred lightyears from *Easy Wind* as the portal closed.

Zarqa moaned and sat up. She spun around in gleeful surprise. "I thought I was still dreaming!"

Flug awoke with a start. His massive fist pounded into the cushion beside him. Everyone stepped away. He blinked in surprise, then embarrassment. "OK. That's not what I expected to see. Hi, Lieutenant Fibari. Is that you, Zuna?"

… … … … … … … … …

Muhammad al-Zawadi watched the lights come down from the sky. They descended to a plain two kilometers from where he stood, watching from his guard post at the site where the excavation of the ancient city of Ur was going on. As the lights disappeared behind a small rise, he got on his horse and galloped across the sand toward them.

"Allah, guide me and protect me," he whispered as he rode. This was sacred ground. Muhammad would allow no violation by the aliens that caused all of this death.

It took Muhammad twelve minutes to reach the top of the rise overlooking the spot where the lights had disappeared. A Rosy flash greeted him as he cleared the ridge. The lights from the lifeboats rose into the air beside the hole in the desert floor that hadn't been there yesterday. Muhammad pulled the rifle from his back and emptied his magazine at the lights. He never felt the laser blast that turned the desert floor around him into fused glass.

… … … … … … … … …

Emperor Cabliux was looking out of the hologram in front of Chairman Grolik. Chairman Grolik was very uncomfortable.

"So what you're telling me is," the emperor began, "a known pirate named Fey Pey planted the dream, for reasons no one but him knows, and hid on the planet for three years, two of which were under an airtight, Ur-directed quarantine. Then he escaped and no one has seen or heard from him since. You're saying Envoy Gart-Disp did an evaluation because this species opened their first wormholes and failed them because they were too warlike without giving them the normal period to correct their failed milestones. And ever since the quarantine has been in place, the species selected for elimination has been attempting to open communications with the Ur to find out how to reverse their failure."

"Yes, Sire. That summarizes what I've been able to uncover."

"Why didn't your quarantine administrator respond to their request for a conversation? What harm would that have done?"

"We didn't see any point, Sire."

"Now, because of that decision, you have this female doing performances that are being sent all over the galaxy while she's committing suicide. Has anyone responded to her? My office has gotten fourteen million queries about her and her damned performances. And that was as of end of business yesterday. My chief of staff expects it will double again today and double again every day in the near future. Within six days, they expect the queries to top a billion. Even the goddamned Mellincon are sending queries and they eat their own children. She has captured the attention of the galaxy and that has captured mine."

"Sire. We didn't want to give them false hope. An elimination decree has never been changed in the history of the Ur."

"And of course, because of that lack of hope, they descended into a world war that almost made the planet uninhabitable. They *were* armed with nuclear weapons, however primitive. What were you thinking? How many members of the species were killed cleaning up that mess?"

"I have no way of knowing," the chairman said. "The blast area from the fusion devices was in a high population region also containing a major country capital. Tens of millions probably died. We also evacuated their primitive fission reactors and all remaining fission and fusion bombs. We didn't want anymore 'accidents'."

"After all that, I'm amazed there's still enough land area to start another species," the emperor said dryly. "Don't let the female die, Chairman Grolik. You won't like what happens if she dies. I want her on Quyl within one day. Within ten days, a full one percent of the Ur will want to meet her. Don't make me tell them she's dead. Are we clear?"

"Yes, Sire. It will be done."

"And I would open up communications with the species. A species with hope won't go to war and destroy their planet."

"Sire, should I tell them the Species Elimination Virus is not reversible? That it has no cure?"

"I wouldn't go that far, Chairman. Let them continue to play at finding a cure. It will keep them busy until there aren't enough of them left to matter. You need to find out why this happened and bring the people who caused it to justice. The whole Species Mining industry is pounding on my door demanding an answer. Let me know if there is any way I can help to expedite your investigation."

"Sire, I understand their concern. Grock has invested fifty thousand years into this planet and spent untold millions of Huz monitoring this species. Our expected failure rate for an individual species over the whole incubation period is eighty-seven percent. If we extrapolate the past performance of similar species that have reached this point in their social evolution, in another hundred years or so, this species would have passed their evaluation. They had already reached a Success Forecast Quotient of ninety-eight percent. We can't afford to lose one that would most probably have succeeded. This cannot be allowed to happen again."

"Keep me informed of your progress, Chairman."

"I will, Sire."

… … … … … … … … …

"Captain Marshall, do you think you could fly an alien lander to rescue Leann?"

Gaye was standing in front of the entire National Security Council. They had called her into this emergency meeting. She was more than a little nervous. "I can fly anything with wings, President Robbins."

"I don't think these landers have wings. The aliens say they will train you. Would you volunteer to be trained to fly it and perform the rescue mission? The aliens have been ordered not to rescue her. It has to be a human at the controls."

She snapped to attention. "Yes, sir. I would. I've seen every one of Leann's transmissions. It would be my honor to be the one who retrieves her."

"Be ready to go on a moment's notice. We don't know when they will contact us. We will also need a maintenance team for the aliens to show how to fix it. We have to do the work. Go collect a team of people you feel can do the job."

"I know just the guy. I met him while we were in Canada. Is the Rosy portal system connected to them?"

President Robbins sighed. Both governments were reluctant to turn the switch so the two countries could exchange goods and people. "I'll ask them." He stared at the blank wall of the warehouse they were using as a national headquarters for a moment. "Yeah. It's time. I am so over this country-to-country protectionism. I'll call them now. Everyone please wait outside."

The meeting participants filed out. President Robbins picked up the Rosy phone he used to talk with Edmonton. The Honorable Glenda LeBec, Minister of Indigenous and Northern Affairs, was the sole surviving minister of the pre-Three-Hour-War Canadian government. She had been visiting a planning session for the First Nations National Aboriginal Day in Edmonton when the Three-Hour War broke out. After it was confirmed that the rest of the government was MIA or KIA, she assumed the role of Acting Prime Minister until elections could be held at some future date.

"Edmonton CFB. Corporal Wright speaking, sir."

"This is President Robbins. I would like to speak to the prime minister."

"Please wait, sir. I will tell her you are on the line."

"President Robbins," the PM's voice came on the line. "How are you? Have you heard from the aliens?"

"Well ... is this off the record, Glenda?"

There was a pause. "If you'd like it to be. Sure. What's up, George? What's so secret?"

He filled her in on the plans for the rescue effort.

"That's wonderful!" she gushed. "How can Canada help?"

President Robbins paused. "I would like to open the transportation portals between our countries. Permanently. Given the current state of affairs in the world, I think country protectionism between the US and Canada is counterproductive."

All he got was silence from Prime Minister LeBec.

"And I need a maintenance team I can send to fix the lander. The person I'm going to send to pilot the lander requested specific people she met in Calgary. She feels they are the best. Could we make this rescue a joint Canada-US operation?"

"I'll need to consult my advisors," the Prime Minister responded after several more moments of silence. "About both requests."

"When do you think you could do that, Glenda? We don't have a lot of time to set this up."

"I'll let you know this afternoon."

"I'll wait for your call as long as I can."

The line went dead.

President Robbins walked to the door and called everyone back in. "I have asked for the people you wanted, Captain Marshall. I want you to prepare a Plan B. Get a maintenance team ready from people available in the US. If Canada decides not to participate, we'll have to use them."

"Yes, sir. I'll get going on that now." She did an about-face and walked out of the room.

… … … … … … … … …

Leann pressed the transmit button on her console.

"Hello my friends. This is the sixth day of my ten-day journey. In the last five days, I have shared poetry, prose, and *Fantasia* with you. Today I want to continue showing you the beauty of humanity that will die if our species is eliminated. I would like to present more of the great music humanity has created. I will present musical pieces with video feed of the orchestras and artists who performed them. I do this to show you the instruments, how they are played, and the emotion behind the music. The first piece is by Wolfgang Amadeus Mozart.

"Mozart began composing and performing at the age of five. He wrote *A Little Night Music* when he was thirty-one years old, four years before he died. It was intended to be performed by a small ensemble of string instruments, but it is now commonly performed with an entire string orchestra. Here is Mozart's *A Little Night Music*."

…

"Ludwig van Beethoven is one of my favorite composers. Indeed, I have chosen three pieces of his to present to you today. The first is a piece that is performed as a piano solo. Its name is *Fur Elise*, which means For Elise. He wrote this when he was almost deaf. No one knows for sure who Elise was. The piece wasn't discovered until forty years after Beethoven died. She must have been quite a woman to have inspired such a beautifully sad composition."

…

Leann waited for a full thirty seconds after *Fur Elise* finished to reappear. The final notes hung in everyone's ears like they would at the end of a concert performance.

"The next piece was created much more recently by Sergei Prokofiev. He grew up in a period of turmoil in a country called Russia. They were in the process of overthrowing a despotic dictator and beginning an experiment in country governance called Communism. It was a period of great passion and Prokofiev captured that energy into his compositions. This one is called *Piano Concerto Number 3*. Such a simple name for such a joyous piece of music."

...

Leann's face appeared after the finale and the applause ended.

"Our next piece is by Antonio Vivaldi. He was renowned for his use of strings. This collection of four concertos is called *The Four Seasons*. Vivaldi tried to capture in music the majesty and beauty of the changing seasons on our world. The music progresses from spring, full of growth and hope, to summer as the world ripens, to autumn harvest, and winter sleep. Here is *The Four Seasons*."

...

The final violin faded as Leann's face reappeared.

"Next I will play the second Beethoven piece I have selected. It is called the *Emperor Concerto*. It was Beethoven's last piano concerto. Like most of Beethoven's concertos, it was intended to be performed by a small ensemble, but it is now almost always performed by an entire symphony. This increases the drama and adds contrast to the breathtaking solos. This is the *Emperor Concerto*."

...

"The next piece is from another Russian composer named Peter Ilyich Tchaikovsky. He created a ballet that was accompanied by a symphony. Both parts were superlative by themselves, but together they are a masterpiece. I give you *The Nutcracker Suite,* but instead of focusing on the orchestra performing the music this time, I will focus on the ballet troop dancing to the music. The performance is set at a time when snow is falling on most of our world and we have an annual gift exchange and celebration between family members. This particular family is the royal family of the land. There are no words spoken in this ballet. All communication is through the music and the body language of the performers. You tell me if this is enough."

Leann's face faded and was replaced by the image of the orchestra performing the overture.

...

As the sugar plum fairies made their last bow, Leann's face returned.

"The next piece was originally written by Johann Pachelbel four hundred years ago. It is called *Cannon in D Major*. For this piece, instead of watching the musicians perform the music, the video feed is displaying places around Earth which match the beauty of the composition.

...

When it finished, Leann reappeared.

"The last performance tonight is a particular favorite of mine. I listen to it when I feel despair. It never fails to fill me with hope and energy to overcome any obstacle. This is the third piece of Beethoven's music I promised you at the beginning of today's performances. He wrote this near the end of his life and he never heard it performed. He had become completely deaf by then. He conducted the first performance and knew when it wasn't being played correctly by how the musicians and singers moved their bodies as they performed. It was his only symphony that was accompanied by a full chorus. Many of us consider this his finest work and possibly the finest of humanity. This is Beethoven's *Ninth Symphony*."

...

As the last notes of the final movement finished, Leann faded into the picture.

"The words of the singers say:
'All men shall become brothers,
wherever your gentle wings hover.
Whoever has been lucky enough
to become a friend to a friend,
Whoever has found a beloved wife,
let him join our songs of praise!'"

Leann switched off the transmission and walked to the observation portal. Each day Earth grew smaller. She was now 3,600,000 miles away from the people she loved. Earth was the size of a tennis ball. For the first time she considered the possibility that she might fail. She wept at the beauty of Beethoven's music, at the beauty of the Earth, and for the civilization that was destined to perish if she did not succeed.

Four days remained before she began her inexorable march to starvation. The water, oxygen, and energy would continue long after she starved to death.

"Time to do it," she decided. She had never created the "letter to your parents" that Lily ordered her to do while they were planning this mission. To do so seemed like an acknowledgment that she would fail. Leann sat at the console of the capsule and collected her thoughts. The first thought that came to the surface was that she hoped she would never have to press the send button on this message. She turned on the camera.

"Hello, Mother," Leann smiled, reached out to the camera, and caressed it lovingly. "I love you. I love you for the wonderful things you have done for me. I love you for deciding to birth me when so many of your friends had no children. I love you for staying up at night when I was sick. I love you for not taking a vacation for twenty years so you could send me to good schools. I love you for teaching me to think and act on what I think is good and right without worry about the consequences. But I especially love you for your support after I decided to do this.

"Here are my final thoughts...."

... ...

Jeremiah's voice came out from the speakers on the front of each truck. "Rojo Diablo! This is the US Marines. Your leaders are dead. Lay down your weapons and come out with your hands up. You will each be treated fairly according to the laws of the land, which are now back in force in Santa Clarita."

One by one, then by twos and threes, members of the gang came out of the surrounding buildings with their hands up and stood in front of the three trucks.

A man on top of a building next to where the gang members gathered opened fire on the Marines, wounding Private McKinty. The sniper saw the gunner on Popeye swing the .50 around and dropped down behind the short brick wall around the edge of the roof. The .50 blew the wall and the gunner apart.

The men and women from Carlos's group moved forward to collect the weapons from the Rojo Diablo prisoners and began moving them toward the containment area that was prepared to secure them as they were ID'ed and charged. Several guys tried to run away, but they were shot. People quit trying to escape after that.

Freddie climbed painfully down from Popeye with his medic kit and began to treat the wounded. Not long after he began, the members of the El Monte Brothers and Free Clarita gangs began leaving town, going north, along with the remnants of the Rojo Diablo gang that were still alive and uncaptured. The battle of Santa Clarita was over.

Jeremiah walked over to Freddie as he was working and kneeled down next to him. "You OK, Chief? You sure are favoring your side."

"Got one in the back. Vest stopped it. Damn that hurts."

"Yeah, it sure does!" Jeremiah remembered the pain like it happened yesterday. "In Iraq, I got an AK round dead center in the front. Bruised my sternum. Still hurts when I do pushups."

Freddie had been waiting for a quiet moment to talk to Jeremiah. He decided it was time. "That niece of Carlos, Josephina? She talked about a woman who saved her life while she was getting raped by some bangers in Mission Hills. Said the woman killed two of 'em and brought her over the mountain to Santa Clarita."

"Cool! Two less bangers to worry about."

"Her name was Rebecca."

Jeremiah looked at Freddie in shock. "Whose name? The woman who helped her?"

"Yep. Josephina said the woman was going to the mountains to be with her husband. His name was Jeremiah."

"When was that?" Jeremiah said, a little too loudly.

"The morning after the bombs dropped."

Jeremiah got up with crazy eyes. "Where is she? Where's Josephina? I need to talk to her."

"She was in Popeye with me. I got her in right before I got shot. Give me a minute to finish this guy up. I'll help you find her."

Chapter 7 – A Smiling Face

The phone rang next to President Robbins's bed.

"Robbins," he said, picking it up.

"President Robbins, this is Captain Xanny." The president recognized the computer-generated voice.

"Hi. What did you figure out?"

"We have evacuated the lander to space. My combat team brought it to my starship by using all our lifeboats together. I need your maintenance team up here so we can show them how to repair it. We will need three repair technicians. All work must be done by people from your planet. And I need someone from your planet whom we can train to fly the lander. The maintenance team and pilot need to be ready for pickup in one hour. I will send a lifeboat to your headquarters."

"I'll have them ready."

President Robbins hung up and called the 24-hour charge-of-quarters for headquarters.

"Yes, sir."

"Tell Captain Marshall and her team to assemble in front of headquarters. Pickup will be in one hour."

"Yes, sir... Uh, sir?"

"Yes?"

"She's already here. So are the Canadians. They camped out in the conference room."

"OK. Well, you might wake them up. I imagine some of them will want to use the facilities before the lifeboat gets here."

"Lifeboat, sir?"

"Just wake them up."

"Yes, sir."

"And tell Captain Marshall she can only take three of the maintenance crew. The rest will have to remain here."

"Yes, sir."

... ...

Lieutenant Fibari pressed transmit on the comm link. "Zindarr Approach Control. This is the Grock Species Mining ship GSMS-77. We request a parking orbit and entrance to your landing queue."

"GSMS-77, Zindarr is a restricted planet. You do not have permission to land here."

"Let me talk to her," Zuna said.

"This is Zuna. I am head witch on Taramon. Let me speak to Kallisha."

"As you wish, mistress."

"Zuna!" a voice came across the speakers. "You've come up in the world. Last time I saw you, you were a cub on your mother's teat."

"Times change, Kallisha. We need to talk."

"You Taramon witches think you can blast in here whenever you feel like it, after the way you treated us when we were told we had to come here. Here! To a planet with no technology, with no infrastructure, with no access to the rest of the galaxy!"

"I don't care about any of that. We have bigger problems right now."

"And, that is important to me, why?"

"Two reasons: Ruatha and a photon torpedo."

There was a long period of silence. The approach controller's voice came back on the channel. "You are assigned parking orbit W-1. Let me know when your orbit is stable. You are to be given immediate access to our star port."

They jumped to the parking orbit, left the hologram decoy display of the Grock Starship, and jumped to the entrance of the approach to the star port.

Kallisha and a group of beings were waiting for them when they got there. The "star port" was a single rundown building in a clearing with jungle on all sides. Kallisha came out of the building to greet them. She was an arachnid. Her eight spider legs carried her along smoothly as she approached the lander. Her entourage, made up of several primates, hyenas, a fish in a water cocoon, and a Melincon, followed behind her.

"What do you know about Ruatha?" she demanded of Zuna in a throaty whisper.

"She was kidnapped by the king of Glycemis to plant a dream in a female on a developing species planet. The dream showed the female how to open a wormhole. When she opened her first wormhole it triggered an alert that caused the developing species to be evaluated and failed. The king transferred Ruatha to Fey Pey's ship. It was Fey Pey who transported Ruatha to the developing planet for the dream plant. The best reason we've figured out so far is that the king wants another aquatic mammal species in the Ur. After Ruatha planted the dream for Fey Pey, he also raised up a species of aquatic mammals."

"Why would Ruatha agree to do that?" Kallisha asked. "We know the rules. So did she. Hostile dream plants are a Galactic offense. The Ur could take out our whole colony for such a violation. We would die before we endangered ourselves in such a way."

"The king planted a photon torpedo here. If Ruatha tried to escape or didn't do what he told her, he was going to detonate it."

Kallisha went white, as much as any spider can go white. "Where? Where is there a photon torpedo? Here on Zindarr? I don't believe it. We would have known."

"Would you like us to scan Zindarr for you?" Zarqa asked casually. "You never know what a scan will turn up." She didn't like or trust Kallisha and her tone said that very clearly. These witches were hiding something.

That got Zarqa a cold look. "Absolutely not. We will conduct our own scan. Wait here."

Kallisha stalked away. Arachnids can go pretty fast when they want to. Her entourage followed behind her, stumbling across the overgrown field as they tried to keep up.

The four of them waited in the sun for what seemed like an eternity. There was no one else in sight at the star port. No other craft landed or took off while they waited. Flug passed the time doing yoga exercises to work out his muscles. The cell where Fey

Pey kept him was too small for most of his routine. Zuna waited in the shade of the lander. Fela watched Flug for a while, then joined him, doing exercises of her own.

Zarqa spent her time recording all that had happened to her and Flug while they were on *Easy Wind*. She got a scalpel from the medical kit on the lander and retrieved a micro storage unit from under a mole on her stomach. She had planted it there while they were on *Easy Wind*. She put a small bandage over the mole, transferred the contents to the lander's computer, then encrypted the contents and sent it to Captain Xanny.

Kallisha came walking out of the building. There was obviously a transportation portal inside it that accessed other places around the planet.

"We've located the photon torpedo," Kallisha said to them. "It is protected by electronic devices, some of which we don't understand. One we do understand is a movement detector, which precludes evacuating it. This is an act of war. I have sent a message protesting this to our Ur representative and to the emperor."

Zarqa stepped forward. "If you would allow it, I would like to see what is protecting it. I'm pretty good with electronic stuff."

Kallisha dismissed her request with a wave of one leg. "I want to evacuate the planet before anyone goes near that device. We're talking genocide here. And I want to know everything you know about this. How many people can your starship transport?"

Lieutenant Fibari tried to think of a way to keep from saying they had jumped all over the galaxy in a lander, then shrugged in resignation. "We have one open berth."

Kallisha stared at her in disbelief. "One? In a whole starship?"

"This is our starship," Fela said, pointing at the lander.

"And that one in orbit around my planet?"

"A hologram."

"Xxjllpedrsss!" Kallisha said in frustration.

Flug coughed and looked away, trying to hide his grin. Kallisha was certainly living up to her reputation as not too politically correct. He was trying hard not to like her and failing miserably.

Kallisha forced herself to calm down. "OK, everyone. Now tell me everything you know about what's going on. I want facts and suspicions. Everything."

Fela began with Fey Pey's meeting with the king of Glycemis. Zarqa added the pieces she found on Fey Pey's ship.

"I have a recording of the meeting between Fey Pey and the king of Glycemis. The king said he would pay Fey Pey ten million Huz to do the dream plant and raise up the aquatic mammal species. He gave him a one million Huz down payment."

When they were done, Kallisha was angrier than she had ever been. "That son of a monkrus! He planned to execute an entire species so he could have another aquatic mammal in the Ur? And I can't believe Envoy Gart-Disp didn't know anything about it—no fix-it period indeed! Just a 'Nope. You're dead!' And Fey Pey! If *I* had put that sleep spell on his ship, he's one fish who would *never* have woken up!"

No one said anything for a while as the ramifications of the story sank in.

Kallisha brought up a communication hologram into the air in front of her. She recited an address.

"Galactic Response Center. What is your emergency?"

"This is Kallisha, regent of Zindarr. Verify my identity."

"Identity verified."

"King Amon of Glycemis has planted a photon torpedo on Zindarr. I am invoking an emergency evacuation of Zindarr. Send all available starships. Use my latest census plus three percent for species and numbers."

"Where are you evacuating to?"

"Use our filed evacuation plan."

"What account will be charged for the cost of the evacuation?"

"Charge King Amon," she said coldly.

There was a pause. "You have no authority to charge to King Amon's account."

"Charge my planetary account."

"Accepted." There was another pause, then the voice came back on. "The first ships should be there within two hours. Have the population collected into regional pickup areas to facilitate the transfer."

"If you will excuse me, I have a few things to do." Without another word, Kallisha walked to the portal building. Before she entered the building, she turned around. "After everyone is off-planet, feel free to play with that bomb all you'd like. But if it were me, I'd leave it for the Ur to take care of. They'll want it as evidence. Fey Pey or King Amon, knowing that, could detonate it at any time."

"We have one berth," Fela called to her. "Would you like us to take one person with us? Someone you can't afford to lose?"

Kallisha paused, then nodded. She motioned to an elderly primate female next to her. The woman walked over to them.

The six of them entered the lander. It lifted off, accelerated, then disappeared in a rosy twinkle.

... ...

Dr. Hehsa stared into the incubator. The zygote was still alive on the seventh day. It had gone through the Cavitation and Zona Hatching phases. Today was the big test: Would it implant into the synthetic uterus inside the Baby Machine?

The Baby Machine was prepped and was waiting. Sridhar reached into the incubator using the gloves that were built into the side. The only way to keep the incubator sterile was to never open it. He picked up the incubation flask containing the zygote, slid it into a sterile transportation box, then sealed the box. He opened the incubator and put the transportation box onto a lab cart, realizing that no one else was in the lab to witness this—possibly the most important and far-reaching event in the history of mankind. He pushed the cart into the hallway and turned toward the gestation room where the Baby Machines were kept. He felt mildly ridiculous, pushing a lab cart with a single, small transportation box on it, but his hands were shaking so much, he didn't trust himself to hold the box as he walked.

Inside the gestation room, he paused in front of the Baby Machine that he prepped an hour ago. The monitor showed everything was ready—all green indicators. He slid the transportation box into the sterilizer, which would kill anything on the outside of the box. While the sterilizer was doing its job, Sridhar washed his hands, put on surgical scrubs, a sterile mask, goggles, and latex gloves. The sterilizer gave a faint ping, indicating it was done. He retrieved the transportation box from the sterilizer and slid it into the opening in the side of the Baby Machine. Sridhar reached into the Baby Machine using the built-in gloves, opened the transportation box, then the incubation flask. He sucked the tiny zygote into a sterile syringe, then squirted it into the synthetic uterus. Closing the cover over the uterus was the last step. He pulled his hands out of the gloves, and waited.

There was no change in the display. When the implantation took place, the display would tell him. He watched the readouts carefully. This was normal. Implantation usually occurred within two to five minutes.

The clock shifted into slow motion. Seconds seemed like minutes. Sridhar couldn't stand it anymore. He walked out of the fertilization room, still in his scrubs, into the canteen. A cup of tea would help. He hands were shaking so much he spilled hot water all over the counter before he realized he was still wearing latex gloves. Then he tore the tea bag, pulling it out of the cellophane wrapper.

"Slow down, Sridhar!" he heard his grandfather's voice say. "Breathe. Center yourself. Find peace."

Sridhar closed his eyes, took a cleansing breath, touched his thumb and middle fingers together with his palms out, and repeated his mantra ten times silently. *Fail or succeed, neither matters. Peace with God is the only important thing. What will happen, will happen.*

He picked up his tea, his hands not trembling at all. He walked back to the fertilization room and through the door, a newfound peace replacing the anxiety he felt just minutes before.

The monitor was unchanged. The zygote had not implanted. Seven minutes had passed since he put the zygote into the synthetic uterus, two minutes past the longest time an implantation had ever taken. Sridhar leaned back against the lab bench, closed his eyes, and tried to stave off the despair that threatened to fill him again. He wanted this to work so badly.

Dr. Splendt walked into the room. "Where did you get the zygote?" he asked, his eyes going wide. "That isn't the new one, is it? The implantation worked?"

Sridhar jerked his eyes back to the display. "Implantation successful" was displayed on the monitor.

He reached down to the floor, then jumped up as high as he could. "Eureka!" he screamed.

People ran into the gestation room from all around the floor.

"It worked!" Sridhar told them, so excited he almost couldn't form the words. "The zygote is still healthy and alive after seven days. The Baby Machine just implanted it. The rest of you stop what you're doing and repeat this process. Do it now. By the end of the day I want fifty-six new zygotes growing, eight for each of our seven remaining Baby Machines. We will implant them in one week. We will continue to monitor this zygote over the next week. At the first sign of abnormal development, let me know."

……………………………

"Captain Marshall, let's try the jump again."

Captain Gaye Marshall had been in the lander simulator for twelve hours straight. All lander pilots were required to qualify using the simulator before they were allowed to sit at the pilot's station in a real lander. The lander controls were, to her, as alien as the physics that made the lander move.

Gaye had been kept segregated from most of the starship and the various species on board. This was done to allow her to assimilate the lander skills without forcing her to endure the culture shock of full immersion into the Ur gene pool.

"I need to pass waste," she said to the trainer, a four-armed primate male named Corporal Vibii.

She had learned the proper way to request a potty-break during the first hour of training. She walked to what passed for a toilet on the starship. With all of the different species on board and the fact that this room must still fulfill its function in weightlessness, most of the appliances in the room were a mystery to her.

Her first jump had been a disaster. She ended up sending the lander into a fatal, descending orbit around a star. Her second jump ended up inside a moon. She was into what she hoped was her last hour of training. The anti-grav drive was a snap. It was easier than flying a helicopter and she was excellent at that. Jumps were another thing entirely.

She couldn't figure out why she was having so much trouble with the jumps: enter the coordinates, accelerate in that direction, and push the frigging button. But somehow, the lander never ended up where she wanted.

She got the clear space rule: always jump to somewhere you know is safe, i.e., free of debris, black holes, solar flares, comets, planets, moons, asteroid belts, Oort clouds. Around the galaxy were lots of known clear areas. They showed up as recommended waypoints when she told the computer where she wanted to go. She got the multiple small jumps instead of single huge ones. It was good to have a general idea of what was going to be where when you popped out into real space. When the instructor did a jump, he ended up precisely where he wanted. When she did it, it was anyone's guess where she would end up.

When she got back to the simulator, she asked the instructor, "What am I doing wrong? Why aren't my jumps working?"

Corporal Vibii looked out at where his supervisor had been sitting until a moment ago. "Your jumps are being overridden by the supervisor," he whispered. "What you are putting in is correct. He's changing it."

"Why would he do that? I don't understand."

"We do this sometimes when a pilot is too confident and sloppy. It gets their attention and makes them be more careful. I've never seen him do it to a new pilot. He is the captain's son. He thinks octopi have an inherent advantage as pilots and navigators because they have an eight-lobed brain." The instructor considered how quickly Gaye had picked up the flight techniques of the lander. "Maybe you're too good."

"What do you mean 'too good'?" Gaye asked. "How can anyone be 'too good'?"

"I never seen anyone learn how to pilot a lander as fast as you did. It normally takes new pilots weeks, even months to learn what you did in hours."

"I've been flying airplanes since I was ten years old. Flying is as natural to me as walking across the street."

"You're an excellent pilot, Gaye," he said, putting one of his hands on hers and looking at her with his violet eyes. "I wouldn't hesitate to fly with you into combat. A little practice with lasers and you could outfly any fighter pilot I've ever seen."

She glanced at his hand, still on top of hers. "Are you coming on to me?" she asked in amusement.

"I don't understand the phrase 'coming on to me'," he said.

She paused, composing an appropriate response without any Earth colloquialisms. Her initial orientation had said to say everything as truthfully as possible and expect just as truthful an answer. "Do you desire a sexual encounter with me?"

He coughed, looked at his hand, then removed it in embarrassment. "Females of my species have pigmentation on their face and body that change with their moods. You do not. And, of course, you only have two arms. You are painfully plain to me, Gaye. Compared to a female of my species, you are deformed. I don't find you attractive at all in a sexual way. But you are the best pilot I have ever met."

Gaye wasn't sure how she felt about what he said. For the first time in her life, she understood what the 'not so beautiful' women around her had experienced. It wasn't a happy feeling.

"So what's next?" she asked him, putting all the emotions aside. "How do I graduate from a simulator to the real lander?"

"Tell the supervisor you want to do a stand-alone certification test," he said in a whisper. "That is what we do for pilot certification. No one can be anywhere near the simulator when a stand-alone test is done. He won't be able to change what you put in. And if you ask for it, he can't turn you down."

Lieutenant Xanny, the supervisor, floated back into the room and settled at his station again. "Are you ready for the next simulation Captain Marshall? Do you think you can get one right this time? Maybe without giving us all a solar sun tan?"

"I would like a stand-alone certification test," Gaye announced.

He laughed. "You haven't made a single successful jump yet. And now you want to be certified?"

"Are you denying me the test?"

The supervisor glared at the four-armed trainer who was busy studying a chart on the console of the simulator. "No, Captain Marshall, I'm not. Please proceed. I will wait in the hallway to pick up the pieces of your simulated crash." He floated away from his station and out of the room. Her trainer got up without any expression beyond a twinkle in his eyes. He closed the simulator door.

Gaye pressed the random mission generator button. She was to jump from an orbit around a category 4 star to an asteroid 2.4 lightyears away. The three-dimensional navigation hologram of space between her point of origin and her target appeared in front of her. Recommended waypoints, known safe areas, were in one color. Objects to avoid were in another. She noted two black holes on the straight line path along with an asteroid field from an exploded planet on the first alternative path. She reached into the hologram and expanded areas where she might want to use as a waypoint, making sure they contained no surprises. One of them flashed blue. It was the sight of a pirate confrontation two days ago. Good one to avoid.

The alien sensor displays used "red" to indicate OK and "blue" to indicate a problem. She was still having trouble adjusting to that.

It would take eight jumps to avoid the unsafe areas. She entered her first jump coordinates, accelerated in the correct direction, and pressed the jump button. An hour later the simulator touched down gently on the simulated asteroid.

The door to the simulator opened and the supervisor floated in. "Well, Captain Marshall, you got one right. You are now officially certified as a lander pilot. I hope one successful mission is enough to rescue humanity's beauty queen." He rotated on his anti-grav pack and floated out.

A moment later the door opened again. Corporal Vibii came in. "Congratulations, Captain Marshall. You did that certification ten minutes faster than Lieutenant Xanny did when he approved it as a certification test. And he's been flying landers for thirty years."

They walked back to where the lander was getting repaired.

... ...

"President Robbins, we have received news about the hidden SHIPS."

President Robbins looked up in surprise at his chief of staff, Patty Kendricks, as she stood in the doorway to his office.

The US created six SHIPS in the years between when BSV had been released and the beginning of the Three-Hour War. SHIPS were Sterile Heritage Protection Sites and were intended to house children who were uninfected by BSV. Those children were the hope of humanity if a cure for BSV was not found. They were going to be used to populate a new colony of humans on an uninfected planet or repopulate Earth if the virus did indeed die out after two hundred years of no humans around to let it reproduce. Four of the SHIPS were public knowledge. Two were kept top secret. He had assumed all six of them had been destroyed during the Three-Hour War.

"What did you find?" he asked sadly, ready for yet another nail to be hammered into the coffin of humanity.

"All of the nonsecret SHIPS were destroyed, as expected. Both of the hidden SHIPS are alive and functioning. We have a total of four hundred and twenty-two uninfected children ranging from four days to twenty-six months of age."

The transformation of his sad face to a smile was instantaneous. “That’s WONDERFUL, Patty!” Then a second thought popped up. “Do you suppose there were other SHIPS in other countries and they also survived?”

“We searched for them before the war, but we never found any. Apparently they didn’t find ours either. No way of knowing now.”

“Four hundred and twenty-two children. I hope that’s a diverse enough gene pool to let them survive across the centuries of the future.”

“If you believe the Bible, we survived from just Noah’s children.”

“There are so many holes in that story. I wonder what really happened.”

“Maybe we’ll find out someday.” Patty walked back out of his office.

“That will be when we start having babies again and donkey’s fly through the air,” President Robbins answered absently to himself as he went back to the pile of work on his desk.

… … … … … … … … …

“Josephina!” Freddie saw her standing with some other people. “Come over here for a minute. There’s someone I want you to meet.”

Josephina walked over. She batted her eyelids at him seductively. “What choo need, Homebre Malo?”

Freddie actually blushed. Every time he saw Josephina, she made it clear that she was drawn to him. She seemed to like his “tough guy” good looks and tattoos. She used her “bad man” nickname as a compliment whenever she could.

“Josephina, this is Jeremiah Silverstein. Could you tell him about Rebecca?”

She frowned, not wanting to recount the circumstances of her rape again. She had put that whole episode into a box at the back of her mind and hoped to never open it again. But because it was Freddie asking, she sucked it in and turned to Jeremiah. "She saved my life. Is she really your wife?"

"I don't know if your Rebecca and mine are the same. Tell me what happened."

Josephina gave Jeremiah most of the story of her rescue and trip to her uncle's apartment, leaving out the gory details at the beginning.

"I think I still have the picture we took before she left in that car José got for her." She dug out her cell phone and paged through the pictures. "Yeah, here it is."

She handed her phone to Jeremiah. His wife's smiling face stared back at him.

Chapter 8 – Stupid Feline

"Remember, porting into an atmosphere can only be done at low relative speeds," Corporal Vibii reiterated his lesson. He was standing behind Gaye in the lander while she sat in the navigator's chair while the repairs were being finished.

"Because if I enter the atmosphere too fast, I will turn us into barbeque," Gaye responded, shaking her head and trying not to smile.

"What is 'barbeque'?" Vibii asked, saying each syllable distinctly.

"Meat cooked slowly over a smoky fire. Very tender."

"My race is vegan, Captain Marshall. I find your metaphor offensive."

"OK, sorry. How about: 'I will turn us into steamed vegetables'?"

He chuckled. "Depending on your velocity, you might simply explode. But, if you aren't going too fast, expect the atmosphere to push against your entry as it escapes through the portal into the vacuum of space. You will need a larger than normal thrust to pass through the portal and the passages tend to be very turbulent. It is much safer and much more comfortable to enter the atmosphere from above where it starts at a low velocity, then descend at a moderate rate. But it does take longer. Use the hull temperature sensors to determine how fast you can descend. As long as they stay in the red zone, you should be fine."

Right! she thought. *Red is good—blue is bad! Why can't I remember that?*

The trainer continued. "I use the 'Auto-Descend' function on the navigation hologram."

Gaye indicated a small button on the hologram.

"Yep. That's the one," he agreed.

Gaye recited the lesson on atmospheric descent. "It will descend at three different speeds. Like a jump, just tell it where you want to end up and it does it for you. High will descend at the maximum safe hull temperature."

"Very good, Captain Marshall! Porting out of an atmosphere into vacuum is much easier. The atmosphere blows you through the portal."

The maintenance team walked on board. "Captain Marshall, we are done. The lander is fully functional." They stored the tools they were given by the maintenance crew on the starship into lockers under the seats. Those tools would be necessary for the maintenance of the lander once they got back to Earth.

Corporal Vibii stood. "I will notify the deck commander that you are ready to depart."

After he left, Gaye retracted the ramp and pressed a button. Both doors in the pressure port closed.

The communicator came alive. "Lander you are cleared to depart."

The wall of the starship disappeared, but there was no outrush of atmosphere. A force field kept it in. Gaye placed her hands on the anti-grav controllers and turned the lander smoothly toward space, transitioning the force field keeping the atmosphere in.

Suddenly they were outside the starship in free space and weightless. Earth was "above" them. The three maintenance technicians were busy taking cell phone pictures of themselves in weightlessness, the starship, the moon, and the Earth. One of them held up a small Canadian flag and left it hanging in midair while the other two took a picture.

She cleared her throat. "Uhhh, you guys? We need to get going. Could you, like, strap in? We have a capsule to catch."

Gaye set the jump controls to ten kilometers away from where the computer said Leann's capsule was now. She turned the lander to the proper direction, accelerated, then pressed the jump button. The cabin was bathed in a rosy glow and they traveled a little more than four million miles. Leann's capsule was in plain sight, illuminated by the reflection of the sun's light. It was also moving away from them at twenty-five thousand miles an hour.

The capsule appeared on her navigation hologram. She jumped to within a kilometer. The capsule flew away from them at seven miles a second.

"We have to match velocities with the capsule. That means acceleration, lots of acceleration. Everyone ready?"

The three techs nodded, with grins on their faces as they snapped the straps on the safety harnesses in place.

"Go get 'er, Captain." "Let's see what this bucket'll do, eh!"

The song "Hot Rod Lincoln" popped into Gaye's head. She started humming the tune and paraphrasing the lyrics as she prepared the lander to catch the capsule.

"Headed out of the starship late one night.
The moon and stars were shining bright
All of a sudden in a wink of an eye
A spaceborn capsule done passed us by.

"Now the fellas was ribbin' me for bein' behind,
So I thought I'd make the Lander unwind.
Took my foot off the gas and man alive,
I shoved it on down into overdrive."

She pressed both hands down on the acceleration panels. Over the course of five seconds, the antigrav thrusters increased up to maximum thrust. All four of the occupants were pressed back into their cushions with accompanying gasps and groans. Gaye had to giggle. According to the nav holo, they were accelerating at almost three g's. That meant their speed was increasing by sixty miles per hour each second the acceleration continued! Her Shelby Mustang didn't have anything on this lander. The best it could do was zero to sixty in three and a half seconds.

Now this *is something I could get used to!* she thought.

But the strange thing was there was no feeling of going faster. Nothing changed in front of them. The stars didn't move or come closer. Nothing went past them at greater and greater speed. There was nothing to give their acceleration any perspective. It just pushed them back into their seat cushions.

Gaye watched the distance between the lander and the capsule in the hologram. Over the course of seven minutes, it stopped increasing. She made a note of the distance remaining between them. When the lander had gone half the remaining distance, she flipped the lander over and began decelerating. It took them a little over thirteen minutes to catch up to the capsule and another couple of minutes to match speeds.

Gaye brought them alongside, aligning the lander's portal with the capsule's portal. The capsule was rotating to maintain the artificial gravity inside.

"Hello, Leann," Gaye said on the radio channel Leann used to listen to Earth.

"Hi. Who is that?" Leann's startled voice responded.

"You called for a taxi, ma'am. We're right outside. Space Taxis Unlimited. At your service."

Leann's face appeared at the window of the capsule. A huge smile blossomed and she waved ecstatically. "Where did you guys come from?"

Gaye waved back. "Oh, we were within a few million miles. We thought we'd drop by to visit. Are you ready to go?"

"I can't leave," Leann said, dismay clouding her sunny smile. "I haven't accomplished my mission. The aliens aren't talking to us yet."

"Actually they are, Leann. Captain Xanny recovered this lander from Iraq where it was buried for four thousand years. He brought me to the starship to learn how to fly it. His maintenance people trained three Canadian mechanics to fix it. He has turned over all of his investigation information of our demise decision to President Robbins. It turns out we were framed! Someone planted the dream that showed Lily Yuan how to open the wormholes. The president has a whole legal team examining the materials to find out how best to move forward with the challenge to our demise."

Leann was having a little trouble getting her head around being ready to celebrate when only minutes ago she was trying to prepare to die in failure.

"Why didn't anyone tell me? I thought I failed."

"President Robbins didn't want you to get your hopes up in case this rescue mission didn't succeed." Gaye thought she understood what was going on inside Leann's head. "You did it, Leann," she said gently. "It worked. Your idea worked. You convinced the rest of the galaxy we have something to contribute. You saved us. It's time to come home."

"Give me a minute," Leann said, excitement building in her voice. "I'll be right out."

"You might want to put on your pressure suit before you do, Leann. It's a little cold out here and breathing is kind of a problem."

As Leann struggled into her pressure suit, she distinctly heard Lily's voice laughing at her. "I knew you'd forget!"

... ...

Lieutenant Fibari activated the ship-to-ship communicator. "GSMS-77, this is the lander. Please open the landing deck."

"What's wrong?" Sergeant Po Fo, the landing deck supervisor, sounded surprised. "You just left."

Fela looked at Zarqa in bewilderment. Zarqa was as confused as Fela. "There's nothing wrong. We need to park the lander."

"The deck is open."

Fela guided the lander through the force field and onto the deck into its normal spot. She opened the exit portal. The piles of dirt the maintenance team had scraped off the recovered lander were still being cleaned up.

"What happened here?" Fela asked Sergeant Fo.

"The other lander," he said, shaking his head. "What a mess!"

"What other lander? We only have one."

"The one we recovered from Earth. It was buried there for four thousand years."

"Four thousand years? And it still worked? Where the hell is it?"

"It's gone. The primates took it to rescue the female in the capsule."

"The primates took a lander? And we let them? How did they know how to fly it?"

"We taught one of their females. She was actually pretty good." Sergeant Fo was enjoying the befuddlement of the great Lieutenant Fibari. It didn't happen very often.

Fela stared at the activity on the flight deck, then at the snickering Sergeant Fo. "I think I'll go check in with the captain. Leave the armament in place on the lander."

... ...

When she got to Captain Xanny's quarters, his door was sealed with a "Busy" hologram hanging in front of it. She began to turn away when Captain Xanny's voice came through the door.

"After two years of being prohibited from even talking to them, suddenly you want me to go get the female and tell them everything? What changed?"

There was a pause. She couldn't hear the response.

"The emperor? The goddamned emperor is involved in this now?"

Another pause.

"Send the female to the emperor? He wants to talk to *her*? How the hell am I supposed to do that? My starship is on quarantine duty. Is someone going to relieve me?"

Another pause.

"So you want me to send the female in my lander to the emperor's palace on Quyl. And what if I need the lander? You guys only gave me one."

Fela rolled her eyes. "I am soooo glad I'm not the captain. This crap would drive me crazy."

She walked to the bridge.

Commander Chirra looked up. "Hi, Fela. Welcome back. Who's the primate?"

"Her name is Beauhi. We went to Zindarr to talk to Kallisha about the dream plant. She's Kallisha's second in command."

"Zindarr?" he gulped. "You were on Zindarr?"

"Yeah. We left there about ten hours ago. We took Zuna back to Taramon, then we came back here. Why?"

"Someone hit Zindarr with a photon torpedo. It's just dust now. It's all over the news feeds."

"Did anyone get off?" Fela asked in alarm. "The evacuation was supposed to start eight hours ago."

"Don't know. Let me see if the exact time of the explosion is in the feed." He pulled up the news feed.

"Breaking news! The Witches World, Zindarr, exploded by photon torpedo! Evacuation underway when the explosion occurred. Three starships destroyed."

The talking heads were being interviewed about where the photon torpedo could have come from and why. A live feed of the expanding debris field filled the news hologram.

One of the commentators was responding to a question. "The Traffic Control Center backup on Zindarr's moon shows the last known ship leaving the area around Zindarr was eight hours ago, right before the torpedo detonated. The lander identified itself as GSMS-77. The lander's exit trajectory established its destination as Taramon. A massive hunt for the lander is underway. The real GSMS-77 belongs to Grock Corporation and is on Quarantine duty on a planet in the EB-31-21-98 solar system."

Commander Chirra pressed his comm button. "Landing Deck?"

"Yes, sir."

"Are both photon torpedoes still attached to the lander?"

"I'll check, sir." He returned several minutes later. "No, sir. One is missing. The display in the lander says they both were there. Because it was *you* asking, I did a visual check as well. I found this." He held up a placebo circuit—a small box with a connector to where the photon torpedo normally was situated. "Someone put a placebo circuit where the missing torpedo used to be. It would make the missing torpedo appear to be present from inside the lander."

"Put that placebo in a sealed bag. Do not touch it any more than you can help."

Fela looked at Commander Chirra in disbelief. "How could that be? There was no time when someone wasn't in the lander. How could someone have replaced the torpedo with a placebo without someone knowing it? Where the hell did the torpedo go?"

Commander Chirra pressed the comm button again. "Sergeant Mixx, please report to the bridge." He turned to Fela, his face hard as stone. "What happened to the torpedo, Fela?"

"I don't know. It wasn't our torpedo that blew up Zindarr. It was one King Amon planted to coerce Ruatha to do the dream plant in the primate female."

"And you have proof of that?"

"Yep. We have a recording of Ruatha telling us that. All five of us heard her. After I told Kallisha about what Ruatha said, Kallisha did a scan of Zindarr and found the torpedo. I sent the recording of Ruatha's statement to Captain Xanny while we were on Zindarr waiting for Kallisha to finish her scan. She found the torpedo and called the Galactic Response Center for an evacuation. She tried to get King Amon's account to pay for it, but the Response Center wouldn't allow it."

"That should be on the recording of the call to the Response Center." He brought up another comm hologram and gave the address of the Galactic Response Center.

"Galactic Response Center. What is your emergency?"

"This is Commander Chirra aboard the GSMS-77. I would like to view the recording of the call from Kallisha, Regent of Zindarr, to the Response Center before Zindarr was blown up."

There was a pause.

"That recording is not available. There is a note attached to the file. It has been marked as evidence. It can only be released to parties involved in the investigation of the destruction of Zindarr."

"Thank you." Commander Chirra ended the call. He turned back to Fela. "Where is the recording of Ruatha?"

"In the lander's storage and, I imagine, in Captain Xanny's mailbox."

Commander Chirra brought up an access window. He connected to the lander. "Where?"

"In a substorage named Ruatha."

He opened the substorage and played the hologram.

Ruatha appeared in the lock of *Easy Wind*. "Aren't you coming?" Zuna called from inside the lander. "We have room."

"No," Ruatha said sadly. "The king of Glycemis planted a photon torpedo on Zindarr before he kidnapped me. If Fey Pey wakes up without my being on board, he'll detonate it. Everyone I love will perish. I have to go. Find that torpedo and evacuate it into clear space." Ruatha slammed the portal closed.

"That's not Ruatha," Beauhi said beside her.

Fela jumped. Damned witches could sneak up on anyone.

"Who is it?" Commander Chirra asked.

"Her name is Plew. She went rogue several years ago and left Zindarr. No one knew where she ended up."

"Rogue from the rogues," Fela said to herself. "That would make her fit right in on *Easy Wind*."

"Could she have planted the dream?" Commander Chirra asked.

Beauhi shrugged. "Probably. She was pretty good at those spells." Beauhi gasped and held her hand to her mouth. She was looking at the news feed on Commander Chirra's news hologram that was still running. "Zindarr is destroyed? Did anyone escape? Were there any survivors?"

"We don't know yet," Fela said gently.

Commander Chirra needed to do some more research before he made up his mind. "Lieutenant Fibari, you are restricted to the ship until we sort out what really happened on your trip to Taramon and Zindarr."

Fela gasped in disbelief. "This is complete crap, Commander, and you know it!" She looked around the bridge. Everyone was staring at her. She shrugged. "OK. I need a rest anyway. Sergeant Mixx, apparently you are still in charge of the security of the ship and the moon base."

Fela walked back to her quarters, pondering how cleverly she was being framed for the destruction of Zindarr. This was pure Fey Pey. He must have known Zarqa and Flug were loyal to Captain Xanny from the beginning. He let them find the evidence, even placed it there so they *could* find it with just the right amount of digging. He incarcerated and tortured the two of them, knowing Zarqa would find a way to contact someone from Captain Xanny's ship. He probably even figured that she, Fela Fibari, his ex-executive officer, would be the one to try to rescue Flug and Zarqa. He distracted Tannl with the Mellincon while someone else took the torpedo from the lander and installed the placebo circuit. He let Flug and Zarqa escape so they wouldn't be found on his ship. And the lander, with me, Lieutenant Fibari, aboard, was the only ship that escaped from Zindarr. The evidence Zarqa and Flug found would turn out to be manufactured and would be inadmissible. They were no closer to finding out what really happened on Earth, three-and-a-half years ago, than they were before they found Fey Pey on Taramon.

The Ur police would be coming to this ship within a day to arrest her for the destruction of a life-supporting planet and the murder of a quarter of a million witches, both capital offenses. Fey Pey had played them like an instrument. It was most likely her missing torpedo that blew up Zindarr. If she had evacuated the torpedo, like Plew suggested, they would have been killed and there wouldn't have been any evidence against Fey Pey or King Amon. You could bet Fey Pey had a perfectly good explanation for why he was on Earth and it had nothing to do with the dream plant, raising up an aquatic mammal, or some covert operation of King Amon's. And King Amon was head of state of a sovereign world. To convict him, you would almost need him admitting in court he kidnapped Ruatha, raised up the mammals, and paid Fey Pey to plant the dream. Like that was going to happen.

She still couldn't believe Fey Pey had duped her so easily. *And I played right into his hands the whole time. Look up "stupid feline" in the dictionary. My picture will be right there.*

... ...

"Are you really a witch?" Leann asked Beauhi. They were both in the canteen. Leann was waiting for Captain Marshall to bring her back to Earth. Gaye was getting some questions answered from her trainer about the lander and how she could have caught up with Leann's capsule without chasing after it.

"Yes, I am, dearie. Why do you ask?"

"I've never met a witch before that I know of. My world hasn't been very kind to them."

"Name me one that has," Beauhi said, a little bitterly.

"What can a witch do? Do you really use magic?"

"Magic is just another force of the universe. Not everyone can touch it and make it do what they want. It's a bit of an acquired skill." Beauhi decided to try something. "Give me your hand."

Leann held out her hand tentatively toward Beauhi. Beauhi took Leann's hand gently in hers and formed a cup with it in her own.

"Now close your eyes and think about your favorite thing when you were a child. It could be a pet, a doll, a favorite place, anything at all. Picture it in your mind. Make it as clear as you can."

Leann closed her eyes and remembered the pet rabbit she raised from a baby. Its name was Snuffles. She felt something move in her hand and her eyes snapped open. Snuffles as a baby was sitting in her palm looking up at her. Leann gasped. Snuffles leapt out of her hand and disappeared into the air.

"What happened to her?" Leann kept looking back and forth from her hand to where Snuffles disappeared.

"It was an illusion created by your memory. It wasn't real. This kind of magic is what the Ur allows. If we had made your pet for real, that magic is forbidden."

"And you could have done that? Made a real animal from my memory?"

"Actually I didn't do anything but channel your energy. With a little training, you could do it as well."

Leann didn't catch Beauhi's subtle sidestep of her question. She didn't know what to say. Finally she stammered, "I c-c-c-could do that? By myself?"

Beauhi chose the aura of a kindly grandmother to present to Leann, trying to lay the groundwork for a lasting relationship between the two of them. "You could do much more than that,

Leann. I could show you. How would you like to be able to know if someone is lying to you or hear what they are thinking behind the words they are saying?"

"I would like that very much."

"I hope we have time together that would allow me to share such knowledge with you."

Beauhi's mind was still recoiling at the power and strength she had felt inside Leann. *This one needs training,* she thought to herself. *Power without training is a danger to everyone. And Leann has created waves that have probably reached to the doorway of the emperor himself. Training her as a witch could only help our cause.*

Chapter 9 – The Mole

"Captain Rousselot, I need some time off." The cleanup of Santa Clarita and Valencia was well underway. The local militias that had kept the gangs out of the hills around Santa Clarita and Valencia joined the Marines in policing the towns and arresting the remaining gang members who terrorized them. Now that Reseda was passed back to the local police for law enforcement and policing, several hundred more Marines were taking part. The Marines had continued over the hills to the north and met up with the Seventh Infantry Division in Bakersfield. The whole I-5 corridor from Canada to Mexico was now clear and secure. Traffic and commerce began to return to normal. Local governments were reestablishing themselves and screaming for federal funds. Repairs to the damage of the war were underway everywhere.

"How long do you need, Gunny?" his Commanding Officer asked.

"I would like a week, sir. I found out my wife passed through here on her way to our home in the mountains, right after the bombing. I want to make sure she made it OK."

"Where is your home?"

"About forty miles east of Sonora."

Captain Rousselot considered Jeremiah's request. "Are you going to go alone? Most of the area between here and there has not been secured. According to what I've heard, Fresno is especially bad."

"I thought I'd go up US-395 through Bishop, sir, on the east side of the Sierras. Bypass the whole San Joaquin Valley."

Captain Rousselot looked out the window of the abandoned storefront he was using as a command center. Jeremiah was too important to his command structure to lose. "Why don't you take Chief Harris with you? I'd feel a lot better about your chances with the two of you together instead of you alone. In fact, your whole team needs a break. You guys kicked ass taking back Santa Clarita from the gangs. Take them and the gun trucks. I want you back in one week. If all of you go, then all of you will come back. Make sure you take enough fuel, food, and ammo. No telling what you'll find along the way. In two weeks we start up Highway 99 to clear the east side of the San Joaquin. Keep your eyes and ears open for any intel."

Jeremiah laughed to himself. *Yeah, some rec time will be well received by the rest of the team!* Jeremiah stood and saluted. "We will be back in one week, sir. Semper Fi!"

"Before you go, they want you up at Brigade."

"Brigade, sir?"

"I think the Colonel wants to thank you personally for the Santa Clarita operation. He wants you there at noon."

Jeremiah sighed. This was going to delay their departure. "Yes, sir." *What the Colonel wants, the Colonel gets.* He saluted.

Captain Rousselot saluted back. "Semper Fi, Gunny. I'm going to issue you orders to do an intel gathering trip to Sonora. That'll cover you in case you encounter any operating military units between here and there. The Reserve and National Guard keep surprising me. I'll have your orders ready after you come back from Brigade. Pick them up from the company clerk before you head out. Go have some fun. You guys have earned it."

"Yes, sir!" Jeremiah saluted again, did a sharp about face and left the storefront.

… … … … … … … … …

The lander settled softly on the white "H" of the helicopter landing pad next to President Robbins's Command Center at Fort Riley, Kansas. The outside of the lander was rough. It was still covered with bits of dirt and dried mud from its four-thousand-year burial. Unlike the helicopters that used the "H" as a landing spot before the Three-Hour War, no wind and dust cloud accompanied the lander's arrival. The camera crews recorded the landing for the president's daily news broadcast.

Somewhere, someone had found a band and it was playing a welcome march for the returning heroes who saved the world.

President Robbins and his cabinet were waiting on a small stage for Leann to appear as the portal on the lander opened. She was the first one out of the lander. She stood at the top of the ramp and waved triumphantly as it extended from the portal down to the ground. The small crowd took pictures of the event to prove they were part of Leann's welcome home.

Leann's mother was waiting in the greeting line with the president. She ran to Leann, giving her a hug while both of them cried. Lily Yuan, Kevin Langly, Douglas Medder, and Clara Medder were waiting right behind the president. They were the four people who befriended Leann before her mission as they helped her prepare for it.

Doug, Kevin, and Lily were nominated for the Nobel Prize for discovering the Rosy wormhole portal three years earlier. As the lander descended with its anti-grav drive, all three of them were studying it. Once the celebration was over and the dust settled, they were tasked with discovering how the anti-grav drive worked and how humanity could use it for peaceful endeavors.

President Robbins walked to the end of the ramp where Leann and her mother were walking toward him. He gave Leann a bouquet of roses, a hug, and a kiss on her cheek. He led her back to the greeting line where the Prime Minister of Canada was also waiting.

After the handshakes and hugs were finished, President Robbins led Leann up to the podium. He leaned over to the microphone. "Leann, you have achieved in one week what I did not in the two-and-a-half years since I was elected president of the United States. The aliens are talking with us. They have transferred to my legal team all of the evidence of the wrongful elimination decision. Everyone, please join me in welcoming the young woman who has saved humanity."

He began clapping and was joined enthusiastically by the entire crowd.

A smiling Leann held the bouquet of roses in the crook of her arm and held up her hand to the clapping audience. She stepped to the microphone. An expectant hush came over the audience.

Leann looked into the camera as it focused on her. "This wasn't an attempt by me alone to get the aliens to talk to us. It wasn't an attempt by the United States and Canada. It was an attempt by the world to get the aliens to listen to our side. *We* have succeeded in getting the aliens to listen. Now we need to succeed in convincing the aliens that humanity is *worth* a second chance. I know we are. You know we are. We just have to convince them so *they* know we are. This is no longer the beginning of the end. It's the end of the beginning. We have a lot of work to do. It will entail sacrifices at the personal, national, and international levels. But we *can* do this. And we *will* do this. Because anything less than success is simply failure."

The audience applauded wildly.

When the applause died down, she continued. "We know what we have to do. We have failed five milestones. Now we have a chance to unfail them. We have to stop fighting among ourselves. We have to stop predatory capitalism. We have to stop pollution and resource depletion. Our success is within reach. It's up to us to grab it and make it ours. The only milestone that isn't a concern anymore is overpopulation. And when we succeed, we will have to deal with that as well. When we're done, I hope 'what to do after we succeed' is the biggest problem facing mankind."

Leann stepped away from the microphone. The crowd in front of her and everyone on the podium joined together in another enthusiastic round of applause. Across the country, at every military base on the Rosy Internet, people stood, clapped, and raised their fists. Hoots, whistles, "Oorahs", and "Yeahs" accompanied the applause.

Captain Xanny watched sadly from his quarters on the starship. He knew none of this would make any difference at all. Wrong or not, the decision had been made and the Species Elimination Virus was released. There was no going back for this species. The clock was ticking. The youngest of them might live a hundred years, but they probably wouldn't last that long. As the population declined and the infrastructure collapsed, so would the healthcare system that allowed such longevity. The last of them would probably die within sixty years.

But for now he must continue the charade. He opened a communication channel to Earth and entered the number of President Robbins. On his hologram, Captain Xanny watched President Robbins reach into his pocket to retrieve his cell phone.

"Robbins." The president's voice came into the hologram.

"President Robbins, this is Captain Xanny. Emperor Cabliux has requested an audience with Leann. When can she be ready for a lander to pick her up?"

"Who is Emperor Cabliux?"

"He is the emperor of our galaxy. He has been watching Leann's exploits with interest. He is equal in authority to the Ur. Together they rule the galaxy as a partnership. It is my understanding the emperor's granddaughter is a great fan of Leann and has watched each of her transmissions with enthusiasm."

"Is she to travel to him unaccompanied or can a team go with her? I fear she will be a little out of her depth."

"You may select five people to accompany her. The emperor may or may not meet with the other people. It will be his decision. Our galaxy has eleven trillion sentient beings. His time is very sought after. But Leann has created quite a following and the emperor is ever the politician."

"She has just returned from her capsule. I will check with her to see when she can leave. Can it wait for a day? She may need to attend to some personal business."

"I don't believe I would tell the emperor of our galaxy to wait while I 'attend to personal business.' He isn't a person who is used to waiting for anything. Especially if you want him to do a favor for you."

"I'll see what I can do."

"Thank you, President Robbins."

... ...

The news feed on Commander Chirra's hologram suddenly started announcing, "Breaking news! Stand by for details!" This displayed for several minutes, then changed again. "The photon torpedo that destroyed Zindarr has been identified as coming from an Ur cruiser abandoned thirty years ago." A live feed of an equine appeared in the hologram.

"We have identified the source of the torpedo that was detonated on Zindarr. Every photon torpedo has a molecular signature that is recorded upon its creation and cannot be changed. The torpedo used on Zindarr came from an Ur cruiser that was fatally damaged some thirty years ago in a pirate confrontation. The Ur cruiser, *Far Galaxy*, was attempting to rescue hostages who were being held for ransom, one of which was the daughter of the Admiral of the Fleet. The pirates and the cruiser were in a running battle for three days. The pirates agreed to release the hostages if the pirates were allowed to escape. To ensure the safety of the hostages, the captain of *Far Galaxy* agreed. The hostages were put in a lifeboat and left for *Far Galaxy* to pick up. When *Far Galaxy* attempted to retrieve the lifeboat, it exploded, killing the hostages and damaging the cruiser beyond repair. The captain abandoned ship and jumped the lifeboats to a nearby waystation. The photon torpedo was launched at the pirates after the lifeboat blew up, but its detonation was never detected. Neither the cruiser nor the torpedo were recovered by the Ur although a massive search for them was conducted."

Commander Chirra keyed the code to Lieutenant Fibari's quarters. "Yes, sir," she answered.

"You are released from confinement. The torpedo that blew up Zindarr was from an Ur cruiser that was destroyed thirty years ago. The torpedo was launched at a pirate vessel, but it never detonated."

"And I'll bet that pirate vessel was *Easy Wind*," she muttered.

"Excuse me, Lieutenant. Could you speak a little louder?"

"I said 'Thank you, sir. I will resume my post.'"

"Carry on, Lieutenant Fibari. Welcome back."

"We need to report the loss of our torpedo, Commander Chirra. I'd be willing to bet it shows up somewhere unexpected and I don't want my name anywhere near it."

"I agree. I will report it immediately."

"Can we get Taramon to ID the Mellincon that got his tail feathers scorched? I'd be willing to bet he was from Fey Pey's crew."

"I will ask, but don't get your hopes up. Taramon makes its living by *not* ID'ing anyone."

Fela walked to the canteen where Zarqa and Flug were giving everyone who was off-duty a scene-by-scene retelling of their exploits. The crew was listening with rapt attention.

When they got to the performance of Plew saying she was Ruatha and sending them to Zindarr, a nav tech asked them, "What was Zindarr like?"

Everyone knew about Zindarr and the dark magic practiced there. Zindarr was the world that mothers scared children with on dark, stormy nights.

"Much like any other unsettled, zero technology world," Beauhi responded from the back of the canteen. She had come in to listen with the rest of the crew. Everyone turned to see who was talking. "We viewed it like a prison. No one was allowed near us. We couldn't interact with the rest of the galaxy. We lived in caves when we first got there. The only supplies we could get were delivered by Ur military supply ships. They would only bring us things that wouldn't allow us to escape. Even our transportation portals were limited to only linked sites that were installed by the Ur military. If we attempted to hack into them, they would stop working. We had one representative to the Ur and she couldn't vote."

"What did you guys do to get sent there?" the nav tech asked.

"We refused to say we wouldn't do magic that changed anything. The emperor said we couldn't even bring rain to a drought area or stop rain in a flood. We refused and got sent to Zindarr."

The canteen was quiet for a while. Fela spoke up. "Zarqa, Flug, Tannl, I need to see you in my quarters."

When they reached Lieutenant Fibari's quarters, she shut the door behind them. "I need to ask you, Flug and Zarqa, if you have ever seen this Mellincon before. She showed the hologram of the Mellincon at the Taramon star port. They both studied the Mellincon's image as he tried to steal the laser and as he was complaining to the star port police.

Flug shook his head. "They all look alike to me. I never could tell them apart."

Zarqa studied the Mellincon. "Let me see those holograms again. From beginning to end." She walked around them as they played. "Stop it. Now back it up about one second." She studied the Mellincon closely. "One second more."

"There. That's makeup." Zarqa pointed to the Mellincon's forehead. "Can you get better resolution on this area right here?" She pointed to the Mellincon's forehead between his ears. Fela stretched the area, magnifying it. "Yep. That's the one that tried to get me to move my bunk when we first got to *Easy Wind*. A lightning bolt scar going from here to here." She pointed from his left eye to his right ear. "You can see how the fur is a different color where the scar is. He was a real jerk."

Fela pursed her lips. "I thought he worked for Fey Pey. Nothing else made sense."

"Well, I never saw him work. But he was sure on *Easy Wind*."

"While he was distracting Tannl, some other people were stealing one of our photon torpedoes."

"What!" Tannl sat up. "No way. I would have seen the alert light when they opened the armament bay."

"Let's make sure that light is working," Fela said, getting up.

They walked to the lander and entered it. Fela opened the armament bay. The armament bay light went from red to blue, indicating the armament bay had been opened. She cocked her head in frustration. She was so sure it would be missing or nonfunctional.

The maintenance tech came in. "Oh, sorry! I was finishing up the maintenance checkout after your trip. You guys must have had a rough one. I can finish later."

Fela was suddenly curious. "Rough one? Why would you say that? You wouldn't have happened to replace the 'armament bay open' light, would you?"

"Not the light—the sensor. There were several sensors missing with the harnesses hard-wired to indicate they were OK." He sat at the console and brought up the maintenance log. "Yep. That one and three others. The strange thing was they weren't just broken, they were gone. That's what I meant when I said 'rough trip.' We normally only see stuff like missing sensors when they were pulled in an emergency."

"What other sensors were missing?"

He checked the log. "Low oxygen, low atmospheric pressure, and Hore energy portal failure."

"Check all three of those systems," she said tersely. "Do a stress test on them. Do it now."

The tech groaned. "All three systems? A stress test, too? That'll take hours."

"Then you better start. I don't want this lander leaving the ship until those tests are complete. Can we help you set them up?"

"Are you saying that you didn't remove the sensors?" he asked, aghast.

"Yep. That's what I'm saying. If they were removed, someone else did it and I want to know why."

The tech sighed, knowing how much work this was going to be. "I can do it. Better to find out those systems have been tampered with here, instead of when you're ten lightyears away from anything."

Fela, Zarqa, Flug, and Tannl walked away from the lander.

Fela stopped. "You guys go back to work or whatever you were doing before I pulled you out here. I have to do my after-action report."

"OK. Fela." Zarqa turned away and walked toward Analysis. Flug walked toward Armaments.

Tannl waited until they were gone. "Do you think we have a mole on board?" he asked Fela.

"Obviously," Fela said. "One or more."

"Who do you think it could be?"

"Don't know. What do you think?"

"I'd look hard at the Mellincon."

"Gwerny?" Fela was surprised. "Really?"

"They're a strange species. You never really know what they're thinking or why."

"Good idea," Fela agreed in almost a whisper, looking around to make sure they weren't being overheard. "I think I'll see where he's been and what he's done."

"Nothing you find would surprise me."

"Thanks for your thoughts. I have to do this damned report."

"Bye."

When Fela got back to her quarters, she began a search of past assignments and employment history. But it wasn't on Gwerny. She began making calls to people on the ships in the profile. There were many people who owed their lives to Fela. They were happy to help her out. And Fela, being the thorough researcher she always was, didn't just check out her primary suspect. She checked out everyone who was in or near the lander since they left GSMS-77 on her trip to Taramon. Some of her calls were to special voice mail boxes that would only be checked when certain ships were in a port of call. While these ships weren't actually pirates, they *were* known to push the limits of what the Ur laws allowed for nonpirate behavior. Everyone had something they hid from everyone else, something they weren't proud of, something they would do differently if they could go back and do it again. And Fela was very good at finding out what those things were.

... ...

"*Señor* Lobo, I have twenty-six men who would like to join your ranks. We would be proud to be part of Lobo Roja."

"What is your name?"

"Arturo, *Señor*."

"Where are you from?"

"Bakersfield. We got driven out by the army."

"Who did you belong to?"

"We were part of Casa Negro. Miguel and I were in collections before the war. Since then we specialized in jewelry stores."

"Did you bring anything with you? Guns? Jewelry?"

"*Sí*. Both." Arturo pulled a packet full of jewelry from his pocket. He skimmed this stuff from what they stole in Bakersfield. The packet contained a magnificent diamond necklace and many loose diamonds and emeralds.

"In our truck we have a .50 caliber, two M-60 machine guns, two grenade launchers, and a TOW missile launcher we stole from the National Guard depot in Bakersfield."

A TOW is a Tactical, Optically sighted, Wire guided missile system—very effective against armor and hard bunkers.

"And ammunition for them?"

"Of course, *Señor* Lobo."

"Come join us then, Arturo. We leave for the mountains tomorrow. All those survivalists living there are like ripe fruit waiting to be plucked."

"I like fruit!" Arturo said, smacking his lips.

"Then we shall all dine well."

Chapter 10 – It Won't Be Long Now

"I'm taking Lily, Clara, and Beauhi."

President Robbins was more than a little irritated and *that* irritated him even more. "I disagree with your choices. None of those people have any background in international negotiations. They haven't any idea what my legal team has come up with. This isn't a girls' campout for a weekend in the woods. This is the future of humanity."

"Clara has legal training and she's Canadian. I'm sure the Canadians would like someone from their country on the team. Tell her what you want, what your ideas are, and I'm sure she will take them into consideration. And I find your comment about the 'girls' campout' offensive. For four thousand years, the men on Earth have screwed up the governance of this world. For the last two and half years, the men of Earth have tried to get the aliens' attention. As usual, when nothing else worked someone tried to blow up the adversaries. The heavy hand won't work anymore, Mr. President. You sent request after request that the aliens ignored. None of Earth's men have gotten anywhere with attracting the attention of the aliens. It was me, a woman, and me alone, who did it. Have a little trust, President Robbins. Men don't have to do everything."

"Beauhi? She isn't even from Earth. And Lily is a physicist. What does she know about negotiations?"

"Beauhi has more insight into people and why they do the things they do than anyone I've ever met and she was second in command to a world leader. She's also had firsthand dealings with the bureaucracy of the Ur. And Lily is my friend. I trust her and her opinions plus she is Chinese. I wanted as diverse a group as possible when we confront the emperor." She started to get up. "We don't have a lot of time, President Robbins."

"Fine," he snapped. "But I'm sending at least one person from my government with you. And he is an expert in negotiations."

"Whom do you have in mind?" she asked, sitting back down again.

"Antoine Garnier, my chief counsel."

Leann already met Mr. Garnier and disliked him intensely. In the two days since she arrived back on Earth, he had fulfilled every negative male stereotype she knew about and even invented several new ones. He had actually patted her bottom and called her "girlie!"

"Not a chance. If you insist on me including someone you know, how about Patty Kendricks? She can get anyone to do anything."

Patty was his chief of staff and his right hand. She could indeed get anything from anyone and have them say "Thank you, would you like some more?"

"OK. Patty," he said resignedly. "But only if she agrees."

"She already has," Leann told him. "And I want one more person. Captain Xanny said I could bring five. I want a man on the team to balance the perspectives of the women."

"Who else do you want, Leann? The Dalai Lama?"

"Good Lord, no! I want you."

President Robbins was taking a sip of coffee. He coughed in surprise and spilled the cup all over his lap and desk.

"Me? You want me to meet the emperor of the galaxy?"

"The person I want to meet more than the emperor is Envoy Gart-Disp. I want to look him in the eye and ask him why he failed us without offering a fix-it period. We were the first species he has failed without one."

President Robbins sopped up the coffee from his lap and his desk with a napkin. "Do you think a fix-it period would have done any good? Remember what the world was like then. There were wars going on everywhere." He started ticking them off on his fingers. "Iraq, Afghanistan, Chechnya, Congo, Somalia, Libya, Darfur, Sudan, Syria, Yemen, Ukraine. And what do you think the world have done if an octopus had appeared on worldwide TV and said 'Quit fighting or we'll cut off your babies'? If I'd been the envoy, I'm not sure I would have given us a fix-it period."

Nevertheless, President Robbins considered her request. He decided he had to ask his next question. “You said you wanted as diverse a group as possible. Are you asking me to go because I’m black?”

She raised an eyebrow. “Your being black has nothing to do with it. I’ve never met anyone who could get more done with opposites and get them working together. Plus you were a lawyer. A really good one.”

“If I go, the Prime Minister of Canada will want to come.”

“Actually, she’s OK with you going. She said she was too busy to break away, *especially* with you going.”

“Now *that* I understand.” His desk was crowded with critical things that needed to be done yesterday. The banking system was just beginning to become functional again. The next meeting with them was tomorrow afternoon. Sprint, AT&T, and Verizon were coming to talk about nationwide Rosy Internet backbones this afternoon. ExAct, the largest dark energy manufacturer before the war, was coming tomorrow morning to talk about replacing the entire electrical grid with local dark energy generators.

President Robbins looked at Leann with a newfound respect. Despite what she had accomplished, she continued to surprise and delight him. “How long have you been setting this up, Leann?”

“Since I got back.”

“You mean you started on this yesterday? Twelve hours ago?”

“Well, more like fifteen hours ago, but, yeah, after dinner with Mom.”

President Robbins realized that Leann was not quite as far over her head as he thought. His decision jelled in his mind.

“Have everyone ready to leave within the hour. Have Clara report to the legal team immediately. I will call them and have them present a thumbnail to us of what they’ve found. I want a pair of Rosy radios to accompany us that will have matched pairs here at headquarters.”

“Yes, sir. You’ve chosen a wonderful team for me.”

He watched the door close behind Leann and snorted. "She made it sound like this was all *my* idea!"

He sighed, started to call Patty, and then stopped, his hand over the phone. She would be packing. He smiled faintly. Time to activate the backup plan to run the country. He put the plan in place in case he died or was killed. Of course he never really expected to use it. The words of his flight instructor at the Air Force Academy echoed in his ears: "If you don't test a plan, you don't have one." He picked up the phone and called his appointed vice president, Louis Barfield.

"Lou, could you come into my office? I've got something I'd like to talk to you about."

While he was waiting for Lou, he called his wife. "Paula..."

Before he could continue, Paula interrupted. "I already know, George. Leann asked me last night if I would let you go. I told her 'Of course.' Go save the world, my love. It's what you're good at. I'll be here waiting for you to return to me. I've packed your bags. Patty put them in her office."

"How did you know I would say yes?"

"George, we've been married for thirty years. When have you ever turned away from a job because it was too hard? You were a pilot in the Air Force Academy and top of your class. You graduated from Harvard Law School while you worked at a PC repair shop fixing computers. You got elected to the House of Representatives from a district that never had a black man represent it before. Then you convinced the whole state of New York to elect you to the senate. Now you are president of the United States. YOU are, George. You accomplished those things because you are a good man. You have changed the world's opinion of black men everywhere simply by being good at what you do. This is the 'hard mission' of a lifetime. If Leann had asked anyone else, I'd have asked her why. You are the perfect person to fill out the team. You six will succeed if for no other reason than everyone else thinks you'll fail."

"So you think I should go?" he asked innocently, waiting for what he was sure she would say.

Even over the phone he could hear her eyes roll. There was a knock on his door.

"I have to go. Lou's here."

"I'm coming down to say goodbye."

... ...

The unmistakable voice of Colonel Donald S. Gall came out of his office. "Gunny Silverstein, get in here!"

Jeremiah walked into the Colonel's office, stood at attention and snapped a sharp Marine salute. Captain Rousselot and Major Dyer, his battalion commander, were there also. "Gunnery Sergeant Jeremiah Silverstein reporting as instructed, sir!"

The Colonel walked around his desk to stand in front of Jeremiah. "Gunnery Sergeant Jeremiah Silverstein, you have brought great credit to your company, battalion, and brigade. You have distinguished yourself and the Marine Corps. It is with great admiration and pride that I promote you to Second Lieutenant in the Marine Corps. The Corps needs as many good, young officers as it can get. You did great as a Sergeant. I know you will do at least as well as an officer, probably better."

The Colonel took the Gunnery Sergeant stripes off Jeremiah's BDUs, then pinned a Second Lieutenant bar in its place. He saluted Jeremiah. "Welcome to the Officer Corps, Lieutenant Silverstein."

Jeremiah had no idea what to do or say. This was so far beyond what he had expected, he was overwhelmed. Finally he managed "Sir, I won't let you down." He saluted the Colonel.

"I know that, Lieutenant. If I'd thought you would let me down, you wouldn't be here today. I understand you and your team have some R&R coming. It's well deserved. You better get to it." The Colonel returned Jeremiah's salute.

"Yes, sir!" Jeremiah did an about face and walked out of the Colonel's office. He wasn't paying attention to where he was going and almost ran over a private walking down the hall. The private saluted him. "Excuse me, sir."

Jeremiah saluted him back. *That's going to take some getting used to,* he thought to himself.

The team's departure was delayed until the next day. It seemed that everyone in the company knew about his promotion except Jeremiah. There is a certain ceremony that revolves around a promotion in the Marines. It involves vast amounts of alcohol, lots of food, and several embarrassing activities. All three were supplied in abundance. After Jeremiah puked for the third time, he crawled underneath Satan onto his sleeping bag. At some point in the night, someone put a blowup doll into his sleeping bag with "Rebecca" written on its forehead in black marker. He put his arm over it and passed out again. The sun was coming up over the mountains to the east.

... ...

"GSMS-77, this is the Bureau of Criminal Investigations. Open your landing deck so we may board you."

"Where the hell did they come from?" Sergeant Fo muttered as he punched the open-deck sequence into his hologram. There had been no proximity warnings.

His backup didn't realize the question was rhetorical. "Those guys have a special back door that lets them go where they want without setting off any alarms. I learned all about it in my Landing Deck Operations class."

"No shit?" Sergeant Fo said, staring at him like this was new information.

The BCI lander settled onto the landing deck. Three armed BCI storm troopers came out of the lander and stood at attention. Their armor covered their bodies and faces. A fourth person exited the lander. The fourth person was a Mellincon in body armor. Only his face was exposed. The boarding ramp folded back into the lander and the portal closed.

"Take me to Captain Xanny," he demanded.

"You watch the store," Sergeant Fo told his backup.

Two minutes later they knocked on the door to Captain Xanny's quarters.

"Who is it?" a voice questioned from the other side of the door.

Sergeant Fo was surprised. The captain never answered a knock on his door like that.

"I am Special Agent Yytti from the BCI. I have an arrest warrant for a Lieutenant Fela Fibari."

"Give me a moment. I am indisposed."

Captain Xanny had heard all about the BCI entering his ship. He was trying to verify the warrant. The agent knocked again.

"I have an arrest warrant for Lieutenant Fela Fibari. I am to collect all materials she brought with her including the witch, Beauhi, an analyst named Zarqa, and a combat sergeant named Flug. I am to bring them back to BCI headquarters."

Lieutenant Fibari entered the corridor from one end and cleared her throat. "Looking for me?"

The agent pulled his laser out and aimed it at her.

Fela put her arms up. "Maybe you ought to look behind you," she suggested.

The agent turned slightly so he could see up the corridor. Corporal Flug had his machine gun aimed directly at the agent's chest. Sergeant Mixx stepped out from behind Flug with a freeze gun.

"Are you sure you understand what this means?" the agent snarled, still pointing his laser at Fela. "You will never be able to escape. We will find you and we will kill you."

"I doubt the BCI will do anything," Fela laughed. "They don't know you're here. I just got off the phone with the head of special ops. He told me nothing was going on out here."

"He doesn't know shit. This is a covert op."

"Well, let's wait until someone knows something. Until then, you and your buddies are going to visit our all-expenses-paid, honored-guest facility."

The Mellincon spun around and fired his laser at Flug. Sergeant Mixx dropped him with his freeze gun.

Zarqa came around the corner from where she was waiting. She walked up to the Mellincon lying on the floor. "Hi, Fuzzy. I knew we'd meet again." She reached up and pulled the makeup off his scar. "Who's the grub now?"

Zarqa and the Mellincon were involved in a confrontation on *Easy Wind* when Zarqa first arrived on board. The Mellincon had tried to bully Zarqa and called her a grub, the not-so-nice euphemism for a new crew member. She stood up to him, toe-to-toe. He backed down.

Flug got an anti-grav stretcher and loaded the Mellincon onto it. As he pushed the stretcher toward the brig, he said brightly, "Right this way, sir. Your companions are already in the spa. I hope you enjoy your stay with us."

Five minutes later, the Mellincon was stripped of his armor and was a furry pile on the floor of his cell. The door to his cell clanged shut.

... ...

The sounds of Jefferson Airplane's "Embryonic Journey" came through the speakers at the party. Dr. Hehsa had declared an Embryonic Day Off. Hermann picked the music. He saw Jorma Kaukonen, of Hot Tuna, perform "Embryonic Journey" live while he lived in San Francisco in the late sixties. A studio version of that song was included on Jefferson Airplane's first album, *Surrealistic Pillow*.

Today was the day the new zygote everyone was pinning their hopes on matured from zygote to embryo. It was two weeks old and still thriving in the synthetic uterus of the Baby Machine. The mesoderm had formed as had the beginning of the amniotic sac. This was as normal a gestation as anyone had ever seen. The other seven Baby Machines, each with eight zygotes, were a week behind this one and paralleling its success.

They weren't out of the woods, by any means, but this was a huge milestone. Not a single test they had run so far survived this long.

From the front gate came the sounds of automatic weapons fire. A Marine Corporal burst into the room. "Dr. Hehsa. A large group of people are at the front gate demanding we give them food."

"Where is Lieutenant Andrews?" Sridhar asked.

"He's talking to them."

"Should I go down, too?"

"I wouldn't do that, sir. Lieutenant Andrews told us to sit back and be ready to defend the installation. He's authorized deadly force. He said if we give them food, they will be back tomorrow with twice as many people. He sent me up here to let you know what was happening."

"I hope Lieutenant Andrews knows what he's doing."

"The last time this happened, he sent them to the civil defense shelter under Peachtree Center. That was a week ago. I guess they finished that one up already."

"Any hope for help from Fort Gordon, Fort Stewart, or Fort Benning?"

"We haven't been able to contact them, sir. We try every morning."

"Did you try Fort Bragg and Fort Jackson?"

"I think so, sir. I'll ask Lieutenant Andrews."

"What is Lieutenant Andrews going to do?"

"I'm not sure, sir." The sounds of multiple automatic weapons firing together came into the room. "I have to go, Dr. Hehsa." He ran out of the room.

... ...

Sergeant Fo pressed the comm button to the landing deck. "Mati, move that BCI lander out to portal four. Put a long-term lock on the portal, then come back in that way. Call me when you're done. Lieutenant Fibari wants to seal it with her own credentials after you're done."

"Yes, sir." Mati opened the door walked into the lander. Several moments later, everyone on the landing deck heard Mati scream "Oh, my GOD!" He did an about-face and ran back out to the waste disposal chute where he donated his lunch.

Everyone on the landing deck watched him without understanding. He got enough control to point at the lander. "Bodies! In the freezer."

The deck personnel crowded into the lander. A trickle of blood painted a crooked line from the open freezer down to the floor of the lander. Three naked bodies were packed into it: a Mellincon and two primates, with bloody stumps where their heads had once been. They were not yet frozen.

Sergeant Fo thought about what to do. *This is one weird day.* He went inside the lander along with everyone else on the flight deck. *Must be what happened to the real BCI people.*

He walked back outside the lander and over to Mati, "When you are finished cleaning out your stomach, this lander still has to be moved. You might put on a pressure suit and don't touch anything you don't have to." He turned back to the lander and shouted, "Everyone, get out of there. It's a crime scene. Don't touch anything."

The proximity alert sounded, then the ship-to-ship communicator activated. "GSMS-77, this is Special Envoy Purr. Please open your landing deck."

"Special Envoy?" Sergeant Fo muttered. "What the hell is a friggin' Special Envoy doing way out here? Where the hell am I supposed to put him?" He walked back to his operations console and keyed the code to open the landing deck. The side of the starship disappeared where the landing deck was. He said, in a very professional voice, "The deck is open. We await the arrival of Special Envoy Purr."

Mati climbed back into the lander, breathing air from the oxygen generator in his pressure suit this time. He sat in the pilot seat without looking at the now-closed freezer door. The console activated.

Another proximity alert sounded and a voice came through to the landing supervisor on the ship-to-ship communicator. "GSMS-77, this is the Grock Corporate Executive Shuttle. Open your landing deck, please."

"Who the hell is this?" Sergeant Fo asked under his breath. "We got all the bigwigs we need on board already."

To the shuttle he said, "You'll have to wait, shuttle. Our landing deck is full at the present time. Give me a couple of minutes."

"I'm running a frigging parking lot," he said to himself. Over the intercom he asked, "Mati, what's the holdup? I need that berth."

The shuttle transmitted again. "If your landing deck is in use, we can use a portal just as easily. Which one would you like us to use?"

"Thank you, Executive Shuttle. Please use portal two," he told them. To himself he thought, *The frigging emperor will show up next and he don't wait for nothin'.*

... ...

The envoy's cruiser took up a parking orbit beside GSMS-77. The crew on Captain Xanny's ship began frantic activities preparing for the Special Envoy to come aboard. There were only eleven Special Envoys in the entire Ur. That one would show up at this remote outpost while they were conducting a quarantine operation was unheard of. A shuttle left the cruiser and made the short hop to the Grock Species Mining starship.

The envoy stepped out of the shuttle after it settled onto the landing deck. She was a Mellincon and a female, the only female Mellincon most of the crew had ever seen. The females of the Mellincon species didn't leave their home world, Gilon, very often. That she had not only left Gilon but ascended to such a position of trust and power spoke volumes about her and her abilities. She looked curiously at the BCI lander as it lifted off the deck and moved out into open space. Captain Xanny floated out of the hatchway that led to the rest of the starship.

"Special Envoy Purr, it is an honor to meet you again."

"It has been many years, Irkoo, too many. Is there somewhere we can talk without being disturbed?"

"Of course. Please come to my quarters."

Once the door closed and they sat down, Captain Xanny asked her, "Envoy Purr, what has brought you here to the edge of the galaxy?"

"Envoy Purr?" She raised her eyebrow. "You weren't quite so formal when we were on Sawajan starving to death."

"My intuition tells me that this isn't a social visit."

"You are correct, of course. The emperor sent me. He wants to know what's going on out here. Grock Corporation is telling him one thing. King Amon is telling him another. Envoy Gart-Disp something else again. Then Zindarr got blown up. And that primate female in the capsule on a suicide mission has the whole galaxy filling the emperor's mailbox. Let's start with King Amon. What proof do you have of a collusion between him and Fey Pey?"

"Let me show you what Zarqa sent me from Fey Pey's personal storage."

She read the text of Zarqa's message. "That's it? You smuggled two people on board *Easy Wind* and one of them sent you this message?"

"That and this." Captain Xanny played the recording Zarqa smuggled out of *Easy Wind* under her mole.

"Why would King Amon allow Fey Pey to record their conversation?"

"He wouldn't, of course. Unless he didn't know he was being recorded. If I was Fey Pey, I would have done it for insurance, in case the King tried to back out at a later time."

"Have you found any proof the aquatic mammals were raised up?"

"Yes, we have. That's the easy part. Here's the before and after DNA. There are still huge numbers of adult animals with the old DNA. All children we have tested who were born after the dream plant have the modified DNA. And they have started interacting with the primates."

Captain Xanny brought up the news clips of the Japanese whale hunt and the interviews with the boy who was saved after his sailboat was run over by a container ship. "And there's the dream plant, of course. That's what started this. The primates had found none of the prerequisite discoveries that were necessary to invent a Hore-field wormhole generator on their own. This species had not discovered the resonance of the Girf particle near absolute zero. They hadn't built virtual transistors. No one had yet found the speed of light anomaly surrounding magnetized argon ions. And, of course, cold fusion had not been discovered in a working form." He played his interview with Lily for her.

She listened to the interview in silence, then added, "And there are those famous pictures of *Easy Wind* rising up out of the water near the dream plant site." The envoy had obviously done her homework. "I'll bet Fey Pey has an unimpeachable explanation about why he was there. What happened to the witch, the one who was kidnapped?"

"Ruatha? No idea. All we have is a clip of the witch Plew, telling us she was Ruatha and sending us to Zindarr to get killed. Let me play that recording also. It was Beauhi who identified her as Plew instead of Ruatha."

"Who is Beauhi?"

"She was Kallisha's second in command. Lieutenant Fibari brought her with them when they left Zindarr."

"That would have been just before Zindarr was destroyed?"

"I don't have an exact time on the explosion but, yeah, it must have been pretty close."

"Did their lander have any photon torpedoes on board?"

Captain Xanny expected this question. "Yes. And one was missing when it got back to this starship. But the one that was missing was not the one used to destroy Zindarr." He paused a minute, wondering if he should show the envoy the clip of the confrontation with the Mellincon at the Taramon spaceport. He decided to go ahead. "We think we know when the torpedo was stolen from the lander. Let me show you this."

After the clip was over, the envoy was quiet. Captain Xanny decided to present Zarqa's idea that the Mellincon was from Fey Pey's crew.

"Zarqa says she recognizes him. That he was on *Easy Wind* and a lightning bolt scar went from his right eye to his left ear."

"I didn't see a scar."

"She said the scar was covered with makeup. Let me show you." He brought up the clip again and stopped at the same place Zarqa had. "If you look closely, you can see the fur is a different color where the scar would be."

The envoy walked around the hologram studying the image. "I see what she meant. Is she an analyst?"

He nodded.

"I thought she would be. No one else would have noticed. The fur is also lying wrong for that part of his head."

"We assume the torpedo was stolen while the guard inside the lander was distracted by the Mellincon. During the after-use maintenance on the lander, after it returned to this starship, four bypassed alert sensors were discovered. Commander Chirra asked the maintenance tech check the armament bay and the tech discovered the missing torpedo. Lieutenant Fibari made him run a stress test on the systems that had missing alert lights. That lander was an accident waiting to happen. The oxygen generator would have failed within an hour. He found two different perforations in the hull and the Hore energy portal would have shorted out after one more jump."

"That would have been a death sentence to the occupants. How did the sensors go missing? Who took them?"

"We don't know who or when. We figure the only reason they got back here without mishap was Lieutenant Fibari did the jump from Taramon in three jumps instead of her normal five. And there are two more things."

"What's that?"

"A placebo circuit installed in place of the missing torpedo. That's why no one noticed it was missing."

"What's the other thing?"

"We have a Mellincon in our brig. I think he's the one who took the torpedo. I think he's the one in the clip from the spaceport on Taramon."

She blinked at him without knowing what to say. "Really? How did you accomplish that?"

Captain Xanny told her about the BCI lander showing up an hour before she did, what the "Special Agent" said, about

Lieutenant Fibari's call to the BCI, and what was found inside the lander when they moved it.

"And Envoy Gart-Disp?" she asked. "How does he fit into this?"

"Other than him being an aquatic mammal and not giving the primates a fix-it period after their failure, I don't have any connection. His decision is public record. No one questioned it."

She stared at the real-time display of Earth Captain Xanny used as wall art while she considered what to do. "I need to talk to each of the people who returned in your lander and the maintenance tech who did the repairs. Keep them separated from each other, both before and after I talk to them, until I finish with the last person. I want my own crew to examine the lander and the placebo device also. And I will need the ID of the missing torpedo so I can report it. Then I need to talk to the people in your brig."

"I will set it up."

"Have you contacted the BCI about their lander and the crew inside?"

"I have. They are on their way."

She sighed and considered what to do. The BCI were renowned for their heavy handed techniques, especially when some of their own operatives were killed. "Maybe I ought to start with the brig people. When the BCI get here, they will want to run the show."

… … … … … … … … …

"Ah, Arturo! Life is good!" He lifted the glass of whiskey to his lips and savored the nineteen-year-old smooth of the amber liquid. Good whiskey seemed to be one of the survivalists' required stores. Invariably there were one or two coveted bottles tucked in next to the survival food.

"*Sí, Señor* Lobo." Arturo exhaled a thick stream of aromatic smoke from the joint in his hand, belched, then slapped the head of the woman who was performing oral sex on him. "Faster, *puta*."

This was the second hilltop community they had pillaged. As soon as this woman finished him, he would kill her. Unless someone else wanted her. There would be plenty more in the next community. Or he could torture her. He loved to hear these spoiled white bitches beg. Yeah. A little torture sounded like a great idea. He grabbed two fistfuls of her hair and started moving her head up and down faster. "*Sí, puta, sí*. It won't be long now."

Chapter 11 – Where's George

Jeremiah was awoken by the pressing need to use the bathroom. "Just a few more minutes!" he moaned. He rolled over, attempted to go back to sleep, then opened his eyes in frustration. His bladder wasn't listening. The first thing he saw through his newly opened eyes was the face of the partially deflated blowup doll with Rebecca written across its forehead in black marker.

"Where'd you come from, sweetheart?" he asked, chuckling as he climbed out of his sleeping bag and hurried to the rear of the truck. Five seconds later, unmistakable urination sounds were coming from back there.

"A shower!" Jeremiah muttered as he finished and zipped up. "A shower is next. Followed by a shave and ..." He opened the driver's door of the truck and was assaulted by the odor inside—a mixture of sweaty men, a brewery, and a week-old latrine. There were three men asleep inside. He grabbed his shaving gear and the least dirty towel from behind the front seat, then closed the door firmly. The world wasn't ready for that smell to be released on the unsuspecting.

"Have to leave the windows down for a while when we leave," he muttered as he walked toward the showers.

"Good morning, sir!" two female Marines snapped a sharp salute as they walked by. He heard them giggle after they passed.

"What was *that* all about?" he wondered, climbing the steps of the shower trailer. It wasn't until he looked into the mirror above the sink that he understood. The face that stared back at him was covered with a full makeup job—base, lipstick, rouge—the works. He studied his face critically. Not a bad job. The mascara and eyeliner were a little overdone, but all-and-all, an excellent attempt. He made a pretty good-looking drag queen. He blew a kiss at himself and walked into the shower room.

And I'd be willing to bet someone took a picture, was his last thought before the hot water of the shower began to melt the cobwebs from the promotion party along with the makeup on his face. His last coherent memory of last night, before it melted into a blur, was standing on a picnic table in a hula skirt and giving a passable luau performance. He was stationed in Hawai'i for a year between tours in Iraq.

By the time he got back to the truck, everyone else was up and moving. OK, maybe "moving" was an exaggeration. At least they weren't unconscious anymore.

"Sergeant Wardell," he called out. "Departure in one hour. Get everyone ready and get the trucks loaded. I want fourteen days of rations, ammo, and diesel leaving with us. You'll need to find a five hundred gallon fuel trailer to pull behind the trucks."

"Yes, sir!" Wardell responded. Then he turned to the rest of the men. "You heard the lieutenant, ladies. Drop your cocks and grab your socks. We've got a trip to the mountains to make. It's the Marine dream, everyone. A damsel in distress needs us manly men to rescue her. We don't want to keep her waiting."

"Has anyone seen Chief Harris?" Jeremiah asked the group. A bunch of people shook their heads "no."

"Crap, now I gotta find him." He walked around the three trucks. Nothing in sight but an old VW microbus parked nearby. Jeremiah blinked. The van was moving—not forward or backward— it was moving kind of side to side. In fact it was still moving. He walked over to it. The unmistakable voice of Chief Petty Officer Freddie Harris came from inside the van. "Yeah, just like that. Oh, babyyyy!"

His voice was joined by a woman's as they both cried out. The van got very quiet until the door opened on the side. Freddie came out pulling on his pants. He saw Jeremiah standing nearby and laughed out loud. "OK, now THAT was a promotion party!" He stretched his massive muscled arms, making his tattoos flex, then finished zipping up his fly.

Jeremiah grinned. All he got for his trouble was passing out next to a blowup doll. "We leave in an hour, Chief. Make sure we have all the medical supplies we're going to need."

"Are you expecting trouble up there, Lieutenant?"

Jeremiah coughed at the title. He still wasn't used to it. "You never know. We've received reports of the gang members that were driven out of Bakersfield, Santa Clarita, and Palmdale working their way up the mountains and raiding the settlements along the way."

"Got it. I'll make sure I bring enough fix-up shit."

"Thanks, Chief."

A beautiful, naked Hispanic woman got out of the van and stretched. Her long black hair framed her perfect face. The Marines who were getting the trucks ready stopped in their tracks, then hooted and whistled. She smiled and waved, making her large breasts sway, then reached into the van to pull on a robe. Everyone moaned. She stepped up to Freddie and gave him a passionate kiss. That got another round of catcalls.

"Sophie, tell Carlos I said thanks!" Freddie said when she was done, patting her on the butt. Freddie figured that Carlos sent Sophie to him to defuse any feelings Freddie might have had for Josephina. As much as Freddie appreciated the gift, Carlos need not have worried. Freddie was Josephina's protector, not her lover.

"I'll tell him, Hombre Malo," she giggled. "You better come find me the next time you come through, Freddie." She wiggled her butt at him as she walked toward the showers.

Jeremiah raised an eyebrow at Freddie. "Hombre Malo?"

Freddie shrugged, wondering how long that silly, ghetto nickname would follow him. He reached into the van for his shaving kit and towel, then walked toward the showers, whistling. *What a great start to a week off!* he thought. *Maybe there's room for two in one of the shower rooms.*

... ...

General Keynan's chief of staff, Colonel Walker, walked into the commanding general's office at Fort Bragg, North Carolina. "General Keynan, we have received a faint radio message from the Atlanta area begging for help."

"We won't be able to get there for at least a week. Charlotte is going much slower than we'd hoped. Who was it? Did they say?"

"It sounded like the CCD or DCD. It was pretty hard to make out."

"Jesus, it wasn't the CDC was it?"

"Could have been."

"What did they say?"

"Something about being overrun by hungry mobs. Their guard force was holding the mob off for now."

"Can't Benning, Stewart, or Gordon pick that one up? The CDC has diseases in there you can bet we don't want turned loose. They have smallpox there, God's sake. No one even gets immunized against smallpox anymore."

"Benning, Stewart, and Gordon say they can't help. Benning is tied up in Alabama and the Florida panhandle. Stewart is committed in Savannah and Florida proper. Gordon and Jackson are working on Columbia and Charleston, South Carolina. No one wants to take on Atlanta. According to the police reports we've picked up, it's mob violence there, approaching an outright war zone."

"So it's the 82nd to the rescue again, is it?"

"Yes, sir, it appears that way."

"Tell General Travis to send the First Brigade. Have him turn over Raleigh/Durham to the Third Brigade and go rescue those guys. I want him to leave here within twenty-four hours."

"Yes, sir."

"And I want Second Brigade to follow them down twenty-four hours later. If we're the ones to tackle Atlanta, so be it. Tell them to take a double load of ammo. We won't be able to extract the people at the CDC. They have too many dangerous pathogens. So tell General Travis we are going to stay for a while. Tell him to make the CDC campus his headquarters."

"The Second Brigade is mopping up Charlotte, sir."

"Then the Third Brigade will have to take over that one as well. They've been in reserve long enough. Time to go back to work."

"Yes, sir."

"Did we ever hear from Dobbins Air Reserve Base? They're a few miles north of Atlanta. Or Warner Robins? They're just south of Atlanta."

"No, sir, they never answered our calls."

"Probably smoking holes. Poor bastards. The Air Force got hit hard."

"Yes, sir. They sure did."

"Any chance we can drop some people in now? At the CDC? Before the 82nd gets there?"

Colonel Walker considered that. "We could drop in a couple of hundred troops with the small aircraft we've scrounged."

"Then do that. Do it now. Send the Special Ops guys. They're just sitting on their asses, dying to do something. We can't take any chances with the shit the CDC has in their vaults. Tell them to defend at all costs. They love it when I say that."

"Yes, sir."

"And alert Womack Medical Center. We're going to need to get medical services going again at the hospitals down there. They will have been pillaged. We'll have to start from scratch."

"Yes, sir."

"And tell the Logistics Readiness Center we will need a supply trains set up to keep the brigades resupplied."

"Yes, sir."

... ...

"Leann, are you ready?" Gaye was waiting in the hallway outside of Leann's room.

The door opened and Leann stepped out with her suitcase trailing behind her. The heavy bags under her eyes told Gaye of Leann's exhaustion.

"Are you OK?" Gaye asked her. "You look like shit."

"I was up all night going over the report from President Robbins's legal team."

"Well, get some rest on the trip. You need to be at a hundred-and-ten percent when you meet the emperor."

"Yeah. I'll get some rest before then." They started walking toward the door at the end of the hallway. "Did you know we were failed because some king on a planet of aquatic mammals wanted Earth? He wanted to raise up the dolphins."

"I thought we were failed because we were too warlike."

"So did I. So did everyone. That was the official version. Everyone's been demonizing Captain Xanny for the quarantine and the elimination decision. It wasn't him at all. It was the envoy who, incidentally, happens to belong to the same species as the king who hired some asshole to plant the dream in Lily and raised up the bottlenose dolphins. The captain has been on our side all along. He's the one who identified the guy who planted the dream, somebody named Fey Pey. It was Xanny who went halfway across the galaxy to track him down. And Xanny is the one who smuggled two people on board that idiot's starship to find out who was behind it all. I can't wait to meet him."

Gaye was quiet as they walked toward the lander. Finally she asked, "Do you think he's really an octopus?"

"I would say 'yes,'" Leann said after a moment's contemplation.

"How does he speak? I mean, octopi don't have vocal cords."

"You're going to have to think outside the planet on this one, Gaye. The galaxy, as we know it, just got a lot weirder."

"I suppose," Gaye said thoughtfully, then she got a gleam in her eye. "I wonder if they allow interspecies sex?"

Leann coughed a little. "The inner primate surfaces! I'd keep your eyes open, Gaye, and maybe not your other body parts. However, I do expect a full debriefing when you come up with an answer to that one."

By the time they got to the lander, everyone else was on board and waiting. Gaye took her seat at the nav station. "Everyone buckle up. I've been told jumping out of the atmosphere can be a little exciting."

... ...

"GSMS-77, this is the Bureau of Criminal Investigations. Open your landing deck for our lander."

Sergeant Fo sighed. For three years, you couldn't pay someone to visit this god-forsaken outpost. Now there was a queue and nowhere to put them. "Our landing deck is full at the present time. Please use portal three."

Where was Mati? He needed that dirty old lander the primates brought moved out to a portal.

Lieutenant Fibari met the BCI agent as the portal door opened. "I need to see your IDs and warrant before you enter our ship."

"I am Lieutenant Ziss. Scan my ID. Here is the warrant."

Fela scanned the ID and warrant. Both were verified by BCI operations. "Thank you, Lieutenant Ziss. Sorry for the caution. After the last 'BCI' people, I guess we are a little paranoid."

"Where is the lander?" he asked, ignoring her remarks.

"You mean the BCI lander with the bodies inside? I would have thought you'd have seen it when you approached the ship."

"I saw no BCI lander on the outside of your ship."

She thumbed her comm link to the deck supervisor. "Po, what port did you put the BCI lander on?"

"Port Three. I thought you were already there."

"The *old* BCI Lander, Po. The one with the bodies?"

"Port Four."

"Is it there now?"

He keyed something into his hologram. "Sensor says it's there." He turned on the camera at the portal. "Camera says it's not."

Fela was already moving toward the brig at a dead run, her claws digging into the deck plates. By the time she got there the shipwide alert was sounding. The doors to the cells were wide open.

She pressed her emergency bridge connection. "Bridge, the brig is open. The pirates are gone. Please check for Sergeant Tannl. Is he on board?"

"Sergeant Tannl shows in crew bay six," Lieutenant Nussi replied.

Fela ran to portal number four. Corporal Mati Qitti was dead beside it, his head crushed in. The lander was gone. She pressed her emergency bridge connection again. "Play portal four's watch camera for the last hour. The hologram started. She fast-forwarded it until she saw Sergeant Tannl lead the four pirate prisoners into the portal. Corporal Qitti attempted to stop them and was killed with a blow to the head with some sort of machinery. She saw it lying on the floor next to him. One of the pirates drew a rune. The Portal Secure light went off on the display next to the door. The door opened and the pirates entered the lander. Before the portal closed, the person who turned off the security lock looked up at the camera, grinned, then pointed at the portal secure light. It went back on.

"That's Plew," Fela said in disbelief. "How the hell did she get on this ship?"

"Bridge, have someone check for the physical presence of Sergeant Tannl in crew bay six."

She already knew what the check would reveal. Sergeant Tannl was gone with the pirates. And they'd left right under her nose. She looked out the portal window to make sure they were really gone and gasped. A photon torpedo was floating right outside the portal where the lander used to be and the display was counting down the final seconds to detonation. "Emergency evacuation!" she screamed into the shipwide comm link. "Move the ship! We have ten seconds to clear the area."

Every navigator kept the coordinates of a safe spot entered into an emergency jump address. That address was used whenever the ship was in imminent danger. The danger could be a meteor, a hostile device, a collision, a solar flare—any number of life-threatening situations unique to starship travel.

Commander Chirra pressed the emergency recall button on his navigation hologram and started the jump sequence. The emergency jump alert sounded loudly, then the ship jumped to the other side of Earth. Emergency evacuation drills were part of the weekly training in which Captain Xanny insisted everyone participate.

Only one injury resulted from the emergency jump this time—one of the BCI troopers didn't know to hold on when the emergency jump alert sounded. Seven seconds after they arrived, the photon torpedo the pirate lander left behind detonated where they had just been, taking out the BCI Cruiser, Special Envoy Purr's cruiser, the BCI lander, and the Grock Corporate Executive Shuttle. The shuttle and the lander were automatically jettisoned from portals two and three as part of the automatic emergency evacuation procedure.

... ...

It was night in Kansas. Paula Robbins, the president's wife, was looking at the stars, wondering where her husband was and how he was doing. Suddenly the night sky lit up with the brightness of the daytime sun. She was blinded momentarily. "What in the world?" she gasped. The fireball faded back to the black of night.

"Please, God," she murmured. "Tell me that wasn't where George was."

Chapter 12 – Feeding the Wolves

"Camp Alpha was taken yesterday," Liam told the assembled homeowners. They were meeting in the Kirkpatrick's house.

"Camp Alpha?" Marvin Schroeder asked, incredulously. "They were Green Berets. Two of them. It was only ten miles from here."

"Must've put up one hell of a fight," Tony said quietly. Everyone had heard the explosions and automatic weapons fire. The noise went on for over an hour. Then there was intermittent fire—one or two shots at a time. Until another hour passed. There was one huge explosion after that.

Liam gave words to what everyone was thinking, "I figure they'll be here tomorrow. We have a choice. We can fight or we can leave."

"Where the hell would we go?" Jonathan asked loudly. "I don't know about the rest of you, but I'm sick a running. This is my home. I say we stay and fight. If that means we die, then I'll take as many a them cocksu…" he glanced over at his children watching him wide-eyed. He gulped and back-pedaled. "I'll take as many a them sons a bitches with me as I can."

"And how would you do that, Jonathan?" Liam asked him, not even trying to hide his sarcasm. "Have you got an infantry company waiting in the woods? Have you got some huge cache of weapons and explosives that none of the rest of us know about? Oh wait! I know! You have twenty barrels of napalm hidden in your basement. Great idea! Let's roll them out and get ready. This'll be better than the Fourth of July! Except for one thing," he said hatefully. "You don't *have* a basement!"

"Does anyone have any Styrofoam?" Tony asked into the stillness that followed Liam's embarrassing monologue.

"Styrofoam?" Liam asked the ceiling. "What the hell does Styrofoam have to do with what we're talking about, moron?"

Tony looked down for a minute, then out the window. His eyes turned cold as steel. "Liam," he said, his voice even, "I've seen you bully everyone up here since I arrived with Rebecca. You seem to delight in embarrassing people and making them feel stupid. Well, it won't work with me. You're an asshole." Tony shifted to a parody of Liam when Liam was talking to Jonathan. "Oh Wait! I know! You're a *world-class* asshole." Tony continued with his voice deadly serious, "If you say another fucking word, I will personally cut off your head, shit down your throat ... and say good riddance."

Those "good riddance" words were the same words Liam had used on Rebecca in the last homeowners' meeting. Their effect was not lost on anyone.

Liam started to say something. Tony unsnapped the release strap on his nine-inch Bowie knife and put it on the table in front of him, never breaking eye-contact with Liam. Liam's face went from red to purple. The veins on his forehead were pulsing like they were going to explode. His wife, Amy, put her hand on his arm. He looked at her in confusion. She smiled gently and shook her head. He deflated like a balloon in front of everyone.

Tony continued as though nothing had happened. "With Styrofoam and gasoline or diesel, you can make napalm. Bury a barrel of the stuff with a stick of dynamite under it and you can take out a whole column of people coming up the road. Effing Viet Cong did it to us all the time. That place where the road goes through that ravine would be perfect."

"I got a shit pile of Styrofoam under this house," Kimberly Kirkpatrick told them. "How much do you need? All my appliances came packed in it. Didn't know what to do with it. No one recycles Styrofoam anymore."

Rebecca spoke up. "Jeremiah brought a case of dynamite with us when we moved up here. It's under our house. He has blasting caps and wire too."

"That's great!" Tony continued. "We'll need that. Once we hit them with the napalm, they'll be a lot more careful. They will try up the road again because there really isn't any other way up here that isn't a pain in the ass. They will send a few people at a time. That's when we pick them off with snipers. They will expect that and have snipers of their own to return fire. Fire once, then move. Watch where their snipers fire from and shoot back at them. Eventually they will get tired of it. They will figure we only had one set of napalm and try a mass charge. We'll hit them with the second set of napalm when they try that. After the second attempt, either they will leave us alone and go on to the next settlement or they will try to flank us." He pulled out a map he had made of the surrounding terrain. "If they try to flank us, they will come up here or here, probably both at once."

Everyone except Liam clustered around.

"When we hit them the first time, they will pull back to here." He indicated a hilltop on the far side of the ravine. "I figure the leader will sit there and watch. If we have enough wire, we hit that with napalm the second time as well. Now there are two ways up here besides the road to flank us. We need a couple of people to watch them and shoot anyone who tries to come up that way. Any volunteers?"

"How are you going to put out the fire?" Liam asked, keeping his eyes on the Bowie knife in front of Tony.

Everyone looked at him, then at Tony.

"What do you mean, Liam?" Tony asked him.

"The napalm will start a forest fire. In case you haven't noticed, California is in the worst drought of the century. There hasn't been any rain in eight months. That napalm would be the match that sets this whole mountaintop on fire. What difference does it make if the fire kills us or whoever took out Camp Alpha?"

"Damn, you're right." Tony said to him. "I guess napalm's out. We'll have to use claymores. They're not as dramatic as napalm, but they're pretty effective, if you aim them right."

"Claymores?" Liam asked dubiously.

"Dynamite with nails in front of the blast. Like those idiots did with those pressure cookers at the Boston Marathon. We'll have to place them where the blast won't start any fires. Does anyone have any bondo?"

Jonathan raised his hand. "I got a bunch. I use it for body repair on cars. Don't know why I brung it with me, but I did."

"Perfect!" Tony said. "We take two sticks of dynamite, cover them with bondo, then stick the nails into the bondo while it's still soft. When it hardens, we put in a blasting cap and camouflage it against something hard like a rock or cliff where all the force of the blast goes out. The claymore will spray the nails all over the road and hopefully into some of the men coming to attack us. What kind of ammunition do you have?"

"Pistols, rifles, what do you mean?" asked Liam.

"We can make booby traps out of rifle cartridges. We drill a hole in a block of wood that's just big enough for the shell to fit in, but not all the way through the block. The end of the shell has to stick out the top of the hole about a quarter of an inch. You put a screw in through the block from the other side so it sticks up inside the center of the hole you drilled. Then you bury the block where someone is sure to step. Cover it with some leaves. They press down on the shell and it goes off, right through their foot."

"Where'd you learn this stuff?" Liam asked. He was clearly impressed.

"By having it done to my platoon in Vietnam, 11th Armored Cav, the Blackhorse Regiment. Never thought I'd ever need it." Tony paused, thinking about what else they could do. "We should also make some punji sticks. We'll put them off the side of the road in the ravine. When they jump off the road to take cover, they'll get a rude awakening." Tony looked around at the assembled people. "We'll have to work all night to get this ready. What do you want to do?"

Liam stood. "Unless someone has a better idea, let's get to work. Tony's ideas just might save our ass."

... ...

The four trucks made good time up Highway 14, north from Santa Clarita. The only resistance they'd received so far was at Indian Wells where Highway 14 merged with US 395. Brutus sent a couple of .50 cal rounds over their heads and the people manning the blockade decided they should be somewhere else in a hurry. The snow plow made short work of dismantling the blockade.

They were coming up on Bishop. The weather was clear and the temperature was borderline hot. No other vehicles were on the road, at least none moving. There were many abandoned vehicles, but most of them were on the shoulder or off the road. A couple of times, Sabre (their name for the snow plow), was used to push cars off the road. None of the bombs in the Three-Hour War fell out this far. There were no strategic or tactical targets on the east side of the Sierra Nevada.

Knowing soon they would be subsisting off MREs, they decided to stop in Bishop to see if they could get anything to eat resembling real food. None of the traffic lights were working, which wasn't a problem since no moving vehicles were in sight. A few pickups that appeared to be farm vehicles were parked outside a café. A white sign with "OPEN" on it in hand painted red letters was nailed to a utility pole with an arrow pointing at the small building.

They parked the trucks in a circle behind the restaurant in the vacant tractor-trailer parking area and everyone got out.

"Corporal Cooper and PFC Jones, you are on guard duty until someone comes out to relieve you. Burgers and fries OK?"

"Yes, sir, and maybe a beer?" Corporal Cooper asked hopefully. "This is R&R, right?"

"It'll have to be when we stop tonight, Cooper. I'll see if they have some to go. Coke OK until then?"

"Yes, sir." Corporal Cooper sounded disappointed.

"Coffee for me, with milk and sugar if they have it," Private Jones said, shaking his head at Cooper. "I'm still recovering from last night."

"Standard guard duty stuff, you two. No sitting in the trucks. Walk the perimeter. If anyone comes near the trucks or even acts like they're going to, tell them to go back the way they came. If they don't, one round over their head. If we hear a gunshot while we're inside, we'll come running. The rest of you, bring your personal weapons with you."

An elderly waitress looked up in surprise as they walked in. When she saw their weapons, her eyes got even wider. "We don't want no trouble," she told them shrilly. "We got nothin' to steal."

Jeremiah gave her his biggest grin. "That's great! 'Cause we aren't here to steal anything but your heart. We're US Marines from Camp Pendleton. We're beginning to reopen 395. I thought we'd get some food before we head over the mountains. Is cash OK?"

She grinned in relief. "Cash is fine, boys. Come on in and have a seat."

Jeremiah saw the cook put down the shotgun he was holding since they came in. The cook picked up the microphone on a CB radio and spoke into it.

Everyone ordered what they wanted, got coffee and soft drinks, then waited on their meals. The door opened and a man with a police department shirt and hat walked in. Jeremiah saw the waitress nod at the cop, then at Jeremiah. Jeremiah figured he should introduce himself. He got up and walked over to the white-haired man with his hand out.

"Hi. I'm Lieutenant Jeremiah Silverstein. We're from Camp Pendleton. We're beginning the reopening of US 395."

"I'm Chief Felix, Lieutenant," the cop said to Jeremiah, shaking his hand warmly. "Took you guys long enough to get around to us."

"Had a few other things to do first, Chief. L.A. was a handful."

"Yeah, I'll bet it was," Chief Felix said, shaking his head. He turned to the waitress. "Miranda, how about some coffee, darlin'?"

"So what can you tell us about the highway north of here, Chief? Are we going to run into any trouble?"

Miranda brought a cup of coffee, then walked away just far enough so she could continue to listen to every word of what they were saying.

"Which way you going next, Lieutenant?" Chief Felix asked.

"Straight up 395."

"All the way to Reno?"

"Not this trip. I figure we'll cut across to I-5 somewhere and head back south. This is a recon trip. Our CO wanted an idea of what we were gettin' into when the rest of the brigade starts up this way."

The Chief added some sugar to his coffee and stirred it for a while. "Lieutenant, I'd stay away from Highway 108 until you get some help. After the bombs fell, I kept in touch with the other police departments and sheriffs within a hundred miles of here via shortwave radio. Last I heard, Highway 120 is OK—pretty ride through Yosemite Valley, if you've never done it before. Not a bomb fell there. But a lot of looters and criminals come up from the Bay area and settled around Sonora and Angels Camp. They were joined by the criminals from Stockton and Sacramento as they were run out by the Army. Not much law enforcement left east of Stockton. One by one, my radio contacts on the Highway 108 corridor east of Sonora quit responding."

A cold hand gripped Jeremiah's heart. Fifty miles east of Sonora, off Highway 108, was where Rebecca was.

Chief Felix saw the change in Jeremiah's face. "That's the way you were going, wasn't it?"

"I thought I would stop by the Marine Mountain Warfare Training Center. It's about halfway across Highway 108."

"I know exactly where it is. I'm sure those guys would like some help," the Chief agreed.

Everyone else was listening also. The men in Jeremiah's team started gobbling their food so they could leave. They knew Jeremiah would want to get down the road ASAP.

"Here's the food for your guys outside." Miranda gave him a bag. "And your meals are on Chief Felix. He charged it to the Police Department."

Jeremiah turned to the Chief. "Thanks, Chief. We'll check in on our next trip."

"You do that, Lieutenant." He got up and held out his hand. "I'll look forward to it. I deployed in Desert Storm. First Marine Division. Semper Fi!"

Jeremiah shook his hand firmly. "Semper Fi, Chief." He turned to the men in his team. "You guys ready to go?"

As one person, they got up, collected their weapons, and walked back to the trucks.

"Here's your food, you guys." Jeremiah handed the bags to Corporal Cooper and Private Jones. "Let's top off the tanks of the trucks and boogie woogie."

Ninety miles farther north, they turned west on Highway 108. The road started to climb up the east side of the Sierras. They could see the top of the pass where the road went over the mountain at ten thousand feet elevation. Four miles after they crested the summit they stopped at the Marine Mountain Warfare Training Center. It was destroyed. There were thirty graves dug in neat rows in front of the main building, each one with a name and ID number on a cross. There were survivors! Someone had dug the graves.

A Marine Major walked out of the ruins of one building to greet them. He saluted Jeremiah. "Lieutenant, you're a sight for sore eyes. I'm Major Goodman, the ranking survivor. Where you from?"

Jeremiah saluted back. "Pendleton, sir. We were passing through and wondered if we could help you out. We didn't know if anyone would still be alive."

"We have five survivors still alive, counting me. Two are seriously injured. Have you got a corpsman with you who can check them out?"

"Yes, sir." Jeremiah turned around looking for Freddie. "Chief Harris, can you come up here a minute? Bring your kit."

Freddie checked them out. They were recovering and would be fine. He changed their dressings and started them on antibiotics.

Jeremiah was anxious to leave. It was getting dark and he wanted to get to where Rebecca was. He asked Major Goodman, "Sir, would you like to come with us or stay here? If you stay, I don't know when we'll be back. We could leave you some MREs and medical supplies and I will tell my command you are here. If you come with us, chances are we'll run into some shit on the way through to Sonora. We're going to stop off and see if my wife is OK on the way. She lives about forty miles farther west on highway 108. We've heard there are looters and gangs that have been driven out of the San Joaquin valley by the Army. We expect to meet some of them somewhere along the road."

"We will come with you, Lieutenant," the Major said without hesitation. Then he grinned. "And if we find some action, so much the better. It's what we Marines do."

"OK, sir. Let's load your injured into the trucks. Our space is pretty limited. Bring just what you need. Glad to have you aboard."

"Thank you, Lieutenant." He turned to the other four men. "Let's get loaded."

The sun was setting as they resumed going west on Highway 108. An hour later they got to the turnoff to Jeremiah's settlement. The sky was sprayed with stars but the moon was yet to rise. They wound through the woods for twenty minutes until they got to the long ravine where the road went up the mountain to the settlement.

Sergeant Raymond was in the snow plow at the front of the column. "LT, I saw movement up the road." He had stopped at the bottom of the ravine. "I don't like this road ahead of us. It feels like a trap. There's nowhere to go if we get hit."

Jeremiah got on the speaker. "Settlement, this is the US Marines. We are here to verify the safety of Rebecca Silverstein. We would like to enter your settlement."

There was no reaction. They waited for five minutes. With a sinking heart, Jeremiah started the same broadcast again. "Settlement..."

"We got more movement again, LT," Sergeant Raymond announced. "Looks to be two people walking down the road, a man and a woman. They have a white flag."

"Let them come closer," he told the driver of the snow plow. Jeremiah got out of the truck with his rifle and protective gear on. He drew a bead on the man. They were just beyond where the headlights hit the road. He couldn't see either person clearly and their faces were covered with camouflage paint. When they were within fifty feet he shouted, "Halt. Who are you?"

The man answered first. "I am Tony Blackeagle. This is Rebecca Silverstein. Who are you?"

"Step into the light, both of you. Hold up your hands so we can see inside your jackets."

They took several steps closer and held up their arms.

"Turn around," Jeremiah commanded.

Rebecca squinted into the headlights after she finished turning around. "Who the hell are you guys?" she shouted. "Can I put my arms down? You're scaring the shit out of me!"

"Ceasefire," Jeremiah commanded into the microphone. There was no one in the world but Rebecca who could say shit like that. "It's my wife."

"Jeremiah!" She shouted to him, finally recognizing his voice. She started to run toward him. He met her halfway, then they were in each other's arms.

… … … … … … … … …

The parachutes blossomed above the CDC campus like two hundred olive-drab dandelion seeds floating down in the dawn light. They drifted down to land among the live oaks and hickories. The equipment bag dangled beneath each soldier on a tether to be released before impact, striking the ground first, followed quickly by the soldier and then the parachute.

Lieutenant Andrews ran to the nearest one. "Who's in command?"

"That would be Captain McQuidey, sir," the soldier said, pointing without saluting. "I think he's over there."

Lieutenant Andrews ran in that direction. "Captain McQuidey?"

"You must be Lieutenant Andrews," the soldier spoke up.

"Yes, sir."

"What is your situation, Lieutenant?"

"The mob has withdrawn for the time being. Did you bring anything nonlethal?"

That got a curious look. "Do you mean like tasers? We're a combat unit, Lieutenant. We're not in the crowd control business. Our mission is to prevent the germs in the vaults inside the CDC from being released."

"How about CS? Did you bring any riot gas?"

"Yeah. I think we have some CS. Why?"

"On their last assault, they put naked women and children tied to carts in front of the crowd. I put snipers in the trees around the perimeter to shoot over them into the body of the crowd before they withdrew. A lot of guys were hurt by return fire."

"Jesus. Let me make a call." He pulled a whistle out of his pocket and blew.

"Secure formation!" his First Sergeant commanded loudly.

The paratroopers ran to him and formed a circle about a hundred yards in diameter, facing out, rifles loaded and ready. The four platoon leaders gathered around him in a cluster of trees.

"Any casualties?" the captain asked the group.

"One broken arm," Lieutenant Givens responded. "Working on it."

"Jones, where are you?" the captain said loudly. He scanned the circle of men for his radio operator.

"Here, sir," one of the men called out, running toward him with the radio handset extended in his hand.

Captain McQuidey grabbed the handset. "Ops One, this is Germ One. Do you copy?"

"Roger, Germ One. This is Ops One."

"We need immediate supply of nonlethal, crowd-control devices—CS, tasers, rubber bullets and launchers, fire hoses, and pumps."

"Roger, Germ One. I will send what we have and see what the other forts can spare."

"Also send what field rations you can spare. That could buy us some time."

"Roger, Germ One."

"And drop all but two pallets outside the CDC perimeter like it was an accident."

"Roger, Germ One," the voice said doubtfully.

"Make sure no more than two land inside the fence. Copy? Do you need my initials? Charlie Juliet Mike."

"You got it, Germ One. All but two outside the fence."

"Send the food, stat. The crowd control stuff by seventeen-hundred hours."

"Roger, Germ One. Food will be there by ten-hundred hours. Crowd control gear by seventeen hundred hours."

"Germ One, out."

Lieutenant Andrews was looking at Captain McQuidey without understanding.

"If we give it to them, they will think we have more. If it appears that we dropped it outside the fence by accident, they will think we are resupplying ourselves—that we're out of food also. Maybe they won't be quite so anxious to sacrifice the women and kids if they think there's no food here."

The captain turned to his lieutenants. He told them about the previous day's attacks and what they could expect today. He talked to them as he studied the terrain, finding the best placement points for the mortar and Squad Automatic Weapons (SAWs). "We cannot allow the germs inside the vaults here to be released. Deadly force is authorized. First and second platoons, reinforce the Marines on the perimeter. I want the mortar set up on that hillock and the SAWs on the roof of the building. Third and fourth platoons set up camp between the pond and the CDC buildings. I want a second and third line of defense dug in. Deploy claymores on each line. I want platoons one and two to swap with platoons three and four every four hours until the fortifications are done."

He paused, then looked his four platoon leaders in the eyes. His voice was cold and serious. "At no time will there be cooking or food of any kind outside of the CDC buildings. Not even a candy bar or chewing gum. Collect all rations the men brought and bring them into the buildings. All eating will be done inside the buildings, out of sight. When the mortar is set up, I want test rounds fired into all expected routes of attack. Make sure there are no people around to get injured when you do it. Same with the SAWs. Test fields of fire but don't shoot anyone. If any trees are blocking your fields of fire that would allow someone to climb over the fence, cut them down. Any questions?"

His four platoon leaders shook their heads.

"Go do it, people."

Lieutenant Andrews was confused. "Why would you give away your armament and their positions?"

"It's called the carrot-and-stick technique, Lieutenant. We aren't fighting a trained aggressor force. These are just hungry people. I want them to know we are armed and dangerous. That we have enough ammunition to waste it on test fires. That's the stick. The carrot is the food we drop. My hope is it's enough to prevent my soldiers from having to kill women and children to keep this place safe."

"What good will giving them the food do? They will be back in two days demanding more."

"Two days is all we need. First Brigade of the Eighty-Second Airborne Division arrives the day after tomorrow. The Second Brigade will arrive the day after that. If we *do* get two days, I will be a happy man."

… … … … … … … … …

"Is everything ready for tomorrow morning, Arturo?"

"*Sí*. The next settlement is waiting for us like a smiling woman."

"They don't have any Green Berets do they?"

"Not according to the woman I questioned. They are a bunch of *gabachos* that escaped from L.A. Maybe a rifle or two."

Gabacho was a demeaning term for non-Mexicans much like the n-word for black people.

"Good. Those Green Berets almost kicked our ass."

"Now they are kicking ass in hell, my friend."

The leader of Lobo Roja got up. "I need some sleep. After today, everyone does. We'll start tomorrow morning sometime. There's no hurry. Those people aren't going anywhere."

"May you have the Conan dream tonight, *Señor* Lobo."

"What's that?" Lobo asked, intrigued. "What is the Conan dream?" Sometimes Arturo came up with the most interesting shit.

"It's from the first *Conan* movie. A bunch of Mongolian warriors are sitting around a campfire. One of the old men asks the young men, 'What are the three greatest things a man can experience in his life?' Each young man tries and fails to provide the correct answer. Then Conan answers. He says:" Arturo lowered his voice and took on Arnold Schwarzenegger's Austrian accent, "'To crush your enemies. To see them flee before you. To hear the lamentations of their women.'"

Señor Lobo laughed and clapped Arturo on the back. "Me too! I hope I have the Conan dream. See you in the morning, Arturo."

Arturo watched him go. In a couple more days, his people would outnumber Lobo's. Arturo always sent Lobo's people in first. Their numbers had steadily declined. By the time they got to Tahoe, he, Arturo, would be in charge and the pathetic *Señor* Lobo would be feeding the wolves he so proudly took his name from.

Chapter 13 – So Important at the Time

Three BCI combat cruisers appeared next to GSMS-77. Landers started going back and forth between the cruisers and Captain Xanny's starship. The investigation was fully underway.

"When did you notice the torpedo was missing?" Special Agent Hlitatta, the BCI agent, had been questioning Lieutenant Fibari all morning. He was a toad. A large toad with opposing thumbs, but a toad nonetheless.

"When the maintenance tech told me, just like I told you the last ten times."

"And that was after Commander Chirra asked him to check?"

"Yep."

"Why didn't you check yourself, before you got back?"

"Didn't think it was necessary. Both the armament bay light and the torpedo light said the torpedo was in place."

"The sensors that ended up missing?"

"Yep, those two and two more."

"The oxygen level warning sensors and the Hore energy portal malfunction sensor?"

"Yep. Those were the ones."

"Who removed the sensors, Lieutenant Fibari?"

"No idea. I suspect it was Sergeant Tannl while I was on Taramon picking up Zuna."

"Yes, the witch. Why did you need to take her to Zindarr?"

"We were going to tell the witches there of Ruatha, the witch who was mentioned in Zarqa's message, the one we thought we met on Fey Pey's ship, *Easy Wind*. We were also trying to get more information about dream plants. How they were done and who could do them."

"Ah yes, the infamous dream plant that led to the elimination order of the primates. But no evidence was ever found about who did it or that it had even taken place."

"Yep. We keep looking. That it was done, we believe to be a given, at least I believe it. None of the research necessary to discover the prerequisite technology has ever been found. Even if she had a dream about wormholes being possible, she wouldn't have known how to create the technology to open one. We are convinced the plant took place and that Fey Pey is the person who orchestrated it. We thought we finally found proof, but it appears the proof was planted for us to find. It would be just like Fey Pey to plant fake evidence to hide the real thing."

The agent pulled up the hologram of the message Zarqa sent from *Easy Wind*. King Amon and Fey Pey had their dialogue again.

"King Amon denies this meeting ever took place. You know that, don't you?"

"I wouldn't have expected anything else. What does he have to say about the aquatic mammals that were raised up on this planet?"

"He says he has no knowledge of it."

"And Fey Pey? What does he say about it?"

"He has disappeared. *Easy Wind* is no longer in orbit around Taramon. Could we get back to questions about you? You were executive officer on *Easy Wind*."

"Was that a question?" Fela asked.

"No. How long did you serve on *Easy Wind*?"

"Three-and-a-half years. Until he lost me to a sex slave trader in a card game."

"There is no sexual slavery in the Ur," the BCI agent said, without emotion.

"Guess you haven't been to Vincar lately, huh?" Fela asked innocently.

The agent ignored her question. "What did you do on *Easy Wind*?"

"What any XO does. I took us from point A to point B whenever Fey Pey told me to do it."

"Did you break any laws when you did that?"

"None I know of."

"Did Fey Pey break any laws while you served under him?"

"Gee, let me think." She looked up into the air and started naming offenses, "Last I heard, extortion, armed robbery, murder, attempted murder, piracy, kidnapping, sex slavery trade, torture, selling state secrets, smuggling, and genocide. Those *are* still against the law, right?"

"What proof do you have Fey Pey committed any of those offenses?"

"Nothing but my own witness of him doing it."

"Are there any other witnesses who could corroborate your accusations?"

"Sure. But they're all dead, just like we would have been, if I hadn't moved the ship before that torpedo blew up."

"And that brings us to the torpedo you lost on Taramon." He checked his notes. "No one saw it being stolen. No one even knew it was gone until you got back here. Then suddenly it shows up after you did and you are the one who finds it, then you sounded the alarm."

"So you're trying to say I brought it back with me, then I tried to blow up myself and everyone else on this ship?"

"Can you think of anything else that may give credence to Fey Pey's being the perpetrator of these crimes?"

"You might check with the mercs that were searching for him on my previous trip to Taramon."

"Mercenaries? Searching for Fey Pey?"

"Yep, in all the bars and brothels in Pirate's Alley."

"Do you know what company they were working for?"

"Nope. Those guys aren't in the give-out-information business."

He made a note on his hologram. "I try to find coincidences. This case has a lot of them."

"Gee, Agent Hlitatta, it's almost like someone planted them, isn't it?"

The agent looked at her coldly. "Don't leave the ship, Lieutenant Fibari."

... ...

"GSMS-77, this is the Grock Corporate Executive Shuttle. Open your landing deck, please."

"How many of those executive toy barges do they have?" Sergeant Fo asked the air above him. To the shuttle he said, "Executive Shuttle, please use portal 3. Our landing deck is full at the present time."

"I copy Portal 3. Thank you."

...

The captain of the Grock Executive Shuttle sat at the table, across from Special Agent Hlitatta.

"No one may leave this ship, Captain Nn." Special Agent Hlitatta's eyes bulged out even more than they normally did. "This is a crime scene."

Captain Nn reached down to his belt and removed his communicator. He press an entry on his contact list and set the communicator on the table between them.

"Emperor Cabliux's offices. How my I direct your call?"

As hard as it was to believe, the toad's eyes bulged out even farther.

"I need to speak to Kat Lollch. Access code 3n45s9."

There was a pause, several clicks, then a low, almost masculine voice came on the line.

"This is Kat Lollch."

"This is Captain Nn, from Grock Corporation. I am trying to pick up the female primate and her companions from GSMS-77 as requested by the emperor. I am not being allowed to leave the starship because the BCI won't release them. Would you please tell the emperor I will not be there tomorrow?"

There was a pause. "Is the BCI agent in charge available for a consultation?"

"Yes, ma'am. Special Agent Hlitatta is here now."

"Everyone but Special Agent Hlitatta, please leave the room. I need to talk to him privately."

Captain Nn left his communicator on the table and walked out of the room, trying very hard to keep a straight face. He was tempted to listen at the door, but he knew generally what was being said and who was saying it. Special Agent Hlitatta's boss's boss's boss was probably on the line.

Three minutes later, the door opened. Agent Hlitatta motioned him to come back in. After the two of them took their seats, the agent swallowed and took a breath. "I have reconsidered your request. You may leave with the female primate and her companions. No one else may accompany them."

"That's wonderful, Special Agent Hlitatta!" Captain Nn said gratefully, trying to ease Hlitatta's embarrassment. "I'm sure the emperor appreciates your help in this matter."

Special Agent Hlitatta got up from the table and left the room without saying another word.

Half an hour later, the Grock Executive Shuttle disconnected from portal 3, accelerated toward the center of the galaxy, and disappeared in a rosy twinkle.

Sergeant Fo looked askance at the filthy lander the primates left behind. He could almost see dirt from it spreading across his spotless landing deck. And it was going to be there until the primates came back from "visiting" the emperor. Some people never did come back from such visits.

"This will never do," he muttered. "If I have to have that son of a monkrus on my deck, it will be clean."

He pulled up the duty roster for the day, studied it, then grinned. His favorite malingerer was at the top of the list. Ex-sergeant Vue, recently of the security team and now *Private* Vue, had wormed his way off the moon base and back onto the starship. Sergeant Vue had always treated Sergeant Fo with disdain and arrogance, considering a Landing Deck Sergeant somehow beneath a Security Sergeant. Sergeant Fo reached for the notification button on his hologram. He entered a message for Private Vue. "Report to the landing deck for assignment. Wear work clothes."

He sat back to wait for Vue to show up. This shift wasn't going to turn out so bad.

... ...

Captain Marshall watched every move the pilot of the Executive Shuttle made. The pilot was an octopus. Following all eight arms as they arranged the jump paths was a stretch.

"Why did you do jumps three and four? I would have jumped straight from where three begins to where four ends."

The pilot's face screwed up into what Gaye now recognized as a smile. "I would have done it that way when I started, also. The problem is that black hole right there." He pointed to a blue dot in his nav hologram his jump path neatly bypassed. "It's so big it was given a name instead of just coordinates. It is called Gargantua. Wormholes are unaffected by everything except monsters like that. Those black holes are so massive they stretch the fabric of the universe. You wouldn't get sucked in, but you would get your path bent along with the bending of space-time as you pass through the black hole. Your wormhole exit would be unpredictable." He paused to give what he said next additional impact. "And 'unpredictable' isn't where you want to exit a wormhole."

Gaye nodded. Exiting a wormhole into a star, a planet, an asteroid belt, or even a black hole, would not have a happy ending. Even if you exited into clear space, who knows where you actually were? It could be in another galaxy or even another part of the universe! That would give "Lost in Space" a whole new meaning.

The pilot continued, "I use black holes like that one as nav beacons—a place to orient to, but also a place to avoid."

"Like a lighthouse on my planet," Gaye said, finally getting it.

"Please explain," the navigator asked.

"We put up light beacons on dangerous points of land at the edges of our oceans. They warn sailors of the danger, but they are also used for navigation into safe anchorages. Once you know where the danger is, you can navigate to safety with confidence."

"Yes," the octopus agreed. "That is exactly how I use them."

Lily was watching over Gaye's shoulder. "Can you bring up a picture of the black hole? I've never seen one."

The pilot was amused. "Visual light. Sure."

He stretched the hologram several times until Gargantua was by itself in the hologram. He tapped "Visual" and the hologram went dark. There wasn't a glimmer of any light anywhere.

"What happened?" Lily asked. Then the "light" of understanding turned on inside her head. "No visible light can escape the black hole. There is nothing to see."

"Hence the name 'black hole.' But if you look at it like this..." the pilot tapped "Gravity" on the hologram. The display lit up like a lightning bolt going through a thunderstorm. "It's a little easier to see. This is a time-lapse display over about a year." The gravity swirled slowly around the black hole, changing colors and direction without any pattern that Lily could see. Instead of the symmetrical gravity surrounding a planet, this gravity had arms that reached out into space around the black hole.

"That's beautiful!" Patty Kendricks gasped.

"Yes, it is. And terrifying, too." The pilot stared at the display. "Any one of those arms could trap or deflect a wormhole. In real space, they pull all surrounding mass and energy into the black hole."

"Why does it have arms like that?" Lily asked.

"We don't know. We suspect it's because of internal explosions that are continuously going on. The explosions are caused by the mass and energy getting too compressed. Only when it explodes, nothing can escape the gravity of the black hole. We think the arms are like gravitational steam vents. Even they get sucked back into the black hole, along with anything else they've trapped."

Clara was watching with them. "Won't everything eventually get sucked into a black hole?" Everyone turned their head to look at her. She continued a little defensively, "I mean, if nothing can get out and the black hole continues to suck new stuff into it, someday everything will be sucked in and nothing will be left."

"Actually, that *will* happen," the pilot said, nodding at Clara with a grudging respect. "The universe is still expanding from the explosion of the universal black hole that happened about fourteen billion years ago. In another twenty billion years, the universe will stop expanding and will begin to collapse in on itself. Thirty-four billion years after that, the universe will again form a single black hole. We call that the Universal black hole. That will explode and make a new universe."

"How could anything escape a black hole that contains the entire mass of the universe?" Lily asked in astonishment.

"We don't know that either. We suspect some new form of physics will come into effect that will allow it to happen. What it is, we haven't a clue. It may have something to do with the balance of visible energy/mass to the dark energy/mass. Maybe gravity inverts for a split second. That's all it would take. The magnitude of the forces involved defy our understanding."

Beauhi spoke up. "It's because none of these regional black holes can tear the fabric by themselves. They aren't big enough. That's why."

Everyone on the ship turned to stare at her, including the pilot. She rolled her eyes. "For hundreds of years, we've been telling the physicists of the Ur why the expand-collapse cycles happen. They don't want to hear it from a witch. We, apparently, don't have the proper credentials to know this stuff."

Everyone was silent. She took a breath and paused for a moment, deciding if she wanted to try to explain it to them. She decided to try. "You've seen these regional black holes are constantly exploding and collapsing?"

"Of course," the pilot said. "We just don't understand why."

"They explode because you can't put that much mass into that little space. When it happens, the mass starts to disintegrate into energy and it starts a chain reaction. The reaction stops as the explosion moves away from the center of the black hole and the extreme pressures there. The gravity arms you're seeing are the result of the mass in the black hole moving around as the explosions work their way out from the middle. Time slows down as you get deeper and deeper into the mass of the black hole, but the energy released doesn't change so the energy over a specific period gets greater and greater, making these explosions more and more violent. But the energy released in these regional black holes isn't enough to break through the barrier to the other side."

"What is the 'other side'?" Clara asked.

The other five people in the shuttle were silent. None of them wanted to show their ignorance.

"Every universe has two parts: the one we live in and the 'other side'. This side has matter. The other side has antimatter. It's all part of the balance necessary for the universe to exist. The two sides have equal mass and they never touch because, if they touch, they cancel each other out, releasing massive amounts of anti-energy on this side and energy on the other."

"What did you mean when you said, 'None of the black holes are big enough to tear the fabric'?" President Robbins asked. "Is that how the perforation happens?"

She tilted her head at him in surprise. "Yes. That's exactly what I meant. When the entire universe finally collapses into a single black hole, the explosions at the center of it get so huge they actually tear the fabric of the universe, allowing the matter and antimatter to mingle. The anti-energy on this side and energy on the other cancel out gravity on both sides of the universe for the duration of the matter-antimatter contact. Without gravity to keep it together, the explosions inside the universal black hole are no longer retained within the black hole. Both sides of the black hole atomize themselves and explode away from the perforation at the speed of light. Because there is so much mass involved, the perforation stays open for several years. This allows the mass to escape the gravity well of the black hole for long enough to spread out into an expanding gas cloud. Over the course of the next four or five billion years, the gas cloud slowly coalesces back into galaxies, stars, and planets."

"What closes the perforation?" Lily asked, still trying to absorb the implications of what Beauhi had said. "The perforation would have to close or the matter and antimatter would continue to interact and ultimately cancel each other out."

"The energy necessary to hold open the perforation is massive. As soon as the black hole dissipates enough, the explosive energy of the black hole goes with it and the perforation closes."

"So where is the net loss of energy in the reaction?" Leann asked. "Every reaction results in a net loss of energy."

"The net loss is what matter and antimatter are consumed during the perforation." Beauhi was amused. These primates absorbed in five minutes what the Ur scientists had ignored since the witches published the physics of the black holes hundreds of years ago.

"So, after enough iterations of explosion-collapse, there won't be enough mass in the black hole to perforate to the other side?" Clara asked.

"Yep. Then the universe dies."

Lily spoke up. "What happens if there's too much mass in the universe? If there is enough mass to form two or more black holes capable of perforating to the other side? Would there be multiple big bangs going off randomly?"

"We don't know. We've never encountered such a universe. But that's what many of our scientists suspect."

"You mean you have visited other universes?" Leann asked in amazement.

The pilot was staring straight ahead, his lips tightly pressed together, like he didn't want to hear the answer.

Beauhi paused, then sighed. "To do so would violate the emperor's command that we do not leave this universe."

Everyone realized she hadn't answered the question.

"How long has this expand-contract cycle been going on?" Clara asked, after a few moments of silence.

"No telling. We look at this as the closest thing to infinity we will ever know."

"Do you think there is life on the other side?" Leann asked. "Do you think the other side could be a mirror of ours?"

Beauhi laughed. "That question has been asked more times than you can imagine. We have no answer and probably never will. But if you like that kind of mind game, I have a couple of ideas for you to ponder." She paused and raised her eyebrow. "Maybe *we* are the mirror of *them*. Or maybe there is more than one 'other side.'"

The pilot began preparing his next jump.

President Robbins stared out the view portal at the stars of their current galaxy and wondered about the expansions and collapses. *Each of those expansions yielded countless civilizations,* he thought to himself. *They were spread across billions of galaxies—intelligent beings who loved, hated, fought wars, celebrated births, and mourned deaths. Their successes, failures, and intrigues, ultimately all of the events that seemed so important to them at the time, ended up making no difference at all.*

The jump alarm sounded.

He chuckled as he belted in. *And that begs the question: What's the point? Did God invent the universe to fulfill some great plan or did we invent God to give meaning to a meaningless cycle of life and death?*

The ship was filled with Rosy light and suddenly the ship was a thousand lightyears closer to the emperor.

Chapter 14 – The Yunia

"So tell me about your defenses," Jeremiah asked Liam and Tony.

Tony pulled out his hand-drawn map and spread it out on the hood of Brutus. "We have claymores set up in ten different places in the ravine..."

Jeremiah coughed in surprise. "Claymores? Really?"

Tony chuckled. "Let me show you one of our claymores. Juan? Go get that last one, will you?"

Juan walked over to Liam's shed and returned with the last of their homemade claymores. He handed it to Jeremiah.

"Thanks for having the dynamite, by the way," Tony said. "Jonathan brought the bondo with him from Fresno and everyone donated the nails and screws. We had a big time cutting up sheet metal scraps into bits."

Jeremiah turned it over and over in his hands, shaking his head. "This is just like the shit we used to find in the Taliban hideouts." He handed it back to Juan. "I hope it works as good as theirs did." There was a trace of sadness in his voice when he said it. "If we need 'em, there are some Marine-issue claymores in the trucks."

"We were worried about fire," Liam told Jeremiah. "That's why we put them in the ravine. There's nothing there that can burn and do any damage. We pulled out all of the brush except what's hiding the punji sticks and claymores."

"Punji sticks?" Jeremiah said in disbelief. "Holy shit! You guys were ready to fight! Did you smear them with shit, too?"

The crew from the trucks had clustered around them and was listening to every word.

"I told you I smelled an ambush in that ravine," Sergeant Raymond spoke up. "I still got it!" He did a little happy dance and spun around. "Oh yeah! Ray's ambush-detection 'brainware' strikes again!"

"Well, they overran the Green Berets at Camp Alpha," Amy Johansson said, ignoring Sergeant Raymond's antics and his software analogy. "We wanted to be ready. Why would we smear them with shit?"

"That was a Viet Cong trick," Tony explained. "Even if the stick didn't hit something vital, a pinprick was enough to start a staph infection. If the stick didn't kill you, the cut would get so infected you became a liability to your platoon. A sick soldier is a lot more work than a dead one. A lot of guys died from those infections."

Jeremiah paused and studied the map. "OK. I agree with where you placed them. The important thing is to not blow those claymores until you get as many people as you can into the kill zone."

"I'm on the detonator," Russell told him. "You give me the word and I'll let 'em blow. We've got the two sides wired separately. We figured they would try a second attack up the road after the first one, thinking we'd used all of the claymores the first time."

Jeremiah was enjoying this unexpected preparation. "You guys should be teaching infantry tactics. That's exactly what they'll try." He pointed to a spot on the map. "I think Popeye should be right here." The position commanded a clear view of the entire approach. He walked over to where that was and looked down the ravine. "Popeye has a minigun and can sweep the whole area before they can withdraw after the second attack. We'll need to keep it hidden until the attack starts." He turned to the driver of the truck. "Joel, park it in that stand of pine trees until the claymores blow. Satan will go here on this knoll. Brutus will go on that one." Jeremiah put an "X" where he wanted each truck. "I remember there is a fire road up each knoll. We can use it to get the trucks up there."

"Why there?" Liam asked cautiously, trying not to sound critical. "Those spots have no view of the attack area and they're behind where the fighting's going to be."

"Because after the second attack fails, the attackers are going to withdraw to here." He indicated an area hidden from the ravine but in clear sight of the knolls where Satan and Brutus would be. "And we'll be ready for 'em. Each truck has two M-60s and a .50. When the attackers retreat from your claymores and the minigun on Popeye, they will retreat right into the crossfire of those trucks. Plus we'll have *our* claymores ready for 'em when they get there. Does anyone know how many fighters they have?"

Everyone looked away without answering. They'd been terrified to go anywhere near the Green Berets' settlement.

"My drill instructor told me a long time ago, 'If you don't know—find out.'"

Major Goodman added: "'Life and death decisions made on incomplete data never turn out well.'"

Jeremiah laughed. They were both reciting from the same Marine tactics manual. "I need someone to reconnoiter the enemy—find out how many people they have, what arms they have, what their condition is. Any volunteers?"

"I'd like to volunteer for that mission." Major Goodman stepped up. "Been a while since I did some real night work. I'm a little tired of teaching other people to do it."

"Sir, if you'd like to do that, I would really appreciate it. Are you sure?"

Major Goodman nodded his head. "Yep. It's not like I have anything to do around here. Between you and these settlers, I'm beginning to feel a little sorry for the other guys."

"Would you like someone to accompany you?"

"Not a chance. I work alone. No one to worry about but me. Be like the old days in Fallujah when *I* was an LT."

"Camp Alpha is about ten miles away," Tony told him. "The access road is seven miles down this road, then off to the right on a fire access road."

"Can I use some of your camo paint?"

"Of course, sir. What else do you need?"

"Well, I brought an M-4 carbine and a 9MM pistol. Some ammunition would be appreciated. All they gave us at the Mountain Warfare Center were blanks." He thought for a moment, then started counting off things on his fingers. "A backpack. A field first-aid kit. A couple of canteens. Night vision goggles would be great! You wouldn't happen to have any grenades, would you?"

"Yep, we do." He turned to Sergeant Raymond. "Roger, rustle up whatever Major Goodman needs."

"I'm on it, LT," Sergeant Raymond told him, walking toward Popeye.

"If you want me back by dawn, I'll need a vehicle to get to the turnoff and back. Something quiet."

"I have a Honda quad I use for hunting," Marvin Schroeder said. "You can use that."

"How noisy is it? It's got to be quiet."

"It's stock and whisper quiet. I never put one a them aftermarket exhausts on. I wanted to sneak up on them deer."

"That'll work. Thanks."

Jeremiah turned to everyone else. "There will be a lot of noise and explosions. Fire may happen. We have to plan that it will. We'll need a reservoir of water to fight any fires that start. Fill every container you have and put them in a common area. Anyone who isn't fighting is on fire duty. And fill your bathtubs. If we need it, we won't have time to wait for a well pump. The rest of you start cutting the underbrush and trees away from your houses—anything that will burn. Throw the brush down the hill where it won't hurt anything if it catches.

"We'll need three lines of defense. The first one is at the top of the hill where the trucks will be. The second will be halfway to the houses. The third will be at the houses. Drop trees so they are perpendicular to the way those assholes are coming. You want to be able to hide behind them." He made eye contact with everyone around the group. "And be careful, people. It's dark. We don't need any casualties *before* the battle starts. Once the trees are down, cut wide V-shaped notches in the trunks so you can shoot from behind them and still be somewhat protected. Put the narrow part of the 'V' toward them and the wide part toward you. That way they have a smaller target, you're pretty well camouflaged, and you have a wide field of fire. If I tell you to fall back, do it. Don't think about it. Don't question it. Do it. Have two safe paths to your next position memorized in case one gets compromised.

"The last thing I have to say, before we get to work, is this is Chief Petty Officer Freddie Harris." Jeremiah pointed at Freddie. Freddie waved his hand. "He is our corpsman. For you non-Marine types, that means he's a medic. He can do almost anything this side of a heart transplant. If you get hurt, come see him. If you can't move, call out. He will find you." He turned to Liam. "Can he use your shed as a first-aid station?"

Liam considered his request. "My house would be better. There's no running water in the shed."

"OK. Freddie, set up in there."

Amy Johansson was recording every word people were saying on her cell phone.

"Why are you doing that, Amy?" Rebecca asked her. She had her arms wrapped around Jeremiah. She was staying as close to him as she could without climbing inside his tunic.

"If we live through this, it's gonna make one hell of a great book! I've already got a plot line set up in my head. You and Jeremiah are going to be stars!"

"I hope I get to read it someday," Rebecca said, knowing people were going to die tomorrow.

"I'll make sure you get a signed first edition!"

An hour later, Satan stopped at the mouth of the fire road it would take to its position on the knob. Major Goodman was on Marvin's quad. He had led their little mini-convoy so he wouldn't have to eat their dust. He waved and continued down the road toward Camp Alpha.

Satan turned left onto the fire road and started its climb to the top of its assigned knoll. A hundred yards further down, Brutus turned right onto its assigned fire road. After the trucks were in place and hidden from view of the road, the crews tried to get some sleep. It was 3:30 A.M. A crescent moon was coming up over the eastern horizon. The sound of falling trees and chain saws still came from the settlement.

... ...

"Lieutenant Fibari, can we please get the primates' lander back to their planet?" Sergeant Fo was going crazy trying to accommodate the traffic back and forth from the BCI cruisers during the investigation.

Fela stared at the lander while she thought about the request. Private Vue had worked on it for two shifts. Most of the major dirt was gone. He was cleaning the jump magnets now. Each one was being disassembled, then reassembled.

"Have you got a replacement for Corporal Qitti yet?"

"No. Corporate tried to give me someone right out of shuttle school. I wasn't having it. I need someone with at least a little experience."

"I'll see if someone can shuttle it down to the surface. Maybe Lieutenant Xanny."

"I'll believe that when I see it," Po muttered to himself.

Fela pretended she didn't hear that. She didn't like the captain's son any better than anyone else. He didn't do one speck of work more than he was required to do. She wasn't looking forward to asking him. Then another possibility occurred to her—Corporal Vibii, the lander trainer. He might have some free time to pilot the lander down to the surface. It was either him, the lieutenant, or Commander Chirra. There weren't that many licensed lander pilots to choose from. She started to leave the landing deck control center.

Sergeant Fo called after her. "If you find someone, be sure to clear the lander's departure with Special Agent Hlitatta. He told me nothing leaves the ship without his written permission."

… … … … … … … … …

Lieutenant Givens ran up to Captain McQuidey. "First Brigade has departed Fort Bragg, sir."

"Dammit! It's about time. They're two days late." He turned to the closed-circuit TV cameras of the approaches to the CDC campus. There was no activity. Maybe the MREs that the Beechcraft Brigade dropped would be enough to hold off the starving people who collected around the CDC each day. The First Brigade wouldn't reach them until tomorrow night, at the earliest. "Have those people who showed up yesterday come back?"

"No, sir. No sign of them."

"And no one gave them anything yesterday? Right?"

Lieutenant Givens hesitated. He had seen a couple of his men throw MREs over the fence to the kids who were begging for food. It was a ceremony as old as soldiers.

Captain McQuidey snapped his head around from looking at the monitors. "Right? No one gave them anything?"

"A couple of my men gave MREs to some kids. They were crying and hungry."

"Shit! What about 'NO FOOD!' don't they understand?" Captain McQuidey asked in frustration. He paused, trying to figure out how to defuse this. "Call Bragg. See if they can set up another MRE drop. Do it now! Tell them this is a crisis. Tell them it may save hundreds of civilian lives."

"Yes, sir."

"Then go to each member of your platoon and tell them again: NO FOOD! If another MRE goes across that fence, I will personally roast the ass of the person who does it and feed *them* to the fucking mob. His will be followed by yours, Lieutenant! DO YOU UNDERSTAND?"

"Yes, sir."

"Get out of here." The captain turned to stare at the monitors. The two days until they were relieved by the First Brigade had turned into four. And now everyone outside the fence knew there was food to spare, food they could give to begging kids. Maybe they'd get lucky and the MREs would arrive before the mob.

... ...

The emperor's planet, Quyl, appeared in front of them. Their shuttle was passed from control point to control point on their approach. Security was huge. The closer they got, the more detail became apparent: continents, oceans, polar ice caps, mountains, enormous lakes, rivers. Leann and her companions were glued to the windows of the shuttle.

"What would happen if we showed up next to the planet unannounced?" Captain Marshall asked, thinking about the no-fly zone that used to be around Washington, DC.

"Any vessel approaching without permission would be sent instantly to a holding area about a lightyear away. It would be boarded and searched. If anyone on the ship responded in a remotely hostile way, their family would be talking about them in the past tense."

President Robbins decided to ask a question that had been bothering him for a while. "If everyone in the Ur gets along and trades without fighting each other, why would any of that be necessary?"

The pilot hesitated, cleared his throat, then said, "I'm sure you've read the Elimination Declaration Envoy Gart-Disp signed."

President Robbins nodded.

"The part where he said 'For a species to be allowed to leave their solar system and begin to intermingle with the other species, peacefully living and trading around the galaxy, the five milestones must have been achieved'?"

President Robbins nodded again.

"Well, that part about 'the other species peacefully living and trading' was more a goal than a reality. I think what he really meant was 'with the problems we have now, trying to keep everyone living and trading without killing each other, we don't want these primates creating more trouble than we already have.'"

"Would you tell me more about what's going on around the rest of the galaxy?" President Robbins asked. "What are the hotspots? Who are unhappy? What is the emperor spending his time on?"

"Actually, Grock thought you might ask for that. They have prepared a short synopsis of current events around the galaxy. I'll send it to a hologram in front of your chair. You can view it while I thread our way through the entrance bureaucracy labyrinth on our way to the emperor's palace on the surface. If you finish that, I can set you up with several of the newsfeeds."

The other five Earth primates clustered around President Robbins's seat as the hologram began.

A BCI agent was under suspension, pending an investigation for killing an unarmed arachnid family on their home planet. Arachnids across the galaxy were claiming species bias and profiling by the BCI. This was not the first time the arachnids had been singled out for special attention by the BCI. The agent said she suspected the female arachnid was smuggling drugs and ordered the female to halt as she walked away. He fired his laser and the whole web caught fire, which spread to her nest, killing her, her husband, and their newly hatched brood.

"She was just spinning a nest. It's what we do," her brother told the interviewer. His three-hundred-forty-three children were crying in the background. "Once you start spinning, you can't stop until you're finished." He looked into the camera and said forcefully, "We never do drugs. We don't have nothing to do with drugs. We don't know anyone that does drugs. That's a stereotype fairy tale the BCI made up about arachnids to cover their ass!"

"Is that a gang mark on your abdomen," the interviewer asked, trying to see underneath the indignant interviewee.

"I got nothing else to say to you. Get off my web!" He turned his back and walked away, keeping the bottom of his abdomen hidden from view.

The BCI refused to comment about an ongoing investigation.

But the last article in the news summary caught President Robbins's interest most of all. The Ur's galaxy was being attacked by a civilization from another galaxy. The attacks were still on the fringes of the galaxy, but over a hundred solar systems had been taken already. The Ur losses were huge. One general after another had been replaced. The attackers were known as the Yunia. Apparently no one in the Ur knew how to fight a war anymore.

... ...

The investigation into the demise of Zindarr had spread to Taramon where the BCI subpoenaed the spaceport's surveillance recordings. Several significant periods came up missing, including the time when the lander from GSMS-77 was on the ground.

"Why those periods are missing is a complete mystery to us," the head of security at the spaceport was saying to the investigator. "We have the required double redundancy in place. Both storage locations have been compromised. How this could have happened, we don't know."

BCI agents could be seen in the background carrying out armload after armload of files and computers while some storm troopers stood nearby in their full armor and very deadly-looking weapons.

"We take you now to the notorious Pirate's Alley where Gati Gotti, our primate-on-the-point, is interviewing a person who was actually on Zindarr only moments before a photon torpedo blew the planet into dust."

A young female primate with large breasts and long black hair was standing next to Zuna. Zuna stared at her with an amused detachment. She assumed the interviewer was chosen by the news feed because she bore a close resemblance to the "witch" stereotype created by the galactic movie industry. Now here she was interviewing a hyena who was the real deal.

"This is Gati Gotti reporting from Pirate's Alley on Taramon. I am interviewing Zuna, proprietor of the Cauldron and Kettle, a famous, some say infamous, witches bar. Zuna, is it true you were on Zindarr just before it blew up?" The interviewer held her microphone down to Zuna's height.

"I was," Zuna said to the interviewer.

"Why were you there?"

"It's a planet of witches. I'm a witch. Do I need a reason to visit?"

The interviewer was flustered by Zuna's reticence and fumbled for her next question from the teleprompter hologram in the air in front of her.

Zuna decided to be a little less hostile. "I went with some friends who needed to warn Kallisha, the head witch."

"What did you need to warn her about?"

"About the photon torpedo concealed on Zindarr."

"You knew the torpedo was there?" the interviewer asked, her eyes going wide.

"Yes. We found out only minutes earlier."

"And you went to Zindarr anyway?"

"Well, someone had to warn them," Zuna said. "They are witches. We tend to protect each other. Historically, there's been a little trouble from the rest of the galaxy in the protection area."

"How did you find out the torpedo was there?"

"A witch on Fey Pey's ship, *Easy Wind*, told us."

"You were on *Easy Wind*?" the interviewer asked quickly. "Do you realize there is an all-galaxy warrant out for Fey Pey and *Easy Wind*?"

"There wasn't then. And yes, we were on *Easy Wind*. We rescued two people who were being held captive."

"What was that witch's name? Did she help you?"

"She told us her name was Ruatha, but she lied. We found out later her real name was Plew. We figured she sent us to Zindarr so we would perish in the explosion along with all evidence that Fey Pey was behind the torpedo."

"Who was with you?"

"Some friends and the two we rescued from Fey Pey's ship. We told Kallisha the torpedo might be on Zindarr. She initiated a planetwide search for it. After she discovered where it was, rather than attempt to defuse it, she called for a complete planet evacuation. We left before the evacuation started."

"You left without rescuing anyone? Knowing the planet could blow up at any instant?"

"We were in a lander. There was room for only one more person. We took Kallisha's second-in-command with us—a witch known as Beauhi."

"Where is Beauhi now?"

"No idea. She may be meeting with the emperor, for all I know."

That got a laugh from the interviewer. "What happened to the rest of the people who were with you?"

"You'll have to ask them. But there is one thing I've heard that I would appreciate your telling people about. Zindarr's representative to the Ur has set up a site where people can search for survivors. I'm sure the families of those witches would love to know if their loved ones are still alive and, if they are, where they are."

The site location appeared at the bottom of the newsfeed hologram.

"I didn't know anyone survived," the interviewer said, surprised.

"The first evacuation ship full of people left before the torpedo detonated. And there were some people off-planet visiting family, taking a vacation, or on business."

There was an awkward pause. Zuna realized the interviewer had run out of questions. She hadn't learned yet you always have a few in reserve for situations like this. Zuna decided to give her an out.

"I have to get back to work, Gati. Thanks for your help in advertising the Zindarr survivor site. Stop in at the Cauldron and Kettle before you leave. I'll introduce you to some people I'll bet you find interesting. There might even be a story in it."

... ...

"Hey," Specialist McKinley nudged his partner. "We've got movement."

Sergeant Baldillez picked up his binoculars and studied the line of houses across the street from the CDC. He saw people hiding in the bushes in front of them. No one was in the street yet. More came around the side of the houses as he watched. He picked up the radio. "HQ, this is Post 9. We've got movement. People are coming from around the houses across the street."

"Roger, movement, Post 9. How many people can you see?"

"At least a hundred. They are hiding behind the bushes in front of the houses. More coming from behind the houses as I watch. Mostly women and children from what I can make out."

"HQ, this is Post 7. We're getting the same thing over here."

Captain McQuidey's voice came over the radio. "All posts, report your status. Are you seeing people collecting in front of you?"

Each post reported seeing the same thing.

Captain McQuidey picked up the microphone for the PA system his team installed. His voice boomed through the silence of the afternoon heat. "People across the street from the CDC, this is the US Army. Do not attempt to enter the CDC grounds. We have been authorized to use deadly force and we will use it. I know you are hungry. I have called for another drop of MREs for you. The 82nd Airborne Division will arrive here in one day to bring law and order back to Atlanta. They are bringing supplies and will be able to feed you. Hang on for one more day. If you attempt to enter the grounds of the CDC, we will kill you."

No one moved away from the houses. More people came from around the back to hide behind the bushes.

"Where are those fucking airplanes?" Captain McQuidey asked the sky in frustration. The storm clouds were gathering above him. Thunder rumbled across Atlanta. The first huge raindrops fell.

The Rosy radio next to Captain McQuidey came alive. "Germ One, this is Drop Control. We are fifteen minutes out and holding. We can't drop while the storm is active above you."

"This is Germ One. How long can you hold?"

"About half an hour. Then we will have to return to Bragg to refuel."

Captain McQuidey made a rude gesture at the clouds. This day wasn't turning out well. Heavy rain started across the CDC campus.

"Drop Control, this drop will stop the women and children gathering across the street from being killed. Is there any way you can just fly over and throw the MREs out? That might work."

"Negative, Germ One. Not until the storm moves off. It's too dangerous flying into a storm cell like the monster above you. The wind shear would send us right into the ground."

Captain McQuidey watched the clouds swirl above him as they passed toward the north. He set the timer on his cell phone for thirty minutes. Maybe they'd get lucky.

Chapter 15 – Return on Investment

Major Goodman returned as the first glow of dawn was appearing over the mountains in the east. He shut off the quad and handed the keys to Marvin Schroeder.

"Thank you, sir. It ran great. Where's Lieutenant Silverstein?" he asked the group who was finishing the final preparations of the defense.

"Over there," Amy Johansson pointed toward Popeye.

The truck had become Command Central. Major Goodman walked over to Jeremiah. Neither man saluted. This was a combat zone. Salutes told the enemy who to kill first.

"What did you find, sir?" Jeremiah asked the major.

"They have about five hundred people. About half of them are injured. Everyone was drunk. Most of them were passed out. There were no sentries. I didn't see any survivors. There were seven dead people tied to trees. They had been tortured. I think two of them were adult male, two were adult female, and three were children, but it was kind of hard to tell. They'd been cut up pretty bad, then burned by the fire at the base of the trees."

The Marines' eyes got hard. They realized there would be no quarter offered from either side. This was going to be a fight to the death.

Major Goodman saw the transformation. "OK, you guys. *This* is what we *do*. We are Marines. We fight. Sometimes we die, but not today. Today we're going to kick the asses of these punks all the way back to the shitholes they crawled out of. You know what will happen if they win. So we're going to make sure that doesn't happen. They've robbed, murdered, tortured, and raped their way up the valley. They think the people on our hilltop are just another bunch of disorganized settlers. They will soon find out we aren't. And by then, it will be too late for them to do anything but die. They aren't taking any prisoners. Neither are we."

The men watched the major while he talked without expression. When he was done they gave a resounding "Oorah!"

"Lieutenant Silverstein, would you fill in the other two gun trucks on what I saw at the camps? They need to know what we're dealing with."

"Will do, sir."

"And have them give us an alert when these guys pass them on the way up here."

"Yes, sir. They already have orders to do that."

Major Goodman chuckled. "This isn't your first rodeo, is it, Lieutenant?"

"No, sir. Until two days ago I was Gunny Silverstein. Two tours in Iraq. One in Afghanistan."

"I'm glad to have you on board, Lieutenant."

"I feel likewise, sir."

"Let's do this."

… … … … … … … … …

Flug watched Lieutenant Fibari mope around the starship for days. She hadn't run any drills. She hadn't held any inspections. When anyone asked her a question, she answered in monosyllables. As hard as it was to believe, he actually missed her sarcastic remarks and blistering critiques.

"Lieutenant, let's go down to the moon base and have a little fun. I got a couple of Huz just begging to get turned into some of that beer they make on Earth. It's not queetle but…"

Fela was surprised by his comment, but, looking back over the last couple of days, she realized how off-kilter she had been. She cocked her head and sighed. "I can't. I promised Agent Hlitatta I wouldn't leave the ship."

"Damn. I haven't seen anyone as down as you since Captain Lyttle abandoned *Far Galaxy*."

Fela's head snapped around. "You were on *Far Galaxy*?"

"Me and a thousand other people. Why?"

Fela pursed her lips, unsure how to respond. She had been Fey Pey's Exec when he kidnapped the Admiral-of-the-Fleet's daughter and held her for ransom. Fela was the navigator on *Easy Wind* during the running battle with *Far Galaxy*. The fight went on for two days as they'd jumped across the galaxy. Finally Fey Pey decided the ransom for the daughter wasn't worth the fight. He put the daughter into a lifeboat and left her for *Far Galaxy* to pick up. He also put a bomb on the lifeboat. When *Far Galaxy* stopped to retrieve the daughter, the bomb exploded. *Far Galaxy* was damaged enough to require abandoning ship. The admiral's daughter and everyone on the lifeboat was blown up. Before the captain of *Far Galaxy* issued the abandon ship order, he ordered the launch of its remaining photon torpedo at *Easy Wind*. Fela saw the torpedo launch and executed a complex series of emergency jumps, enabling her to avoid the attack.

A week later, Fey Pey sent Fela back to the torpedo in a lander to deactivate it and bring it back to *Easy Wind*. The captain of *Far Galaxy* had set the torpedo to follow *Easy Wind*'s electronic signature and explode when it got close enough. Having a different electronic signature, the lander was able to approach the torpedo as safely as anyone could approach a live bomb capable of exploding a sun. The bonus Fey Pey had offered for the retrieval was insanely huge. She volunteered mostly because she was having a hard time dealing with Fey Pey's murder of the admiral's daughter. The daughter's courage had captured Fela's admiration as the daughter had resisted Fey Pey's questioning and subsequent torture. As Fela approached the torpedo in the lander, she wondered if the reason she volunteered to recover it was because, deep down, she hoped the torpedo *would* explode. Fela could still remember feeling the cold fingers around her heart as she exited the lander and floated toward the live torpedo, wearing only a pressure suit.

That was how Fey Pey got the torpedo that blew up Zindarr. But to say this would tie her legally to the exploding of Zindarr, the destruction of *Far Galaxy*, and the death of the admiral's daughter.

Flug waited for Fela to respond. He didn't know what was going on inside her mind.

Finally she asked, "Did anyone ever find *Far Galaxy*?"

That was not what he had expected her to say. "Not until Zarqa did while we were on *Easy Wind*. *Far Galaxy* was about a lightyear away from where the captain reported her disabled."

"Really? And Zarqa found her?"

"Yep. Then I pulled the Graftium out of the drives. Fey Pey gave me a big bonus that I split among the security team."

"I bet Fey Pey got a chuckle out of that! That Graftium must have been worth a million huz or more on the black market. The main drives on a starship won't work without it."

Flug cocked his head. "Yeah, he did. And I didn't get a Huz of it anyway after he locked me and Zarqa up. It sounds like you know him."

"We've met," she said. Then an idea occurred to her. "Do you think you could find *Far Galaxy* again?"

"Not me, but I'll bet Zarqa could. She's a magician with those scans."

"It's not where the captain said it was," she said, looking at Flug out of the corner of her eyes. "Everyone has searched for it there." She left out the part about Fey Pey ordering her to return to where the lifeboat blew up, after she recovered the torpedo. He wanted to salvage anything of value from the hulk, claiming pirate's privilege. All they had found was the expanding debris cloud from the lifeboat explosion. Fey Pey was furious.

"Yeah. Far Galaxy still had enough power left after the lifeboat exploded to make one more jump. He told us he didn't want the pirates coming back to strip her, but everyone figured it was so he could do the salvage himself. After everyone was in the lifeboats, he jumped us all to the military planet Hollum, then cleared the jump history from the lifeboats. All that work for nothing."

Fela didn't understand. "What do you mean?"

"He died a month later in another battle. He never came back to salvage the hulk."

"Do you think the computers are still intact and functional?"

"I have no idea. It's been, what, fifty years or more since it was disabled?"

"Yeah, at least that." Fela got a faraway look in her eyes. "If we could find *Far Galaxy* again, if the computers still work, and if the signature of the pirate ship that attacked them is still in the memory banks, we may have the first hard evidence of who it was that attacked *Far Galaxy* and therefore who retrieved the photon torpedo that blew up Zindarr."

'That was a lot of 'ifs'," Flug said gently. "And you left out the big one."

"What's that?" Fela asked.

"If Special Agent Hlitatta will let you off this ship to try."

Fela sighed again. "Yep."

"Maybe you should ask him," Flug said gently. "I get the feeling he's an honest cop trying to run this investigation by the book. I'll bet he would send someone along or even accompany you himself. It wouldn't hurt to have an impartial witness when you pull that signature out of the memory banks."

Fela gave Flug a sideways glance. *How much does he know?* she wondered. *Sometimes he acts like he's just a dumb grunt and other times he has an insight that amazes me.*

… … … … … … … … …

"Sure, I'll fly the lander down to the surface," Corporal Vibii said to Fela. Where do you want me to leave it?"

"The coordinates of their governmental headquarters should still be in the jump computer history file. That's where they left to come up here."

"Are the primates going to attack me when I get there?"

"These primates are at the world government headquarters. I think you're safe. But I'll let them know you're coming. You may have to open the hatchway and say hello."

"No problem. When do you want it gone?"

"Yesterday would be fine."

"Can I finish breakfast?"

"Of course. After you park the lander, use the lander's Hore delivery portal to report back up here. I'll tell portal operations to expect you. I appreciate you doing this."

"Glad to help, Lieutenant."

"I'll clear the lander's departure with the BCI."

… … … … … … … … …

Special Agent Hlitatta was at the next table. Fela padded over to him.

"Agent Hlitatta, could I have a moment of your time?"

He looked with distaste at the blob of generated protein on his plate. "Sure. I think I'm done anyway."

"I have two things. The first is that the landing deck supervisor would like to move the primates' lander back to the planet surface. Corporal Vibii has volunteered to fly it. We need your permission to allow the lander to depart."

"I'll have a team search the lander and clear it for departure. What's the other thing?"

"I think I can find the remains of *Far Galaxy*."

That got a hard stare. "And how did you come into this information?"

Fela gave him the whole story of her discussion with Flug and Flug's announcement that Zarqa had found *Far Galaxy* from the pirated scans while she was on board *Easy Wind*.

"If the computer banks are still viable, the signature of the pirate ship would still be in them. That could tie the explosion of Zindarr to a ship and a captain."

"I understand exactly what it means, Lieutenant. I need to speak to Sergeants Flug and Zarqa immediately," he said, getting up with his tray. "Have them report to the conference room. I will meet them there."

"And the lander?" she called after him.

He pressed a button on his belt and talked into a hologram that appeared in front of him while he walked toward the tray drop-off area.

... ...

"Here they come," Post 5 reported.

The people streamed out from around the houses, but there weren't any naked people tied to carts in the front of an angry, armed mob. And they weren't acting like they were going to storm the fence line. Instead they silently gathered in a circle around the entire campus and stood fifty feet away from the cordon. An old black woman stepped out from the mob and hobbled halfway to the fence as the rain poured down on everyone. A man tried to help her, but she waved him off. Her clothes were torn and dirty. Her white hair hung in soggy dreadlocks. She smiled at the soldiers with their guns, then awkwardly got down on her knees, bowed her head, and began to pray. The entire crowd behind her did the same thing, spreading in both directions around the one-mile circumference of the perimeter. There were at least ten thousand people kneeling silently in the rain.

Captain McQuidey got on the radio. "Drop Control, we are out of time. Pass over the drop zone and release all cargo."

"Germ One, we are out of time as well. We must return to Bragg to refuel. We will return in three hours."

Captain McQuidey wasn't having it. "Drop Control, I am invoking emergency wartime authority. You will pass over the drop zone and release all cargo. Do you understand?"

"Roger that, Germ One. I copy emergency wartime authority. May I have your initials, sir?"

"Drop Control, this is Germ One. I reply Charlie Juliet Mike."

The planes reversed direction and flew back toward Atlanta, knowing they would not have enough fuel to make the return flight to Fort Bragg. Instead, they would have to land at one of the small, unsecured private airports between Atlanta and Fayetteville, North Carolina. There they would wait until someone could bring them the fuel to return to base. The rest of their critical resupply missions would have to go on hold. But first they had to find a reference point so they could see where to drop the MREs. The GPS system didn't work anymore. So they flew through the clouds around Atlanta searching for a landmark, something they could identify from the air. Once they identified something, they could vector from that to the CDC.

There was nothing quite as frightening to a pilot as descending into an unknown air space full of tall buildings through a storm cell when he couldn't see the ground or any other reference point, not knowing if in the next second he would enter a wind shear that would blow the plane into the ground or, worse, into a building.

"Drop Control, this is Drop Three. I've got Peachtree Center," the pilot announced over the radio. "On my starboard wingtip."

The Drop Control Officer breathed a sigh of relief, checking his map. "The CDC is four-and-a-half miles due northeast of Peachtree Center. Drop formation, people. Follow me. We don't have time to make two passes. I want every other plane to follow me clockwise around the CDC. The rest of you go counterclockwise. We will meet back up on the other side. When I say drop, let 'em go. No questions."

Two minutes later the planes passed over the CDC. The pilots had threaded the needle—a hundred feet above the trees and a hundred feet below the clouds. A roar went up from the people as the planes became visible. The pallets of MREs crashed into the ground and homes around the CDC in a rough circle outside the fence line as the planes banked back to the north and began climbing out of the storm. As one body, the people turned their backs on the CDC campus and ran toward the sites where the pallets smashed to the earth. The planes were not high enough for the parachutes to open before the pallets hit. The loads had burst open upon impact, spreading the MREs around them like confetti.

In moments, the old woman, still on her knees, was the only one remaining in the street. As the rain sheets blew across the campus, a lightning bolt flashed above her, followed by a huge thunder clap. She looked up at the low-flying clouds, closed her eyes, and mouthed, "Thank you." She used her cane to get to her feet, then hobbled away to join everyone else as the food was distributed.

… … … … … … … … …

Lobo studied where the next settlement was on his map. His scouts said it was larger than this one, ten houses instead of two. But the houses were well built with expensive vehicles parked around them. This settlement would be a plum, a very rich plum. They would have cash and jewelry hidden in those pretty homes. There was a single road that led to it. He liked to hit these little settlements from the front and rear at the same time. The shock effect overwhelmed the defenders. That kind of attack would be difficult with this one. The terrain was steep and brush covered. On the other hand, there was no way for the settlers to escape with their wealth.

"Arturo, how do you think we should attack this settlement?"

Arturo had already studied the map. This was his chance to eliminate most of Lobo's men. "I think we should send everyone up the road as a mass. The sight of so many armed men coming at them will scare the shit out of those people. They'll lay down their rifles and run away. They won't have time to take their wealth with them."

"*Sí*, that's what I thought, too."

Arturo had told his own commanders to lead their men around both sides of the mountain and attack in a pincher movement while Lobo's men got blown to bits and everyone was distracted by the conflict coming up the road.

"Where do you think we should put the mortar?"

"On that hilltop right there." Arturo pointed. "They'll have a clear view of the whole attack area and can hit any hot spots."

The 88-mm mortar they stole from the National Guard armory had saved their ass on the last hill. Those Green Berets had booby-trapped every approach. Luckily, two of Arturo's men were ex-infantry and expert in using this particular mortar. They could hit an anthill at four hundred meters.

"Just keep the mortar out of sight until we need it."

"*Sí, Señor* Lobo. That makes sense." He had already told the mortar crew where to place themselves.

"There's nothing to do now but wait," Lobo said, finishing the Booker's Bourbon from the Green Berets' stash. "Let's follow the men and find somewhere to watch."

"I have the perfect place picked out," Arturo said. "We should be able to watch the whole thing."

"Arturo, how did I manage without you?" Lobo said fondly, putting his arm around the younger man as they walked toward the Humvee recently "acquired" from the Green Berets. They got in, Arturo driving, and started down the rutted gravel road that led out of the settlement. The other vehicles were far ahead of them.

... ...

Guillermo Villalta and his younger brother, Gael, set up the mortar on the hilltop they were assigned by Arturo.

"I want to be Forward Observer this time," Gael said.

They served two tours in Iraq together in the Fourth Infantry Division. The FO would tell the gunner by radio how to adjust fire to hit the target. The gunner was usually out of sight of the target. The FO's job was to watch where the rounds struck and adjust fire, saying things like "Drop 80, left 10," meaning bring the aiming point eighty meters closer and ten meters to the left. But to watch where the rounds hit, the FO had to see the enemy and that meant they could see the FO.

"Not gonna happen, *Culo*," Guillermo told him affectionately. *Culo* was the gutter word for a human rear end. He started putting propellant charges on the ten rounds they brought with them. "I'm FO. You're gunner. It's a team that works."

The greater the propellant charge, the higher the round flew and farther it could go. The distance to the settlement was known, so calculating the needed charge was easy. The ten rounds were all set to go, ready to grab and drop them down the mortar tube, once the proper distance and direction was established. It was called "firing for effect." There weren't words to describe the fear of being underneath a "fire for effect" barrage.

"You're always FO. I'm as good as you. I want to be FO this time."

"What part of 'no' don't you understand, Gael?"

"You know, mother was right. You are a bully sometimes."

Guillermo grimaced. Bringing up their mother was a cheap shot. She had died in the bombing. He walked to the top of the hill. The settlement was a quarter mile away. It would take a pretty good marksman to shoot someone hiding behind a tree with a pair of binoculars.

"OK. You be FO. I'll be gunner," Guillermo told him sternly. "Don't fuck up."

"You drop 'em where I tell you," his brother replied, just as sternly, trying hard not to smile. "Don't fuck up."

Guillermo didn't have time to worry about his brother before the attack. He wiped his forehead and went back to setting up the mortar. Gael studied the settlement through his binoculars. The heat rising from the countryside made the images waver like a dream. He made a fairly accurate estimate of the distance and compass heading to each building and point of defense.

... ...

"They're coming," the Brutus announced over the radios.

The first trucks appeared at the entrance to the ravine a few minutes later. They paused at the bottom of the ravine as the commander in the lead truck studied the sides of the ravine and the tree line at the top through his binoculars. The air was hot and still, almost as if the hillside were holding its breath. The commander signaled the convoy to continue up the hill. As they turned the corner near the top of the ravine they encountered the first fallen tree across the road. All of the trucks and cars stopped, bumper to bumper, and the people got out with their guns ready, studying the hillside. A hawk screamed high above them.

"Bring up that chain saw, Miguel," the commander ordered, shouting back down the line of trucks. He pointed to two groups of five men nearby, then up the sides of the ravine. "You guys get up there and see what you can see."

Jeremiah gave Tony the signal. The claymores blew along one side of the road, filling the air with the noise of the explosions and smoke. Several of the men standing near the claymores were almost cut in half by the spray of screws, nails, and cut-up sheet metal that was blown into them by the explosions. As the echoes of the claymore detonations died away it was replaced with the sounds of screaming men and automatic weapons firing into the trees on both sides of the ravine. The men who were not in the kill zone and those who weren't badly injured ran down the road the way they came, abandoning their vehicles. Some men jumped into the brush in the ditches beside the trucks and were impaled on the punji sticks. Brutus backed out of its hiding place and opened up with the minigun on the fleeing men, leaving dead men everywhere the tongue of fire touched. The two M-60s joined it, shooting people who were still returning fire. From each of the settlers' hiding places behind the logs, a steady stream of deadly rifle fire accompanied the barrage from Brutus.

A mortar round hit the top of the settlement area, landing past Brutus by seventy yards. No real damage was done but some shrapnel hit the side of the truck and some pine needles at the impact site caught fire. Caitlin and her children ran to put it out. Thirty seconds later, the next round hit twenty yards on the other side of Brutus, next to one of the defense logs killing Marvin Schroeder and his wife and sending shrapnel into one of the rear tires of Brutus.

"They're on that hilltop!" Jeremiah screamed at the minigun operator, pointing across the ravine.

Knowing the next round from the mortar would be dead on top of them, the minigun operator and both M-60s covered the top of the hill with bullets until the minigun went empty. The driver put Brutus in drive and drove up to where they had hidden until the fight started. Apparently their firing stopped the mortar. No new rounds hit the settlement. The minigun operator connected the next tub of ammo to the minigun and prepared to re-enter the fray.

… … … … … … … … …

Guillermo Villalta held the body of his younger brother in his lap as he rocked in agony. Gael had been killed by Jeremiah's attack on the mortar site. When Jeremiah told Brutus to open up on the hilltop where the mortar was set up, the tree Gael was hiding behind was cut in half by the fusillade. His brother was hit at least twenty times. He died instantly. Guillermo ran to his brother's aid and been shot as he did. Blood still gushed from his shattered right arm.

Because he had run to his brother's aid, he hadn't dropped the round that would have landed right on top of Brutus. The eight remaining rounds were lined up next to the mortar, ready for his brother's command to "fire for effect." That fusillade would have obliterated Brutus, the settlers, and the Marines on the hilltop.

Guillermo turned his face toward the sky and muttered, "Forgive us, Father, we have sinned. We were weak." He made the sign of the cross on his brother's chest, then on his own.

He stroked his brother's face one more time, then estimated the distance to the mortar, trying to figure out if he could crawl back there and drop the rounds. He decided he must try. He laid his brother down and began to crawl toward the mortar, using only his left arm and knees while he left a thick trail of blood from his ruined right arm in the dirt behind him.

He got to the mortar and wiped his face, trying to make sense of what was going on. The world was getting fuzzy. He knew he was supposed to do something with the mortar rounds stacked up beside the mortar. He picked up a round with his left hand and held it without comprehending what it was. He tried to put it into the mortar tube, more from habit than anything else. The round seemed two feet wide and the tube was only a one-inch hole. He fumbled with trying to fit the round into the tube several times before he succeeded. But it was upside down. This caused the detonator on the nose of the round to fall onto the firing pin at the bottom of the tube. Nothing happened. The round did not explode because the detonator didn't arm until after the round was fired out of the tube.

Guillermo sat down next to the mortar and put his head against the tube, trying to figure out what was going on, why he was here, what he was trying to do. The world faded. He closed his eyes and died.

... ...

When the last of the retreating attackers disappeared around the bend in the road, Jeremiah shouted, "Cease fire!"

Nothing is quite as spooky as the silence after a firefight. The adrenaline in the combatants is at an all-time high. As the gun smoke slowly dissipates, the situation goes from absolute terror, bullets whistling past their heads, the chaos and noise of machineguns firing, claymores detonating, men screaming, and mortar rounds exploding to ... nothing.

Jeremiah called out, "Who's hurt?"

No one answered.

"Freddie, go check out the Schroeders." Jeremiah pointed to where he was sure their bodies lay.

The sound of a bullet discharging came from one of the alternate approach paths.

"OK, people, we've got visitors. They're coming up one path, probably both. You know the plan. Take your preassigned stations. Wait until you have a clear shot, then shoot anything that moves. There aren't any good guys coming up those trails. Cooper, you man the claymore detonators on the east side. Jones, get the west side. Brutus, position yourself in the middle of the settlement. Shoot anyone you don't recognize. People, if you have to retreat to Brutus, do it with your arms waving that red cloth I gave you."

"I'm going to see what they've got," Major Goodman picked up a handheld radio, his rifle, and trotted away from the settlement toward the north in his boonie hat.

"Tony, you keep watch on the road. You have your rifle, right?"

Tony nodded. "Yep."

"Watch out for people from the road trying to work their way up here, injured or not. If there is any kind of concerted attack, blow the second bank of claymores when they're in the kill zone."

Everyone took up their positions.

The radio in Brutus came alive. "This is Popeye. We got a bunch of people coming down the road."

The remnants of the attackers were trying to retreat back down the road.

"Fire when they are in the kill zone," Jeremiah told them.

The sounds of Popeye and Satan opening up with their claymores and machine guns came to the hilltop. Smoke filled the air in the settlement, making their eyes water and giving the hilltop a surreal appearance. Apparently some of the brush in the ravine had caught fire from the claymores.

The radio in Brutus crackled to life again. "LT, we got about fifty people still alive who want to surrender. They got their hands up and have thrown their weapons away. We figure another twenty or so escaped. Got a lot of wounded enemy. None of us are hurt. Could you send Freddie over?"

"Freddie's pretty busy up here. Secure them before you give first-aid. Make 'em sit where you can see them in the road. Keep 'em covered. Tell them if anyone tries to escape you will shoot them. Don't hesitate to use deadly force and don't take any chances. These are the assholes that raped and murdered their way up here. I've got another bunch coming in the back door up here. I'll come down after we finish this up."

... ...

Lobo watched his men get slaughtered without emotion. He turned to Arturo. "You did this," he accused Arturo. "You knew they were waiting for us."

"I figured they were," Arturo agreed.

"Why? Why did you do this, Arturo? Both of us could have been rich."

Lobo turned to look at his men sitting in the road while the Marines searched, disarmed, and bound them. Popeye was a hundred feet away with its machine guns ready, waiting for the slightest aggressive movement from the prisoners. While he was facing the road, he pulled his pistol out of his waistband. He spun around, ready to kill Arturo.

Arturo was ready. He fired one shot, catching Lobo in the eye and blowing his brains out the back of his head. Arturo walked over to him and watched with interest as Lobo died. Each death was unique. He kept a mental photo album of the people he killed. When the blood stopped and Lobo's remaining eye went wide, Arturo unzipped his fly and urinated on the pile of meat and bones that moments before was one of the most feared banditos in the San Joaquin valley. Then he got into the Humvee and drove back down the hill, passing over Lobo with two wheels as he left the hilltop. At the bottom of the hill, he turned toward Sonora.

Arturo estimated there was at least two million dollars in cash and jewelry in the back of the Humvee. Law and order was returning to California. Two million dollars should be enough to start a bank, like Amadeo Giannini did in 1904. Giannini started the Bank of Italy in San Francisco. His bank offered services to people the other banks wouldn't touch—working people, immigrants, people who couldn't speak English, people who weren't rich. Unlike his competitors, Giannini's branches stayed open until ten o'clock at night to fit the hours of its patrons. After the Great San Francisco Earthquake of 1906, while the other banks were still trying to dig out of the rubble, he set up a table in the middle of the devastation and offered loans to help people rebuild the city. In 1930, in the heart of the Great Depression, the Bank of Italy became the Bank of America. By 1945 the Bank of America was worth over five billion dollars. He figured the current situation roughly paralleled the one in 1906. Thirty-nine years—that was how long it took Giannini to make B of A worth five billion dollars. He could wait thirty-nine years to be worth that much. Now that everyone who could tie him to the bandits were dead, courtesy of the US Marines, there was nothing to worry about.

As he drove west, Arturo began considering names for his bank. He wanted one that said "Let's start over together."

"Bank of the Resurrection—nah, too Christian...Bank of Arturo—nah, too Mexican...Bank of the World—nah World Bank was taken." He could wait for a name.

A brightly colored parrot flew across the road in front of him. "What's a parrot doing up here?" he asked himself. "Must have survived someone's house getting blown up—a bird from the ashes." Then the name popped into his head. "Bank of the Phoenix...yeah, that might work. Not too foreign. Not too ethnic. A name filled with hope for the future. The bank to help everyone as this country rose from the ashes. Yeah, that's it: The Bank of the Phoenix.

"Just don't miss a payment," he said quietly. Collections were his specialty. He knew how to do collections. Bandits could make a living stealing from people. But to get really rich, you had to start a government or a corporation. Then you could steal as much as you wanted and no one could say anything as long as you did it within the law. He couldn't start a government, so he had to make sure the government passed the laws he needed. And that was easy enough to get done. A few investments into the bank accounts of key legislators. Such a great return on investment those deposits would make. He would make sure the police departments were well funded. Maybe he would run for office. That would make it even easier.

... ...

Jeremiah's handheld radio came to life. "This is Goodman. There are about twenty-five men coming up the east trail. One is injured. They are being very careful, checking for booby traps. They should arrive at the settlement in about five minutes." There was a hesitation, then Major Goodman talked again. "They aren't just punks from the city stumbling through the woods. These guys look to be ex-military. They have M-4 rifles, body armor, and twenty-five meter spacing. There's one M-60, four men back from the point. Leader is three men back from point. Be careful. Going to check the west trail."

Jeremiah passed Major Goodman's information to everyone as they waited.

Five minutes later, Jeremiah's radio came alive again. "This is Goodman. The west side has ten men, one M-60." There was a rifle shot, then a second followed by a rattle of automatic weapons fire.

"Got the leader and the M-60 operator," Major Goodman said quietly over the radio.

"Are you OK?"

"Yep. Going back to the east side."

The sound of automatic weapons fire and grenade explosions came from the other side of the hilltop where Popeye and Satan were located.

"What's happening, Popeye and Satan?"

After a pause, the radio came to life. "Some people tried to pull off a counterattack when Satan went down to the road, LT." There was a pause. "Uh, Lieutenant, I don't think we have to worry about prisoners or casualties anymore. At least not with this group. Freddie can stay up there."

... ...

Jeremiah turned on the PA system in Brutus and pulled the microphone to his mouth. "People coming up the hill. This is not an undefended survivor settlement. We are the US Marines from Camp Pendleton sent here to stop and defeat you. You heard what happened to your friends. They are all dead or captured, but mostly they are dead. We are waiting to kill you. Surrender now and we will give you a fair trial. Continue up the hill and you will die."

The group on the east trail continued coming up the hill. Major Goodman waited until the first three men were in the kill zone for the claymores. He shot the leader of the group. The machine gunner began to deploy his machine gun. Major Goodman shot him also, then detonated the claymores. Five men at the head of the team on the trail were killed. Most of the rest threw down their guns and held up their arms in surrender. Four men at the end of the group ran back down the trail.

The surviving men on the west trail retreated and began their walk back to the Green Berets camp to figure out what to do. *Señor* Lobo would know. He said he would be waiting for them there.

Major Goodman followed them, killing them one at a time, as he got clear shots.

Chapter 16 – That Makes Two of Us

The lander descended rapidly through the atmosphere. Corporal Vibii saw the "H" on the ground next to the building that was the obvious target of the descent. He had no idea what the "H" meant, but he didn't care either.

"Drop this antique lander off and open a portal back to the starship." Those were his orders and that was what he intended to do.

As he settled onto the "H," a group of primates ran out of the building and formed a group as they stared at the lander. Corporal Vibii was surprised by the greeting. He wasn't sure what they wanted—no one else accompanied him. This was just a drop-off, no big deal. He decided to open the hatchway and say hello before he ported back to the starship.

When the hatchway opened, he walked halfway down the ramp and waved. He was greeted with complete silence. A man walked out from the group, then up the ramp. He held out his hand uncertainly, not sure which of Corporal Vibii's four arms to aim for. He said some words the Corporal didn't understand. Corporal Vibii touched the Interpret button on his utility belt, activating the interactive interpretation computer.

"I didn't understand what you said. Please start over."

"Welcome to Earth," the man repeated. "I am Vice President Barfield."

"I am Corporal Vibii. I was told to bring this lander back to Earth."

"What has happened to our delegation that left to visit the emperor? They were in this lander."

"I don't know. No one tells me anything. They left the starship yesterday in an executive shuttle. They should be arriving at Quyl sometime today."

"Where is Quyl?"

"About fifty thousand lightyears …" he brought up a navigation hologram, looked around at the orientation of the Earth to the sun, turned the hologram so the orientation matched, then pointed about thirty degrees up from the southern horizon. "that way."

"Fifty thousand lightyears? So far?"

Corporal Vibii wasn't sure how to respond so he nodded in agreement. Distances like that really had no significance to him, not when, if you were stupid enough to try, you could jump the whole fifty thousand lightyears in a single jump.

"Is that where the emperor lives?"

"Yes."

"Corporal Vibii, do you have time to eat before you return to the starship? When the starship alerted us to your impending arrival, we prepared a meal to share with you."

"I am vegan," Corporal Vibii told the vice president, remembering Captain Marshall's comment about barbeque. "Can you accommodate my diet?"

"Fruits, nuts, vegetables, cooked grains, breads. Are these acceptable?" the vice president asked.

"Yes, as long as they are prepared with vegan ingredients. Uncooked fruits and vegetables are preferable."

"I will make sure they are served. Give us a few minutes to arrange this." The VP signaled a person next to him, then whispered to her to go set up a vegan meal.

Corporal Vibii decided to see how far he could push this "visit." He was at the end of his shift on the starship and he had watched this beautiful world for over two years from space without being able to visit. "Would you happen to have any of Earth's fermented beverages? I've heard about them on the starship and would like to try several. I think you call it 'beer.'"

The vice president was amused. Of all the things he expected Corporal Vibii to ask, beer was nowhere near the top of the list. And Vice President Barfield was a connoisseur of beer. "Do you have a preference? Light? Dark? Bitter? Cold? Warm?"

"Cool, dark, bitter, with a thick creamy head," the corporal responded, smacking his lips.

"Now *that* I can provide...all in the interest of good galactic relations, of course." The VP rubbed his hands together in anticipation. "We have a local microbrewery making that very kind of beer. It's one of my favorites. Once we've tried that one, there are several others I could recommend."

They walked into the building and turned toward the presidential dining room.

As soon as they entered the building, Doug and Kevin walked into the lander. They had been studying the maintenance manuals and schematics Captain Xanny's maintenance crew gave the Canadians as part of their maintenance training.

Kevin removed the access panel that covered the anti-grav drive mechanism. "There it is, Doug."

They both stared at it in awe.

Doug said quietly, "If we can duplicate it, it will ...,"

"Don't you dare say those words!" Kevin interrupted him.

Lily's dream, the dream that showed her how to create a Rosy field wormhole generator, had said "Build it and it will change the world." That dream led directly to the elimination order for humanity and the sterilization of the human race. Kevin had expected Doug to use those same words: change the world.

"... eliminate the need for highways," Doug continued, ignoring Kevin. "No more cranes. No more helicopters. Do you know what this means, Kevin?"

"What?"

"We could build a Jetson car."

Kevin looked at Doug in confusion. *The Jetsons*, a futuristic cartoon sit-com popular in the 60's, 70's, and 80's, had never been a part of his childhood. He had no idea what Doug was talking about.

"I mean, not the part about George Jetson pushing a button and his car folding into a suitcase. I mean the part about it lifting off from his house and putting away through the air without propellers, jet engines, or rocket motors."

"I'm not sure I want most of the drivers on the roads today to have three-dimensional access. They screw up regularly in two dimensions. And what about drunk drivers? Right now the worst they can do is hit a bridge abutment or another car or even a pedestrian. With an anti-grav car, they could really do some damage. Imagine a drunk senator running into the Capitol building."

"Quidditch." Doug was still not paying attention. "We could actually have a Quidditch match with anti-grav broomsticks!"

Kevin snickered. "Until Lord Voldemort showed up with Fey Pey's team of pirate Quidditch players and stole the Golden Snitch."

That finally got through to Doug. He turned, wide-eyed, to Kevin. "Do you think he would?"

Kevin snorted and started to reply. Doug laughed and poked him in the arm. "Got cha!"

... ...

Special Agent Hlitatta stared at Corporal Flug. "So what you're telling me is you pulled the Graftium out of the drives on *Far Galaxy* and convinced Fey Pey the computers were nonoperational."

"I figured there was a reason he was so happy about finding *Far Galaxy* and I didn't believe it had anything to do with 20 kilograms of Graftium."

"Do you know what that much Graftium is worth?"

"A couple of million Huz on the free market. Maybe half that on the black market."

Agent Hlitatta looked again at the transcript of Flug's time in the Combat Corps. It showed his assignment to *Far Galaxy* about two months before the ship was lost. "Your career in the Combat Corps was cut short. Tell me about it."

"Not much to tell. We were cleaning up the insurrection on Klaverdamonous. My lieutenant ordered me to kill some suspects. I refused. He arrested me."

"And his order was found later to be illegal."

"Made no difference to the Corps. I was handed my resignation and told to sign it. I did."

"How did you end up on GSMS-77?"

"Captain Xanny liked that I refused to kill innocent beings because some kid was scared of those people. It was the lieutenant's first mission, right out of the academy. Those heavy-worlders can get pretty intimidating to a kid born in zero-grav on an asteroid miner."

"Did you refuse to kill them because you are a heavy-worlder yourself?"

"I don't think that had anything to do with it. But who knows? It was a knee-jerk reaction to what I thought was an illegal order. He may have been afraid of me also."

Agent Hlitatta sat back in his chair. "Who do you really work for, Corporal Flug?"

"I work for Captain Xanny and Grock Corp. I thought you knew that."

"Your transcript is too clean. No one gets thrown out of the Combat Corps for disobedience without at least a fine and jail time. There is no record of you even taking a leave."

"Got no one to see. Both parents are gone. I have no extended family, both my parents were only children. I got all the adventure I needed serving in the Corps."

"What do you do for fun, Corporal Flug?"

"Why, I talk to BCI agents, of course," Flug said, then put on a thoughtful expression. "We're both on the same side, Agent Hlitatta."

"What does that mean, Sergeant?"

"Just what you think it means. I want to bring Fey Pey to justice as much as you do."

"Who says I want to bring Fey Pey to justice? He hasn't been charged with a crime yet."

Flug raised an eyebrow. "You're a cop, Agent Hlitatta. You know he's guilty, like any good cop would. All you're doing now is finding out how to prove what he's really done so you *can* bring charges against him and make them stick. You've been on the BCI Fey Pey team for three years. None of this can be a surprise. He's the slipperiest pirate I've ever seen."

Agent Hlitatta continued to stare at Flug without blinking. The Fey Pey team was top secret—*beyond* top secret. There's no way this ex-Combat-Corps-senior-sergeant could possibly know it even existed, let alone that a specific agent was assigned to the team and how long he had been assigned there.

"How about this?" Flug suggested. "How about I get someone to vouch for me, someone you can trust?"

"Who would that be?"

"Don't know yet. Let me work on it."

"OK. You have two hours. After that, I'm going to lock you up for divulging top secret information."

"Fair enough." Flug got up and left the conference room without saying another word.

... ...

Headquarters Company of the First Brigade of the 82nd Airborne Division rolled onto the campus of the CDC, two days late. The rest of the brigade took up positions around the area and made their situations secure. The brigade immediately started implementing the preplanned food distribution program, providing hot meals to the hungry citizens. Combat teams began performing patrols of the interstate highway system around Atlanta, removing roadblocks and taking out areas of resistance.

The brigade legal teams began collecting evidence of who broke the law during the absence of any legal authority, what they did, and who they did it to.

Emory University Hospital reopened a day later, under tight security. The brigade medical staff was kept busy with the surviving casualties from the attack on the CDC.

Word spread quickly that law and order had finally returned to Atlanta. Farmers began delivering the truckloads of produce and meat that was waiting in the farms and pastures of north Georgia for the anarchy to end. Peace and capitalism slowly returned to chaos-torn Atlanta.

The old woman who led the prayer vigil outside the CDC became a local hero. Her name was Mary King. Although she was no direct lineage to Dr. Martin Luther King, she had devoted her life to living in his nonviolent footsteps. People credited her with preventing the slaughter of the starving people around the CDC. She became the focal point and coordinator of the entire Atlanta recovery effort.

Dr. Hehsa met with his staff about the research that had been underway since the siege of the CDC began.

"Our body doesn't recognize this virus as a pathogen," he recapped. "Without the virus being recognized as a pathogen, our bodies won't produce any antibodies. Without antibodies, there is no immunity."

"What if we make it a pathogen?" Dr. Splendt suggested.

"You want to change this benign virus into something virulent?" Dr. Hehsa asked, amazed.

"Well, no, not exactly. Just something the body *thinks* is virulent."

"And what happens if we do our job too well?" Dr. Hehsa said after a few moments of deliberation. "What if we end up turning something loose on our population that has no cure and is more lethal than Ebola, Dr. Splendt? The idea of creating another disease scares me to death. The world has enough diseases."

Dr. Splendt's face flushed red. He wasn't used to being dismissed out of hand.

Sridhar saw this and backpedaled a little to let him save face. "I'm not saying that we won't try your idea, my friend. If everything else fails, let's use it as plan Z. But first we have to try everything else."

There was a pause in the meeting. Tensions were running high.

"Dr. Hehsa," a pretty lab tech named Sylvia Davis stood in the silence. "I have an announcement to make."

"Yes, Sylvia," he said, grateful for anything that would defuse the stress in this meeting. "What would you like to say?"

"I'm pregnant!"

Shirley Perez stood next to her. "Me, too!"

Both women beamed ecstatically.

Dr. Hehsa looked back and forth between them, unsure how to proceed. “I am assuming this was not done in the traditional manner?”

“I did it,” Dr. Splendt said, standing, unable to hide the smug expression on his face. “I created two zygotes from *their* eggs and *my* sperm, all of us infected with BSV. I used the same process we used to create the embryos that are gestating in our Baby Machines. Both of these women were willing to try the implantation process. It succeeded.”

“And the babies will be born infected by BSV,” Dr. Hehsa said sadly. “What does this prove?”

“It proves that couples can have a baby from their own genes without waiting in the Baby Machine queue. It proves they can have a baby that is theirs instead of a clone or a child who is simply a member of their gene pool. It proves that all over the world, people can begin having their *own* children again, children of a woman and a man who want a child who is *their* offspring. The process to make the eggs and sperm fertile is complicated, but not impossible, for any competent genetic lab to perform. And there are a lot more women than there are Baby Machines. The labs won’t have to wait nine months before they can begin working on the next customer’s zygote. And the cost of the lab’s efforts and implantation will be much less than the cost of a gestation in a Baby Machine. It may not be a cure, but it is certainly a work-around until we *can* find the cure.”

Dr. Hehsa let himself begin to get excited. “You have ultrasound of this? There isn’t any doubt?”

Dr. Splendt slid two grainy photographs across the table. They showed healthy embryos inside two separate uteruses. “No doubt at all. I’m going to be a daddy!”

... ...

“How did you find *Far Galaxy*?” Agent Hlitatta had been questioning Zarqa for an hour.

"I saw an anomaly on a scan that had no business being there. Fey Pey wanted to exercise his 'security' personnel. It seemed worth a look. He wanted an abandoned ship within a couple of lightyears of the reported site of abandonment of *Far Galaxy*."

"Why did he want you to search there?"

"Don't know. I suppose he wanted to find *Far Galaxy*. Everyone had looked for it. Just the Graftium in it would make someone rich for the rest of their life."

"Did Corporal Flug give you any guidance in where to search?"

Zarqa cocked her head at that question, then took a full minute thinking about it without responding. Until that moment, she thought it was solely her idea. But thinking back, Flug had brought her attention to the anomaly. He did it by asking her what it was. She was about to examine the next scan. The anomaly was so small, she had missed it. "Well, now that you mention it, he did." She told him about the incident.

Agent Hlitatta's communicator buzzed, indicating an encrypted message was is the queue. He picked it up. "You need to wait outside for a moment, Sergeant Zarqa."

She left the conference room.

Agent Hlitatta retrieved the message and decrypted it. It was from the Director of the BCI. It was comprised of two sentences: "Corporal Flug is reliable. You may trust what he tells you."

He studied the message. It had come in a direct, encrypted send from the desk of the Director at the headquarters of the BCI. There was no chance it was hacked. The BCI messaging system was the most secure in the galaxy. This message had been created by the Director himself, not an administrative aid.

Agent Hlitatta sat back in his chair to think about this. The Director of the BCI had taken time out of his schedule to send a secure message any flunky could have created.

"The frigging Director?" Agent Hlitatta asked the air above him. "The Director doesn't know the name of my boss's boss's boss. And now the Director himself tells me that a lowly ex-Combat-

Corps Sergeant on a species mining ship at the edge of the galaxy is OK? Who the hell *is* this guy and why is he here?" There was only one reason he would have done it—that Corporal Flug was part of an operation so covert only the Director and a select few even knew about it.

He picked up his communicator and did a secure erase of the message, then called Captain Huerrai, commander of one of the BCI cruisers stationed next to GSMS-77. "Captain, prepare for an immediate departure. I will be coming aboard with two people from GSMS-77. We will leave when I arrive. I will give you the coordinates of our destination when I arrive on-ship. No communication will be allowed off the ship after I arrive. Shut down all Hore communication portals. Wartime security protocol. Do you understand? I need a verbal acknowledgement."

"Yes, sir. I understand. I will make it so."

He walked out of the conference room. Sergeant Zarqa was waiting for him. He told her, "You will accompany Corporal Flug and me on a trip. Pack what you're going to need."

"Where are we going?" She had already guessed, of course.

"I will tell you when we are aboard the cruiser. You will talk of this to no one."

"I've got to clear it with Captain Xanny."

"I will do that. Go pack. Be at my shuttle in ten minutes."

He called Flug and told him the same thing.

"I'm at your shuttle, waiting for you," Flug replied. "Did you shut down all Hore communications on GSMS-77 as well?"

Agent Hlitatta paused, wondering if his phone was bugged. "I was about to do that."

"Great minds," Flug said.

"Excuse me?"

"I guess I've been on quarantine duty here too long. That's a truism from Earth. It means great minds think alike. It's a way of complimenting us both for coming to the same conclusion at the same moment."

"I will be at the shuttle in five minutes," Agent Hlitatta said without emotion.

… … … … … … … … …

Leann was tired of the primping and people who treated her as a fragile and priceless artifact. She had been bathed and shaved and sprayed with perfumes. Her auburn hair was highlighted with varying shades of white, yellow, and red. It was piled in curls on top of her head. Her face was smeared with more makeup than she had worn in her whole life. She was here to meet the emperor, not be a fashion plate on some newsfeed somewhere.

A little girl, maybe seven years old, entered the room where the prep team was working on Leann. Her skin was greenish, her hair was white, and her eyes were orange. But it was her head that caught Lean's attention. Her head was a little larger than "normal" on Earth. The women working on Leann went silent, bowed, and backed away from both Leann and the little girl.

"Are you Juliet?" she asked, ignoring the people who had been working on Leann. The words appeared in Leann's ears, but the girl's lips didn't match the sounds.

Leann was at a loss for a moment. Then she connected the dots. This girl thought she was Juliet from the play she performed on the capsule.

"No honey, my name is Leann Jenkins. I played Juliet in *Romeo and Juliet*. Did you like the play?"

"Yes, I did. Did she really die?"

"She did in the play."

"It was so sad and so beautiful all at once. Why didn't you bow to me? Everyone bows to me."

"Would you like me to bow to you?"

The girl thought about that. "No. Juliet didn't bow to anyone either."

"She bowed to the Prince."

"But not to the Prince's granddaughter."

"Is your grandfather a prince?"

"No. He's the emperor." She said it without the hesitation that would have indicated it was a name drop. It was just a statement of fact. "Are you going to perform a play while you're here?"

"Would you like me to?" Leann asked.

"Oh yes," the girl clapped her hands together in excitement.

"What kind of play would you like?"

She didn't hesitate. "*Romeo and Juliet,* it's my favorite of your performances."

"You saw them all?"

"Yes. Many times. I liked *Tom Sawyer,* too. *Treasure Island* scared me. Grandpa wouldn't let me watch *The Diary of a Young Girl* more than once. I made him promise not to let the Nazis capture me."

"I don't think I can perform *Romeo and Juliet* on a stage by myself. It was hard enough doing it in the capsule with two cameras."

"What do you need to perform it?"

"Some more people to act the other roles. My drama coach would know who else I should ask." Leann did a quick count. "We'd need eleven other actors who knew the roles. And some people to help with the scenery and costume changes."

"I'll have Grandpa approve it. Wait here." She walked out the door.

Leann stood without moving, staring at the empty doorway. She giggled and motioned the prep people to come back. "Let's get this done. I think I'll be seeing the emperor shortly."

They pulled an exquisite floor-length dress over Leann. The material felt like silk, but was not. It was almost sheer and clung to every curve of her body, but nothing important was visible. The color was deep black with sparkling dots spread around it randomly. On her left hip was Earth. Leann spun around and looked in the full-body mirror on the wall and gasped. The dots were arranged in the constellations as seen from Earth. And the constellations and Earth moved around her body as she spun! Her auburn hair became the sun, the shadows of the curls appearing to wrap around her head and disappear into the air above her. Even the makeup she had objected to without effect became part of the whole illusion. Leann had never seen the magnificent young woman staring back at her in the mirror.

The girl returned, pulling a handsome elderly man behind her. A retinue of assorted people followed behind the two of them. Three people circled them with what Leann assumed to be recording devices. The elderly man was dressed in a simple black tunic with a single adornment over his left chest. It was a gold and silver galaxy that slowly turned without moving. She stared at it, wondering how something that didn't move could rotate.

"Grandpa, this is Leann Jenkins. She played Juliet in the play. She said she would perform it here for me, but she needs eleven other people to do it. Please, Grandpa, please let her do it for me."

Leann bowed to the emperor, then held out her hand, as she was instructed to do.

He took her hand and brushed his lips over it. "So we finally meet, Leann. You have caused me quite a bit of trouble."

"How did I do that, Sire?"

"By telling the truth. No one ever tells me the truth. It was quite refreshing. You have met my granddaughter, Tablique?"

"Yes, Sire."

"She says she would like you to perform *Romeo and Juliet*. Is this something you would like to do?"

"I would love to, Sire. I will need some other people from my planet to play the other rolls, some stage people to help with the scene changes, and my coach to direct."

"I will tell my chief of staff to facilitate this. May we transmit your performance to our member states? Tabi has generated significant interest."

"Of course, Sire."

"How long will you need to prepare for the performance?"

Leann paused to consider this. "Six weeks, I think."

"Make it so. I need to return to my duties." He turned to Princess Tablique. "Give Grandpa a hug. I have to go back to work." She reached up to him and hugged his waist. He patted her on the back. Without another word, the emperor left the room. Everyone but Leann followed him. The audience was over.

… … … … … … … … …

"How could you plant the bullet booby traps without recording where you put them?" Jeremiah was frustrated with their lack of foresight. "What if you miss one? Someone will get hurt, maybe killed."

No one met his eyes. Finally, Amy Johansson said quietly, "We didn't think we'd live to worry about cleaning them up."

"I remember how many we made," Jonathan said. "We made forty-two."

"OK. Everyone start collecting the ones you can find. And be careful! Bring them back to Jonathan. When we find forty-two, we'll be done. Tony, go check the claymores on the east side of the road to make sure all of them exploded. And retrieve the ones from the west side. Does anyone have a tractor or bulldozer? We need to dig a mass grave for the dead people."

"Why are we going to bury them?" Liam asked. "I think we should burn them." He looked back at everyone's hostile stares. "Except for the Schroeders, of course. They should be buried."

"It's too dry to burn them, Liam," Rebecca reminded him. "We really don't have much choice about the hole. Either we plant them or live with the stink for weeks. Didn't Marvin have a tractor?"

"Yeah," Liam answered. "So does Bill Maloney. Maloney's has a backhoe on his."

Jeremiah decided to take control of the situation. "OK. Someone needs to dig a grave for Lucy and Marvin Schroeder. Then dig a hole big enough to bury these assholes who were going to kill us. It doesn't have to be neat and tidy. We chuck 'em in the hole and cover 'em with dirt. Don't waste time making it pretty with markers and such. I need to collect any IDs they have on them. I'll get my guys going on that. Liam, can we use your truck and trailer to collect the bodies?"

"Someone will have to pay for the diesel," Liam said, defensively. Everyone stared at him like he was a worm. Liam crossed his arms and shrugged. "What the hell, go ahead, use it.

Could you at least put a tarp on the trailer so the wood doesn't get soaked with blood?"

"I can run the backhoe," Jonathan said. "Where do you want me to dig the hole?"

Jeremiah studied the area around the settlement. An idea occurred to him. "Have you got any of that dynamite left? From under my house?"

"Yeah," Jonathan said. "There's a little over half a case. We only used twenty sticks for the claymores. We ran out of bondo."

"Let's throw the bodies into the ravine and start an avalanche with the dynamite to put dirt on top of them. It's more than those assholes deserve. And it'll save everyone a lot of work."

Everyone nodded in agreement. "Tony and I will set the charges. Jonathan, you dig a grave for the Schroeders. Corporal Rawlins, get to work on Brutus, changing that flat tire."

"Yes, sir." Rawlins got up and walked toward the truck.

"I'm on it." Jonathan walked toward Maloney's house to get the tractor with the backhoe.

"Sergeant Raymond, you take the rest of the people to collect the bodies onto Liam's truck and trailer. Throw them into the ravine. Freddie has examination gloves for everyone to wear. Do not come in contact with the blood or bodily fluids. There will be a lot of it. Lord knows what kind of diseases those bastards carried with them. Carry your weapons with you, people. Be on the lookout for survivors and ambushes. If you find someone who is still alive, give a call to Freddie. He will save their life if he can."

"What about the trucks and cars?" Sergeant Raymond asked Jeremiah. "There has to be seventy or more of 'em."

"If they start and move, put 'em up that hill where the mortar was. If they don't, thrown 'em in the ravine with the rest of the corpses. Push 'em over the side with the tractor or Sabre. Has anyone been up to check on the mortar?"

"Yeah," Sergeant Raymond spoke up again. "I did. Both the gunner and the FO were dead. 88MM mortar. Still had seven rounds ready to go. There was one upside down in the tube. Don't know if the gunner was trying to commit suicide or too out of it from blood loss to realize he dropped it that way. I brought the mortar and ammo down with me. It's broke down in the back of Popeye. Brought the two dead guys down, too."

"OK, I want the road passable by nightfall—into the ravine or up the hill—don't matter to me as long as the cars are gone."

"Yes, sir."

Major Goodman waited until everyone had left the area around Jeremiah. "Lieutenant Silverstein, you might think twice about collecting the IDs."

"Why's that?"

"As long as you bury the IDs with the people, no one knows who they were or if they died up here as a result of your action. If you collect the IDs and turn them in, the lawyers will have a field day saying they were just walking in the woods and the big bad Marines killed them because they were Hispanic."

Jeremiah considered what the major said. "Sir, those people had family who loved them. If the tables were turned, I would hope they would turn in my ID."

"Do you think they were going to turn in the IDs of the Green Berets and their families? Maybe you need to go see how their three kids were hung upside down above a fire and roasted to death while their parents watched. They were animals and the world is a better place because you killed them. You are opening a can of worms with the IDs. Let dead dogs lie."

"I appreciate your advice, sir, but I will follow the standing orders I followed in Iraq and Afghanistan. They said to collect the IDs of enemy combatants and turn them in. I intend to do that."

"Then take pictures, Jeremiah. Fill your phone. Get everyone in the camp to do the same thing. Photograph every one of those assholes where they fell with their weapons in their hands before they are moved. And be sure to preserve the dash cam recordings from your three trucks."

"Yeah, that makes sense, sir. I can do that."

… … … … … … … … …

The sun was going down when the last of the cleanup was completed. The bodies had been collected and thrown off the bridge into the ravine. There were about thirty cars and trucks on top of the corpses. The sun disappeared behind the clouds that had been blowing in from the west all afternoon, getting darker and lower in the sky above them. The temperature dropped steadily all afternoon, giving them a welcome relief from the heat of the morning as they went about their chores. There were thirty-two survivors among the attackers. Eighteen of them were injured. Freddie worked all afternoon on them, trying to save their lives. Three weren't expected to live through the night. The others would probably live to go to trial. Jeremiah moved the uninjured prisoners to Liam's shed after he removed the tools Liam kept in there. There were no windows, heavy wooden walls, and a stout, locking door. He screwed two-by-fours across the door as added insurance in case they somehow got the hinge pins out.

"Hey! We got no water in here," a voice shouted. "I'm thirsty! And I got to pee!"

"Damned shame," Jeremiah answered back. "Hope you can hold it until morning. There's a plastic trash can in the corner if you can't."

He walked down the hill to the bridge. The entire settlement had assembled to watch the explosion and landslide.

"Is everyone ready?" Jeremiah asked the group.

The people in the crowd nodded.

"Open your mouths and cover your ears! That lets the pressure equalize without blowing out your eardrums."

Jeremiah signaled Tony to detonate the dynamite. The explosion ripped the side of the ravine loose, sending it like a cleansing tsunami over the bodies and cars of the people who had hoped to kill and rob the settlers. When the noise stopped and the dust cleared, there were many feet of rock and dirt covering what would soon come to be called Dead Man's Gulch as long as people lived in the settlement.

Jonathan stood on the side of the bridge over the ravine. "Have fun in hell, assholes," he shouted loudly. He made a rude gesture at the rocks covering the bodies and followed that with a big gob of spit.

The first drops of rain from the clouds caught the settlement by surprise. No one expected rain in May. By the time everyone got somewhere dry to hide, the rain was torrential. Jeremiah told the Marines to use the Schroeders' house for rest and shelter. The gun trucks were clustered around it, draped with tarps from Schroeder's shed to keep the water out of the gun access holes cut into the canopy. The guns were taken inside to be cleaned and oiled.

... ...

Rebecca looked out the window of their cabin at the hill on the other side of the valley as she dried her hair with a towel after her shower. She could barely see the hillside through the rain and darkness. Jeremiah came out of the shower with a towel wrapped around his waist.

"It's beautiful," he said, putting his arms around her from behind and pulling her to him.

She put her cheek on his arm and pulled his arms tight around her. Then she turned around to face him. "Do you have to return, tomorrow?"

"No, not for another four days."

She kissed him passionately. When she was done, she said seductively, "We have some catching up to do, my warrior husband."

"Before or after we make love," he asked.

"I don't know," she whispered, rolling her eyes, then she kissed him again. "That's actually the kind of catching up I had in mind, unless you have other plans, of course."

"Let me check my calendar." He picked her up as easily as if she were a little girl and walked into the bedroom with her across his arms. He set her gently on the bed and started thumbing through an imaginary calendar in the air in front of him. "We're in luck, the rest of my day is wide open."

Rebecca pulled off her robe and stretched out on the bed. “Well, that makes two of us. Come to bed, Jeremiah.”

Chapter 17 – We Wait

"Mr. Langly, Mr. Disney will see you now."

Kevin got up and walked into Mr. Disney's office. Elias Disney became CEO of the Walt Disney Company after the previous CEO was killed during the Three-Hour War. He was the great-grandson of Walter Disney.

Elias got up and walked around his desk to shake Kevin's hand. "Mr. Langly, this is an honor. I don't get to meet many Nobel Laureates. Have a seat. What can I do for you?"

"I have an idea for a unique ride. I thought I would see if you have any interest."

Mr. Disney cocked his head, a bemused smile on his face. "OK, you have my attention. What's your idea?"

"A free fall portal through the center of the Earth to Australia and back."

Elias stared at Kevin, then out the window of his office in Burbank, California, for a full two minutes without speaking. "If anyone else had suggested this, Mr. Langly, I would have laughed and shown them the door. How would it work?"

"We dig a shaft, say ten feet in diameter, almost straight down in Disneyland for, say, five hundred feet. No big technology there. At the bottom of the shaft is a Rosy portal synced to the bottom of another five-hundred-foot shaft in Australia. Perth is the point in Australia closest to the exact opposite side of the Earth from Anaheim, California. The actual opposite side is about a thousand miles west of there, in the southern Indian Ocean. People would jump into the top of the shaft in Anaheim, free fall five hundred feet, accelerating by gravity. They would reach about a hundred and twenty miles an hour. After they pass through the portal, the gravity that had been accelerating them would begin decelerating them until they reached the top of the shaft in Perth. They would be motionless for a split second, then gravity would pull them back toward Anaheim. They would bounce back and forth until you pulled them off at one end or the other."

"The lawyers would have a field day when someone got hurt. It's too unsafe to allow someone to free fall. They could hit the side of the shaft, spin out of control, collide with someone else, and what would happen if the power to the portal failed after the person began their free fall?"

"Well, the portal stays open and functional for five seconds after power is cut. If the power failed at the instant the person left the top of the shaft, he would still pass through the portal before the Rosy field collapsed. But to make it even more reliable, we could power it with its own Rosy energy portal. You could build a sensor system that would detect where in the shaft a person is and use air jets to move them back to the middle when they stray to the side. Or maybe the solution to the safety issue is to have two shafts. One for certified skydivers who sign a bulletproof liability waiver. And one for everyone else. The 'everyone else' ride would have a capsule that would invert at the other end so you would come back to Anaheim heads up."

"Only one person could go at a time. It would never make enough money to cover the construction costs. And the lines would be out of the park."

"So build more of them. Or... " Kevin got a faraway look. "The fall only takes about ten seconds from Anaheim to Perth. Even going back and forth a couple of times, you're only talking about a minute and that would get boring after one or two rides. But if you had a killer roller coaster on the Anaheim side that would do a ninety-degree turn straight down into the Earth only to pop out going straight up into a killer roller coaster on the Perth side, then do the whole ride again *backwards*. Now that would be a ride everyone would want to go on again and again. And all riders would be buckled in. No safety problems. A hundred people could go at a time. And the seats could begin facing in either direction—two completely different rides."

It was Mr. Disney's turn to get that faraway look in his eye as he envisioned The Roller Coaster Through the Center of the Earth. Nothing like this had ever been conceived before. Using the

Earth's own gravity to accelerate and decelerate the ride. A thousand-meter gravitational trampoline with no net! He could make it a theme ride from the Disney movie *Journey to the Center of the Earth*. Dinosaurs and giant spiders jumping out at people as they go by. A T-rex chasing the car into the opening to the portal. Boulders barely missing the occupants. A volcanic eruption on the other side blowing them out into Australia. A world-class restaurant/hotel where you can eat and visit Perth and vacation across the rest of Australia. And that would open up Australia to come to Anaheim to visit the full-blown theme park and greater Los Angeles area.

"Mr. Langly, your idea is fascinating. I'll have to run this by my design team, my legal team, and the board. If we decide to go ahead with the design, could you participate in the project with my team, as a consultant? I mean, we would do all of the work. I'm sure you are pretty busy."

"Absolutely. It would be my pleasure. And you might also consider hiring Douglas Medder. He designed the Rosy transportation portals that are in use all over Canada and the US. He's the one who figured out how to connect two ends of the portals together so they line up reliably."

"I'm sure having Doug as part of the team wouldn't be a problem. Thanks for coming by. I'll let you know what they say."

... ...

As *Señor* Lobo specified, the surviving bandits from the attack on Jeremiah's settlement collected at the Green Berets' compound. Five-hundred-seventy-one men left there to attack the settlement. Thirteen returned. Four of them were injured, one seriously. Neither *Señor* Lobo nor *Señor* Arturo were among the survivors.

"What do we do now?" one of the men asked. "Wait for one of them to show up?"

"If either one was alive, he would be here now," another said.

"I say we go back and kill those *pendejos*," an injured man said angrily. "They killed my brother! Look what they did to me!" He held up his blood-soaked arm.

"OK. You go back," a man with his arm in a sling said in disgust. "I've had my fill of Marines, their bombs, and their machine guns!"

"Mateo, settle down," one of the other survivors said to the guy who wanted to go back. "Everyone knew this wouldn't last forever, your brother included. I think it's time to think about Plan B. I say we go back to L.A. and see what's cookin'. Life is getting back to normal. Someone is supplying drugs and whores to the people who want to buy them. Someone is selling the stuff we stole. Let's find them and get on board. The vacation is over. Let's get back to work."

He looked around the group. Most of them were nodding. "I figure we need at least three cars or trucks. Who wants to go back to get them with me? It's raining and they think they won. No one will be expecting us to return. Or we can walk and find something along the way."

No one volunteered to go back—even Mateo kept silent.

"OK. It's walking then. We start in the morning. Everyone get something to eat from the Green Berets' survival food, then get to sleep. We got a long walk tomorrow. Daniel is going to need a ride. He can't walk on that foot."

"There was a garden cart in the Green Berets' shed. He can ride in that."

"Until we find a vehicle, we can take turns pushing and pulling it. It's mostly downhill to Sonora."

... ...

"Professor Flamé? This is Leann Jenkins."

There was a pause on the other end of the line. "Hi, Leann. Where are you? Are you still in the capsule?"

"No. The emperor of the galaxy decided to intervene on Earth's behalf. I am on his planet. He wants me to perform *Romeo and Juliet* for him. It will be telecast to all of the worlds of the Ur."

"By *yourself*? How will you do that on a stage?"

"I can't, obviously. That's why I'm calling you. I need you to assemble a cast and crew to put it on and send them here. They want me to play Juliet. And would you direct it?"

He was silent for a while, then he asked, "How many people will we be presenting it to?"

"I don't know. Maybe ten thousand in the on-site audience. There aren't that many people who actually live here on the emperor's planet. Across the galaxy, the emperor's chief of staff expects an audience penetration of somewhere around ten percent. That would be around 1.1 trillion people, but it could be more. He wasn't sure."

Professor Flamé coughed. "Excuse me? Was that trillion with a 'T'?"

"Yes. Trillion with a 'T.'"

"And all of them understand English?"

"No, of course not. They have translator computers that convert what we say into the thousands of languages in use. They even translate our inflections and meanings."

"Where exactly is the emperor's planet?" He asked. The enormity of the audience was still soaking in.

"I don't know. Lily said it was fifty thousand lightyears from Earth. It took the pilot a day to get here. He made a bunch of jumps."

"Let me contact some people who might be interested. I'll get back to you in one day. Is this a good number?" He checked the origin display. It said "Ft. Riley, KS."

"No. I'll have to call you. This is a Rosy phone that Lily brought along. It calls Ft. Riley and I call out from there."

"You mean you're still on the emperor's planet? Fifty thousand lightyears away?" That part hadn't sunk in yet. "You sound like you're next door."

"Yes. I'm on the emperor's planet. And we have to be good—no opening night heebie-jeebies. Shakespeare apparently tapped into a common thread of empathy that's present throughout the entire galaxy. This could generate enough good will that the emperor will change the elimination decree and humanity would be allowed to join the Ur."

"How long will we have to rehearse and design the sets?"

"We have six weeks."

"Call me tomorrow around now."

"OK. See you then. Bye...and thanks, Professor Flamé."

"Goodbye, Leann."

... ...

The entire crew aboard the BCI cruiser stared out at *Far Galaxy*. It had reached "ghost ship" status throughout the galaxy, like the *Flying Dutchman* on Earth. There were many on the crew who hadn't believed she even existed, that she was born from the imagination of old sergeants to terrify recruits as they began training.

Zarqa led them to *Far Galaxy* in a roundabout path. When the first place they'd arrived at was empty, she realized she'd transposed two digits in the coordinates. On her second attempt, they'd popped out of the wormhole about a kilometer from the ship.

The damage from the exploding lifeboat was plain to see—the side of the fuselage was peppered with holes. The engine cowlings were gone, testament to Flug's previous visit.

Now that they had found it, many of the crew wanted nothing to do with the abandoned starship, no matter what kind of reward or incentive was offered. Tales of ghosts surrounding and protecting the ship abounded during late-night storytelling sessions in the canteen. And the stories of the Admiral's daughter were especially gruesome. She was waiting inside for some hapless young explorer to rescue her. She would lure him into the captain's bedroom chamber from which he would never return.

"Is there any chance there's still power on board?" Agent Hlitatta asked Captain Huerrai.

Captain Huerrai was quiet for a few moments, considering the agent's question. "If the Hore energy portal was left on, it's still functioning. Hore energy portals don't like being shut off for long periods. The backup batteries go dead, then the portals can't start by themselves." He pressed a button on his belt. "Analysis, scan for energy portals."

"Negative, sir," the response came back a moment later. "The ship has no Hore emissions. No emissions of any kind."

"You told Fey Pey the portal doors were booby-trapped. Are they really booby-trapped or was that a diversion?"

"They are really booby-trapped, Agent Hlitatta. At least they were fifty years ago. And without any power, there's no way to turn them off and the trips were mechanical. The captain wanted the whole ship blown if it wasn't him coming back to salvage it. The only safe way in I can see to get in safely is to cut a hole in the hull. Can you get the plans to the ship from BCI archives? They would show us where to cut without hitting anything important."

"I'll ask BCI Central, Captain," the Executive Officer said, bringing up his communication hologram.

"Until the plans arrive, we wait," Agent Hlitatta told everyone.

... ...

"Captain Pey," the synthesized, metallic voice came through Fey Pey's communicator, "are the bribes in place?"

"Yes, Lord Quilp. The defenses around Quyl will be turned off in..." he checked his timer, "forty-eight minutes."

"And they will remain off?"

"We will have a fifteen-minute window. After that, we can expect the defenses to begin coming back online. The scans will reactivate first followed by the laser batteries, then the evacuation targeting computers."

"Fifteen minutes should be enough, Captain. Will the emperor be in his quarters?"

"He is expected to be. His schedule says he will have finished a meeting and will have twenty minutes of free time. That usually means he will visit his granddaughter in her classroom."

"How about the three cruisers? Are they disabled as well?"

The cruisers had been a problem for Fey Pey. Ever since the Yunia began attacking the galaxy, three military cruisers had been stationed around Quyl, the emperor's planet. Fey Pey had tried to find a way to disable them or smuggle people and bombs on board, to no avail.

"Their scans will be turned off, along with those on the planet and moons. Other than that, they will still be functional."

"Thank you for your efforts, Captain Pey. You will be rewarded appropriately."

... ...

A few minutes were unassigned until his next audience. The emperor walked into his granddaughter's classroom. The teacher and the other twelve children looked up as he walked in. They didn't care. The emperor was a regular visitor to the classroom. But his granddaughter wasn't there.

"She's with the actors," the teacher said. "The actors" was what the palace workers called the Earthlings.

The emperor walked over to the quarters that were assigned to the Earthlings. Leann was practicing her lines while the other five people were reading the parts of the other cast members of *Romeo and Juliet*. They were doing the balcony scene. President Robbins was reading Romeo's lines and thoroughly enjoying doing it. The emperor's granddaughter was sitting next to Lily and Patty while they watched the scene unfold. The play script was open in Gaye's lap. She was checking Leann's lines as Leann said them.

... ...

Corporal First Class Unigh Flassa was bored. She was watching her hologram of the area around Quyl—ships in, ships out: a steady progression of inbound ships delivering supplies for the emperor's staff and supplicants hoping to get one minute of the emperor's time, a steady progression of outbound ships, empty freighters, and disappointed supplicants. She sighed for at least the tenth time since she began her shift. Her cruiser, *Galactic Protector*, was one of three combat cruisers assigned to guard the emperor's planet since the Yunia began attacking the Ur's galaxy. She longed for actual combat. She had volunteered for it three times, but her captain wouldn't let her go. He said she was too valuable being bored watching this damned hologram. She sighed again.

She realized her hologram hadn't changed in a few minutes. She pressed the refresh button. Nothing moved very fast on a display covering the immense area that hers did. But they did change a little with each refresh. She pressed refresh again. Nothing. She called Systems.

"Thank you for calling Systems, all of our agents are busy. Please keep your communicator open and your call will be answered in the order received."

She ended the call and pressed refresh again. Nothing. No movement. She checked out the time display on the hologram. It displayed a value almost fifteen minutes ago. She pressed refresh again. Everything moved. She gave a sigh of relief, then noticed three new ships, ships that hadn't been there fifteen minutes earlier, were approaching the third circle. The third circle was the innermost controlled region to Quyl. The ships were within a thousand kilometers of the three cruisers.

Unigh pressed her comm button in panic and called the nearest ship. "Ship by waypoint AZ25-412, identify yourself."

There was no answer. A chill went down her back. She pressed the captain call button and alerted the evacuation batteries. The sergeant in command of the batteries had been bored as well. He didn't hear the alert button on his hologram. He was in the latrine enjoying a new porn magazine he received from a friend on another cruiser.

The captain returned her call. "What's happening?"

"The scans were down for fifteen minutes. Three ships have penetrated to the third circle. They refuse to identify themselves ... one of them just opened a Hore portal to within a hundred meters of us, Captain."

The combat alert sounded throughout the ship. The torpedo exploded next to the cruiser before the captain was able to reach the bridge. The other two cruisers disappeared in similar explosions.

... ...

The emperor's granddaughter gave the emperor a huge smile and waved just as the attack alert alarm sounded throughout the palace. The emperor looked up in confusion.

Beauhi recognized the alarm and its consequences. "Sire, come close." She motioned him to join her and the five Earthlings. "I can't protect you from there."

His granddaughter held out her arms to him. He walked to her and picked her up. Beauhi threw up a concealment spell around the group.

"We must be silent and motionless," she whispered.

The buzzing sound of laser batteries firing filled the air around the palace, until they stopped abruptly after huge explosions rocked the room.

... ...

After the Ur cruisers were destroyed, the laser batteries activated on Quyl's smaller moon. They were destroyed in a counterstrike as soon as they fired their first volley. The laser batteries next to the palace were destroyed in similar fashion. As the Yunia cruisers approached Quyl, the automated defense response systems on the planet sent one evacuation device after another at the Yunia cruisers. But before the Quyl devices were able to deploy, each device was evacuated into the sun by the Yunia's own evacuation devices, followed by the launch site from which the Ur evacuation device had been sent.

The combat troops on Quyl, the last line of defense around the emperor's palace, prepared to defend the palace on the ground. Their fortified emplacements were evacuated into their sun. In the course of half an hour, Quyl had gone from the most heavily guarded planet in the galaxy to defenseless.

Lord Quilp's voice filled the cockpits of the waiting squadrons of landing crafts. "Prepare to land. Kill anything that resists us. But *not* the emperor. We need him *alive*."

Chapter 18 – Perhaps You Should Hire Him

Several minutes after the laser batteries exploded outside the palace, the group of people protected by Beauhi's illusion spell heard the sounds of shouting and running feet in the hallway on the other side of the door. A laser firefight erupted.

The evil-sounding snap of a laser hitting a body was a sound no soldier ever forgets. The laser destroyed the immediate tissues around the strike point, of course, but it was the water in the tissues surrounding the strike site that did most of the damage. Within a microsecond of a laser strike, the water in those tissues turned into steam, which expanded with all of the power of an explosive round. The tissues around the strike area popped like a balloon, causing massive damage to the individual unlucky enough to have been targeted.

The snap-pop-scream went on for a while like popcorn in a pan, then slowly became less and less frequent. The barrage ended and the door opened.

A strange-looking, six-legged soldier with the two legs nearest its head used as arms scanned the room with its laser at the ready. "They're not here!" it called out, then left the door open and ran down the hallway toward the next room. Smoke and the smell of burned flesh filled the room from the hallway.

"What are those things?" President Robbins whispered to the emperor.

"The Yunia, I expect. I've never seen them before. We must leave here. There's an escape passage in the next room. Do you think we can get to it?" He remained motionless like everyone else.

"Where does it go?" Beauhi asked.

"To an escape lander, but I can't fly it. I don't know how."

"I can probably fly it," Gaye said.

He looked at her doubtfully. "Maybe the cruisers are still in action. My pilot is supposed to be down there waiting for me."

"I doubt the cruisers are still functioning, Sire," President Robbins chimed in. "Those Yunia soldiers wouldn't be down here if there was still fighting going on above this planet."

"Let's check the hallway," Leann suggested.

Beauhi walked across the room and peeked out the doorway cautiously. There was no one in sight. She heard some laser fire from around the corner. There were flashes outside, visible through the windows in the hallway. She prepared two separate illusion spells. In one, she put the image of the hallway to the right. In the other, she put the image of the hallway to the left. She cast them so someone entering the hallway from either end would see the other end of the hallway instead of them walking to the next room.

"Let's go. Those spells will degrade in a couple of minutes."

Once they were in the other room, the emperor opened the secret panel and led them into a dusty passageway. The panel closed behind them. The passageway wound down until they entered a vast cave with a complete lander in it. There was no exit path for the lander to the surface. There was about three feet of clearance between the top of the lander and the top of the cave.

"How did you get it down here?" Gaye asked in amazement.

"In pieces through a transportation portal that was carried down here one piece at a time." The pilot was nowhere in sight. "The pilot who was supposed to fly it must be dead or he would be down here."

Gaye walked around it. It was much newer than the model on which she had been trained. Or maybe this one was just cleaner. This lander was so new, it was still shiny. She pressed the ramp-open switch and walked into the lander, after the ramp extended.

"You guys stay out there," she called back to them. "I'm going to make sure the controls are the same as the lander I was trained on." She glanced at the people. They hadn't moved. "Maybe you should stand over there." She motioned to a spot against the wall of the cavern, protected by an outcropping of rock.

Everyone got her meaning and moved.

She sat at the navigator's station. The lander even smelled new. She brought up the navigational hologram and keyed in the coordinates of Earth from memory. The hologram was exactly like she had hoped. Halfway to Earth was Gargantua, the monstrous black hole.

She put her hands on the movement panels and the lander lifted off the ground about a foot.

"The ramp, Gaye!" Leann shouted. "Retract the ramp!"

"Dammit!" She pursed her lips, lowered the lander to the floor, and pressed the retract ramp button. "Going too fast. What else did I forget?"

She went over the mental checklist that Corporal Vibii made her memorize. Power supply—fully functional. Check. Air pressure—check for leaks. She closed the hatchway and did the check. Pressure was holding. Check. Oxygen generator. Check. CO2 scrubbers. Check. Emergency escape coordinates. She checked where they were set for: a close orbit around Quyl—probably where one of the cruisers was stationed. If the cruisers were destroyed, that would never do. She changed the coordinates to clear space about ten lightyears away from Quyl, then added four more in a zigzag, switchback path, changing directions in three dimensions, ending up about three lightyears away from Gargantua. The last preparatory task was to set her actual path to where she wanted to go. She drew a blank. Where the hell *were* they going to go? She opened the hatchway and walked out.

"OK, I can fly this. Where are we going?"

The emperor looked confused. This wasn't supposed to happen. His whole life, someone else had taken care of the day-to-day details. It was his job to worry about the big stuff: merging of civilizations and smoothing the trade relations between worlds.

President Robbins spoke up, "They will be expecting the emperor to bolt. They will be waiting for us to try and will follow us if they can. Can you evade them?"

"No one taught me anything about how to cloak our exit path." Gaye paused to consider her options. "But I know whom to ask. President Robbins, did you grab one of those two Rosy radios this morning. The ones we brought with us from Earth? They are linked to the command center at Fort Riley."

President Robbins had forgotten all about the two radios. This morning he put one on his belt today purely by habit. There had been a beeper on his belt for most of his adult life and he felt a little naked without one there. He handed the radio to Gaye. The other radio he brought with them was on the table next to his bed.

She pressed the power button, then the transmit button. "Hello, Earth. Come in Earth."

"This is Headquarters, Colonel Johnson speaking. How may we help?" The radio was on speaker. Everyone could hear him.

"Colonel Johnson, this is Captain Marshall."

"Hi captain, I thought you were off planet. What can I do for you?"

"We *are* off planet and we're in a jam. The Yunia have taken control of Quyl, the emperor's planet. I need to talk to the pilot trainer from the starship. His name is..."

"Who the hell are the Yunia?"

"Colonel, I can't explain that now. I need to talk to the pilot trainer, Corporal Vibii. He's on the starship. Can you patch us through?"

"Captain, have you been drinking? This is a joke, right?"

President Robbins grabbed the radio out of Gaye's hand. "Colonel Johnson, this is President Robbins. Connect us to the goddamned corporal."

"Yes, sir. He's in the next room sleeping off some beer."

"Take the phone to him, Colonel. Do it now—RUN COLONEL!"

Thirty seconds later, a sleepy voice came onto the radio. "Corporal Vibii, whaddayawant, Captain?"

"How can I hide the path of a lander?"

"Gaye?" the sleepiness was out of his voice in an instant. "I thought this was Captain Xanny."

"Nope, this is Gaye. The Yunia have taken over Quyl. The emperor is with us in his escape lander. We expect the Yunia are waiting for us to leave so they can follow us and capture the emperor. Is there anything I can do to hide our path?"

"A gravitational singularity left at your point of departure. But it will eat Quyl unless someone evacuates it."

She thought about the Yunia swarming through the palace, shooting anything that moved. The rest of the planet was unpopulated. "There's no one left on Quyl but us and the Yunia."

"Then you will have to do multiple, random-direction jumps. They will be able to see the direction you left, but not how far you went."

Gaye turned to the emperor. "Does this lander have any of those gravitational singularities Vibii is talking about?"

"I have no idea."

"Corporal Vibii, how would I know what a gravitation singularity looks like and if this lander has one?"

"What model is the lander?"

"How would I know that?"

"Press the setup button on the nav holo."

"You mean the button you told me never to touch."

"Yeah. That one."

Gaye did. "Merktobl Corporation. Model 43590-x0010."

"Wow. I've never flown anything that new. Is there a button on the setup holo that says armament?"

"Yes."

"Press it."

"Two lasers, two evacuation devices, three of something I can't pronounce. I'll try to spell it for you—ZHHGBDELIT."

"Excellent! Those are gravitational singularities. I figured they would be there on the emperor's escape lander."

"So how do I deploy them?"

"You only need one," he cautioned. "When two singularities get together, physics goes upside down. You won't like what happens. Bring up the main nav holo again. You will see the armament button, upper right. Let's go through the setup. You'll need to know how to use the other armaments also. Thank God, you're a fighter pilot."

Half an hour later, Gaye figured she was ready. "Everybody on board. We're leaving."

The people strapped in. The emperor sat with his granddaughter in his lap, his arms around her. Her eyes were huge and her lower lip trembled a little, but she wasn't crying. He held her hands as they waited.

Gaye retracted the ramp, sealed the portal, and lifted the lander off the ground. It bumped the ceiling of the cave. Everyone looked up, then back at Gaye. She lowered the lander a bit, then moved it to the end of the cave without bumping the ceiling again. She wanted to have the longest acceleration distance when they left. The door at the other end of the cavern opened and twenty Yunia soldiers poured out into the cave. They started firing at the lander. She let loose a blast from the laser cannons at the ceiling above the soldiers. She was expecting a real blast, like a rocket or cannon would have made. All she heard was a faint hum. The ceiling exploded, then collapsed onto the soldiers. She chuckled. "Now these lasers are something I could get used to!"

She moved the lander to where the collapse happened and studied the rubble. The arm of one of the soldiers, still clutching his laser, stuck out from under a large rock. She extended the ramp again.

"What are you *doing*, Gaye?" Lily asked in alarm. Every moment they delayed was another chance for the Yunia to capture them.

"I've got to get a tissue sample," she called back, sprinting down the ramp onto the floor of the cavern and pulling her pocket knife out. She grabbed the arm, sliced a finger off, and ran back to the lander, clutching her prize. "No one knows what their DNA is like. Corporal Vibii said there were standing orders to get a sample at the earliest opportunity."

Lily felt vaguely nauseous, not really believing what she had just witnessed.

Gaye retracted the ramp and moved the lander back to the end of the cavern. "Here we go, everyone. Hold on!"

"Trigger the Hore field generator now, Gaye," Vibii called out from the radio. "Remember, it takes five seconds to activate. Direction is more important than speed. Set your jump direction down the long axis of the chamber. You have to get to passage speed before it opens the portal."

She activated the Hore jump field generator, then started accelerating carefully. With only a foot-and-a-half of free space under and over the lander. The lander had to rotate as she accelerated and avoid the rocks blown from the ceiling by her laser blast. She scraped the ceiling, then the floor. One of the landing pads clipped a rock on the floor. The other end of the cavern was coming at her way too fast.

Gaye leaned forward and pressed the release button to deploy the singularity. The end of the cavern looked like it was ten feet away. She threw her arms up, bracing for the impact, then the Rosy aura from the Hore jump field activated the portal and they were blown into clear space by the atmosphere in the chamber. The nav hologram showed they were ten light years from Quyl.

A pleasant voice came across the shuttle PA system, "Hull breach. Twenty minutes until total loss of atmosphere."

The pressure inside the lander was dropping. The O2 generator kicked on full blast. She had left the radio on for just such an emergency.

"Vibii! What do I do?" she asked a little too loudly. Her training had never addressed a hull breach.

His voice came back, clear and calm. "There's a sealant kit under one of the seats."

Everyone reached under their seats to search for it.

"Got it," Lily said loudly, holding up the kit.

Corporal Vibii continued, "Gaye, press the flashing blue warning button on your hologram. It will expand until it's a picture of the lander."

She did. The navigational hologram was replaced with a hologram of the lander. A blue area flashed on both sides of the ship. Apparently one of the Yunia lasers had found its mark.

"Turn off the artificial gravity."

"Hull breach," the voice told them. "Nineteen minutes until total loss of atmosphere."

"Can I turn off that message?"

"Later. Turn off the gravity."

She did. Her ears popped with the decreasing air pressure.

"Now shake some of the powder in the kit into the area near each leak. Watch where the dust goes. Do NOT put your finger on the leak! There is a tube of glue in the kit. Squeeze that into the hole. It will dry as soon as it hits the vacuum outside the lander."

"Stay where you are, Gaye," Lily told her, pulling Leann out of her seat. "We can do this."

"Hull breach," the announcement continued happily. "Eighteen minutes until total loss of atmosphere."

They released their belts and floated up to the area indicated on the hologram. Both of them heard the air escaping through a quarter-inch hole in the hull. They didn't need the powder to tell them where it was.

Leann pulled a panel off the wall. The hole went through a relay box. She couldn't get at the hull.

"Hull breach," the announcement told them. "Seventeen minutes until total loss of atmosphere."

"I can't get at the hole. I need a screwdriver!" Leann was on the verge of panic.

"I've got one," Lily called out. She pulled the multitool out of her belt holster, extended the screwdriver, and handed it to Leann. "Remind me to kiss Kevin when we get back home. He gave this to me when we graduated from Stanford."

Leann unscrewed the cover screws and wrenched open the relay box. The hole went through the back of the box, then through the hull.

"Hull breach," the announcement said. "Sixteen minutes until total loss of atmosphere."

They were down to seventy-five percent of normal pressure. Leann squirted some glue into the hole. The hissing stopped, then the plug was blown through with a pop. The hissing started again.

"Try this." Lily held out a patch about two inches on a side. "It was in the kit also."

Leann squirted some glue around the edge of the patch and slapped it onto the hole. The hissing stopped, for good this time.

The other hole was much easier to access. Leann used another patch in the kit.

The pressure began coming back up.

Leann was pumped! "Just like fixing my bicycle tire when I was a kid!"

"For the record, there was a toolbox in one of the lockers," Corporal Vibii told them. "But Gaye, you have to jump again. Right now! They will be following your exit path from Quyl. But they won't know how far you jumped because of the singularity. Get the hell out of there. Do the jumps we set up. Then come to Earth. Captain Xanny will know what to do."

Gaye executed the preplanned series of Yunia-confusion jumps. Corporal Vibii had modified the ones she set up, making them even more random. She dropped a new singularity after each set of two jumps. After the sixth crisscrossing jump, she began her careful navigation around Gargantua. By the time they reached Earth, the emperor was asleep with his granddaughter across his lap.

"GSMS-77, This is the Imperial Lander. Request permission to board."

"Imperial Lander, the deck is open. Welcome back, Captain Marshall."

"Sergeant Fo, is that you?" Gaye asked. His voice greeted her like a welcome home.

"The one and only. I wouldn't have missed the arrival of the emperor on Captain Xanny's ship for anything. Been a little exciting around here getting ready."

"Been a little exciting around here, too."

"I've heard. You did well, Captain. Congratulations."

… … … … … … … … …

The Hore energy portal had been reactivated and most of the holes in the hull of *Far Galaxy* crudely repaired. The ship held pressure for now, although the ship still couldn't move, since the Graftium was removed from the drives. Flug, Agent Hlitatta, and Zarqa were on the bridge ready to see if the computers could be brought back to life. Flug was in the Tech's seat. He pressed the power-up button for the master console computer. Nothing happened. He pressed it again. Still nothing.

"Let me try, Flug," Zarqa suggested.

"What else is there to try?" he asked, irritated. "It's a frigging button."

She gave him "the look" and rolled her eyes. He got up.

She opened the panel where the button was mounted. Someone, probably the captain before he left, had pulled the link to the computer off the back of the button. She pushed it back on, then pressed the button again. The tech hologram appeared in front of her.

"Starting main computers," the hologram announced. "Enter current star-date."

Zarqa entered it.

"Damage found," it told them a few moments later and began listing the damaged areas.

"It's got to do this. It's part of its turn-on procedures. We can't access anything until it's done. But while we're waiting, Agent Hlitatta, you could call Fleet Command and get the master decryption key for the ship's data store. Then we can copy *Far Galaxy*'s memory stores into the cruiser's."

Fifteen minutes later, the hologram ended with, "Graftium missing from main drives. Drives inoperable."

Zarqa set up a link to the cruiser's storage.

"Computer, decrypt and copy all data in memory store to storage on linked ship."

"Local or master decryption key is required. Do you want to copy the data in their encrypted form?"

Fleet Command had sent the master decryption key to Agent Hlitatta's communicator. He held it up to the hologram. The key exchange took place.

"Master decryption key accepted. Substorage named 'Captain's Data' is separately encrypted. Do you want to copy the data in their encrypted form?"

Zarqa rolled her eyes again. The captain had set up a private encryption key for his personal data beyond the ship's encryption key. That was *so* against military regulations.

Flug considered the problem. The captain had been more stubborn than creative. "His son's name was Eaple," he said, spelling the boy's name.

She tried it.

"Decryption key not accepted. Do you want to copy the data in their encrypted form?"

"What was his wife's name?" Flug muttered to himself. "Kalluia? Klullia? Klushia! I think that was her name. Try that."

She tried it.

"Decryption key not accepted. Do you want to copy the data in their encrypted form?"

"BCI can crack the key," Agent Hlitatta told them impatiently. "It's what they do."

"Try it backwards," Flug suggested. "He was always entering things reversed."

Zarqa tried the son's name backwards.

"Decryption key not accepted. Do you want to copy the data in their encrypted form?"

Zarqa tried the wife's name backwards.

"Decryption key accepted. Substorage named 'Captain's data' will be decrypted and copied," the computer reported.

… … … … … … … … …

"Lord Quilp, the emperor has escaped."

"How did this happen, General Asga?"

"The pilot left a gravitational singularity in the subterranean shelter where the escape lander was housed. We were able to track the lander to its first exit point by using the squadrons of fighters to sample the vacuum. We got lucky and found an expanding cloud of atmosphere at one point. Someone must have hit the lander with a laser. We picked up the next trajectory and found the exit point for that one as well. The next trajectory contained another singularity at its exit point. We were unable to track the lander beyond that."

"Was there any order to the exit points, General?"

"No, Lord Quilp. The pilot was apparently experienced in escape tactics. The exit points displayed no pattern that we were able to determine."

"I thought the emperor's pilot was killed in the fighting."

"He was. We don't know who was flying the lander. He was very good. Not many pilots could have exited that underground shelter without catastrophic damage to the lander. He was able to pilot the lander to escape velocity in a cavern a mere meter taller than the lander while under fire from the team tasked with capturing the emperor."

"Perhaps you should hire him to train your pilots, General."

General Asga didn't know if he should laugh or not. Lord Quilp had never displayed anything close to a sense of humor. He decided to change the subject.

"Sire, about the singularity in the subterranean shelter. I must evacuate it or it will eat the planet. Some of the palace will be damaged."

"Do it now, General. Salvage what you can. I need some quiet. I must prepare my report for *our* emperor."

"By your command, Sire."

Chapter 19 – Yeah. Sure. Whatever.

Agent Hlitatta watched the video of the confrontation between the Mellincon and Sergeant Tannl during the attempted stealing of the laser while the lander was on Taramon. This was perhaps his twentieth viewing. The confrontation was obviously staged. His cop instincts kept bringing him back to this one piece of evidence. But he was missing something. He didn't know what it was and it was driving him crazier than having the emperor on board. People were constantly coming and going, interfering with his crime scene and investigation.

This must have been when the torpedo that almost destroyed GSMS-77 was taken from the lander. It was really the only window of opportunity. If he could prove that Lieutenant Fibari didn't try to blow up her own ship or have anything to do with the demise of Zindarr, he could offer her immunity for her testimony against Fey Pey. He had no doubt that her time with Fey Pey wasn't quite as unsullied as she would have him to believe.

He went over the things he thought were true about Lieutenant Fibari's visit to Taramon, in no particular order, and put them into the hologram hanging in the air in front of him.

According to the ship's clock on the video, the first confrontation happened about an hour and a half before Lieutenant Fibari returned with Zuna.

The second confrontation took place after Lieutenant Fibari returned to the lander.

The Mellincon was part of Fey Pey's crew.

The torpedo was on the lander when they arrived at Taramon.

It was gone when they arrived at GSMS-77.

The missing torpedo was *not* the one that blew up Zindarr, but it *was* the one that almost blew up GSMS-77.

The torpedo that blew up Zindarr was from a pirate/BCI confrontation that took place fifty years earlier. And the pirate was never identified.

Lieutenant Fibari had trusted Sergeant Tannl enough to leave him in charge of the lander while she went to Pirate's Alley to talk to Zuna.

Lieutenant Fibari was away from the lander about three hours.

That same period was missing from all of the spaceport security recordings and their backups.

Zuna's coven put everyone to sleep on *Easy Wind* so Lieutenant Fibari and Sergeant Tannl could rescue Flug and Zarqa.

Lieutenant Fibari and Sergeant Tannl were aided by the witch on board *Easy Wind* who said her name was Ruatha but, in actuality, her name was Plew. She refused to accompany them to Zindarr, but she told them about the torpedo on Zindarr.

The four of them, Lieutenant Fibari, Flug, Zarqa, and Sergeant Tannl, went to Zindarr and warned Kallisha.

Kallisha found the torpedo and said it was protected beyond her ability to deactivate it. She started an all-planet evacuation. She tried to charge King Amon for the cost.

Beauhi left with Lieutenant Fibari.

Zindarr blew up after a single evacuation ship was able to depart.

The fake BCI crew showed up shortly after the news reported Fela had escaped from Zindarr before the explosion. The fake BCI crew were, in fact, a team from Fey Pey who killed the real BCI team and tried to kidnap Lieutenant Fibari, Zarqa, and Flug. The Mellincon from the Taramon confrontations was the same Mellincon as the fake BCI agent. Plew was apparently part of the crew on *Easy Wind*.

Sergeant Tannl facilitated the escape of the team from Fey Pey. Plew helped him with the locks on the lander.

Agent Hlitatta knew a lot but it was not enough. He started listing the outstanding questions.

If Plew and Tannl were working for Fey Pey, why would they help Lieutenant Fibari rescue Flug and Zarqa? Why would Sergeant Tannl go to Zindarr knowing it was going to be blown up?

Obviously Lieutenant Fibari was *supposed* to rescue Flug and Zarqa. Even if the ship had not been put to sleep, he suspected Lieutenant Fibari would have been allowed to escape with the prisoners. The sleeping crew may have been staged. Why? What was in it for Fey Pey?

The only thing that made sense was that Lieutenant Fibari and her companions were supposed to go to Zindarr. And the only reason Fey Pey would want that to happen was so they would be killed by the explosion. Or take the blame for the planet's destruction. But Sergeant Tannl was with them. Why would he accompany them if they were supposed to be blown up with the planet? He wouldn't, obviously. So they weren't supposed to be blown up at Zindarr. Unless Tannl didn't expect Fey Pey was going to blow up Zindarr.

When the news feeds announced that Lieutenant Fibari had escaped, Fey Pey captured a BCI lander and sent Plew and the Mellincon to kidnap them. And when they couldn't kidnap them, they tried to blow them up again with the second torpedo.

Why would he take such a chance? It all came down to Lieutenant Fibari. Fey Pey wanted her out of the picture. She must know something that was particularly damning to him. Lieutenant Fibari was Executive Officer for Fey Pey for three years almost fifty years ago. She said she saw him do awful things. There was probably a case for making her an accomplice, but no one knew what Fey Pey had done. And without any corroborating witnesses, it was his word against hers. Which pirate would you believe in court?

He needed some real proof. Something that would hold up to courtroom scrutiny. Previously he always watched the video starting at when the Mellincon showed up to steal the lasers. This time he started it from five minutes before the Mellincon showed up. He stared at the landing gear of the lander on the next pad. Nothing moved. Not a being walked by. Five minutes later, the Mellincon appeared, looked both ways, and then approached the laser. Agent Hlitatta blinked. The shadow from the landing gear on the next pad moved just before the Mellincon showed up. The ship's time in the display only changed one second, but the shadow from the landing gear moved a good thirty minutes farther toward sunset from where it was a moment before the Mellincon arrived. He backed up the feed and watched it again. Then he noticed a second thing. The camera on the lander next door was aimed directly at Fela's lander.

Agent Hlitatta picked up his communicator and pressed the speed link to the agent on Taramon. "Ghoti, what ship's lander was to the north of Lieutenant Fibari's lander?"

There was a pause. "*Kaneabris*, I think. Let me check." A moment later he returned. "Yep. *Kaneabris*. They're still here. They're going through a refit. They said their computers were down when I asked them for their feed two days ago."

Agent Hlitatta recognized the name. *Kaneabris* was one of those marginally legal ships that made a living by finding and salvaging the satellite and ship debris that was floating around every colonized Ur planet like a cloud. Some of it was actually very valuable. But most of it was worthless trash. There were many complaints that *Kaneabris* sometimes "salvaged" functioning satellites, but no one had ever proved anything. *Kaneabris* probably considered themselves pirates, which was why they were trying to protect Fey Pey, another pirate.

"Honor among thieves," he grumbled, wondering if the idiot captain aboard *Kaneabris* knew Fey Pey would sacrifice both *Kaneabris* and its captain without a moment's hesitation or remorse.

Agent Ghoti answered him back. "Excuse me, sir?"

Agent Hlitatta came back to the present. "Send an agent to their ship—no, wait. I want you to go to their ship with a combat team. Do it immediately. I want the unmodified camera feed for the period Lieutenant Fibari was on Taramon. Take a Customs lander and tell them you are Customs until you board. Don't tell them what you want until you are in the ship's data center with all comm to the rest of the ship cut off. I don't want anyone to have the chance to delete or modify their video. And don't let them tell you their computers aren't functional. Take some heavy techs with you. If it's encrypted, bring it in its encrypted form. As soon as you get it, send it to me. And don't forget to check the lander. It may still be in the lander's data store, even if they deleted it."

"Yes, sir."

... ...

The space around Earth was filled with Ur battleships, cruisers, and destroyers. The emperor was in constant meetings with the admiralty about the Yunia. As a courtesy, because they were the heads of the remaining governments on Earth, President Robbins and the Prime Minister of Canada were allowed to attend the meetings. Neither the president nor the prime minister had spoken yet.

The admiral of the fleet was giving a presentation about the defenses around Earth's solar system. He was a large male lion in his adult prime. "If they come from any direction, we will detect and repel them. We have over three hundred ships covering all possible avenues of attack."

President Robbins couldn't stand it anymore. "Why are you waiting for them to attack you? Why aren't you attacking them? You will never win a defensive war."

The admiral tried to ignore the president and continue with his presentation.

"Admiral Nam," the emperor interrupted. "President Robbins has asked a question that has bothered me since the Yunia started attacking us. Please answer him."

"Because we don't know where they are, Sire. If we did, we would attack them."

"How many battles have taken place with the Yunia, Admiral?" the emperor asked.

"Eighteen, Sire."

"And how many of their ships have been destroyed?"

"We're not sure, Sire. No one has returned from those battles to tell us."

"Why is that?"

"We're not sure, Sire. They may have a weapon we don't know about and have no defense against. They may...we just don't know, Sire."

"Well then, why don't we find out," President Robbins suggested.

"How would *you* suggest we *do* that?" The sarcasm in the admiral's voice was hard to ignore.

"That's easy, Admiral. We set a trap and watch what happens."

"Are you suggesting we sacrifice one of our ships and crews simply to find out how the Yunia kill it?"

"Well, not exactly. Don't you have a starship graveyard where you put the old out-of-commission ships?"

"Of course."

"How much work would it be to make four or five of them functional again, enough to make a small taskforce? Populate it with computer-driven human simulations. Have them show up at a known Yunia stronghold and take pictures of what happens next. Knowledge is power, Admiral. If you don't know, find out."

"Except for one thing." The admiral spoke slowly, like he was talking to a child or an idiot. "We don't know where they are."

"I'd bet they are still mining data from my computers on Quyl," the emperor interjected. "Could we use Quyl as our testing bed? And along the way, put a photon torpedo into Quyl. There's too much that's too valuable there to just give it to them."

The admiral hesitated. Showing disrespect to a leader of this primitive world was one thing. They weren't even a member of the Ur. He couldn't do the same thing to the emperor.

"I will give your idea to my planning team, Sire. They may decide this is a good way to go."

The emperor put his hands together in front of his face, thinking. He reached a decision. "Admiral, you have one day to put this plan into action. My computers on Quyl have the keys to our galaxy. They have the troop strengths, armaments, and location of every outpost and combat ship in our fleet. It has the access passwords and decryption keys for our whole military network.

But the most damning thing that was on those data stores was everything we know about the Yunia, which isn't a pile of shit in a snowstorm. They will know how much we *don't* know about them and use that against us, too. If it hasn't already, that information must be prevented from falling into their hands. If you can't get retired ships to populate the raid, I will use yours and you will be on it. Am I clear?"

The admiral's face was red. His mouth was opening and closing like a fish out of water. Finally he said, "Yes, Sire. I understand. I must leave this meeting at once to set this in motion."

"One day, Admiral," the emperor told him again. "You have one day."

Admiral Nam picked up his communicator and left the meeting without saying another word. The rest of the room of advisors was silent. The stress of the Yunia attack on Quyl was showing on everyone. No one knew where the next attack would be. It might even be here on Earth. No one believed the Admiral—that the attack would be repelled.

President Robbins decided a little levity might break the tension. He turned to the emperor. "There is a curse known to a group of my species." The emperor looked at the president blankly. The president continued. "It goes like this: May you live in interesting times."

"Interesting times!" the emperor chuckled. "Yes, I understand. 'Bored' is a luxury I rarely get to enjoy. There are days when I wish that something, anything, on my schedule didn't involve the survival of billions, sometimes trillions, of beings."

... ...

The communicator on Agent Hlitatta's belt buzzed, indicating he had received an encrypted message. He pressed the decryption key to retrieve the message and play it. It was from BCI headquarters.

"Agent Hlitatta, we have recovered the signature of the ship *Far Galaxy* was pursuing from the data recovered from *Far Galaxy*.

The signature is consistent with *Easy Wind*—with less than one thousandths of one percent chance of error."

Well, Agent Hlitatta thought to himself, rolling the ramifications of the message over in his mind, *That means we can charge him with four counts of murder and kidnapping for the deaths of the people on the lifeboat and multiple counts of attacking an Ur warship for four days, both death sentences. But we still don't have him possessing the torpedo. That would lead to a charge of genocide.*

His communicator rang again. "We have recovered the camera feed from the lander. They had deleted it, but it was still in the lander's storage, like you thought it would be."

"What does it show?"

"It shows the Mellincon and four others, including Sergeant Tannl, removing the torpedo and replacing it with the placebo circuit. Then it shows them doing the singeing of the Mellincon's fur with the laser." The agent laughed. "They rehearsed it twice. By the end of the second filming, there wasn't much fur left."

"Excellent work, Agent Ghoti."

"Do you want me to arrest the captain of *Kaneabris* for lying to the BCI and interfering with a BCI investigation?"

"No. I want you to impound his ship and tell the captain he has three days to find out where Fey Pey is or he will be charged with conspiracy to commit murder, five hundred times, conspiracy to commit grand theft for the attempted destruction of a starship belonging to Grock Corporation, and conspiracy to possess a weapon of mass destruction. The torpedo Fey Pey stole from the lander was intended to kill an entire starship and its crew, but it could just have easily been used to destroy a planet and the people on it, like Fey Pey did with Zindarr. And let's offer him something positive for his help, too. If he does turn up Fey Pey, tell him he will get his ship back *and* the reward. The reward should be up to a couple of million Huz by now. And it will probably double when I tell BCI headquarters about the video feed you found."

"Yes, sir."

… … … … … … … … …

"I don't know where he is!" Captain Pild screamed. "How can I tell you where he is if I don't know?"

"Not my problem, Captain. You have three days." Agent Ghoti walked to the door of the captain's quarters. Without breaking eye contact with the captain, he opened and closed the metal door several times. The door made a heavy clunk each time as it closed. "Get used to the sound of metal doors closing, Captain. You're going to hear it for a long, long time. If you have any favors to call in, now would be the time. Someone knows where Fey Pey is. You have to find out who it is and get him to tell you."

"I'll need a lander."

"Only if we can put a tamper-proof, linked-Hore tracer in it."

"You don't think he'll find it? Are you stupid?"

"Not this one, he won't. That's the deal. You interested? I'm kind of hoping you don't find him." Agent Ghoti looked around the captain's quarters. "I've got an uncle who would love this ship, especially since your refit is almost complete. Probably get it for a tenth of its value."

Captain Pild stared at Agent Ghoti in disbelief. This had been his ship since he murdered the owners and stolen it a hundred-and-fifty years ago. He realized that there was really no choice. He shrugged. "Yeah. Sure. Whatever. When can you get the thing installed?"

"I think it's already done. They started the installation before I came in here. It's installed in the same lander that took the pictures of Fey Pey's crew stealing the torpedo. Remember that one? The one with the video you ordered deleted? All the rest of your landers have been disabled and sealed. And I wouldn't try to remove the tracer. You won't like what happens if you do. And there's one more thing."

"What's that?" Captain Pild asked in resignation.

Agent Ghoti pulled a vial from his jacket and poured a pill onto the table. "Swallow this."

"What is it?"

"A neurotoxin. It will kill you in about five seconds if you get more than a kilometer away from the lander or take longer than three days in your search."

Captain Pild picked it up and examined it. "Will you turn it off when I get back?"

"Sure." Agent Ghoti smiled broadly. "And because you're cooperating so fully, we'll even remove the tracer, too."

Captain Pild popped the pill in his mouth and swallowed it.

Agent Ghoti held his communicator up to Captain Pild's body and scanned it. The pill was in his stomach. A red light came on the display indicating the pill was attached to the stomach lining.

He picked up his communicator. "Link the pill to the transmitter."

A voice over the communicator came back in ten seconds. "Linked."

Agent Ghoti opened the door to the captain's quarters. "See you in three days, Captain Pild."

"One kilometer isn't enough. I'm going to have to be all over Pirate's Alley. Make it ten."

"OK. I can do that." Agent Ghoti picked up his communicator again.

Chapter 20 – Bait

The fleet of five Ur cruisers popped into space above Quyl. All five were under remote control from Admiral Nam's battleship, *Emperor Xull*, which was sitting in clear space about a lightyear away. The shielded, linked-Hore feeds gave them a complete view of the planet area in nine different formats. All five cruisers started launching evacuation devices at the fleet of Yunia ships. The devices were easily deflected until two devices arrived at the same ship at the same moment. The ship disappeared amid wild cheers by the Fire Control section aboard *Emperor Xull*. Their celebration was short-lived. The five cruisers and their feeds disappeared moments later, just before the planet Quyl erupted into space as three of the five photon torpedoes sent to the surface by the Ur cruisers detonated.

Lord Quilp watched the expanding cloud of debris from the planet's explosion with frustration. The data transfer from the emperor's computer center into his starship's computers was only minutes into the task.

"How much did we get, General Asga?"

The general checked the feed. "Something on the order of three petabytes, Sire."

Lord Quilp sighed. That was not nearly enough. The emperor's datastore had contained several hundred thousand times that much. "When will you have it decrypted so we can see what the lives of the people on the surface and in that cruiser bought for us?"

"The decryption teams have started on it, Sire. And we've started the transfer back to Sibia. They should crack the encryption before we do."

"Have the sniffers begun following the inbound trails of the five Ur starships?"

"Yes, Sire."

"If they find anything, let me know."

"Yes, Sire."

Lord Quilp went back to his view of the destruction of the planet. The molten center was still expanding. The Ur had sacrificed five cruisers to destroy the emperor's planet and the information stored there. The first casualties were inflicted on his fleet. As much as Lord Quilp didn't want to believe it, he was faced with incontrovertible evidence: the generals of the Ur were learning how to fight. The conquest of this galaxy was going to take longer and cost more than the Yunia leadership had expected. How much more, only the future would show.

He spread his wings in frustration then emptied the poison reservoir at the end of his abdomen. The poison production was an automatic reaction to combat in his species. It wouldn't do to have any pressing bodily functions interfere with the status update to his emperor. He knew what her reaction would be. "Unhappy" didn't begin to describe it.

... ...

Doug watched the drone hover silently in midair in front of him. There were no propellers, turbines, or rockets. It was powered by a dark energy portal and supported by the anti-grav drive. Kevin and Doug had created the anti-grav drive after studying the anti-grav unit in the lander and the schematics in the repair manuals.

He moved the drone left, right, up, then down. He sent it to the end of the lab and back. He deployed the grappling claw and picked up a pencil. The pencil dropped out of the claw and fell to the floor. Doug sent the drone after it.

Kevin and Venkat watched Doug exercising the drone. Venkat was from Canada. Doug had met him while he was deploying the Rosy transportation portals to connect the surviving military bases in the US and Canada. Months before, Venkat had joined Kevin, Doug, and Lily to help create the Rosy internet backbone that was replacing the fiber optics internet infrastructure across North America. The fiber optics switching centers were blown up during the Three Hour War.

"Doug, the building's on fire." Kevin said.

Doug did not react at all, his concentration on the drone was all encompassing.

"Doug, there is a king cobra crawling up your pant leg." Still no reaction. Kevin turned to Venkat, chuckling. "Sometimes you have a discussion with Doug and, in the middle of the discussion, you realize Doug isn't listening anymore."

"He is a brilliant man," Venkat said reverently. "Very proud am I to be working with you two."

"You're not too shabby yourself, Venkat. We never would have gotten the Rosy Internet working without your help. Did you hear Verizon wants to use it to replace their trunk lines that were destroyed in the Three-Hour War? I expect AT&T and Sprint to do the same thing. You're going to be a rich man."

"A rich man with no children. Who cares?" he said sadly.

Doug turned to them. "I wonder if I can get it to do a flip." He tried and the drone crashed into the floor, shattering into pieces.

"Well, maybe you shouldn't do that with the next one, Doug," Kevin suggested.

Doug started picking up the pieces and putting them onto the lab bench, triaging them into piles of ruined, salvageable, and still OK parts. "I think the problem is that we never got the anti-grav unit to reverse its thrust. It doesn't behave like an electromagnet. With an electromagnet, when you reverse the polarity, you reverse the poles."

Kevin bent over to help Doug pick up the pieces. "How about we make the drone a sphere and put six anti-grave emitters on it, one for each of the six directions. Then the computer can adjust the thrust to them based on whatever is down and where the pilot wants to go."

Doug stared at Kevin for a moment in silence. "Kevin, that's brilliant! You build the unit. I'll program the on board computer. We should be able to test it tomorrow. The on board computer will figure out what I want and accommodate it."

"USB interface to all six?"

"Yeah." Doug scratched the stubble on his chin. "That'll let me control each one independently."

"Let's go to work, Venkat," Kevin said, getting up. "Daylight's burnin'."

Venkat coughed. "Uh, Kevin? Have you been outside lately? The sun is being down for over an hour." He held his hand up to his forehead like he was shielding his eyes from the imaginary sun. "I am seeing another all-night building session on the horizon."

"Battle stations, everyone," said Kevin, pulling a plastic mixing bowl over his head and swatting at imaginary drones buzzing around him. "The fabulous, fantastic, never-to-be-believed, upside down, downside up, anti-grav ball is about to become the next wonder of the world!"

Venkat shook his head. "Kevin, you are non-stop entertainment."

"Let's get to work."

They both looked at Doug. Doug was staring at his computer screen, completely absorbed with his program modifications. The world around him, the world beyond his computer screen, had ceased to exist, replaced by a massive case statement that would control the six emitters based on the navigator's commands and the direction of gravity down. "First I have to establish the orientation of each emitter to down … "

… … … … … … … … …

The bar was smoky. Captain Pild sat in the corner, nursed his queetle, and considered his options. None of them were very good. This was the sixth bar he had been into on Pirate's Alley. No one admitted to seeing Fey Pey in at least four weeks. Actually, it was even worse than that. After he asked and they said no, they left quickly and went different directions. He glanced at the clock on the wall. The seconds were ticking by.

It's amazing how fast time goes by when you want it to slow down. If you knew you were going to die in one minute, each second would be something you'd cherish, something you would try to grab as it went by. "Hey, wait! Don't go!" you'd be shouting as each one slipped through your fingers.

"You want another queetle?" the bored bar maid asked, snapping him out of his reverie. She was covered in tattoos. Even her face.

"How long did it take?" he asked.

"Huh? My tats?" she laughed. "God, days at a time for months." She paused as a question occurred to her. "Why? You want one? I know a good tattooist here in the Alley. She's a real artist. Give you something to remember."

"No time," Captain Pild said to her, a tinge of sadness in his voice. "Waiting for someone."

"So you want another queetle while you wait?"

"Sure. What difference does it make?"

She left, walking toward the bar.

A woman slid into the booth on the other side of the table from him. She was a primate—big, muscular, and hairy with almost purple skin, maybe a heavy-worlder. Her eyes were completely dilated and black. It felt like she was staring right through him. "You lookin' for Fey Pey?" she whispered hoarsely.

He studied her. "Yeah. I've got a message for him."

"He's off-planet. He won't be back for a couple of days."

Captain Pild sighed hopefully. "Would a 'couple of days' translate to less than three?"

"Why?" she asked, suddenly suspicious. "You in a hurry?"

"I have to leave in two and a half days," he said. "If it's longer than that, it won't matter. I won't be here."

"Give me your name. If he shows up before that, I'll let him know you want to see him."

"Tell him Captain Pild of the *Kaneabris* wants to see him."

"*Kaneabris*, huh. I've heard of her."

"We've worked this side of the galaxy for over a hundred years. I met Fey Pey a couple of years ago when I was selling some satellite parts I 'found.' He was able to find me a buyer and only charged me twenty percent."

"Where will you be, if I need to find you?"

"Either here or in my lander at the spaceport, on pad 13-BD."

"I'll let you know." She slid out the booth and walked out the front door of the bar.

The barmaid came back with his bottle of queetle. She set it on the table and looked around. "Your friend leave or does she need a bottle as well?"

"How much do I owe you?" Captain Pild asked.

"Ten Huz," she answered.

He pulled the money out of his pocket and paid her, then he picked up the bottle, drained it, and walked out of the bar. At the back of his mind, a clock kept going tick-tock. It was driving him crazy. "A couple of days." That's what the woman said. A week ago, a couple of days wouldn't even have been an irritation. Suddenly, "a couple of days" was the rest of his life. Captain Pild wasn't used to being on a schedule. He wasn't used to answering to anyone else for anything. He didn't like it.

"I'm too damn old for this shit," he muttered, walking into the next bar.

... ...

"Jeremiah, do you have to leave tomorrow?"

Jeremiah tried to wake up. Why did women always ask this stuff just as their men were falling asleep? He sighed and collected his thoughts. "Yep. I told Captain Rousselot we'd be back in a week."

"But what if the bangers come back?"

"They're long gone, Rebecca." He rolled over and put his arm around her, spooning their bodies together and cupping her breast. "Why don't you come back with me," he whispered into her ear. "We'll get a place together and set up house. It'll be like the old days."

"And do what? Get a job waiting on tables? Wait for someone to tell me you were killed by some asshole who wasn't ready for law and order to return to his little piece of the pie? Why don't you stay up here where it's safe? The Marines will be fine without their newest second lieutenant."

"I can't do that, Rebecca. You know that. My country needs me."

"I need you, too, Jeremiah. Doesn't that count for anything?"

"It counts for a lot." He squeezed her. "I missed you so much. I thought someone had killed you or worse. I met Josephina."

Rebecca sat up in bed and twisted around to face her husband. "Josephina? Josephina Sanchez? Really?"

"Yeah. Her uncle and his militia supported us while we cleaned out the gangs from Santa Clarita."

"How was she?"

"She's fine. At least she was. She had a crush on Freddie. He kept trying to keep her at arm's length. She kept trying to make it a lot more personal. She's the one who showed me your picture and told me you were on your way up here. She told me all about you saving her life. If I hadn't met her, I never would have come back up here trying to find you."

"Small world."

"So will you come back with me?"

She was silent while she considered life without Jeremiah again. She lay back down in the bed and resumed her spoon position, pulling his arm around her. She came to a decision. "If I come back with you, I will volunteer to be a Marine."

It was Jeremiah's turn to be silent. He pulled her over so they were face to face. His expression was very serious. "If that's what you want to do, I will support you a hundred and ten percent. Of course, as soon as you enlist, we can never make love again. That would be fraternization."

She giggled. "Then I guess we better do it while we can. Think you're 'up' for it?"

… … … … … … … … …

The emperor was ecstatic. "No new weapons, Admiral Nam! Just evacuations. And we took out one of their cruisers with ours."

President Robbins was deep in thought. "I may have an idea for you to use against the Yunia."

The admiral started to say something, but the emperor held up his hand. “What is your idea, President Robbins?”

“I’m not particularly proud of what I’m about to say, but here goes. My country built a series of remote launchers for bombs. We had ten launch silos, each with ten bomb launchers in them. The remote silos would send a bomb to a remote relay launch site that would send the bomb to where it was intended. The sites we were attacking would see a bomb sent at them from the remote site, but not from the silos. They would send a bomb back at the remote site. As soon as one remote site was taken out, another remote site, in a different location, would take over the bomb delivery function. This technology was also put in place by at least four other countries on my world. It directly led to the war that devastated Earth.”

Admiral Nam snorted and looked away.

The emperor ignored him. “Please continue, President Robbins.”

“Here’s my idea. Let’s build a bunch of remote launchers. Launch *them* into space near the Yunia fleet. They will acquire a target and launch evacuation devices at the Yunia, one ship at a time. If we hit each ship with twenty or thirty evacuation devices concurrently, they won’t be able to defend themselves and they will be evacuated into the sun. When one remote launch device gets evacuated, we send another one to a different location nearby, replacing the one that was taken out. They talk to each other via linked-Hore radios so they coordinate their attack on one cruiser at a time. The cruisers, sitting a lightyear away, would be feeding them the evacuation devices as fast as they can be passed on to the Yunia starships. In fifteen minutes, the whole fleet could be annihilated.”

“And what happens when the Yunia figure out where the feeder cruisers are located?” Admiral Nam asked. “That would take *our* cruisers about thirty seconds to locate and destroy any remote launching device.”

“How about a double indirect system?”

Admiral Nam stared in disbelief.

President Robbins had to bite his tongue. This guy was like some of *his* generals. There was always a reason why an idea they didn't have wouldn't work. "You said they could figure out where a remote launcher was being fed from. What if we built a system where the cruisers fed a remote launcher that fed a second remote launcher and that one was the one that targeted the Yunia fleet? I am assuming that would take a little longer, especially if they weren't expecting us to use a double indirect system, *especially* if they were under intense pressure from the rest of the launchers."

"And when they do figure it out? Will you tell the parents of the people on the cruisers why their sons and daughters were killed?"

"It's a battle, Admiral Nam, not a police action. It cost us five cruisers to take out one of theirs in the battle around Quyl. You have to expect some casualties. But we can limit the exposure by jumping to another location, say every five minutes. We should make *them* suffer the 5:1 loss rate next time."

The admiral couldn't hold back anymore. "And how, pray, will you encourage the Yunia to send a battle fleet into your little trap, President Robbins?"

"To set a trap, all you need is bait. The more tempting the bait, the better the trap. They've already shown they want the emperor. All we have to do is show them where he is."

"You want *me* to be the bait?" the emperor asked, shocked.

"No, Sire, of course not. But I want the Yunia to *think* you are." President Robbins paused, taking a moment to collect this thoughts. "We will need a world that can be sacrificed without costing billions of lives. Do you know of one we can use?"

Chapter 21 - Fey Pey Wants to See You

"Lieutenant Silverstein reporting for duty, sir." Jeremiah saluted sharply and stood at attention in front of Captain Rousselot's desk. A duffel bag was slung over his shoulder.

"Welcome back, Jeremiah. How was your week off?"

Jeremiah coughed. "It wasn't what I expected, sir."

"Did you find your wife? Was she OK?"

Jeremiah chuckled. "Yes, I found her, sir. She's fine. I brought her back with us."

"What's she going to do now?"

"She wants to join the Corps, sir. At least that's what she said on the way down here. But about the week off. It wasn't quite as relaxing as I'd hoped, sir."

Jeremiah related to Captain Rousselot the chronology if his trip—about retrieving the personnel at the Mountain Warfare Training Center, then about repelling the gang attack.

"I have their IDs and personal effects here." He patted his duffel bag.

Captain Rousselot patted his desk. "Let's see what you got."

Jeremiah opened the duffel bag and poured the contents onto Captain Rousselot's desk. The wallets and personal effects of the people who had died in the attack covered the top and overflowed onto the floor.

After the last of it came out of the bag, Jeremiah said, "I didn't know what to do with this stuff. I'd hoped you would know."

Captain Rousselot stared at the pile without speaking for a while. "How many of those guys did you kill?"

"Four hundred twelve, sir. We also have fifteen injured and fourteen captured. We brought them back with us."

"Let me get this straight. The fourteen of you killed four hundred and twelve of the gang members that had been attacking the settlements in the Sierras? And captured twenty-nine prisoners?"

"Well, we got some help from the people who lived in the settlement and a few got away."

Captain Rousselot stared at the pile of wallets, IDs, personal effects, and the scattering of dog tags that some of the ex-military gang members were still wearing when they died. The command was getting a lot of heat from local leaders about the Marines using unwarranted deadly force. The captain figured most of it was because the Marines had taken out the criminals that were supporting the corrupt local government leaders.

There was a call to attention in the company orderly room outside of Captain Rousselot's office. A knock came shortly after.

His first sergeant stuck her head in. "I'm sorry to interrupt, sir. There's a Major Goodman here to see you."

Captain Rousselot came around his desk and opened the door. "Major Goodman, welcome to Charlie Company." He saluted sharply, then held the door open. "Please come in. What can I do for you?"

Major Goodman returned the salute and walked into Captain Rousselot's office. He nodded to Jeremiah. "I wanted to tell you what a fine officer Lieutenant Silverstein is. He rescued me and my staff from the Mountain Warfare Center, then kicked the asses of the murderers and rapists attacking his wife's settlement. I will be submitting an after action-report that includes a recommendation that you submit him for the Bronze Star. If there is any question about what happened or if there is any doubt about the justification for his decision to use deadly force against civilians, let me know. Those assholes deserved every bullet they got. The only reason the lieutenant and his men returned to you unscathed is because of the fine leadership and planning Lieutenant Silverstein displayed. We were vastly outnumbered by a battle-hardened, heavily armed aggressor force. He kept a cool head and led his men to a resounding victory that I suspect saved the lives and property of every settler between Sonora and Lake Tahoe. His performance brought great credit upon himself and the Corps. We only lost two friendlies in the entire battle. Those were from a mortar the aggressors were using."

Captain Rousselot was amazed. "A mortar? They had a mortar?"

"And squad and heavy automatic weapons they stole from the National Guard armory in Bakersfield. There was even a TOW missile system in one of their vehicles. Lieutenant Silverstein used surprise, overwhelming firepower, and entrapment to engage and overcome the enemy. He and his men performed in highest tradition of the Corps. I would be proud to have Lieutenant Silverstein in my command."

"You helped too, sir," Jeremiah spoke up. "Without your reconnoitering, we never would have known what to expect. And you kept the people who were flanking us from coming up the hill."

"I was glad to do my part, Lieutenant Silverstein. Mostly I sat back and watched you make the right decisions for the right reasons at the right time. If you hadn't, I would have intervened. I didn't have to. Your success in the battle is witness enough to what you did and said."

Captain Rousselot didn't know what to believe. Four hundred-twelve dead civilians was going to be a hard sell to battalion. "I need to debrief the other members of your squad, Jeremiah."

"I have a video of the entire battle, sir, if that will help. One of the civilians in the settlement, a woman named Amy Johansson, caught the whole thing on her cell phone camera. We have loads of after-action photos and I saved the dash cam feeds from the three trucks."

"Not Amy Johansson—the author?"

"Yep, the same person. She said she was going to base her next book on the battle. She said the Marines are going to love it."

"My wife has every book she ever wrote."

"I wish I'd known that. She offered us all a signed copy of her last book while we were leaving. I didn't know anything about her. I turned her down."

Major Goodman stood. "I have to leave, Captain Rousselot. I will send you a copy of my report. I have to submit it to General Blakesly, my commander."

"Where is he stationed, Major?"

"The Pentagon."

Captain Rousselot pursed his lips. "The Pentagon is gone, Major, along with most of the east coast from New York to North Carolina. We think the aliens were cleaning up the nukes someone dropped on Washington."

Major Goodman sat back down, shocked. "My God. I had no idea." He hesitated for a moment. "But that explains a lot. Even our emergency radios, the ones that were supposed to be manned 24-7 in the Pentagon, weren't being answered. We didn't know what was going on, why we didn't get any response."

"You could submit your report to the base commander here," Captain Rousselot suggested. "He would love some good news for a change. After the Three-Hour War and the gangs took over, everyone wanted us to bail them out. They beat up General Langlitz every day over the lack of progress. Now that law and order is restored, they want us to get the hell out of their business."

"Until they get in over their heads," Major Goodman said to them. "Then they'll want us to come running to help like a trained attack dog. Are they really calling it the Three-Hour War?"

"Yep."

"Damn." He got up again. "I guess I ought to report to HQ and see how I can help."

Captain Rousselot stood and saluted. "Thanks for filling me in on what happened up there, Major Goodman. That cleared this mess up a lot."

Major Goodman saluted back and left the office.

Jeremiah was still standing. "I'll go create an after-action report, sir. When do you want to talk to the rest of my team?"

"Now. Have them report to the orderly room and tell them not to talk about what happened until after I talk with them."

"Yes, sir." Jeremiah saluted and left.

... ...

"I won't do it!" Doug said quietly.

Everyone in the room turned to look at him, not understanding.

"I won't help you make a new weapon. You turned our last invention into a weapon and it destroyed our world. And the emperor is the leader of the government that gave humanity its death sentence. Why should I help the people who did that to us? Clara and I can never have children because of the Ur."

President Robbins spoke into the silence that followed Doug's announcement. "Doug, the Ur are the only hope we have to get our fertility back."

"Do you even know if they can reverse what they did?" Doug asked. "The way I see it, the Yunia are God's way of punishing the Ur for being a corrupt, self-serving government that benefits no one but itself." Doug paused. He hadn't said the Earth's governments had reaped the same reward for their selfish exploitation of wormhole technology, but the words were hanging in the air. "They let a *fish* give us a death sentence while *another* fish planted the dream that would cause us to be failed *after* he had already raised up our replacement species. How can the Yunia be worse than that? Hell, they might be better." He turned to Lily, Kevin, and Venkat who were sitting next to him. "You guys can make up your own minds. As far as I'm concerned, they can go fuck themselves. I wouldn't help the United States turn wormholes into weapons and I won't help the Ur do it either."

"I'm with you, Doug," Kevin said emphatically.

"Me, too," Lily said, putting her hand on Doug's and staring belligerently at President Robbins.

"I am with them also," Venkat said, putting his hand on Lily's. He tried to smile at the president in apology, but his hand was firmly on the pile.

Kevin reached across Doug and added his hand to the stack, symbolically cementing their unity.

Doug glared at President Robbins from behind the stack of hands. "We need something that shows the Ur's good intentions. You get them to give humanity back its fertility and give Earth full membership in the Ur or we don't help."

Doug pulled his hand back. The rest did also. All four of them stared at the president, waiting for his response.

President Robbins considered what his next move would be. No one else on Earth understood wormholes like these four. Rosyville was a hole in the desert. The emperor did not reestablish his communication lines to the rest of the galaxy's civilian centers after the demise of Quyl. No one in the command structure wanted the Yunia to be able to find where the fleet and the emperor were hiding. Without contact to the science and technology developers of the Ur-controlled galaxy, there wasn't a chance of developing the remote repeater station functionality without the help of these four scientists. And without that, the Ur had no chance of defeating the Yunia. This might be the club he needed to get the Ur to release the cure for BSV and give Earth an admission to the Ur.

"If I get a promise from the emperor that he will give us the antidote for the infertility virus and give us full membership into the Ur, will you agree to work on the project?"

Doug was skeptical. "Is his promise binding on the Ur? I thought they were equal in power and neither controlled the other."

"I don't know," President Robbins responded thoughtfully. "In the absence of Congress and the Supreme Court, I have binding powers over the operation of the United States. I would expect he has the same kind of authority."

Lily spoke up. "If he said those things, would you believe him?"

"Yes, I would," President Robbins answered without hesitation.

She knew he was lying. Beauhi had taught her how to watch people's aura and what changes happened to it when they told a lie. When a person said the truth, their aura turned pure sky blue. The less truthful the person became, the more their aura turned nonblue. Red indicated anger. Yellow indicated doubt. Orange was doubt and anger. Green was hope what was said was the truth, but deep down you doubted it. Purple was a pure lie. The deeper the purple, the more deliberate and malevolent the lie. President Robbins's aura was green with tinges of purple.

She decided to see how far he would lie. "Really? You would trust them so completely? President Robbins, you ran for president on the promise to stop the lying. Do you really trust another politician to tell the truth?"

The president hesitated again. He was also having major doubts that any promises made by the emperor in the heat of the moment would be implemented after the crisis was over. If he said that, these four would walk out. He decided his only chance was the almost full truth.

"Lily, I don't know if the emperor will honor any promises made to us under duress. I understand your doubt. I guess I misspoke when I implied I would believe him without question. But I don't know that we have much choice. The Ur is a democracy. Even with its faults and corruption, a democracy is still the only form of government that attempts to represent the people it governs and be bound by their wishes. We don't know anything about the Yunia and they aren't talking. In the absence of any other information, I would rather go with the devil we know than the devil we don't know. But I will ask the emperor for his promise for both our admission to the Ur and the antidote for the infertility virus. I don't know what else I can do? Do you?"

The president's aura was much more blue than it was before. There was still something he wasn't telling them. Maybe that was as honest as a politician ever got.

"I want you to have Beauhi in the room when you ask him," Lily told him. "She will be able to tell us if he means what he says."

"All I can do is ask," he said, rubbing his temples. "But I *will* ask."

... ...

Captain Pild had drunk too much queetle. He staggered out of the bar and stood swaying in the alley, looking one way and then the other. He didn't recognize either one.

How the hell did I get here? he wondered.

The night had become fuzzier and fuzzier as it progressed. The hallucinogenic chemicals in the queetle were affecting his eyes. The lights in the alley were changing colors and the floor of the alley was moving up and down. Captain Pild dropped to his knees and puked. He hadn't been this wasted in a long time. He didn't know how to get back to his lander. Not that it mattered. This was the end of the third day. Tonight was the last night of his life.

He tried to focus on the puddle of puke in front of him. "What th' hell did I *eat*?"

The various shapes and colors swam in front of him. "That isn't Pite, is it? Please, somebody tell that isn't Pite."

He coughed and spit, trying to get the taste of puke and Pite out of his mouth. Pite was a worm that grew in the manure of a pachyderm on a world in arm one of the galaxy.

"What'm I complainin' 'bout? This jus' makes up fer all th' times I shudda died and didn'."

He struggled to his feet and wiped his mouth, grabbing onto a light post to keep the world from moving quite so much. Pirate's Alley had been a long shot for finding Fey Pey. That fish was so hot he glowed in the dark. If he knew what was good for him, he was in another galaxy.

The moon was coming up over the end of the alley to his right. He started staggering toward it. Was the spaceport to the east or west of Pirate's Alley? He couldn't remember. If he walked to either end of the alley he was on, he could be going toward the spaceport or away from it. A medium-sized pachyderm came out of another bar and stood stretching and farting. Elephant farts, once they start, went on for a while and smelled as bad as elephants did.

"Whic way's th' spaceporrrt?" Captain Pild slurred, grabbing onto the pachyderm's arm for support.

"It's that way." The pachyderm pointed at the other end of the alley.

Captain Pild turned in that direction.

While the captain was distracted, the pachyderm emptied Captain Pild's pockets with his trunk.

"Hey! Whddaya doin'?" he shouted, "Gimme back m' money!" He swung drunkenly at the elephant, then grabbed at his empty laser holster.

"Looking for this?" the pachyderm asked, waving the laser over his head as he walked away.

"Bastard!" Captain Pild screamed.

All he got back was laughter. He tried to decide if the pachyderm had been telling the truth or not. He decided it really didn't matter and started walking in the direction the pachyderm pointed. Ten minutes later, he was as lost as when he started. Halos that sparkled and changed colors moved around the lights.

"Whoever laid out these streets was an idiot," he muttered.

A cloth bag was pulled over his head from behind.

"What the *fuck*?" he screamed, striking out with his fists. This night was *not* turning out like he wanted.

A woman's raspy voice whispered in his ear. "Shut up, asshole. Fey Pey wants to see you."

Chapter 22 – Let's Stay in Touch

"We won't help you against the Yunia unless we get two things." President Robbins told the emperor. Beauhi sat quietly at the president's side at the conference table.

The emperor had been expecting this. He even knew what those two things were, or he thought he did. He sighed. "You want your fertility back and membership into the Ur."

"Correct. Can you agree to them?"

"Of course, I can. And I do. Effective immediately, Earth is a member of the Ur. Your fertility reversal will have to wait until the crisis with the Yunia has been dealt with. I have no way to contact the genetics lab to tell them to create the reversal virus."

"Can't GSMS-77 do the reversal now?"

"No, I'm sorry to say they cannot," he told President Robbins, brushing aside the question. "They have the virus to set the infertility in place, but not the virus to undo it. But I have a question for *you*. What are you going to do about the aquatic mammals that were raised up? Your species hasn't done very well dealing with variations among your own species. How are you going to mutually coexist with another sentient species who will expect and demand equal rights and privileges? What are you going to do when they demand you stop polluting their homes with the waste from your factories and cities?"

"It will be a learning experience for both of us," the president said confidently. "But we will make it work, somehow." He didn't tell the emperor that this was his biggest concern also. Scenes of black people getting lynched filled his nightmares with the black people morphing into dolphins crying out for help as they died. "We want it in writing."

The emperor pressed a button on his communicator. A hyena walked in with a piece of paper in her mouth. The emperor waved his hand over the paper. His signature appeared. He handed the document to the president. "Here you are."

The president got up from the table, contract in hand. "I will ask Doug, Kevin, Lily, and Venkat to begin development on the weapons."

"When do you think a trial of the new technology can be demonstrated?"

"I'll let you know."

"The Yunia may show up at any time."

"I will let you know, Emperor Cabliux. I have confidence that these scientists can produce technology that will allow us to overcome the Yunia. They are the best we have."

President Robbins and Beauhi walked out.

"He was lying," Beauhi said to him. "Not about the Ur membership, but about the infertility virus reversal."

"I know. What difference does it make? It's our only chance. Maybe he'll help us when the dust settles. Do you see any alternative?"

They walked in silence to the lander where Gaye waited to take them back to Earth.

... ...

As much as they disliked being part of the effort to build new weapons with Rosy, Kevin, Doug, Lily, and Venkat were doing their best to supply what the president had promised and make it work. Kevin and Lily, especially, hated having to spend even more time away from their daughter, Lan. She was being cared for during the day by a young woman from Manhattan, Kansas, named Pájara Benito. Her mother was a colonel at the hospital on base. Lan liked Pájara very much, almost too much, for Lily's taste. Pájara treated Lan like the child she would never have. Lily found herself liking Pájara in spite of her reservations about Lan having two mothers for the duration of this effort.

"I have an idea about them tracing the source of the indirect fire," Doug said thoughtfully, staring at the Mt St Helens photo they had taped on the wall of the lab. "The double-indirect technique may not be necessary."

Kevin and Venkat glanced up from their work on making the remote launchers jump to a new location after each launch of an evacuation device. As soon as they arrived at their new location, they would sync to the mothership, receive a new evacuator, launch it, and jump again. It wouldn't be at the new location for more than ten seconds. They called it the Jumping Jack.

Doug's face was covered with that faraway look he got when his brain was working at warp speed. "What if the repeater station detected a wormhole opening near it and evacuated itself and whatever comes out of the wormhole? In addition to taking out the attack module, the evacuation would take with it all vestiges of where the evacuation devices were coming from that it was forwarding to the battle. We could use my wormhole detection resonator to know when the attack module appeared."

"What's the point?" Kevin asked, trying to understand. "All you're doing is what the Yunia wanted to do when they sent the evacuator at the remote launcher."

Doug shook his head. "Yeah, you're right. A dumb idea."

"Why aren't they using dumb bombs like we did in the Three-Hour War?" Kevin asked. "No emissions to detect. Send those bad boys right up the ass of those Yunia ships. End of story. End of problem."

"I was having the same idea," Venkat said to them. "The Ur says it won't work—that the ships can deflect a wormhole opening up inside their ship." He left out the part about the general ridiculing him in front of the entire command center for suggesting it.

"Did you ever watch a game of beach volleyball?" Lily asked.

The other three stared at her, wondering where the question was going. Lily never asked a question without having a reason for asking it.

"I was beach volleyball king of Marin County," Kevin said proudly, sucking in his gut.

All three of them stared at him in disbelief. Kevin was overweight and couldn't run a hundred yards.

"Hey, what's with the looks?" he asked. "I used to be a jock before I turned into a nerd."

"Then you'll remember how to block a spike?" Lily asked.

"Sure, you jump up at the same time as the opponent. When he smashes the ball, it hits your hands and gets deflected right back at him."

"Exactly," Lily said with an evil grin. "The general said every starship can deflect a wormhole opening within it. But we don't have to open a wormhole into their ship. When they send an evacuation device at our repeater, they've already done that for us. And wormholes go both ways. Why don't we send them their own evacuator back through the same wormhole? Every wormhole stays open for at least five seconds. All we have to do is deflect their evacuator back through it like a volleyball. A little high explosive should create enough pressure to send it back without damaging it in the process."

"We can do better than that, my love," Kevin said with a huge grin on his face. "As soon as the wormhole opens, how about we send a solid fuel rocket right up their ass through that same wormhole—instantaneous ignition, very deadly. Much better than their own evacuator, which they can probably turn off, or even a laser, which may or may not hit anything important. I could add a wormhole sniffer in the guidance mechanism. The wormhole wouldn't even have to be right next to the launcher when it opens. It detects the wormhole, fires, and goes right through—a little rocket-express love letter right into their launch room. I dub that one The Orient Express in honor of my wife."

Lily had been a Chinese national until she was smuggled out of her homeland in the middle of the night, right before her parents were arrested as dissidents.

Venkat was a little overwhelmed by Kevin's vehemence. "Please make sure your rocket won't be following the linked-Hore portal to the mothership, Kevin. That would not be a good thing."

"Yeah. Good point," Kevin agreed, making a note. "I'll make sure it ignores the link to the mothership."

"Another thing we must be doing also," Venkat reminded them. "We must make the remote unit evacuate itself into the nearest star if the link breaks to the mothership or if the unit is captured. Simple self-destruction is not enough. We must not allow these launchers to be captured and replicated by the Yunia."

"Also if the mothership gives the repeater a self-destruct command," Kevin added. He remembered the debacle of the bomb launchers during the Three-Hour War and the president not being able to turn them off.

Doug was staring out the window. He hadn't been listening to them at all. "Lily, remember when we lost our first Rosy wormhole generator?"

She grimaced at the memory. It happened while they were graduate students at Stanford. They had discovered wormholes only a couple of days before and were trying to figure out what they could do with them. "Yeah. We opened up a wormhole into space, a million kilometers out from Earth. The generator, the laptop, even the power supply for the laptop got blown out into the vacuum. You were pretty mad. You'd just bought that laptop. Then our advisor, Dr. Johnson, walked in the door right after the generator disappeared and wanted to see it work."

"So what would happen if we opened a wormhole into the middle of a star?"

She went pale. "That would be like opening a wormhole into the middle of an exploding nuke."

"And if the wormhole generator was right next to a Yunia starship when it did that?"

"End of starship," Kevin said quietly. "Nothing could withstand the force of a star in full burn with a couple of trillion tons of pressurized hydrogen at twenty-something million degrees exploding out through the wormhole."

"OK. Here's my idea," Doug said. "We launch a wormhole generator so it's in a direct line between the star and the Yunia starship we've targeted. The generator opens two wormholes about a half a second apart. The first one would go to the Yunia starship and the second one, a half a second later, to the center of the nearby sun."

"Five seconds later, the Yunia wouldn't know what hit them," Lily said. "That's what we found out about wormholes that day at Stanford. Five seconds to open. Five seconds to close. How close can we get to the starship before they can deflect the end of the wormhole?"

"I don't know. We'll have to check," Doug continued. "The wormhole generator would be vaporized, but the wormholes it generated would stay open for another five seconds. And there's no way anyone could find where the generator had been launched because the explosion from the star would obliterate any traces of the wormhole that was used to launch the generator."

"And there's no defense against it," Kevin added. "because nothing actually comes through the wormhole until the twenty-five-million-degree blast from the center of the star shows up half a second after the wormhole opens. Let's call that one the Fry Daddy."

Venkat chimed in. "The only thing we would be having to worry about is how we are getting the coordinates of the starship so the wormhole generator could put the end of the wormhole next to the Yunia starship."

The four of them pondered that problem.

Suddenly Doug spoke up. "That's easy! During a battle, there are wormholes opening everywhere. All we have to do is make sure this thing targets the bad guys and not the Ur starships or remote launchers. But I just thought of something else. If we can find a Yunia base, we send tiny listening posts all over the solar system waiting for the Yunia starships to open any kind of wormhole. The listening posts will collect the coordinates of all wormhole activity, then periodically open a shielded, linked-Rosy communication channel to the mothership. It may take a day to collect enough data points to predict the orbits of the Yunia starships and bases. Once we can predict where they are going to be, the mothership launches the dual-wormhole generators to the correct spot, one for each starship and base. Voilá, they all go up in smoke."

"Doug," Lily asked, "when does your wormhole detector detect the wormhole?"

He furrowed his brow, trying to understand what she was asking. "What do you mean?"

She restated her question. "We know it takes five seconds to open the wormhole. And the wormhole exists for five seconds after the generator shuts off. When, in that five seconds of start-up time, does your detector figure out a wormhole is being created? At the end of the start-up five seconds, at the beginning, or somewhere in between?"

"I don't know," he said. "I've never bothered to find out."

"Let's find out. If it's before the end of the five seconds, I have an idea."

They set up a generator and a detector. Venkat powered on the generator. One second into the start-up cycle, Doug's detector went off.

"But we don't know if it was detecting the generator or the far end of the wormhole," Doug protested.

"That means we do the old thousand-meter test," Kevin suggested. "Like we did at Stanford."

They set up a detector a thousand meters away and sent a wormhole right next to it. One second after the start of the wormhole, the detector went off.

"OK," Lily said, "here's where I was going with this. How about combining our two ideas? We launch a repeater somewhere between the Yunia starship and the sun. We have it launch an evacuator at the starship. They deflect it and respond with an evacuator of their own. As soon as the wormhole starts to form next to the repeater, the repeater opens a wormhole into the sun. The Yunia wormhole opens and, one second later, the starship gets a sunburn to die for. And if they figure out what's happening and quit trying to take them out, we deluge them with evacuators being fed from the mothership until one of them works."

"We could also put a nuke on the repeater," Kevin suggested. "If the repeater can't get into a straight line between the Yunia starship and the sun, it could pop the nuke when the Yunia wormhole opens. A sun only needs twenty-five million degrees to continue its fusion reaction because of the incredible gravitational pressure at the center of a sun. A nuke has to reach somewhere around a hundred and twenty-five million degrees to make the fusion work because it doesn't have the gravity. A hundred twenty-five million degrees should do the dirty deed. I name that one the Bar-B-Que."

Lily slammed her hand down on the table, an expression of pure hate on her face. "I think we should build all of 'em. Hit 'em with everything we've got. If they figure out one, we'll have four others that will kick their ass. This is *our* galaxy, goddammit! They attacked us!"

Doug gasped in shock. He hadn't wanted to create any weapons and now they had created a series of them that would undoubtedly kill countless Yunia and proliferate nukes again. He had gotten caught up in the gestalt of their creativity and forgotten what they were really doing.

"I have to leave for a while," he said, looking like he was going to throw up. "I'll see you guys tomorrow."

… … … … … … … … …

"Why did you want to see me, Captain Pild? What was so important that you asked for me all over the Alley for three days?"

The voice of Fey Pey was unmistakable. Captain Pild figured they were still in Pirate's Alley somewhere. They had to be. He was still alive even if the cloth bag was still over his head.

"The BCI wants to talk to you," Captain Pild told the voice.

"And that is a surprise to me, why? My name and picture are on every hologram in the galaxy."

"I don't get the idea they want you for that. I think they're terrified of the Yunia. I think they want you to help them set up a trap."

"Are you wearing a transmitter, Captain Pild?"

"No. My lander has a tracer though. They planted a neurotoxin in me and gave me three days to find you. If I fail, the toxin gets released. What time is it?"

"It's 15:30." The voice was indifferent.

"I have twelve minutes left to check in or I'm dead."

"Could you set up a linked-Hore meeting between me and the BCI agent that you're dealing with?"

"Probably. How would I connect to you?"

"I'll give you a shielded linked-Hore communicator. It will take them ten minutes to break the shielding and trace it to my location. That should be long enough."

"I have to leave now or I won't have a chance to get to my lander in time. I won't be able to deliver your message or the communicator."

"Then you better leave, Captain Pild. The communicator is next to you. You are already in your lander."

Captain Pild's hands were cut free and the bag was pulled off his head. The black primate walked out of the lander without saying another word. Fey Pey was nowhere to be seen.

"He must have been talking through a communicator carried by the primate," Captain Pild muttered as he got clearance to leave. Two minutes later he was exiting from his second jump. The BCI cruiser was a hundred meters away. Every laser on the side of the cruiser was aimed at him.

"Open the frigging landing deck!" he screamed. "I need to talk to Agent Ghoti! NOW, ASSHOLES!"

… … … … … … … … …

"President Robbins?"

"Hello, Dr. Hehsa. What great news it is that the CDC has survived intact after the Three-Hour War!"

"Yes, sir. We have just been given access to the secure military Internet and voice network."

"That's terrific! What is the status of the CDC? We didn't know what became of you."

"We are alive and well, sir. The 82nd Airborne rescued us from the hungry mob in Atlanta."

"Is there anything you need from us?"

"No, sir. But we have some news for you."

"What is that?" President Robbins braced himself for more bad news.

"Well, sir, there are two things. One is that we have semidefeated BSV. We have two pregnant women in our lab."

The president was dumbfounded. “Really? That is WONDERFUL, Dr. Hehsa! Tell me more!”

“It was much less complicated than we had feared, once we figured out how our DNA was modified to stop the implanting of the spermatozoa into the ovum. We were able to change the DNA back inside the gametes.” Dr. Hehsa realized that President Robbins may not know what a gamete was. “The gametes, of course, are the sperm and ovum. This allowed us to get the two gametes together for fertilization. We have fifty-seven embryos growing in our Baby Machines from normal fertilization, not cloning. And we have two of our staff who volunteered for the experiment entering their fourth week of pregnancy.”

“You said you have ‘semidefeated’ BSV. What did you mean?”

“Well, sir, the virus is still alive and well. We can reverse the virus within individual gametes, but not within a whole living human organism and certainly not worldwide. What this means is, for a woman to become pregnant, the actual fertilization must be done in a genetics lab. She will need several of her eggs harvested and her husband or a male donor would need to provide some viable sperm. The lab would modify each of the gametes to enable the fertilization to take place, then the zygote…”

“Dr. Hehsa, excuse me, what is a zygote?”

“I apologize, sir. A zygote is the fertilized ovum. It would have to be introduced into the woman’s uterus where it would implant.”

This wasn’t quite the “cure” President Robbins had been hoping for.

Dr. Hehsa sensed President Robbins’s disappointment. “Sir, I know this isn’t a cure. But it *will* allow men and women all over the world to begin having children born from their bodies again. The babies won’t have to be clones of relatives or strangers who died before BSV and would not have to be gestated in Baby Machines. There were perhaps fifty thousand Baby Machines worldwide before the Three-Hour War. They were capable of producing approximately sixty-five thousand babies per year. By using our new technique, any competent genetics lab could impregnate several thousand women per year. And there are thousands of genetics labs worldwide. At least there were before the war. That would create millions of babies instead of tens of thousands."

"That is truly good news, Sridhar. Please forgive me for sounding disappointed. What you have achieved is nothing short of miraculous. I believe you have saved the human race. Everyone, including me, was hoping for a cure. This may have to suffice. And if it does, so be it. There may be no cure for BSV."

President Robbins considered how to proceed. The emperor was promising to give Earth the antidote for the antifertility virus in return for Earth's help in defeating the Yunia. But, he knew the emperor was either lying about it or, at least, wasn't telling him everything. Beauhi's input had reinforced his misgivings. Maybe it was because the president himself had been forced to lie so many times that he knew when another politician was doing it to him. And if the emperor was lying, there was no telling what would happen if it became known that our own solution was waiting in the wings.

"Dr. Hehsa, please don't tell anyone about your discovery. I can't tell you why right now. But I think your continued secrecy is vital to the survival of the human race."

There was a long pause at the other end of the conversation. "Yes, sir," Dr. Hehsa told the president, trying not to sound disappointed. "Can I at least begin to spread the technique to other genetic labs? So they can begin to use the procedure?"

"I need you to wait for several months before you tell anyone, no longer than that. I will tell you when your discovery can be made public. You said there were two things to tell me. What is the second?"

"The other thing is we have analyzed the tissue sample that was retrieved from the alien invaders. We can plant it into the same infertility virus that was used to infect us. If the opportunity presents itself, it might be a good way to return the favor."

"Do you mean the Yunia or the Ur?"

"I do not know either of those names, sir. Captain Gaye Marshall gave us the sample. It was DNA, but very different from ours. We were able to insert the DNA into the virus, but, without having any subjects to test it on, we don't know if it will work or not."

This was all a surprise to President Robbins. No one had told him what the tissue sample Captain Marshall had collected as they escaped from Quyl would be used for. This was all new information to him. "Continue your research on that as well. I need to gather some more information before I can tell you how to proceed beyond that."

"Yes, sir."

"Dr. Hehsa, please accept my deepest thanks for your efforts. As I have said before, I believe you have saved humanity."

"Thank you, sir. But it was a team effort. I am not claiming to be the only one who made the discovery."

"Thank you again, Dr. Hehsa. I will be in touch."

"Goodbye, Mr. President."

Chapter 23 – The Heat Is On

"General Langlitz, I am J. Yousef Hamani. I represent a group of fifty-one families who had their sons, fathers, brothers, and husbands murdered near Sonora, California, by Lieutenant Jeremiah Silverstein and his squad of Marines. We would like you to convene an Article 32, grand jury, to investigate the murders. We desire that you convict Lieutenant Silverstein and his squad of thirteen Marines for the murder of four hundred and twelve innocent men while he was on a vacation visiting his wife. I have filed a wrongful death lawsuit against the US government, and Lieutenant Silverstein's entire command, ending with you, sir, in the Los Angeles Superior Court for those deaths."

Mr. Hamani handed the summons issued by the Superior Court to General Langlitz. When the general didn't take it, Hamani dropped it on the desk. General Langlitz looked at the summons without touching it like it was a pile of shit that wouldn't go away.

General Langlitz finally responded in the gravelly voice that was his trademark. "Those four hundred twelve men you call 'innocent' had murdered, raped, tortured, and robbed their way up the Sierras from Bakersfield to Sonora leaving a trail of bodies and burned settlements. I have no interest in convening any kind of grand jury. I fully intend to give Lieutenant Silverstein a medal for ridding the world of the vermin that attacked him and the twelve people in his wife's settlement. My only regret is that there weren't more of those assholes for him to kill."

"Then I suppose I will see you in court, General." Mr. Hamani rose from his chair, smiled, and offered the general his hand.

The general walked to the door to his office and opened it. "Good day, Mr. Hamani."

Mr. Hamani walked out.

While he was still in hearing distance, the general called out to his secretary, "Kathy, call a cleaning crew. I want this office scrubbed from top to bottom to get rid of the stench."

He walked back to his desk and picked up his phone and dialed a number.

A young voice answered, "Camp Pendleton Judge Advocate General office. Corporal Youngblood speaking, sir. How may I direct your call?"

"This is General Langlitz. Let me talk to Colonel Letson."

"Yes, sir. I will connect you."

There was a click. "Colonel Letson speaking, sir."

"Colonel Letson, I got another one. This one is for Lieutenant Silverstein and his defense of his wife's settlement." He listened for a while. "Yeah, yeah. Same shit. Four hundred twelve innocent men on a walk through the country picking daisies, holding hands, and singing 'Kumbaya.' He also filed a wrongful death with the L.A. Superior Court." He listened for a while longer, then gave the head of the base JAG office (the lawyers of the military) a recap of the whole conversation.

"Did you really say you wished there were more of them for Lieutenant Silverstein to kill?"

"Yeah. He was a worm. I wanted to step on him."

There was a pause. "No offense, General, but I wish you hadn't said those words."

"Too late now."

"Yes, it is, sir. I expect he was wearing a wire. He'll use it against you in court."

"Shit."

"When the next one shows up, sir, please do this: listen to what he has to say, then show him the door. Do not respond in any way. When they show up like this, they are on a fishing trip. This guy left with a lot more than when he arrived."

There was an awkward silence between them. Neither one knew what to say next. The colonel broke the silence. "Well, I'll send someone over for the summons. I figured this would happen, so I've started collecting evidence. We'll need to have a team follow the gang's path up from Bakersfield to take pictures and find any witnesses that are still alive. Didn't you tell me Lieutenant Silverstein brought back a personal movie of the attack?"

"Yeah. One of the civilians in the settlement took it while the fight was going on. And he has the dash cam recordings from the three trucks and a bunch of stills they took after the battle. I'll tell him to bring them over to your office."

"And we'll need to depose the people in Lieutenant Silverstein's settlement and his squad."

"Don't forget Major Goodman and the rest of the survivors from the Mountain Warfare Center."

"I won't. But in all truthfulness, military witnesses don't carry much weight in a civilian court when a soldier is on trial. Juries tend to view them as protecting each other's ass instead of telling the truth."

"That's a sad statement all by itself, Colonel" the general told him.

The colonel sighed, then answered. "Yes, it is, sir."

They were both silent for a moment, then Colonel Letson continued, "The world didn't exactly turn out like we thought it would when we were young men, sir. But civilian witnesses are what we need—the more injured and devastated, the better. Live accounts of mom or dad, sister or brother, grandma or grandpa, getting murdered, tortured, or raped. Eyewitnesses who can identify the perps from a picture. We might get lucky and one of the relatives of the fifty families will be ID'ed as one of the gang members."

... ...

"Admiral Nam, what do you think about the weapons proposed by the Earthlings?" The emperor stared at the monitor. The image of Earth and its moon was displayed as the battleship orbited Earth about a million miles out.

The admiral considered his response. "I think this species has demonstrated very clearly why it was given a death sentence. They are descended from killer apes. No matter how you wrap it up with bows, ribbons, and brilliance, they are still predators."

"In case you haven't noticed, Admiral, we need predators right now. Predators to fight the predators."

"And after the fighting is done, Sire? What then?"

"Then the problem will take care of itself. There is no cure for their infertility. In a hundred years, they will end the problem of their existence for us. For now, we build the weapons to defeat the Yunia that they have invented. We'll take one problem at a time."

"Yes, Sire."

"When can you have the modifications made to your cruisers and battleships to launch the remote launchers and support feeding the remote launchers their evacuators?"

"That can be done relatively quickly, Sire, possibly as soon as two weeks. The fusion devices will take more time. We have outlawed that technology for thousands of years. However, we have an adequate supply of small-yield photon torpedoes. If we substitute them for the fusion devices, we could be ready when the evacuation feeders were done."

"Will they work as well as the fusion devices?"

"Better, Sire. They are smaller, hotter, don't leak radiation, and don't degrade over time."

"Make it so, Admiral."

"Yes, Sire."

... ...

"Special Agent Hlitatta, it's a pleasure to meet at last." Fey Pey's voice over the call was smooth as silk.

"Will you help us trap the Yunia?"

Fey Pey was silent for a moment. "OK, Agent Hlitatta, let's cut to the chase." His voice got very serious. "Why would I do that? What's in it for me?"

"We could reduce the charges against you. Take away the capital offenses. You would spend some jail time, but not be executed."

"How could I possibly turn down such a kind offer? Let me think? Uhh—no. Sorry. The Yunia have offered me the solar system of my choice anywhere in the galaxy. And one percent of everything they 'collect' from the subjugated peoples of the Ur after they are freed. Somehow being rich beyond what even I can imagine doesn't compare with doing some undetermined amount of jail time in one of the Ur's maximum security criminal rest homes."

"I'm not going to get into a bidding war with you. You are a criminal. It's my job to bring you to justice." Agent Hlitatta felt dirty even talking to Fey Pey. He wanted to see Fey Pey in the sights of his laser.

"Is there someone else I can talk to?" Fey Pey asked casually, unimpressed by the agent's hostility. "Someone with a little bigger view of the issues here?"

"You must mean someone who thinks your treasonous interaction with the Yunia is worth more than the hundreds of thousands of lives you took when you detonated the torpedo on Zindarr."

"Torpedo on Zindarr? You must have me confused with someone else. But I think you are beginning to understand, Agent Hlitatta. I was hoping to speak with the emperor instead of some low-level worker in the BCI."

"The emperor doesn't talk to criminals."

That brought a round of raucous laughter from Fey Pey. When he got his voice under control, he said, "You *do* have a sense of humor, Agent Hlitatta. The emperor has more criminals working for him than I do. Only they are called advisors, ambassadors, ministers, and generals."

"He won't talk to you."

"That's too bad, Agent Hlitatta." There was a pause. "You work for Minister Sri Yeblana, don't you? He *is* head of the Justice Ministry, isn't he?"

"What does that have to do with anything?"

"Did anyone ever think to ask where he went on his last vacation? And who paid for it? And what about those 'entertainment' ladies and the cost of their 'entertainment' as well?"

"No. Where did he go and who paid for it?"

"Oh, I don't know. I just ask questions now and again. Our five minutes is almost up, Agent Hlitatta. I'll call back sometime. Bye."

The call ended. An incoming call activated it again. "Did you finish the trace?" the agent asked.

"No. He broke contact before we could get closer than somewhere on Taramon."

"Damn."

"Maybe next time."

"Yeah. And snillers can fly to the moon."

"Excuse me?"

"Never mind. Thanks for trying."

... ...

"Lord Quilp?" The hologram in front of him sparkled into a three-dimensional image of the leader of his galaxy. She was a large insect-looking being with six legs, the front two of which were used as arms. She was covered with orange and black stripes. Her violet eyes appeared to rotate as she talked. She was the same species as Lord Quilp and everyone else in Lord Quilp's armada. Unlike the Ur, which was made up of thousands of species, these beings were apparently a single species.

"Yes, Sire."

"Have you found the emperor?"

"No, Sire. He has gone into hiding."

"I'm not surprised after your bungled attack on his home planet."

"We will find him, Sire."

"You have a deadline, Lord Quilp.

"Yes, Sire. I will find him."

"You better, Lord Quilp. And when you do, I expect you to make an example of his demise. I want the emperor, his defense fleet, and his government crushed. This has already cost more and taken longer than expected. This circus-galaxy of so many species can never stand against the might of the Mux. We will crush them and feed them to our babies."

"The Ur has provided more resistance than expected, Sire." *And it was only going to get worse*, he thought to himself, *based on the last battle around Quyl.*

"That's your problem, Lord Quilp, not mine. If you can't subjugate these primitive beings with the fleet I've given you, I'm sure a hundred other generals would love to have the chance."

"Yes, Sire. I will do my best."

"Eight weeks, Lord Quilp. If you haven't completed your mission in eight weeks, I will find someone else who can. And you can count on that being the end to your career as a general and Lord."

"I understand, Sire."

"I hope you do, *Lord* Quilp." She stretched and extended her claws, looking directly at him.

The image of his leader disappeared. Lord Quilp reactivated his communicator. "Where the hell is Fey Pey?"

"He hasn't checked in for two days, Lord Quilp."

"Have you sent a new page to him?"

"Yes, Sire. Two hours ago."

"How is the campaign in the inner arm going?"

"One success after another. These beings have no idea how to fight."

"How are our losses?"

"Minor ground troop losses. We haven't lost another cruiser since the one at Quyl."

"Let me know the minute Fey Pey contacts you."

"Yes, Sire."

... ...

Dr. Hehsa's phone rang.

"Dr. Hehsa, CDC speaking."

A woman's voice answered him. "Dr. Hehsa, please hold for the president."

There was a click, then President Robbins came on the line. "Sridhar, how much of the BSV virus does it take to infect a target audience?"

Dr. Hehsa considered the question. "It depends on how the virus is disseminated. Airborne into the atmosphere of a planet, it would take quite a lot. Individually administered doses would require much less."

"How about an accidental infection of several candidates in a small room? Candidates who would spread the infection to the rest of the population?"

"That would require a very tiny amount, sir, perhaps a hundredth of a gram. We would need some form of propellant to make it airborne so they would inhale it."

"I need ten thousand devices. They have to be small enough to be hidden inside a larger device without being noticed. I want them to become armed when the device enters a vacuum and deploy when the device becomes pressurized again. When can you have them ready?"

Dr. Hehsa thought about it. "We can make the virus, sir. And we can create ampules that can be crushed and presented to the propellant, but we do not have the facilities to make the devices you describe."

It was President Robbins's turn to pause. He came to a decision. "You make the ampules. I need some samples as soon as you can make them, say ten prototypes without any virus inside, just sterile water. When can you provide them?"

"I can have the prototypes ready today, sir. The live ampules will require about two weeks."

"Great! Create the prototypes. I will have a courier pick them up. And get to work on the live virus ampules using the DNA from that tissue sample Captain Marshall gave you."

Chapter 24 – The Trap

The cruiser popped into space next to the dead planet. Fifty other assorted warships appeared in space all around the planet. They started conversing with each other electronically and sending evacuation devises to the surface at places where they had been told the emperor was hiding. A battleship appeared in the middle of them and took control of the fleet. On the three moons were passive recording stations. A red giant star glowered at them from two hundred million miles away, covering the ships in a red aspect that appeared to be dried blood.

"Begin the attack," Admiral Nam ordered. He was on the bridge of *Emperor Xull*, about a lightyear away from the planet. The area around the planet was displayed on three separate holograms fed by the observation stations on the moons.

One repeater appeared about half a million miles away from the planet. It was followed by twenty others. They formed a million-mile diameter sphere around the fifty ships and began launching evacuation devices at the cruisers.

The warships defended themselves, deflecting the evacuation devices and launching their own. None of the evacuation devices the warships launched evacuated anything but empty space. The Jumping Jacks were gone by the time the warships' devices reached them. Several of the warships disappeared, victim of three devices arriving simultaneously. The battleship disappeared in a red ball of exploding hydrogen gases, millions of degrees from the middle of the red giant. The rest of the fleet erupted in various balls of flame as the rockets and torpedoes entered their launch rooms. The whole battle took less than one minute to complete. Not a single warship survived the onslaught.

"Send the repeaters into the sun," the admiral commanded. This was the final item on the test plan—would they stop when ordered. Over the course of ten seconds, he watched them disappear from the hologram.

General Nam walked off the bridge of his battleship. The primates' weapons had performed flawlessly. Not one of the warships being attacked were able to track the path back to the feeder ship, which was also running on remote control.

Now the hard part was waiting for the Yunia fleet and the trap. None of this mattered if the Yunia fleet couldn't be drawn into one place where the attack could be made.

... ...

The emperor was in a quandary. When he was a young man, a boy really, he met another young citizen of the Ur—an aquatic mammal. He had never met one before. He knew about them, of course. But this one was different from his other contacts. Fey Pey had listened and been interested in *him* instead of trying to use him to get access to his father. They became friends, at least he thought they had. When his friend began asking him for innocuous things like shipping lists and freight schedules, he hadn't questioned it. What harm could it do? Then he began to hear about ships being waylaid by a new pirate who seemed to know which ships were transporting precious cargo and which were carrying ordinary cargo. He asked his friend, Fey Pey, if he knew of the pirate, thinking they could capture him and finally get his father's approval. Fey Pey had laughed and said no. Then he had left the room and the boy's life.

Several weeks later, the boy received a communication crystal. Inside it Fey Pey's unmistakable voice said, "If you ever need my services, you have only to call." It also contained a communicator number.

Years later the new emperor was trying to negotiate a peaceful settlement between the sides of a particularly bloody civil war on a planet named Plendor. It was the emperor's first major impasse since his father had died. One person stood in the way of a successful ceasefire. This Plendor person was the leader of one of the sides of the civil war and was resisting all his efforts to bring him to the negotiating table. The emperor was frustrated with his inability to find a way to end the conflict. He was certain, if this person were removed, he could reconcile the three sides of the war and end the struggle. Not wanting to get Ur troops involved, he had reached out to his former friend.

"Just remove him. Get rid of him," he told Fey Pey. "I want him gone."

Fey Pey had listened quietly. "I will take care of it."

The person disappeared that night. The third side's resistance to the ceasefire and the negotiations collapsed. The emperor was able to stop the civil war and bring peace to the planet.

The emperor read the message in his hologram again. A full pardon for any and all unspecified crimes committed across his entire lifetime. That was what Fey Pey was demanding for his help in bringing the Yunia into the Ur trap. That and the right to seed ten worlds with whatever species of being he chose. And he wanted—no, demanded—there be no interference from the Galactic Species Control Board with the species he chose to raise up on those planets or how they grew.

The emperor sighed. He had used Fey Pey several other times across his lifetime—always for the good of the galaxy. If he did agree to Fey Pey's demands, how could he justify it to the rest of the galaxy who were clamoring for Fey Pey's head? If he didn't agree to it, how would Admiral Nam attract the Yunia fleet to one place so they could be annihilated? A hundred more planets had fallen to the Yunia since he arrived on Earth. They now occupied almost a quarter of the Ur-controlled galaxy. None of their attempts at drawing the Yunia armada to one place or another were succeeding. Rumors of the location of the emperor were carefully planted. The trap set. And no one showed up.

It was almost as if someone was telling them these hints were false.

For the first time in his life, the emperor didn't know what to do. It wasn't a feeling he liked at all.

… … … … … … … … …

"We have another report of where the emperor is."

"Lord Quilp, it is false. The Ur is trying to lead you into a trap." Fey Pey was amazed these morons were still taking the bait. "I told you I would find the emperor and I will. I have spies all over the galaxy trying to find out where he really is. Let them do their job. We will find him."

"We have already spent four weeks searching. One more week, Fey Pey. You have one week to find him or you will be the one hiding from me."

"I understand, Sire. I won't let you down."

Lord Quilp turned on his heel and walked out of the conference room.

Fey Pey watched him leave. This wasn't turning out like he had hoped. Why wouldn't the goddamned emperor make up his mind? The water cocoon surrounding him swirled in reaction to his turmoil.

A low-level analyst approached Lord Quilp as he left the room. "Sire, I have an idea you may not have considered."

"Doubtful, but I'm listening."

"The aliens left behind a shielded linked-Hore communicator on the emperor's planet. I have just completed triangulating to where it communicates. It is a small planet at the edge of arm two of this galaxy. I feel there is a strong probability that the emperor is there."

Lord Quilp stared at the clerk. "Have you told anyone else about this?"

"No, Sire. I thought you should know first."

"You will tell no one. Thank you for your discovery. I need those coordinates."

"Yes, Sire."

… … … … … … … … …

Emperor Cabliux began his daily status meeting. "Admiral Nam, has the fleet been fitted with the new weapons?"

"Yes, Sire. The installation is complete."

President Robbins decided it was time to unveil his last request. “One ship must escape.”

Admiral Nam grunted in disgust, as usual, then replied, “Why would we do that, President Robbins? To return to their galaxy and tell them how we beat them?”

“Exactly,” President Robbins answered with a sigh. Admiral Nam was *so* predictable.

“So they can build defenses against our new weapons and attack us again?”

“You know so little about battle, Admiral Nam.” Their sparring in these meetings was becoming legendary. “They will come back unless we let someone tell their command how thoroughly we defeated them. You may not know this, Admiral Nam, but warriors respect someone who defeats them. They will hate us. They will tell stories about us. But they will come back as equals and ask to be trading partners instead of adversaries. If we don’t let someone return, they will come back with another fleet to find out what happened. This battle and death will happen again.”

“Let them come back!” Admiral Nam shouted, hitting the table with his paw, his claws leaving deep furrows in the surface. “We will defeat them as many times as they return!”

“I would much rather have them as trading partners than I would as enemies, Admiral Nam,” the emperor said gently. “I’m going to agree with President Robbins on this one. Let one vessel escape.”

“Sire, this is idiocy,” Admiral Nam said resolutely.

“Your disagreement is noted, Admiral,” the emperor said. “Let’s move on to our biggest problem. How can we get the Yunia to send their fleet into our trap? Does anyone have any new ideas? I refuse to do business with the criminal Fey Pey.”

“You may have to, Sire,” Admiral Nam said. “None of our planted clues have yielded anything. He may be our last hope.”

“He murdered your daughter, Admiral Nam. How can you suggest I give him a full pardon for any and all crimes?”

Admiral Nam sighed. “That was a long time ago, Sire. I hardly remember her.”

An aide burst into the room. “Sire, the Yunia have entered this solar system! The battle has begun!”

Chapter 25 – The Battle of Star EB-31-21-98

"Sire, you must leave!" Admiral Nam was vehement. "I cannot ensure your safety if you remain here."

"They will be expecting me to bolt, Admiral Nam. If I leave, they will follow and this opportunity will pass us by. I will remain here. They want to capture me. I will invite them to try. You will prepare the trap."

Admiral Nam hesitated, then bounded out of the room, knocking over an aide who was coming in the door.

President Robbins walked into the war room and immediately saw a three-dimensional hologram of the solar system.

The emperor's face appeared on the display. "Warriors of Yunia, I believe we can resolve this amicably. You want to expand. So do we. I invite you to become trading partners with the Ur instead of adversaries. If you attack us, we will defeat you. There is no need for this. Come to my table and let us discuss how we can become allies instead of enemies."

The first Ur starship disappeared from the display.

President Robbins watched the Yunia starships hop from position to position as they closed in on Earth, obviously expecting a counterattack. The emperor's message had given them a target and that target's name was Earth. "Not yet, Admiral Nam. They aren't in the kill zone yet. We need them where we can kill them."

Another Ur starship disappeared.

A Yunia starship disappeared, then another. "Not yet, Admiral," President Robbins muttered. *How many people are on a starship,* he wondered. *Five hundred? A thousand? All of those beings had other beings who loved them.*

The progress of the Yunia fleet slowed. More and more starships appeared. President Robbins realized the counterattack was causing them to wait until the entire fleet showed up. "That was brilliant, Admiral. Good job. Now we'll get the whole fleet."

Starships started appearing all over the solar system. There were hundreds, then thousands of them. The dots representing starships began to look like the Milky Way on a clear night. They started to converge on Earth.

An Ur starship disappeared. Then a Yunia starship. The Ur fleet appeared to be badly outnumbered.

"Now, Admiral. Open up on them!" President Robbins shouted.

The admiral couldn't suppress a smug smile as pressed the attack button. Five seconds later, Yunia starships began disappearing all over the display. Some went out with small explosions. Some were massive. Some turned into fireballs. A small inset display in the hologram gave the number of Ur starships in action and lost. Another readout gave the same numbers for the Yunia. Both totals climbed as the battle progressed. But the Yunia losses increased much faster. The Yunia were losing ships at a ten to one rate over the Ur.

President Robbins felt a dizzying surrealness, watching this interplanetary battle play out as far removed from him as a child's computerized video game.

"When do you think the Yunia will realize the Ur ships they are blowing up are dummies?" Lily asked the president. They had placed old, decommissioned Ur starships around the solar system to camouflage the repeater stations. Those junk starships were producing lots of radio traffic and wormholes to nowhere so the Yunia would think they were really attacking the Yunia fleet.

"Pretty soon, I'd guess."

"What if we're doing the same thing?" she asked.

"What's that?"

"Blowing up dummies." The actual Ur fleet was beyond Pluto in the Oort cloud.

President Robbins turned to look at her in shock. "What an awful idea!"

"I'm just saying," she said solemnly. "That's how my mind works sometimes. If we could do it to them, why couldn't they do it to us? I mean, in a battle of this magnitude, I would test the water before I dove in."

He turned back to the hologram of the battle raging in front of them. The number of remaining starships were about equal now. The ratio of destroyed starships was up to twenty Yunia for each destroyed Ur starship. Both fleets were down to about a hundred ships. They watched together as the Yunia numbers descended toward zero.

"Leave one, Admiral," President Robbins whispered. "You have to leave one."

The display of Yunia starships dropped precipitously toward zero. It passed ten, then five, then two. And stopped at one. That one starship opened a wormhole to Earth. Then it winked out of existence.

"You were supposed to leave one, Admiral!" President Robbins shouted.

"Go copulate with a monkrus, you disgusting primate!" he bellowed back. "They were about to blow up your world and us with it. Maybe you want to commit suicide, but I certainly don't."

The emperor spoke from behind President Robbins. "Admiral, please send sweep teams to the locations of the destroyed Yunia starships. Search for survivors. Some of the crew may have made it to lifeboats. We could send them back to their home planet and achieve the same effect. And postpone sending any undestroyed devices into the sun for at least a day—deactivate them but don't destroy them."

... ...

Lord Quilp watched his ghost fleet of captured starships and derelicts disappear into dust. This changed everything. Not only had the Ur learned to fight, they had created a whole new technology of weapons that were incredibly deadly and effective beyond anything he had ever seen. His real fleet would have been decimated if he had allowed them to attack like they wanted.

He opened a communication channel to his analysis section. "Have you figured out how their new weapons work yet?"

“There are at least three, and possibly even five, different types being employed. They’ve been busy, Lord Quilp. I don’t know how we would counter two of them. One of them is apparently opening two wormholes concurrently, one wormhole into their sun and the second to the target starship. We would very much like to see how they do this.”

“Is the emperor on the planet from which the transmission emanated?”

“I would say not, Sire. They couldn’t be that stupid, not with the creativity these weapons demonstrate.”

“We must consider our next options. I want to withdraw to the edge of the galaxy. Before we leave, is there any chance of capturing some of those devices?”

His analyst paused to consider his request. “Doubtful, Sire. We could try, if you’d like. But it may allow them to realize that they have been fooled into believing they have defeated us.”

“They will figure that out as soon as they scan the first wreck.” Lord Quilp came to a decision. “We have to try. The benefits are great enough to offset the risk. I want to see how those weapons function. Let’s see if we can get one of each.”

...

The sweep teams were able to find two functioning Ur weapons: a Jumping Jack and an Orient Express. They didn’t know those were their names, of course.

"Should we disinfect them, sir?"

The weapons deck supervisor considered this as he studied the two devices inside the biological containment. The containment was still in vacuum.

"That will take at least a day. I don't think we have time. Lord Quilp said he needed to know if either device is functional as soon as he can. Otherwise the sweep teams will have to find another one and risk detection by the Ur. They have been in vacuum for days. Anything organic would be long dead. We should be fine, but we'll quarantine ourselves for a couple of days to make sure. If we aren't dead or sick by then, who cares?"

The supervisor pressed the quarantine button on his tool belt. The doors to the lab swung shut and hermetically sealed themselves. The tech began to bring the atmosphere in the containment up to normal pressure. Neither of them heard the tiny puffs of propellant that blew the contents of the ampules into the inner workings of the devices.

When the pressure in the containment was equal to the room, the tech opened the containment. He glanced at the sealed door to the corridor, sighed, then began his disassembly of the Jumping Jack. Two days with his supervisor in this little room and he had a date tonight with that hot female in personnel. Dammit! At least he was going to get hazardous duty pay for these two days. And the trip home was going to take weeks. There was plenty of time to "mingle" before he got to home base.

...

"Set a course for home," Lord Quilp told his Exec. "The continuation of the offensive here is going to take a policy decision at the emperor's level. We still have to finish analyzing the data we took from Quyl and everyone needs a rest and time to visit their families. There are families all over our galaxy who want to see their loved ones. There's plenty of time to return to the Ur and try again."

Lord Quilp's weapons sections had gleaned enough data from their disassembly to re-create the weapons. They were actively working on creating working copies and working defenses for them. Their hope was, once they could re-create them, they would be able to figure out a way to counter them.

"And what do you want to do with the fish?" his second in command asked. Fey Pey had been restricted to quarters ever since he recommended they attack the Ur in force at this little solar system.

"Kill him," Lord Quilp said quietly, his voice dripping with malice. Then he hesitated, his face hard and cold. "No. Wait. Killing would be too easy. I have a better idea. Drop him off in a lifeboat where he will be found by the Ur. And include the holograms of his interactions with us. I suspect the Ur loves a traitor as much as we do."

"As you command, Sire."

... ...

"They're all wrecks," the people reported in the sweeps of the Yunia starships. "There are no survivors because there were no Yunia on board."

"Well, who the hell was attacking us?" Admiral Nam asked, perplexed.

"The Yunia, Admiral Nam." President Robbins laughed but there was no mirth in it. "They were testing the water. Something tipped them off that we had set a trap. And we played right into their hands. We used every new weapon in our new playlist. And they saw how each one works. Now they can go home to figure out how to counter them without losing a ship or a single fighter to get that knowledge."

"And that means..."

"Yep. That means they will be back, bigger, badder, and smarter than they were before."

... ...

"We've found one survivor," one of the search teams reported later in the day.

"Ours or theirs?" Admiral Nam asked.

"We're not sure. He says his name is Fey Pey and claims that he's the one who caused the Yunia to retreat. He said he saved the entire Ur. There's a galaxy-wide Arrest-On-Site order out on him."

Admiral Nam turned to President Robbins and gave him a quizzical look.

"Bring him in, Admiral Nam," President Robbins said grimly. "I'd be willing to bet the emperor would love to see him. And when he's done, if there's anything left, I expect some of my legal team would like a shot also."

Chapter 26 – One Thing at a Time

Intragalactic communications was reestablished after the war. The largest audience in recorded history was watching the culmination of Fey Pey's trial. The two months of the trial were a movie-maker's dream. It had political espionage, rape, murder, money, high level corruption, slavery, torture, exploding planets, payoffs, and kidnapping. Through it all, Fey Pey stared out placidly from his bubble of water without saying a word. His legal team presented him as *the* hero of the war who had risked his life to save the Ur-controlled galaxy. The prosecution team painted a very different picture.

The defense and prosecution were finishing their questioning of Fey Pey's crew. Throughout the trial, he had shown no reaction, other than a faint amusement, to almost all of the witnesses. He listened impassively while Lily Yuan described how the dream plant had changed her life and her world. The witch, Plew, described how her life had been a hell living in solitary confinement, knowing any false move would have cause Fey Pey to detonate the photon torpedo on Zindarr. The only witnesses he showed any reaction to at all were his ex-Executive Officer, Fela Fibari, and the analyst, Zarqa Shaia. Lieutenant Fibari had described the three-and-a-half years she served under Fey Pey. She told about retrieving the photon torpedo deployed against them by the Ur warship, *Far Galaxy*, thereby tying Fey Pey to the destruction of Zindarr. It was only after she ended her testimony by saying he had lost her in a card game to a sex trader, Fey Pey gave his only display of emotion so far: he had laughed out loud. When Sergeant Zarqa, whom he deliberately allowed to be inserted into his ship's crew by Captain Xanny, described her finding of the hologram of Fey Pey and King Amon of Glycemis, he laughed again. Fey Pey's defense team subsequently proved that the hologram was computer generated.

After the last member of his crew was finished, Fey Pey asked his legal team to put him on the stand. His questioning went on for days.

He was being questioned by the prosecutor about his own part in the dream plant and raise up of the aquatic mammals on Earth.

"I was just doing what I'd been paid to do by an envoy of the Ur. Who was I to question the inner workings of the galactic government?"

"You keep saying that, but you have no proof of any meeting."

Fey Pey turned to the magistrate in frustration. "I have incontrovertible proof that Envoy Gart-Disp contacted me about the dream plant and aquatic mammal raise up. That he paid me to do the job and gave me the DNA to do the raise up. He gave me a witch to do the plant."

The magistrate was irritated. "Unless you will produce such proof, I don't want to hear about it again and neither does the jury."

"I want an unbreakable guarantee that I will be pardoned for any and all crimes committed in my past before I turn it over to you."

"I can't give you a pardon like that. Only the emperor can."

"Then you better get busy and tell him."

"You want me to tell the emperor that you deserve a pardon on the promise that you have proof of high level corruption? Without even seeing what you have to offer?"

Fey Pey paused, then came to a decision. "There is a communication crystal inside my Hore energy unit. Please retrieve it and play the hologram inside."

The security team leader retrieved the crystal and handed it to the magistrate. The magistrate placed it in his viewer. A hologram appeared in the middle of the courtroom of a deserted starship bridge. Envoy Gart-Disp appeared. Fey Pey's unmistakable voice asked the envoy, "Why have you asked me here, Envoy?"

"I want you to perform a mission for me. One that is illegal."

"'Illegal' is a very expensive word, Envoy."

"I am prepared to pay you one million Huz now and two million more upon completion."

"Please continue, Envoy. You have my attention."

"I want you to plant a dream in a primate on a planet near the edge of the galaxy."

"And that is worth three million Huz to you?" Fey Pey laughed a little nervously.

"You need to find the correct primate for the plant, first. Then I want you to raise up an aquatic mammal on the same planet. I will give you the modified DNA for distribution to the aquatic mammal species."

Fey Pey in the hologram took a moment to think about what the envoy was asking him. Glycemis was the only planet with an aquatic mammal species in the Ur. This would double the clout of aquatic mammals when the Ur met for legislative sessions. While Fey Pey cared not the least bit about the politics of the Ur, he *was* a member of the aquatic mammal species.

"When can you transfer the funds to my account on Glycemis?"

"As soon as you agree to the tasks."

"I have no one who can do a dream plant. Only the witches have that ability and they don't rent out."

"We have a person who can do this. She will accompany you. She will also choose the recipient of the dream. Her name is Plew."

"I will also need a biotech team to prepare the Species Inoculation Virus. I am not a species miner."

"It has already been arranged. All we need is your agreement to perform the task."

"I'll need the coordinates of the planet."

"Here they are." The envoy handed a communication crystal to Fey Pey.

"When do you want this done, Envoy?"

"Immediately."

"I will need a week to prepare the quantity of SIV needed for the raise up."

"Then you had better start. Do we have an agreement?"

"Yes, Envoy. I will notify you when these tasks are complete."

The envoy turned without saying another word and left the hologram.

… … … … … … … … …

The court was silent. The magistrate watched the hologram three times. The prosecution objected they needed time to verify that the recording was real.

The magistrate was in a tailspin. This was so far beyond his jurisdiction, he didn't know where to begin. Corruption at the envoy level. Envoys were just below the emperor in authority. And the live feed had gone out across the galaxy.

Fey Pey watched his discomfort with amusement. "Declare a mistrial, Magistrate. Say new evidence has been presented. Say the prosecution needs time to prepare."

The magistrate ignored him. "Take Fey Pey back to his cell," he commanded. "I have to communicate with my superiors. This court is recessed."

… … … … … … … … …

"Ur citizen, Fey Pey, rise and face the judge." The magistrate spoke the words so everyone across the galaxy could follow what was being said.

"Have you any words to say before the jury retires to deliberate on verdicts for the charges?"

"Yes," he said, in a deep rumbling voice. The water cocoon around him rippled as he spoke. "I have information that can only be viewed by the emperor himself. Information that has a direct bearing on this case and, indeed, on the future of this galaxy."

The magistrate coughed and glanced down at his notes. He was tired of Fey Pey's slippery tactics. Yet he hadn't refuted any of the allegations against him. Indeed, he seemed to enjoy the witnesses recounting the murder and mayhem he had performed during his career as a pirate. The recording of his meeting with

Envoy Gart-Disp was declared real by the GBI. The envoy had disappeared without a trace. A mistrial was deemed unnecessary.

"The emperor isn't here Citizen Pey. Anything you have to say must be said here."

"May I meet with you in your chambers, Magistrate?"

The magistrate considered his request. The meeting couldn't pose any danger to the conviction he was certain the jury would return. And he was curious as to what Fey Pey could have to say that he thought would cause any change to this verdict. "This court will take a short recess while I hear what Citizen Pey has to say." The magistrate turned to the security team. "Please escort Citizen Pey into my chambers."

When the door to the chambers was securely shut, Fey Pey floated in front of the magistrate, supported by his anti-grav unit. The security team trained their freeze guns on him. He ignored them. To the magistrate he said, "I want you to give a message to the emperor. Tell him I will divulge what I did on Plendor and who told me to do it unless he meets with me."

The magistrate laughed at Fey Pey's audacity. "I don't have any way to communicate with the emperor. He doesn't talk to people like me."

"I believe you, Magistrate. So here's a communicator number." He passed a slip of paper to the magistrate. "Call it. It will be a recorder. Tell it what I said, then end the call. Be sure you use my exact words and my name. You should also tell it your name and where the hell we are. Then get ready for a visit."

The magistrate looked down at the number, turning the paper over and over.

"We are done," Fey Pey announced, his anti-grav unit lifting him to eye level. "I will return to my cell."

... ...

"You will announce Fey Pey has escaped," the emperor told the magistrate.

"Escaped from the most heavily guarded security facility in the galaxy?"

"Yes. I have people who will help make it believable."

"When will this 'escape' happen?"

"Tomorrow, just after midnight. You will tell no one."

The magistrate shrugged. There wasn't much else he could do. This was the emperor telling him to do this, not some local hoodlum.

"OK."

… … … … … … … … …

Easy Wind, Fey Pey's ship, orbited around the planet hosting Fey Pey's trial. Fey Pey appeared on the bridge, porting up from the planet surface.

"Emergency departure!" he screamed. "NOW!"

His exec pressed the jump alert. *Easy Wind* accelerated and disappeared in a rosy ball. But as it went into the portal, things changed. Instead of ending up a lightyear from Gargantua, they exited into an area of space that fit none of their guidance computer's knowledge base.

"Where are we," Fey Pey asked Byteen, his exec.

"I have no idea," came the response. "This isn't a known part of the universe."

… … … … … … … … …

"Is he gone?" the emperor asked Beauhi.

"Yes. Gone from this galaxy, gone from this universe."

"Thank you for your help in this."

"Thank them," she told him, indicating the auditorium full of witches behind her. They were the surviving members of the Zindarr witches. Together they formed a coven powerful enough to move the end of *Easy Wind's* wormhole into another universe. "All I did was ask. They were the ones who altered his wormhole and sent him to where he'll never come back."

"You will receive a new planet and this one won't be a prison."

"Actually, we have a different idea. Let me tell you about it."

... ...

"President Robbins?"

"Yes. Who is this?" His phone never rang without one of his staff announcing who was on the line.

"This is Emperor Cabliux. I have some good news for you."

"What is that, Emperor? Is the antidote for our sterility ready to be deployed?"

"No. That will take some more time. Humanity has been accepted as a full, voting member of the Ur. You will need to send a delegate to Arawon."

"That's great news. When can we expect the antidote?"

The emperor paused. "There is a problem with the antidote, President Robbins. It cannot be administered worldwide. All it can do is reverse the effects of the virus on a person-by-person basis. If any treated person comes into contact with the virus again, they will be made infertile again. I know this isn't what you wanted to hear, but we've never previously wanted to reverse the effects of a virus deployment."

"So what you're saying is that, unless we get treated for the virus and migrate somewhere where the virus has never been, we will remain sterile?"

"Yes. That's what I'm saying."

"How long will the virus live, Emperor?"

"One hundred years after the last person of your species dies a natural death on your planet, President Robbins. But because of your planet's help in defeating the Yunia, we are willing to make an offer to your citizens. We offer you an uninfected planet to which you may migrate. This planet is undeveloped and has no intelligent species on it, much like your world was fifty-thousand-years ago when humanity was raised up from the primitive apes that inhabited it before. Each individual who elects to migrate will be disinfected of the virus and allowed to leave Earth. Earth itself will remain in quarantine until the virus dies. Anyone who migrates will not be allowed to bring anything with them because of the difficulty of cleansing those items of the virus. However, we will help you build a new infrastructure on your new planet, which will make you self-sufficient."

"You would migrate an entire planet? Some six billion people? Who would pay for this migration and resettlement, Emperor Cabliux?"

"The personal assets of the people who started this mess, King Amon, Envoy Gart-Disp, and the pirate Fey Pey. Once those monies are exhausted, the Ur itself will fund your migration and resettlement. We owe humanity a huge debt of gratitude for your help in defeating the Yunia. Without humanity's participation, the battle with the Yunia in your solar system would have had a much different ending."

"What of the people who elect to remain behind?"

Again the emperor paused. "They would live their lives and die without having any children. One hundred years later the virus would die with them."

"And could we return then?"

"As much as I object to the manner in which the aquatic mammals were raised up, now that it is done, they are considered a species-in-development and, as such, they are protected by the GSCB. If you elect to leave, this planet would become the sanctuary of the aquatic mammals, administered by Grock Corporation and monitored by the GSCB. You could not return."

"And if we don't elect to leave?"

"You would die as a species and this would still become a sanctuary."

"Why can't the dolphins be resettled instead of humanity?"

"At this point in their development, they are too fragile as a species to collect and move. They are perhaps fifty thousand years away from being able to make that kind of decision."

"And if we find a way to resolve our infertility without Ur consent or help?"

The emperor sighed. He had expected this question. They were primates, after all. "Then you would be carefully monitored to ensure the successful development of the aquatic mammals was not interfered with. President Robbins, please consider this carefully. We are offering your species a new start on an undeveloped planet full of untapped natural resources. We will help you create a pollution-free environment where you can grow and prosper with the rest of the Ur. Your technology can be brought there if you like, but the massive technology of the Ur will also be available. You can make this world into a paradise or a hell. But it would be your world. If you remain here, you would be forced to make this a shared world with the aquatic mammals taking an equal footing in the running of it. Do you think humanity would accept that? If they didn't, the Ur would be forced to intercede on their behalf. If we did that, infertility would be the least of your problems."

It was President Robbins's turn to pause. He was a black man. His lineage dated back into slavery in South Carolina before the Civil War. His relatives had lived through reconstruction and the Jim Crow era of the South. His grandmother had walked with Martin Luther King in Selma, Alabama, when she was a young girl. Then he thought about the waring between factions of Islam and the constant waring between the Muslims and the Hindus and the Christians and the Muslims, even among sects of Christianity there was constant sparring, if not open warfare. Then there were gays and straights. Chinese and whites. Koreans and Japanese. Tolerance of differences between humans wasn't something humanity was very good at. He could easily envision the conflict between the dolphins and the humans. It had already begun.

"I cannot make this decision by myself. We need to inspect the world you have to offer. We will also need your offer in writing with your personal signature on it. My staff will create a presentation of the pros and cons that we will distribute around the world."

"When do you think you might come to a decision?"

"One thing at a time, Emperor Cabliux."

Chapter 27 – The End of the Beginning

President Robbins stood at the podium on a spit of land that looked out over the body of water that had replaced the East Coast from North Carolina to New York City. Twenty-one million people had died when that land had been sent into the sun because of radioactive contamination.

"In the eighteenth and nineteenth centuries, we had a symbol that represented all that was good in the young United States. When someone wanted to show the good side of our country, Columbia was used. Her name and image appeared all over the world as the poetic name for the young United States. That goodness was the reason we named the land where our government was headquartered The District of Columbia.

"That goodness still exists today. The partnership of Canada and the United States has already begun to lead the world to a new future of peace, growth, and prosperity. In the spirit of all the things that were good about the previous United States, in remembrance of the people who lived here, and in the hope that good can come from their sacrifice, I name this body of water The Gulf of Columbia. We must never allow such a disaster to occur again."

... ...

The committee from Earth included President Robbins, Captain Xanny, Canadian Acting Prime Minister LeBec, and twenty other select members of both the US and Canada governments. They were in orbit above a beautiful world, slowly rotating beneath them. The starship was a thousand miles above the surface of the planet. The world had a twenty-one-degree tilt from the solar plane extending out from its sun. There were two moons visible, one significantly larger than the other. The larger moon was closer in to the planet than the smaller moon. The sun seemed a little bluer than Earth's Sol and a little farther away, but there were no reference points to judge its size, distance, or color.

On the planet there were blue oceans, continents, rivers, lakes, polar ice caps on both poles, storms, clouds, and vast forested areas. They waited for a complete orbit to check out the geography of the whole planet. There was a single large ocean that went from pole to pole and covered two-thirds of the planet. A "single ocean" was probably a misnomer. Earth could be considered to have a single large ocean, since all its waters meet and intermingle at various points.

There were three major continents. One large U-shaped continent wrapped almost all the way around the northern hemisphere. It reminded them of Asia on Earth if Asia extended all the way around the world to include Europe, the North Atlantic, and Canada. This continent filled most of the northern hemisphere, with the northern polar ice cap filling the inside of the "U." There was an arid band in the "U" that followed the middle of the continent and was apparently a desert. A second smaller continent in the southern hemisphere was on the side of the world under the base of the "U" about the size, shape, and location of Africa on Earth. A third even smaller continent was in the southern hemisphere, roughly on the other side of the world from the second one, a little to the east of the mouth of the "U" of the first continent. It reminded the committee of Australia on Earth, being about where Australia was in relation to Asia.

Both poles seemed to be in water areas, but it was hard to tell since the water appeared to be frozen. The northern polar ice cap was larger than the southern one. The northern hemisphere was in its winter season. Snow and ice extended halfway down to the equator.

Several island archipelagos existed, one between the smallest continent and the large continent, another in the mouth of the "U" of the large northern continent. The middle-sized continent was shaped like a bent triangle with the base parallel to and slightly below the equator and the point aiming at the South Pole.

The third and smallest continent was more oval-shaped, with the long axis of the oval running east-west.

They decided to explore the smallest continent first. The shuttle carrying them descended into a small clearing in the middle of a huge forest. After it settled onto the ground, they disembarked. The tops of the trees, at least they appeared to be trees, waved in the wind a thousand feet above them. The trees had to be a hundred feet in diameter. The deep blue sky was visible between them. The gravity seemed a little less than Earth's, but it was hard to tell. The air smelled the sweet smell of healthy forest duff.

The only sound was the wind through the limbs. Then they heard some chittering. They turned around and a small critter ran up to them, sniffed, then scampered to a tree and went twenty feet up the trunk. It turned around and chittered some more. It was about the size of a medium-sized dog, about thirty, thirty-five pounds. Its fur was brown and black with white areas around its neck and under its belly. Around its eyes were circles of black fur that gave the appearance of making its large eyes even bigger than they were. It's ears were in constant motion, listening in all directions. The group heard answering chitters from all around them. More of the critters showed up and checked them out.

"You said there was no intelligent lifeforms on this planet," President Robbins said to Captain Xanny.

"There aren't," he answered. "The communication that you're hearing is nonverbal alert and curiosity noises. These don't qualify as intelligence on the galactic lifeform guidelines. In ten thousand years, who knows? But for now, these are not considered to be an intelligent lifeform."

A grunt came from the bushes uphill from them.

The critters disappeared in every direction. Two seconds later, there wasn't one in sight. An animal about the size of a wolverine trotted into view. It paused where it had emerged around a bush and eyed the visitors, then ignored them. It looked around, tested the air. A rock the size of a softball fell from the tree the wolverine was standing beside. It thudded into the dirt next to the creature. A second hit it on the head. The animal looked up into the tree and hissed. More rocks started to fall. The wolverine turned around, hissing and looking up, then disappeared into the forest from where it had come.

"Let's check out the largest continent," President Robbins suggested.

"There are large feline predators in the steppes of the largest continent," their guide informed him. "We will need guards to explore there."

... ...

Doug and Clara turned into the driveway of their farm near Calgary, Alberta. The horses lifted their heads from their grazing to watch them.

"Stop, Doug," she told him. She leaned out the window of the truck and whistled. Her horse perked up her ears, then trotted over to the fence line that separated them. The horse stood beside the fence and blew her greeting. Clara leaned out the window and scratched her horse between the eyes, then held out one of the carrots that she had gotten on the trip up for just this purpose. Doug's horse came walking over to investigate. He got his share of carrots as well.

"Home at last! Home at last!" Clara intoned, paraphrasing Martin Luther King's famous line. "Praise God, Almighty. Home at last!"

"How appropriate and here comes Martin, himself, to welcome us."

They watched Martin, Mindy, and Bill walk down the driveway from the house. Doug got out as they reached the truck, picked up Martin, and spun him around. "I am so glad to see you, little boy."

Martin squealed in delight and gave Doug a big hug.

"How's the farm, Bill?" Doug asked.

"Long winter. Spring is a beautiful thing up here."

Doug approved of what he could see of the pasture. The wind blew waves through the knee-high grass. "Horses are fat."

"They need some exercise. I rode 'em in the winter when I could. Got down to forty below some nights."

"Wouldda been here if I could," Doug told him.

"Yeah. I heard. You done good, Doug. You kicked them assholes back to their own galaxy. I'm proud a ya." Bill held out his hand. "I figured takin' care a this place was my part a the plan. I were proud to do it."

Doug's protest that he hadn't been a willing partner was cut short by Mindy.

"YOU AREN'T!" Mindy screamed at Clara, grabbing Clara by her arms and spinning around in joy. Everyone turned to look at them.

"Yes I am," Clara hugged Mindy back. "I'm due on December twenty-second. And it's TWINS!"

"Does this mean the virus is dead?" Bill asked, looking back and forth between the women.

Clara sighed. "No. It doesn't. The virus is alive and well. And will be as long as there are humans to keep it alive. I got pregnant using a new technique the CDC discovered. President Robbins sent us down there after the emperor left. Dr. Hehsa, head of the CDC himself, did the procedure. Two eggs ended up getting fertilized so he used them both. The procedure doesn't kill the virus, but we can still get pregnant. I'm the mother and Doug is the father. They're going to roll the procedure out to all the functioning fertilization clinics worldwide. All you have to do is want it to happen, then go to a fertilization clinic to perform the procedure."

Mindy stopped to think about that. "No more accidental pregnancies. The world will be a changed place."

"That's just the beginning of the changes that are coming," Doug told her, wondering how the world would receive the idea of sharing the oceans with intelligent dolphins. "Did you hear about the new world? Atlantis is what they're calling it."

"Yeah. I heard. Why would anyone want to leave Earth?"

"It's a whole new world, Mindy," Doug told her. "Why wouldn't you want to be part of it?"

Mindy looked at Doug, then turned in a slow circle with her arms wide—her friends, the farm, the Canadian Rockies west of them, and ended up looking at Martin and Bill. "This is as close to Heaven as I can imagine," she said, hugging Martin and Bill. "I don't want to leave."

Clara hugged Doug. "We hoped you'd feel that way. We've already told the Prime Minister we aren't leaving."

… … … … … … … … …

Lily and Kevin were silent as the devastation that had been Rosyville spread out around them. Even Lan was quiet for once. There were no MPs at the front gate. There was only a hole where the front gate had been. At least a hundred bombs were sent to Rosyville during the Three-Hour War. There wasn't a whole building left standing. What hadn't been destroyed by the bombing was destroyed by the fires that raged unchecked until they burned themselves out. The mountains were black with burned vegetation. No one came to greet them. No one else was there. The wind never seemed to stop blowing as it passed across the burned hills around what had formerly been a lovely town nestled among them. If they listened closely, they could almost hear the wind whispering of the spirits of the people who had died when the bombs fell. Kevin's father died along with most of the rest of the residents. Kevin, Lily, and Lan stood in front of the ruins that had been their house. The only recognizable things were the charred remains of their heat pump and water heater.

"Doug and Clara invited us to live with them in Calgary," Kevin reminded her.

Lily hugged Kevin. "What do you think about moving to Atlantis?" she asked tentatively, looking up into her husband's eyes. "President Robbins said that the provisional government in China would allow Mother to join us. I think they want to get rid of her. She can be a royal pain in the ass when she gets her tail feathers up. Kevin, we could start a new life and help build a new world. They're going to need physicists."

"I can't wait to meet your mother." He paused. "Calgary is very cold in the winter."

"She's from Tibet. Calgary doesn't have anything on Tibet. But in Atlantis we could really be part of making something wonderful. There won't be any countries. The whole world will have a single government. And it will be a democracy."

"How about your father? Did they find him yet?" Kevin was avoiding the discussion about Atlantis. Both of them knew it.

"No. He 'disappeared,' according to China." "Disappeared" was what happened when the old government killed people.

"OK then." He didn't know what else to say. "Atlantis? Are you sure? Once we go, we can't come back."

"I'm sure I want to go with you, Kevin." She hugged him again. "I'm sure I don't want to go without you."

The stars were beginning to appear in the darkening sky above them. Kevin came to a decision. "Then let's go! What an adventure this will be!" He picked up Lan, spun her around, and pointed, trying to get excited. "Look up there, Lan. We're going to the stars!"

... ...

"This Article 35 hearing will come to order," Colonel Murray, the military judge announced, slamming down his gavel. "The purpose of the this Article 35 hearing is to determine if Lieutenant Jeremiah Silverstein and his patrol warrant a trial by courts martial for the death of four hundred twelve civilians on June 23 at the settlement camp near Sonora, California. Is the prosecution ready to proceed?"

Captain Reynolds rose and said, "We are, your honor."

"Is the defense ready to proceed?"

"Captain Mark rose and said, "We are, your honor."

The prosecution presented the pictures of the men who were killed, their lives as devoted fathers, sons, brothers, and husbands. According to the prosecution, they were trying to find a place to bring their families to escape from the lawlessness and mayhem in the urban areas around Southern California. The pictures depicted men holding their children, wedding parties, graduation ceremonies, entrance to the military events. Then the prosecution shifted gears. They showed closely cropped pictures of the dead men lying in pools of their own blood on the road approaching the settlement. Wives, children, mothers, and fathers took the stand to tell about the fine men who had been murdered by the out-of-control Marines. The surviving members of the attack testified that the attack had been a complete surprise and completely unwarranted.

The defense presented a vastly different picture of those same men. Arrest records were entered into evidence: murder, armed robbery, burglary, grand theft, rape, drug sales and distribution, possession of stolen goods, felony assault, attempted murder, extortion, pandering. The pictures the defense presented were shown in their uncropped versions, revealing the stolen automatic weapons the assailants had died with, surrounded by spent cartridges on the ground. The array of weapons stolen from the National Guard Armory in Bakersfield were rolled into court and left on display. All of the settlers from the camp testified. Major Goodman testified as to what he saw and did. Jeremiah testified about what he encountered when he arrived at the settlement, how they arranged their defenses, and how his men had reacted during the attack. The video that Amy Johansson made of the battle was presented in its entirety. The dash cams from the trucks were viewed from end-to-end. Pictures were presented of the settlements that the gang had pillaged before reaching the one that Jeremiah and the Marines defended. The grisly images of the three children who had been roasted to death as they were tied to a tree in the Green Beret's camp was left on the screen as the defense rested.

Jeremiah and his patrol were found not guilty of any wrongdoing. The gang member survivors of the attack were turned over to civilian authorities for trial and punishment. As they were leaving the Provost Marshal offices where the Article 35 hearing had taken place, Major Goodman asked Jeremiah to wait for a moment.

"Would you be interested in working for me at the Mountain Warfare Center?" he asked. "The Marines want me to start up the training center again. I need some good people to help me get it organized and functioning. I thought I'd ask you first."

Jeremiah's mind was still reeling from the Article 35 hearing. What he was going to do next was the furthest thing from his consideration right then. He blinked. Twice.

"You could live with your wife in the settlement and work at the Center," Major Goodman suggested.

"Oh, honey!" Rebecca gushed, hanging on his arm. "That would be wonderful!"

"I still have that Wrongful Death lawsuit in Federal Court to deal with," Jeremiah said.

Major Goodman chuckled. "I'd be willing to bet that will go away pretty quickly once the prosecutor sees what happened at this hearing. But, absolutely, deal with that first. Once it's dismissed, please come see me."

Jeremiah started to get excited. He had been wondering what was going to happen with his future, now that this was behind him. "I will, sir! Thank you!" He saluted Major Goodman. The major saluted back and walked away.

... ...

"Are you sure you want to do this, Chief?" Captain Rousselot asked Chief Petty Officer Freddie Harris.

"Yes, sir." Freddie stood at parade rest in front of the captain's desk. "The emergency is over. I'd like to return to Montana to raise the children I was entrusted with at the SHIPS."

"The Marines still need you, Chief. People are dying every day."

"My kids need me too, sir. There're lots of other medics to save those injured Marines."

"I can't tell you 'no.' You didn't sign a contract when you came on board after the president's invitation. You can leave at any time. You know that. You don't need my permission."

"I'd like to have it, sir."

Captain Rousselot came around the desk. "Chief, it's been my pleasure to have you in my command. If you change your mind, please come back."

"I won't change my mind, sir. But thanks for the offer. Could I have a letter of release?"

"Of course, let me get my clerk to prepare one."

Five minutes later, Captain Rousselot signed the letter and handed it to Freddie. Freddie saluted the captain. The captain saluted back. Freddie did an about-face and left the captain's office.

Freddie hoisted his sea bag onto his shoulder and walked to the portal to Fort Lewis. At Fort Lewis, his truck was where he had left it. The battery was dead. A passing truck gave him a jump, then he was through the front gates and on his way back to Montana.

It took all day to drive to the SHIPS in Montana where he had been stationed before the Three-Hour War. He walked around the grounds in silence with only the wind to greet him. There wasn't much left. Anything that could be used or stolen was gone. The barracks that had been full of sleeping workers and soldiers were now just a few burned poles sticking up into the air. The motor pool contained the burned-out hulks of the vehicles that no one could use.

In front of the rock slide covering the main entrance, he pounded the sign into the ground that he had made at Fort Lewis before he left. On it were listed the names of the fellow submariners at the SHIPS who were killed by the bombing of the war. He also included the names of the eight children in his care who had died before he could pull them out of the nursery. Every time he hit the posts with his hammer, the echo of it returned to him a second later, sounding like applause from the ghosts of the people on the sign, like they were helping him erect the memorial.

When he was done, he looked around the bowl one more time, then got back into his truck for the drive to the O'Flynn's farm. The sun was going down behind the mountains to the west when he pulled up to the driveway that led to the farmhouse. He stopped the truck on the road and watched for a while. Ray had built a swing set for the kids. He turned into the driveway and parked the pickup next to the farmhouse.

"He's back, Ray! Freddie's come back to us!" Andrea ran out the door into Freddie's arms.

Ray came out, leading both children. Wilson broke away from Ray's hand and ran to Freddie. "Fweddie! You're back!"

Freddie picked him up and spun around. Shannon came running right behind Wilson. He picked her up too and fiercely hugged both of his children. "Yep. I'm back to stay, kids."

... ...

A hush came across the gathered crowd that was seated at the small University of Calgary theater. The emperor and his daughter were in the front row, next to President Robbins and his wife. The curtain went up on act one, scene one, of Romeo and Juliet. The narrator began his monologue:

"Two households, both alike in dignity,
In fair Verona, where we lay our scene,
From ancient grudge break to new mutiny,
Where civil blood makes civil hands unclean."

...

The prince reflected gloomily on what had transpired in the last four days:

"A glooming peace this morning with it brings;
The sun, for sorrow, will not show his head:
Go hence, to have more talk of these sad things;
Some shall be pardon'd, and some punished:
For never was a story of more woe
Than this of Juliet and her Romeo."

The curtain fell. Professor Flamé came on stage. "OK, everyone, great job. Get ready for the encores. Supporting actors first. Three-two-one. Curtain up."

They were greeted with enthusiastic applause. "Everyone but Leann and Jason next."

Much more applause. "OK. Leann and Jason—by yourselves.

The applause was thunderous. "Now everyone together."

The applause didn't stop. The cast pulled Professor Flamé out and he bowed as well. The whole cast bowed one last time, then the curtain fell for good.

... ...

"How many beings saw this, Emperor Cabliux?" President Robbins asked. The emperor had returned to Earth with his granddaughter for the show.

"The numbers aren't in yet. I expect something on the order of two trillion were watching live. Another several trillion will watch the reruns. Leann has quite a following."

"How do you think she will do as Earth's representative to the Ur?"

The emperor hesitated then smiled. "I expect she will get a grand welcome." He remembered seeing her in the capsule and the pressure her exploits had brought on his office. "She'll do fine, President Robbins. I look forward to working with her. Not many people enjoy telling the truth as much as she does."

President Robbins laughed at that one. He had squirmed under Leann's truthfulness as well. "I understand, Sire."

"President Robbins, not many of your species have volunteered to migrate to the new planet. I believe you are calling it Atlantis. And the ones who have volunteered are mostly the unskilled poor. Why is that? I would have thought humanity would embrace a new start."

President Robbins considered the emperor's question. "There are two categories of people I see volunteering. Most of them are the people who think they have no future here on Earth. They have no money and no education, but they do have a desire to better themselves. They think their chances of providing a better future for themselves and their families lie in our new world. They are motivated and desperate. Many have skills that we will need a lot of: carpenters, electricians, masons, farmers, mechanics, people who work with their hands. The other category are people who are educated and moneyed. They are going on an adventure. They may be bored with their lives of leisure or simply want to help a new world begin and grow. I would expect great things from Atlantis. My country was formed from the same two groups of people three hundred years ago. In the past hundred years, we have led our world in almost every area of endeavor."

"This is an experiment that I will watch with great interest," the emperor told the president, getting up. "Thank you for allowing my granddaughter and me to attend this presentation."

"The honor was ours, Sire."

"Several hundred movie companies have contacted me about licensing the plays and books that Leann performed during her 'capsule' period. After tonight's performance, I expect that number to increase dramatically. Grock Corporation has a vested interest in this. You will require their approval and participation to go forward. The terms could be very beneficial to your world. I have a liaison unit that normally helps new members to the Ur begin these negotiations. Have you set up a similar unit on Earth?"

Intragalactic commerce! President Robbins had not expected this to happen so quickly or on this scale. "Not yet, Sire. I will get my staff working on it immediately."

"Let me know if I can help. When your unit is ready, contact me and I will have my liaison unit help them gain the proper licenses and explain the laws and regulations that abound across the Ur. Their first challenge will be to receive and distribute the revenue generated from tonight's performance."

"Revenue, Sire?"

"Nothing happens for free in the Ur, President Robbins. Over two trillion beings watched this performance. With replays, the number may reach twice that. I expect each group of four or five beings has paid a Huz to watch. After taxes and the twenty-five percent that Grock Corporation will deduct, Earth will have a substantial opening balance in its planetary account. These funds can be used to buy products and services on the open Ur marketplace, remunerate the participants in the performance, and add to your general fund for repairs needed from the unfortunate war that devastated large areas of your world. And I expect you will see a number of inquiries about other artistic endeavors. Leann seems to have struck a chord of emotional empathy."

President Robbins decided he would need a new cabinet-level secretary to handle this aspect of being a member of the Ur. "You have given me much to think about, Sire. I will have my Secretary of Intragalactic Commerce contact your liaison unit."

... ...

"Dr. Quigee, have you noticed that the rate of people coming in for start-finish appointments has been declining?"

Dr. Quigee was checking his patient queue in his office hologram. "Nobody has figured out they made a baby last month, Ziklet. Next week they'll be beating down the door. One thing you can count on in this business is you never run out of customers. The Yunia aren't known for idle hands, if you know what I mean. Speaking of, how long is your husband home from that awful galaxy he was sent to? The one with so many different species?"

"He has another week's leave, then everyone's being called back. The admiral gave everyone in his fleet a month off. They returned to their homes all over the galaxy."

"Wow. He's been home for three weeks already?"

"Yep. I wish he had never signed up for the military. The kids are just getting used to him being around."

"You're not the first woman who wished for that." Dr. Quigee checked her watch. "My next appointment is here. See you later."

Book One: The Beginning of the End

Book Two: The Three Hour War

Both titles are available on Amazon in either paper or e-book format.

Music Links from Chapter Six

Here are the YouTube links for the music Leann played in Chapter Six.

Mozart's *A Little Night Music.*
https://www.youtube.com/watch?v=FVTXlRxVdEY

Beethoven's *Fur Elise*
https://www.youtube.com/watch?v=yAsDLGjMhFI

Prokofiev's *Piano Concerto Number 3.*
https://www.youtube.com/watch?v=q4TyQ97Jcr0

Vivaldi's *The Four Seasons.*
https://www.youtube.com/watch?v=GRxofEmo3HA

Beethoven's *Emperor Concerto.*
https://www.youtube.com/watch?v=hDXWK3W477w

Tchaikovsky's *The Nutcracker Suite.*
https://www.youtube.com/watch?v=xtLoaMfinbU

Pachelbel's *Cannon in D Major*.
https://www.youtube.com/watch?v=NlprozGcs80

Beethoven's *Ninth Symphony.*
https://www.youtube.com/watch?v=r0jHhS5MtvA

Fredrick Hudgin

I have been writing poetry and short stories since I took a Creative Writing class at Purdue University in 1967. Unfortunately, that was the only class I passed and spent the next three years in the Army, including a tour in Viet Nam. After leaving the Army, I earned a BS in Computer Science from Rutgers and struck off on a career as a computer programmer.

I find that my years of writing poetry have affected how I write prose. My wife is always saying to put more narrative into the story. My poetry side keeps trying to pare it down to the emotional bare bones. What I create is always a compromise between the two.

Short stories and poems of mine have been published in Biker Magazine, two compilations by Poetry.Com, The Salal Review, The Scribbler, That Holiday Feeling, a collection of Christmas short stories, and Not Your Mother's Book on Working for a Living.

My home is in Ariel, Washington, with my wife, two horses, two dogs and three cats.

My website is **fredrickhudgin.com**. All of my books and short stories are described with links to where you can buy them in hardcopy or e-book form. I've also include some of my favorite poems. You can see what is currently under development, sign up for book announcements, or volunteer to be a reader of my books that are under development.

Other books by Fredrick Hudgin:

School of the Gods is an Action/Fantasy novel about the balance between good and evil.

The idea for this book began with a series of "What if…"s. What if we really did have multiple lives? What if God made mistakes and learned from them? What if our spiritual goal was to become a god and it was his job to foster us while we grew? What if we ultimately became the god of our own universe, responsible for fostering our own crop of spirits to godhead? If all that were true, there would have to be a school. I mean, that's what schools do … give us the training to start a new career.

School of the Gods is not a book about God, religious dogma, or organized religion. Instead, it's a story about Jeremiah: ex-Marine, bar fly, and womanizer. Jeremiah's life of excess leads to an untimely end. There is nothing unusual about his death other than he is the 137,438,953,472nd person to die since the beginning of humanity. That coincidence allows Jeremiah to bypass Judgement and get a free pass into Heaven. It also begins the story.

Jeremiah's entry into the hereafter leads to him becoming the confident of the god of our universe. As Jeremiah begins his path toward godhead, he discovers the answer to many questions about God that have confounded humanity from the beginning of time like why transsexuals exist, the real reason for the ten commandments, why the Great Flood of Noah actually happened, and where all of the other species that couldn't fit on the boat were kept. Along the way, God, Jeremiah, and three other god-hopefuls throw the forces of evil out of God's Home, create a beer drinker's guide to the universes, and become all-powerful gods of their own universes.

Ghost Ride is an Action/Fantasy novel about how ghosts share our lives and interact with us daily.

David is a Green Beret medic. At least he was for thirty years until he retired and returned to his parents' home without a clue what to do with the rest of his life. While he is trying to figure out how to recover from the violence he'd faced in Afghanistan and Iraq, he meets a woman who shows him the way, then disappears. As David rebuilds his parents' home and attempts to start an emergency care clinic in his rural town, he meets the woman's granddaughter. Together they figure out how to bring down the meth lab that has poisoned their rural town, overcome state licensing regulations preventing the clinic from opening, help their friend attempt to beat his cancer, and discover David's roots buried in an Indian sweat lodge. Ghosts abound in this story of love, betrayal, supernatural guides, and unfaithful parents. The good guys aren't entirely good. The bad guys aren't entirely bad. Nothing is what it seems at first glance in Chambersville as the book leads the reader on a merry Ghost Ride.

Green Grass is an Action/Fantasy novel in which a magical world collides with our technological one.

It features five archeology students who find a scroll at a dig in the Dead Sea which describes in great detail how to open a portal to Paradise. Paradise has no war, crime, lawyers, or politicians. Everyone just gets along and grows together. Instead of turning the scroll over to their professor, they decide to try it and find it works. They send one of their own to Paradise and, amazingly, get someone from Paradise in return.

Once the swap happens, they learn that they can't undo it for a year. Each of the swapped students has to learn to survive in a world that is completely different from the one in which they have grown up. Paradise, as it turns out, is not the quiet nirvana that was described in the two-thousand-year-old scroll. The Earth students drop into the middle of a civil war with dragons, mages, swords, smuggled technology from Earth, and double agents on both sides of the portal.

Sulphur Springs is a Historical Fiction novel about two women who settle in the Northwest.

Duha (pronounced DooHa) is the daughter of a slave midwife. Her mother and she are determined to escape the racism in Independence, Missouri, by migrating to Washington State in 1895. But her mother dies in Sheridan, Wyoming, leaving Duha with no money, no job and no future but working in the brothels. She meets Georgia Prentice, a nurse in the hospital where her mother dies. Georgia takes her in and, together, they begin a life together that spans sixty years and three generations.

They settle in the quiet, idyllic settlement of Sulphur Springs, Washington, nestled between three volcanoes: Mt Rainier, Mt Adams and Mt St Helens. The beautiful fir covered hills and crystal clear rivers belie the evil growing there that threatens to swallow Duha's and Georgia's families. Three generations must join together as a psychotic rapist/murderer threatens to destroy everything that they have worked and suffered to create.